"A masterful coming-of-age novel . . . Rice's characters are complex and real, his dialogue pitch-perfect, and his writing intelligent and strong. He builds suspense beautifully . . . amid enduring philosophical questions about what it means to be human."

—*Publishers Weekly* (starred review)

"Christopher Rice never disappoints with his vivid people and places and masterful prose. He will hold you captive under his spell as his images and emotions become your own."

—Patricia Cornwell, #1 *New York Times* bestselling author

"Christopher Rice is a magician. This brilliant, subtly destabilizing novel inhales wickedness and corruption and exhales delight and enchantment. Rice executes his turns, reversals, and surprises with the pace and timing of a master. *The Heavens Rise* would not let me stop reading it—that's how compelling it is."

—Peter Straub, #1 *New York Times* bestselling author

"Christopher Rice has written an amazing horror novel with more twists and turns than a mountain road. You'll think you know your destination . . . but you'll be wrong."

—Charlaine Harris, #1 *New York Times* bestselling author

PRAISE FOR CHRISTOPHER RICE

A Density of Souls

"An intriguing, complex story, a hard-nosed, lyrical, teenage take on *Peyton Place*."

—*Publishers Weekly*

"A chillingly perverse tale in which secrets are buried, then unearthed . . . very earnest plot."

—*USA Today*

"An imaginative, gothic tale."

—*Rocky Mountain News*

"Solid debut novel . . . an absorbing tale."

—*Kansas City Star*

"Tormented families . . . unspeakable secrets . . . a blood-thirsty young man. No, it's not Anne Rice, but her 21-year-old son, Christopher."

—*Village Voice*

"[Rice's] characters speak and act with an ease that proves [him] to be wiser than his years."

—*Austin Chronicle*

"He's learned . . . a storyteller's sense of timing. And he capably brings a gay teen's inner turmoil to life."

—*Seattle Weekly*

The Vines

"His best book yet."

—Geeks OUT

"Does not disappoint and grabs you from the opening chapter straight to the end with plot twists that are dark and thrilling . . . The transitions between modern-day and French colonial slavery are exquisite and leave the reader intrigued throughout the narrative. Rice also creates a beautiful mythology infused with a thriller that gives you many shocks and oh-my-God moments in every chapter."

—Buzzfeed

"As gothic as one could expect from the author (*The Heavens Rise*) and son of Anne Rice, this tale of evil vegetation that feeds on the blood of those seeking revenge for past wrongs is gruesome . . . there are dark thrills for horror fans."

—*Library Journal*

The Heavens Rise

"This is Rice's best book to date, with evocative language, recurring themes, and rich storytelling that will raise the hairs on the back of the neck. It rivals the best of Stephen King at times and sets a standard for psychological horror."

—*Louisville Courier-Journal*

BONE
MUSIC

OTHER TITLES BY CHRISTOPHER RICE

A Density of Souls

The Snow Garden

Light Before Day

Blind Fall

The Moonlit Earth

The Heavens Rise

The Vines

The Flame: A Desire Exchange Novella

The Surrender Gate: A Desire Exchange Novel

Kiss The Flame: A Desire Exchange Novella

Dance of Desire

Desire & Ice: A MacKenzie Family Novella

WITH ANNE RICE

Ramses the Damned: The Passion of Cleopatra

BONE MUSIC

A BURNING GIRL THRILLER

CHRISTOPHER RICE

THOMAS & MERCER

Published by Thomas & Mercer, Seattle

www.apub.com

Amazon, the Amazon logo, and Thomas & Mercer are trademarks of Amazon.com, Inc., or its affiliates.

ISBN-13: 9781542048309 (hardcover)
ISBN-10: 1542048303 (hardcover)
ISBN-13: 9781542047784 (paperback)
ISBN-10: 1542047781 (paperback)

Cover design by M.S. Corley

Printed in the United States of America

First Edition

To Jacque Ben-Zekry
and
Eric Shaw Quinn,
who helped bring Charlotte to life over a fateful,
last-minute lunch in Seattle

They didn't plan to kill my mother.

She wasn't like the other women, the ones they stalked and captured. The ones who came to in a cold root cellar miles from where they'd been abducted, hog-tied and disoriented, their faces pressed to the dirt floor.

My mother wasn't like those victims. She was an accident. A flat tire and a rainstorm conspired to place her in their path. And by the time Daniel Banning had reached through the passenger window of her Celica and placed his stun gun to the side of her neck, they still hadn't noticed the baby in the back seat. When they did, their choices narrowed. Leave me by the side of the road, along with all the forensic evidence that might involve. Or add a nine-month-old girl to their list of victims.

People have made so much of the fact that two of the most notorious serial killers in American history couldn't bring themselves to kill a baby. It blinded them to what the Bannings really did to me, which on some days seems much worse.

Did I cry that night?

I still don't know if my infant brain sensed their evil, sensed the wrongness in the sounds my mother made when the electricity surged through her body before she went rag-doll limp across the steering wheel.

To this day, to any interviewer that will listen, Abigail insists I didn't. (Daniel hung himself in prison before he went to trial.) She's told three of her biographers I was silent and docile as she peeled me out of the car seat and shielded me from the rain with one open flap of her coat.

To hear her tell it, I barely cried at all during the seven years she and her husband groomed me to be a killer.

I remember the mobile made of stars and half-moons they hung over my baby bed.

I remember them carrying me across the cow pasture, pausing so I could run my hands along silky flanks and marvel at how oblivious those great beasts seemed to the touch of my tiny fingers. There were horses, too, but their long, angular heads and great huffing breaths frightened me, and I didn't feel the same affection for them as I did for the cows.

I remember Daniel taking me to a wooded hillside so blanketed with ferns he used them as a kind of slide and sent my little body gliding downhill. It felt almost like flight, and I squealed and threw my arms skyward into the diamonds of sunlight filtering through the dense branches above.

I remember the day I sneaked out of the house, ran clear across the pasture, and, after stumbling a few paces into the woods, came across the root cellar for the first time. I remember the explosion of force from someone throwing themselves against the other side of the door half-buried in the hillside; I remember the low keening sounds, the whispers, the begging; and I remember thinking that it made no sense for someone who sounded grown-up to be begging for anything from a child as young as me.

Then Abigail came running. She scooped me up as if I weighed nothing and carried me back toward the house. I would like to believe there was some desire in her to protect me from the horrors taking place on that farm, but she was simply biding her time until she could present *those horrors in the correct way, in a manner that would allow me to find my own role and purpose in them.*

That day, the day I found the root cellar, is like a tent stake that anchors a swirl of memories.

Because it was around that time that the lies started, and the burnings.

People came at night, they told me. People came at night while we were sleeping to steal the cows. And sometimes Daniel and Abigail would have to chase these people, and when they chased them, sometimes these people dropped their belongings. Their purses, their watches, their phones. And their rings.

Because these people had come to steal something of ours, it wasn't right for us to return their belongings to them, was it?

It was time, they said, for me to start learning about the wrongness of other people, the badness of people who came to harm the special place we had on the farm.

It was time for me to start using the incinerator.

Abigail placed a plastic tub of wallets, watches, and jewelry in my small hands and followed close behind me as we crossed the field.

Until then they had taught me to steer clear of the strange machine, which looked as if someone had removed the smokestack and front part of a locomotive and set it just behind the barn. That first time Abigail picked me up by the waist so I could drop the tub's contents inside the chamber. Then she turned and held me up to the control panel so I could start the burning.

The second time a stepladder was waiting for us when we got there, and she stood back, beaming with pride, as I dropped two leather wallets and three slender gold watches into the chamber below. A spread of photographs in plastic cases slid free of one wallet as it thunked against the chamber's bottom. When I peered farther in to see who the pictures were of, Abigail jerked me back. She didn't want me to look too closely at the life she was compelling me to erase.

She was so proud when I was done that she picked me up and kissed me. I remember the feeling that I was contributing to the specialness of our home. That I had somehow helped keep it pure. That I had kept the cows from being stolen in the night.

There was no way for me to know that the nickname that would follow me for the rest of my life was born in that moment.

Imagine witnessing a murder before you know what death is.

When parents explain death to their children, they are, even if they don't intend to, giving every life equal value, equal weight. They're saying we all end the same—no matter who we are or what we have acquired in the interim. Even a seven-year-old can understand this.

Daniel and Abigail Banning didn't do that for me.

Instead they taught me that all living things could be broken up into three groups. Those that provided us with something—the cows and their milk, for instance. Those that provided us with nothing and could be extinguished without thought—like the bluebird whose neck Abigail broke with her bare hands while she and Daniel studied my reaction. And then there was a third group: the corrupters. The living things who would try to steal from us, take from us, turn us against our better selves. Like the people who came in the night to take the cows, the ones who dropped their watches and purses in their haste to get away.

It was their job as my mother and father, they said, to teach me how to deal with all three.

In some respects they were like other parents. They masked what they thought to be hard truth inside a fabric of comforting lies. In their view, the corrupters were not cow thieves. They were the women Daniel Banning blamed for his abominable appetites.

Women like Lilah Turlington. They followed Lilah and her boyfriend, Eddie Stevens, for two days as the couple backpacked along the Appalachian Trail before approaching their campground around dusk, posing as two hikers in search of company, earning their trust, before beating Eddie to death with a large rock and binding Lilah with nylon rope. Women like Cassie Murdoch and Jane Blaire, the two road-tripping University of Georgia students they struck up a conversation with at a roadside diner so they could find out which motel cabin they were spending the night in. They broke into their room while they slept and beat Cassie and Jane so swiftly and savagely the poor girls might have mistaken the first few seconds of the assault for a nightmare before they were knocked unconscious.

These were the real corrupters they sought to cleanse from the earth, the women Daniel Banning had an overwhelming desire to rape, a desire Abigail would allow him to indulge for three days before she went down to the root cellar with a knife and cut his victim's throat. But not before whispering in her ear, "You are now nothing."

Today Cassie and Jane are buried almost side by side at Oaklawn Cemetery in New Orleans, their hometown; Eddie and Lilah are in a small, woodsy cemetery in Asheville, North Carolina. I've visited them at least twice.

I've been to visit all the victims at least once, all the people they killed during my time at the farm.

To prepare me for my first kill, they set bird traps through the branches that surrounded the path we took on our sunset walks—small steel cages that glinted amid the foliage. Because I had watched them kill four birds with their bare hands, I now saw birds as a nuisance, their skittish *flight evidence of some mania or disease. But when Abigail reached inside one of the traps and placed the chirping creature in my tiny hands, cautioning me to grip it tightly so it wouldn't fly away, a resistance rose in me, as primal and fundamental as thirst.*

At least that's how I choose to remember it. That something deep within me, something untouched by the Bannings and their evil, was still alive, and that this fundamental goodness prevented me from taking that bird's life.

But truth be told, I'll never know for sure.

For that was the precise moment when men dressed entirely in black, their goggles and helmets reflecting the evening sun, burst from the woods on all sides of us, ordering us to hit the ground, facedown, hands up. For an instant their long guns were like fingers of darkness sprouting from the shadows. Daniel and Abigail made sounds I'd never heard them make before. Not just cries of alarm but furious wails and profanity I wouldn't learn the meaning of until later.

A boot heel pressed Abigail's face to the leaf-strewn soil. Daniel made a run for it before he was tackled to the ground. I was knocked backward and dragged away, the bluebird alighting from my suddenly open hands. What saved its life? My refusal to kill, or chance?

I wish I knew for sure.

I

In light of the conflicting and in many cases inaccurate press accounts of a recent event in the Burnham College Talks Series, the program coordinators have decided to post both a partial and a full transcript of the event to their website. The partial transcript appears below.

"OF HUMAN MONSTERS," A TALK WITH LOWELL PIERCE AND HIS DAUGHTER, TRINA PIERCE, DISCUSSING THEIR BESTSELLING BOOK OF THE SAME TITLE AS WELL AS THE *SAVAGE WOODS* FILMS THE BOOK INSPIRED—BURNHAM COLLEGE, COLORADO SPRINGS, CO

(Excerpt)

AUDIENCE MEMBER 1: Mr. Pierce, we've certainly heard a lot from you today, but we haven't heard much from your daughter, and so I'd like to direct this question to her.

LP: Sure. Of course.

AUDIENCE MEMBER 1: So this week the fifth film in the *Savage Woods* franchise was released, and while it's common knowledge these films are based on your exp—

TP: They're not based on my experiences.

AUDIENCE MEMBER 1: Right. But ... I mean, not literally, but they're inspired by—I guess what I'm saying is if you'd been forced, I mean ... they were holding you hostage, so it's not like people wouldn't understand if they made you—

TP: Are you asking me if I killed someone on that farm?

AUDIENCE MEMBER 1: I'm asking you if what we saw in the first *Savage Woods* film might have some more basis in reality than you've been willing to discuss.

TP: So you're asking me if I shoved someone into an incinerator while they were alive? When I was seven?

LP: Trina, let's just—

TP: Let's just what, Dad? I mean ... again? Again with this question?

LP: (inaudible)

TP: (inaudible) ... No. The answer's no. I've never killed anyone. The movie's a bunch of lies. It doesn't have anything to do with me at all.

AUDIENCE MEMBER 1: But it was based on your life, I mean—

MODERATOR: All right, maybe there are some other questions that can steer us back toward the book so we can focus on—

TP: It was based on a book my father wrote about my life when I was eight.

(Murmurs onstage, inaudible. Crowd noises.)

LP: What Trina means is that in order to give an accurate picture of what she went through at the time, a lot of us had to work together to make the book a reality. There was not only the matter of her age but also the trauma she'd been through and—

TP: Translation: I had nothing to do with that book.

LP: Well, of course you didn't; you were only eight years old. I mean . . . an eight-year-old can't write a book.

MODERATOR: Do we have another question?

AUDIENCE MEMBER 2: Yes, I . . . I mean, is it OK to ask about the movies, like, at all?

(Laughter.)

TP: No.

(More laughter.)

TP: No, I mean, whatever your question about the movies is, the answer's no. No, I haven't spent my life being stalked by the Bannings' cannibal cousins. Because the Bannings weren't cannibals, and they didn't have any cousins. And, no, everyone I get close to isn't horribly murdered.

AUDIENCE MEMBER 2: OK. But is it true you die in this one?

TP: Fingers crossed.

(Laughter. Some applause.)

LP: Trina, that's enough. Why don't we—

TP: Is it enough, though, Dad? Is it finally enough? Can we finally stop doing this every time a new movie comes out?

MODERATOR: OK. Now I'm confident that someone out there has some questions about the book, which presents some very valuable, if harrowing, lessons on how we can spot and avoid psychopaths who might seek to—

LP: Exactly. Why don't we take one more question about the book, and then we'll begin the book signing? There's a hand up in the back, I think.

AUDIENCE MEMBER 3: So . . . um . . . Burning Girl.

TP: Don't call me that.

AUDIENCE MEMBER 3: Excuse me?

TP: I said don't call me that name.

(Crowd noises. Scattered boos.)

AUDIENCE MEMBER 3: I wasn't going to call you that; I was just bringing it up as an example . . . OK. You know what? This is cute and all, like, this little display, I guess you'd call it. But you've been profiting off what happened to you for almost a decade now. I'm just wondering where all this self-righteousness comes from all of a sudden. Why are you upset now?

(Light applause.)

TP: *I've* been profiting? You do know I'm sixteen, right?

(Laughter.)

LP: OK. That's enough. Look. Trina and I have devoted our lives to turning her terrible experience into a set of tools people can use to avoid falling prey to monsters like the Bannings. This is our life's work. It always will be. Now, as I have said repeatedly, we can't be held responsible for the creative license Hollywood takes with Trina's story. We're not producers on the *Savage Woods* films. We never granted script approval, so it simply isn't—

TP: He gets a percentage of the gross. Do you guys know how that works? It's a Hollywood thing—

LP: Trina!

TP: If they promise you a percentage of the net, you'll never get anything because they've got accountants who can make it look like the movie never made a profit. But if you get part of the gross, you always get paid. He gets a part of the gross on every *Savage Woods* movie, including the one where I supposedly shoved someone in an incinerator. Where are you going, Dad?

(Lowell Pierce removes his microphone and leaves the stage.)

TP: It was supposed to be a miniseries, you see? Real fact based, true to life. But then they came to him and they said it would make a lot more money as a horror movie franchise. They could make them real cheap. They wouldn't have to cast any stars. Maybe pump out a lot of sequels. And he said yes as long as they gave him a cut of the profits. As long as he could quit his job. Cheap torture porn about his own daughter. That's his life's work. And mine, too, apparently. Now, are there any other questions before I go vomit like I always do after these things?

AUDIENCE MEMBER 3: Yeah. I got one. Why are you such a bitch?

TP: I don't know. Why are you a basement-dwelling psychopath who gets a boner watching women get tortured?

(Inaudible outburst. Sound equipment distortions. Security escorts Trina Pierce offstage.)

1

Jason Briffel reads the transcript again.

His hands are shaking. If anyone inside this roadside diner notices how badly he's sweating, they'll probably blame the baking desert heat outside.

But it's not the heat.

It's the same full-body reaction he experiences every time he reads the ten-year-old record of the last time Trina appeared onstage with her birth father.

Normally the transcript focuses him, which is why he picked it up after the plate of steak and eggs in front of him failed to ignite his appetite. He thought it would collect his scattered thoughts, channel his anxiety and doubt into action.

It's been seven years since he showed up on the doorstep of her grandmother's house in California, even longer since he mailed her those letters explaining how her birth father and her so-called rescue by the authorities had averted her true destiny. Her soul was being starved. Together, the two of them could reawaken that exceptional and enlightened young girl Daniel and Abigail Banning had coaxed into being.

But today the transcript hasn't worked its usual magic. Reading it has left him angry and confused.

He's gripped now by the humiliating memory of what happened to him that fateful night at Burnham College. He's feeling the vise grip of the two blazer-clad security guards who'd appeared out of nowhere right after he entered the auditorium. The ones who'd threatened to call the cops as they carried him out so quickly he could practically feel the wind in his hair.

A hopeful, perhaps foolish part of him had been convinced that someone in Trina's inner circle would have seen the wisdom in his letters.

Abigail Banning certainly had.

Unlike Trina, who responded to his attempts at honest communication with a restraining order, Abigail replied in great detail to every single letter Jason mailed her at Haddock Penitentiary. She recognized Jason as the vehicle for her adopted daughter's restoration, a daughter who'd been divinely gifted to her and then cruelly removed by a world that did not understand the spiritual necessity of life taking. Abigail blessed Jason with words he'd been desperate to hear since he'd first laid eyes on Trina.

You will be the Daniel to her Abigail, she'd written. *And in so doing, you will become my son, too.*

Why hadn't he read that letter instead of this transcript?

He's brought it with him, along with several others. They're at the bottom of his backpack, along with the coil of rope, the rolls of duct tape, and the Ziploc bags in which he plans to put the bullets he's going to strip from the three different guns she keeps in her house.

Should he read it now?

No, there's no telling what effect it might have on him.

Instead he searches the diner for corrupters. There's one sitting a few tables away: pretty and young, with a blonde ponytail and a halter top that reveals just enough suntanned skin to corrupt. She taps at the screen of her smartphone. The mustached man sitting across from her gazes out at the passing eighteen-wheelers with a vacant stare that reveals all the damage she's done to his soul.

She ignores the man on purpose. Jason knows this. That morning, or possibly the night before, she denied the man sex and took great, silent, delight in the pain this caused him. Right now she's texting a girlfriend, or maybe several, and they're reveling in the power she lords over the man, in the pain her withholding creates in him. And she does this because she is a corrupter, one of many. And once Jason has awakened Trina to their combined destiny, she will give herself entirely to their union and help him remove women like this blonde whore from the earth. Trina will burn away the evidence of his work, just like she burned away the detritus of Abigail and Daniel's victims. But first he has to break down her walls, show her there's no escape. From her true calling. From her real mother.

From him.

These thoughts, these plans—this *vision*—finally give him the confidence he's been seeking since he stopped off at this diner.

He has only a few hours left in his drive, a few hours until he'll reach the isolated parcel of Arizona desert she now calls home.

Today is a day like no other, and it will require a great deal more strength and confidence than it did to write those letters.

Because a few months ago, all those years of not knowing where she'd disappeared to came to an abrupt end, thanks to a single miraculous e-mail. As thrilled as he'd been to have the information, the knowledge brought with it a distinct challenge: to return to the mission he'd almost given up on entirely—to stoke the flames that would turn Trina into Burning Girl once again.

As for the name she calls herself now, he must never let it pass through his lips. He would be doing her a disservice if he did. His job is to free her of her delusions, not strengthen them.

So he avoids thinking it now. To him, she will always be Trina Pierce. And if he succeeds this time, she will become his Burning Girl.

2

"Charlotte, why don't you step away from the window?"

She knows it's a good idea.

Most of Dr. Thorpe's suggestions have been good ideas, or at least the 30 percent she's been willing to try.

It's true. If she doesn't stop staring at the movie theater across the street, she won't be able to focus on his advice. But a crazy part of her believes that if she turns her back on the bold cluster of words on the old-school marquee, they'll somehow strike at her like a snake. They're the same words that stopped her in her tracks when she first saw them, that have turned every night for the past two weeks into a prolonged battle with terrible dreams.

HALLOWEEN DOUBLE FEATURE—*SAVAGE WOODS* & *SAVAGE WOODS II: THE RECKONING*

The Blake is a restored movie house, one of the new jewels of Scarlet, this tiny, once-abandoned mining town in the Arizona desert turned hippie enclave and aspiring tourist trap. Its stucco facade is painted a shade of hunter green that from a distance makes it look like an oasis rising from the parched Sonoran desert. At night the vertical neon sign that spells out the theater's name is visible for miles around.

At dusk, however, the sign looks skeletal and hungry; the unlit neon letters cast spidery shadows along its length. And then there are the posters flanking the ticket booth; the same blood-dripping art that used to stare back at her from the T-shirts worn by all those horror movie fans who'd pack the house at the events she used to do with her father.

"OK," Dylan says. "Then describe what you're seeing right now."

"A movie theater," she says.

"Is that all?"

"Invasion. Injustice."

"Fear?" he asks.

"That, too. The girl on the poster looks very afraid, just like she always does."

"The girl that's supposed to be you."

"Well, she doesn't look like me. Her hair's still brown, for one, and I've got about fifteen pounds on her. And they changed some of the letters in her name, so there's that. One in the first, one in the last. My father saw to that part, you know, 'cause he's such a kind, considerate, selfish, motherfu—sorry."

"Since when did I say you couldn't curse?"

"Well, if you had, I'd probably just do it anyway and then leave."

"You're free to leave at any time. You know that."

"I do."

"But I wish you wouldn't, Charlotte. I wish you'd keep talking."

"Honestly, it's easier when you try to read my mind."

She sits, looks at him for the first time since she stormed into his cramped office, which always smells of burned coffee from the AA meetings downstairs.

It's not easy looking Dylan Thorpe in the eyes, and not just because he's basically appointed himself her psychiatrist now. It's hard because he's one of the most astonishingly handsome men she's ever seen. The kind of handsome that seems two-dimensional and unreal even when it's sitting across from you, like it might slide from view if you swipe up on your phone.

Another woman, a woman without Charlotte's walls, might have tried to seduce him after their first chat downstairs. Even after it became clear that he'd sought her out as a kind of pet project.

By his own admission, Dylan had sensed she didn't truly belong in the AA meetings at the Saguaro Wellness Center. That she gravitated to them because there was something about the sharing—all those honest, unguarded expressions of hopes, insecurities, and fears—that quieted her soul, even though she'd never been what anyone would call an alcoholic.

It would take another few weeks before Charlotte admitted she liked the meetings because they made her feel close to her late grandmother, with whom she'd lived for almost a decade after fleeing her father.

They were both survivors, she and her grandmother. The woman almost drank herself to death following the disappearance of her daughter and grandchild. But even before Charlotte's rescue—*Trina's* rescue, if they were going to be technical about it—Luanne found sobriety and became a pillar of the small 12-step community in Altamira, a little town just south of Big Sur and a short drive inland from the Pacific Coast Highway, a place she'd called home for thirty years. After Charlotte went to live with her, Luanne made a habit of bringing her to the open AA meetings in town, the ones that allowed nonalcoholics to just sit and listen. That's where Charlotte first heard slogans like "First things first," "Easy does it," and her personal favorite, "Keep it simple, stupid." That's where she had seen that people really could change. That we're not all doomed by our genetics or our pasts.

The eight years she'd spent with her grandmother, three of them as an almost-normal high school student and the rest as an assistant manager in Luanne's pet supply store, were the happiest in her entire life. Idyllic compared with what came before and after. The long walks they took together along Altamira's rocky coast, the open skies that were often filled by great, towering clouds, the steadiness of her grandmother's grip, and the quiet wisdom of her recovery, even the biting chill of the Pacific winds—all these things made her time on the Bannings' farm seem like a memory so distant it might one day fade entirely.

Then one afternoon, walking home from the store, Grandma Luanne died of a sudden, massive heart attack, a quick and painless death, but one that tore a hole in Charlotte so deep she could barely speak for weeks afterward. *This is what it means to have real family,* she'd realized as they lowered the casket into the ground. *This is part of loving and being loved, and without it, you cannot have the other parts, the joyful parts.*

In her will Luanne left Charlotte her house and the small pet supply store she'd run for thirty years. Six months later, one of the big chains opened in the next valley over, close to the 101 freeway. Sales dropped precipitously. Her grandmother's AA friends chipped in what they could, but it was obvious that even selling her grandmother's house would not be enough to keep the store afloat.

When her father refused to help, Charlotte snapped.

Desperate, she decided it was time to demand at least a respectable portion of the money she'd earned for him over the years—something she could use to start a new life. And it was time to demand it with a lawyer.

She won, but with her victory came the sad realization that there was a lot less money saved than her father had led everyone to believe. Still, she got enough to pay for a legal name change and her house outside Scarlet.

In short, combined with the sale of her grandmother's house, she managed to get just enough money out of him to become Charlotte Rowe.

In the three months since they started these chats, she's shared all this with Dylan. She doesn't harbor any delusions about him, about what their sessions mean to him. She's just something rough and real for him to cut his teeth on after years of listening to big-city, high-paying clients whine about their perfect lives. And she's fine with that. It keeps her safe, installs the kind of boundaries and structure her life has always lacked.

But still, there are moments, moments when the heroes in the Nora Roberts novels she reads before bed start to look like Dylan in her mind, or when her hands start to wander under the sheet as she wonders what things would be like if she wasn't quite her and he wasn't quite him and her past was someone else's.

When she reminds herself that she's just a hard-luck case, then Dylan's good looks don't inspire childish romantic fantasies in her. Instead his twinkling blue eyes, determined jaw, and short, jet-black hair, which he always keeps combed to one side like some TV dad from the 1950s, are just additional reminders that he's passing through, while she plans to hide out here for as long as she can.

And it was all going so well, she thinks. *Until the Blake decided to have a Halloween film festival.*

"OK then. Well, is it safe to say you assumed that by moving to a town as small as Scarlet, you'd never have to look at that poster again?"

"Something like that, yeah. And technically, I don't live here."

"Your grocery store is here," he answers. "And your PO box."

"And you."

"Exactly. So it's got to feel as if they're getting ready to play that movie just down the street from where you live, even though it's a forty-five-minute drive."

"Movies. Plural."

"Exactly. Go deeper, Charley."

It gives her a warm feeling the way he says even the shortened version of her new name. *Charlotte* is what her grandmother wanted to name her when she was born, and *Rowe* is the last name of a

22

Canadian author who wrote a vampire novel her grandmother had loved.

"What does that mean, Dr. Thorpe?"

"It means you call me Dr. Thorpe when I ask you to do something you don't want to do."

"What are you asking me to do, Dylan?"

"Spell out how you feel, without judgment. So that we can walk you back to a healthier perspective together, one step at a time. "

"OK . . . I feel like the movies are a sign someone knows I'm here."

"Even though you changed your name. Even though you live behind the kind of security system that's usually used to protect bars of gold."

"And the guns. Don't forget about the guns."

"The point, Charlotte, is that when I asked you to describe what you were seeing out the window, you used the word *invasion*."

"Did I?"

"You did, yes. Is that an accurate description of what you feel when you look at that marquee?"

"Yes," she answers.

"So it's safe to say that what you're feeling now is akin to what you felt when Jason Briffel made threats against you in the past?"

Like ice water in her face, hearing the guy's name again.

"Do we have to use his real name?" she asks.

"What would you like us to call him?"

"I don't know. Maybe we can come up with some term for him, some nickname."

"How about we just call him your stalker?"

"Maybe something more . . . I don't know . . . benign."

"I'd caution you against downplaying it. Dismissing the seriousness of the letters he sent to you and Abigail Banning won't make you stronger."

"I'm not dismissing it. I just don't want to say his name, OK?"

There's a flash of something in his eyes, an emotion she can't quite read. Is he offended? Did she bruise his Harvard-educated ego?

She doesn't have the energy to apologize just yet, because she's seeing Jason Briffel all over again. His ruddy-cheeked baby face and his mess of dirty-blond curls. The way he used to linger too long next to the signing table after the events she did with her dad; his hungry, probing looks as he fingered the latest copy of her dad's book, which he'd just purchased yet again so he could secure a place in line and have an excuse to get close to her.

How many times had she told her dad she thought the guy was stranger than the rest? When he'd reach the table, he'd fall to a crouch so they could be at eye level with each other, and he'd start asking her all kinds of concerned questions about how she was holding up, as if her rescue had been only months before and not years. And then there was the time he'd tried to reach for her hand. She'd withdrawn it quickly, and something dark had flashed in his eyes.

Her father had dismissed her concerns, of course. He hadn't taken them half as seriously as he did the computer hacks they were subjected to by crime scene junkies searching for proof she was lying about what she'd had to do on that farm. When it came to Jason Briffel, her father had just given her some lecture about how they couldn't control who their work touched. To this day, she isn't sure if her dad really believed, or still believes, his old pabulum—that those leering horror movie fans were truly concerned with the psychology of serial killers. That they came to their events so they could learn how to protect themselves and their loved ones from psychopaths, not just to savor the gory details of the Bannings' crimes, to worship the dark mystique in which those awful movies had shrouded her.

Then Briffel had found their address.

That's when the letters started.

It was her dad's fault, something with how he'd registered to vote in his district that had made his address available to the public. And as she'd read the first letter, she'd realized where all Briffel's concerned questions came from. He wasn't worried she'd been traumatized by her time with the Bannings. In his twisted mind, the trauma was that she had been "removed from the Bannings' care," as he put it, her destiny thwarted.

The letters contained crime scene photos, some real, some fake, all designed to stir memories of her time on the farm, even though she'd never personally laid eyes on any of the victims. He included passages from letters Abigail had exchanged with him, letters in which she'd praised the work he was trying to do to "reawaken Trina to her destiny."

If she hadn't alerted her father's publisher herself, nothing would have changed. When Stonecutter Books found out about their young star's stalker, they'd insisted her father relocate them and they'd contributed to the expense of extra security at their events. They'd also provided legal assistance so Charlotte could go about filing a restraining order.

Now, thanks to the work she's done in this tiny office with this exceedingly handsome man, she can see that it was her father's refusal to treat Briffel as a threat that had caused her to go so far off script that fateful day at Burnham College. Because that's when she'd realized as long as they kept doing those events, there would be more Jasons. That's when she'd decided she could never set foot onstage with her father again.

Three years had passed between the evening security escorted Jason out of the event and the sunny afternoon he appeared on Grandma Luanne's front porch in Altamira. Now it's been twice that. Maybe Jason's moved on to a new obsession. If changing her name and moving to the middle of nowhere doesn't make her feel safe, then nothing will.

"Sorry," she says. "I didn't mean to snap like that."

"It's fine," Dylan says. "How are you sleeping?"

"Badly. Ever since I saw the . . ." She gestures to the window behind her, to the marquee across the street. "You know."

"Is it affecting your work?"

"I work from home in my pajamas, so not really."

"I'm aware your clients can't see the bags under your eyes, but is it having an impact on your ability to keep up with your call load?"

"I have bags under my eyes?" she asks.

"Charley, is it affecting your work?"

She sucks in her best attempt at a deep breath. It turns into a shallow grunt. "The other day I got a client's origin city mixed up with the one from the previous call."

"What does that mean?" he asks.

"It means I booked him a ticket from Singapore to Boston instead of Paris to Boston."

"I understand those cities are very far apart."

"Yeah, well, on a computer screen, they're just a bunch of letters and airport codes, you know."

"Especially if you haven't had any sleep."

"I caught it before he left for the airport. Got him on a flight that left the next day. Put in a comp request for an extra night at the hotel."

"Has he complained?"

"Survey review's at the end of each month. We'll see."

Dylan nods.

"I don't want to take anything, Doc," she says once the silence between them becomes uncomfortable.

"All right, well, let's talk about that."

"I don't want to swallow a bunch of pills just to feel normal."

"That's not exactly an accurate description of the treatment options we've discussed."

"Please, I just . . . I don't want to talk about it."

"That's exactly why we *should* talk about it. It's not about the medication. It's about your belief that accepting that kind of help is admitting unacceptable weakness."

"There's no pill out there that's gonna change my past."

"True. But we're not talking about changing your past."

"Then what are we talking about?"

"We're talking about a bridge, Charley. A temporary solution that will allow you to get some sleep. That will reduce your anxiety just enough you can leave the house for longer than it takes to come here or run to the grocery store. Maybe for as long as it takes to start forming some meaningful social relationships. Once you get in the habit of those things, they'll be easier to do in the long term. Any medications we explore would be about helping you take the leap."

A bridge. A leap. Which one is it, Doc?

"How sad is it that making conversation with the checker at the grocery store is taking a leap?" she asks.

"Charlotte, you were kidnapped as a baby. Your mother was murdered. You were held hostage for seven years by two psychopaths who isolated you from the world, who lied to you about who you were. Who tried to turn you into someone like them. And when you were returned to your father, he exploited you at every turn and without your consent. And, ironically, none of these traumas in your past are the source of your current anxiety."

"You're kidding, right?"

"I'm not. These events I just listed, they've made you incredibly strong. Resourceful, even." Her expression must betray her doubt, because he sits forward, planting his elbows on his knees. "Charley, you emancipated yourself from your father as a teenager after you rejected his agenda for you in front of an audience of hundreds. As an adult, you went on to sue him—successfully, I might add—for money that was rightfully yours, money that allowed you to change your name and relocate.

"These are not the actions of a broken bird, Charley. You're tired, for sure. You're tired, and you're still grieving your grandmother. Those two conditions have tricked you into believing you're weak. And the longer you stay barricaded in that house, the bigger this lie becomes in your head."

How long has he been waiting to say this to her? It's the first time she's seen him look nervous. On edge, even. Maybe he's afraid she'll walk out.

"You can admit that what happened to you made you stronger without celebrating the people who did those things to you. But to do that you're going to need a bigger push than I can give you in here."

Maybe this is why she keeps coming back to Dr. Thorpe. Because he's the first person she's met in years who can make her cry just by stating the truth.

And if I can cry, she thinks, *if I can cry, then I'm not the sick and damaged killer those movies made everyone believe I was.*

His expression is fixed as he reaches across his desk and hands her a box of tissues.

There's a soft buzz that sounds like it's coming from her phone, but when she looks to where she thought she left it, on the edge of Thorpe's desk, it's not there.

"It's mine," Dylan says. "Sorry, I thought I turned it off."

"Where's mine?"

"Stay focused, Charley. I think we're onto something here."

"OK. It's just . . . it's hard to focus right now."

"Because you need some sleep?"

"Yeah," she finally says. "I need some sleep. It's just . . ."

"What, Charley?"

"There were pills before."

Dylan seems genuinely concerned. For Christ's sake, it's not like she's about to disclose she was molested. But that's how he's acting.

"You've tried medication before?" he asks.

"My father tried medication. On me. When I was ten."

Dylan nods, and his expression is grim. "And what prompted your father to put you on medication back then?"

"I started complaining. About the appearances. The movies."

"I see."

"Do you?"

"Your father drugged you to silence you, and so you're afraid that's what I'm trying to do to you now."

"It's not like it worked. I started hiding the drugs after a few weeks."

"But you stopped complaining, didn't you?"

"For a while."

"From age ten to age sixteen is a long while."

"I guess." Christ, she sounds sixteen. She's even staring down at her lap now like a sullen teenager.

"I'm not trying to silence you, Charley. I didn't reach out to you and offer my ear because I thought what you needed was more silence. Quite the opposite, in fact. And I can assure you that if you decide to go the medication route this time, it'll be entirely different."

"How can you assure me of that?"

"Because this time the choice will be yours."

3

Access Denied.

Jason isn't surprised when these words appear on the keypad's display.

He never expected to crack her code on the first try.

There's no telling exactly what type of security system she has; she hasn't posted a sign next to her driveway like a suburban family would.

She doesn't really have a driveway. Just a strip of tire-scuffed earth that looks a little smoother than the surrounding desert. It leads to a reinforced-steel garage door that, like the rest of her squat, one-story stucco house, is painted the common colors of the Sonoran. The paint does its job. The house is pretty much camouflaged from the nearest road. But he had no trouble finding the place with the directions the Savior gave him.

Given his research into alarm systems, he figures he's got about three more tries before he's locked out or the alarm company alerts local law enforcement.

The nearest police station is just inside the Scarlet town line, a thirty-minute drive away. So if he does get locked out, he'll have time to race back to the dried-out arroyo where he hid his car. Then he'll have to reassess.

He has to teach Trina that her defenses against him are useless, and he can only do that by getting inside her house, by showing her that he belongs there, that their union is inevitable. On the basis of his e-mails, the Savior seems to understand this. He sent Jason a list of possible code words—objects and places with a special meaning to her, terse descriptions of her favorite memories—and strings of relevant numbers—her birthday, her birth mother's birthday—that might be the basis of her alarm code.

If he cracks the code, he's in.

She's afraid of keys, the Savior told him. They're too easily lost, too easily stolen or copied. The idea behind a security system like hers is to make sure no door is ever left unlocked by mistake and to eliminate any exposed mechanisms that might allow an intruder access to the locks themselves. The cylinder inside each is several inches deeper than your average dead bolt, too deep to be jimmied open by even the most skilled locksmith. And in the absence of a key mechanism, you'd have to tear apart the door frame or the adjacent wall to even try for access to the lock itself. The code unlocks a specific series of doors for several minutes, and then they lock again automatically. It's the kind of system usually reserved for vaults or other storage facilities that rarely see human visitors, and Trina's installed it in her own home.

Can she not see how desperate this is, how it smacks of someone denying the inevitable?

Chances are the system includes smoke detectors that disengage all the locks in case of a fire. But what if something else happened to her out here? What if she had a heart attack or was bitten by a snake and she couldn't enter the code and so EMS couldn't get to her?

Stupid. So stupid.

Not stupid, he reminds himself. Just misguided, that's all.

He scans the words and numbers again.

The meaning of some are clear to him thanks to his study of Lowell Pierce's book—*bluebird*, for instance, *Joyce Collins*, her birth mother's maiden name—but the others he doesn't understand. As he reads over them now, he feels a surge of jealousy.

The Savior knows why these words are precious to her. The Savior knows more about her than Jason's managed to learn in a decade.

Whoever the Savior is, they've come to the same conclusion Jason did years ago. That Trina was taught the cleansing power of murder at a young age, and with every day she refuses to put this lesson to good use, her soul dies a little bit more.

As evidenced by this secluded prison in which she now lives.

It's literally in the middle of nowhere, this tiny house, surrounded by parched desert sliced by arroyos and dotted with sparse stands of blue paloverde trees that give only teasers of shade. On his walk in, he'd passed the old fence lines, spotted a few crumbling stakes. His Internet research into the area told him this used to be part of a sprawling housing complex for the workers in the copper mine just up the road, which probably explains its water and electrical lines. But the mine's been closed for years, and most of the houses were abandoned after a big fire swept through the area. Trina's is the only one within view.

A courtyard sits between the solid-metal entry door and the front door of the house itself, which he can't see from where he stands. The wall is eight feet high. She poured a river of concrete along the top and studded it with huge, jagged shards of glass that give off rainbow reflections in the dusk. Did she set each piece by hand? If so, she didn't do it to keep out snakes; she did it to stop him, and so the sight of all that jagged glass now makes him angry. But if he gets angry, he'll get distracted, and that's unacceptable.

BBIRD474

It feels like a wild guess. But it isn't really.

The code's the average length of most computer passwords; eight characters, with a mix of letters and numbers.

And how many times did he sit in the audience and listen to her tell the story of how she came to see the bluebird, the one she didn't kill, as a symbol of her rebirth?

As for the numbers, 474 are the last three digits of her mother's birthday, if you chop off the month, which is March. And in all her years of signing his books, her handwriting would always place the emphasis on the final letters in her name and not the first, as if her hand always needed a second or two to gather energy before exploding with it at the end. That's why he's assumed she would cut off some of the first few letters of the word *bluebird* and drop the number of the month in the sequence of digits in her mother's birthday.

And it's wrong.

Which shouldn't surprise him. When it comes to Trina's life story, bluebird isn't the most secret of passwords. How many times did he sit in the audience and listen to her tell that story about the bird flying out of her hands right as the SWAT team exploded out of the woods?

He's not willing to jettison the rest of his guess—not yet. He refuses to believe Trina has let go of her birth mother, and that's part of her problem, her inability to see her mother's death as a necessary sacrifice, a fundamental aspect of her rebirth. When it comes to the code, he just needs a word, a token, a thing from her more recent, and more secret, past. The life she made for herself after she legally changed her name and disappeared from that town in California where her grandmother's friends had threatened to beat him to a pulp if he ever came back again.

He consults the list.

Altamira, Luanne (grandmother), Bayard Rock (Altamira landmark, used to visit with grandmother on her walks), Fisher Pit (copper mine near her house, closed 1986).

While he's sure Bayard Rock is probably the most meaningful item on the list, it's not exactly secret, a local landmark in a town where she'd lived while she was still Trina. And Fisher Pit, which is just up the road, isn't exactly the most covert, either.

He should just wait. He should just wait until her headlights appear out of the darkness and then slip in through the reinforced-steel garage door as soon as she opens it. It won't be the easiest maneuver, but it's doable.

But where would he hide until then? There are no trees close to the house. There's pretty much nothing close to the house. The nearest arroyo, where he hid his car, is a fifteen-minute walk if he moves at a clip, way too far for him to make it through the garage door before it closes. And that's the idea, isn't it. Nothing but wide-open desert on all sides of the house, no obstructions, easily surveyed with the night vision cameras she's got attached to her security system.

I have to get in, he tells himself. *If this is meant to be, then I'll be able to get in.*

While his gut tells him Fisher Pit is probably the basis of her code, he doubts she used a name that could be easily found on a map of the surrounding area. So he goes for the year it closed and adds it to his previous string of digits; *1986474.*

A single beep. *Access Granted.*

The flood of adrenaline makes him dizzy at first, then breathless with elation.

He almost forgets to follow the Savior's next instruction, which is to pass the code along if he cracks it. He has, and he does. He's proud of how it looks on the burner phone's screen next to all the nervous preparatory texts they've exchanged over the past few hours. A task completed, a goal met.

In another few seconds, he's crossed the courtyard and slipped inside the house. She's left the air-conditioning on, a necessity even in October, and the cool air kisses his skin in an undeniably welcoming way. He's in. And just as he expected, a few minutes later, the locks all click shut behind him, the sounds a confirmation of his speed and smarts.

Not just that. But his destiny as well. *Their* destiny.

Now he just needs to find her guns.

4

"Describe them to me," Dylan says.

"I can't. The dreams are too vague," Charlotte answers.

"Can you remember any of them?"

"Not really. It's more like I wake up with an awareness that they were bad. Or that I was being chased."

"Dreams are funny things."

"These dreams aren't funny. I mean, I don't wake up laughing."

"Figure of speech," he says. "Forgive me. What I mean is that most neuroscientists believe dreams don't actually have a chronology when we're in them. When we're asleep, we're not tuned in to the type of physical stimuli our bodies use to detect the passage of time."

"So what does that mean?" she asks.

"It means our brains have been firing a stream of random images at us and our waking minds instinctively place them in a coherent order. A narrative that makes sense to us."

"So dreams have less to do with our subconscious and more to do with our mental state when we wake up? Is that what you're trying to say?"

"Actually, I'm trying to get you to describe your dreams over the past two weeks."

"I can barely remember them. I just wake up sweating and with a sense of anxiety and dread. Like someone's in the house with me."

"Is Jason Briffel in them?"

She shoots him dagger eyes before she can stop herself. He shakes his head. "Sorry. Your stalker, is he in any of the—"

"Like I said, they're vague. They're more like . . . I don't know . . . swirls of feelings."

"Swirls of feelings. That's an interesting description."

"Is it?"

"What about the other agreements that you've made with yourself? How have those gone?"

"Other agreements?"

"The Mask Maker. It was very upsetting when you first read about it. We agreed you'd make an effort to avoid anything further about the case."

"Have they found another body?" she asks.

"I feel like this is your way of maybe answering my question."

"Because if I'd broken my agreement, I'd know whether or not they'd found another body."

She smiles. He smiles back.

"So maybe you're answering my question. Or maybe you're using me to get around the agreement you made with yourself."

He smiles again. She smiles back.

"Does that mean you're not going to tell me?"

"Well, if you remember correctly, they didn't find a body. They found a face."

"I remember. And if they haven't found another one, then it's not a serial."

"That's not what you felt when you first read about it. You thought the gruesomeness of the crime, the fact that the face was displayed in public like some kind of mask meant—"

"Maybe it's a mafia hit. Isn't there a lot of Russian mafia in LA?"

"The police don't seem to think so."

"That it's a hit, or that there's a lot of Russian mafia in LA?"

"Charley. We're off the point."

"There's a point?"

"There hasn't been a high-profile serial predator like this in a while."

"You mean a good reason for me to avoid all news everywhere."

"Pretty much, yes."

"So they *did* find another face?"

"I'm not answering that."

"Why not?"

"Because it's not the point."

"Again. What *is* the point, Dylan?"

He bows his head, closes his mouth, as if he's reconsidering his initial response. For a long while, there's just silence and the low murmur of the AA meeting downstairs. Occasionally a motorcycle backfires in the street below, probably snarled in the little knot of traffic that always develops around that crosswalk they just installed between the movie theater and the new ice-cream parlor next door to the center.

"So it's not the movie," she says, trying to control her anger. "It's that I'm not over those letters from Jas—my stalker. It's this Mask Maker psycho. I mean, I don't understand what you're trying to say."

"I'm saying it's all of them. I'm saying the number of potential triggers in your life is expanding by the day, and it's expanding because you're on too fragile a foundation. You live in isolation. You have no meaningful friendships—"

"That's not true. I have Kayla."

"I'm not including the lawyer who helped you sue your father. That's a business relationship. And she lives in San Francisco."

"We talk once a week."

"You've got all your grandmother's friends back in Altamira, and you've been to visit them how many times?"

"That one's hard."

"Why?"

"Because my grandmother's still dead."

"She's still dead whether you visit her friends or not."

"Jesus, Dylan."

"You need a breath, Charlotte."

"Well, I'm not going to get it talking to you right now. And what happened to the bridge? I thought I needed a bridge. What? Are we building a whole city here?"

"You need something that's going to reduce your anxiety levels so that you can start acting contrary to your instincts right now."

"And what are my instincts right now?"

"To isolate, self-obsess, and convince yourself of things about yourself that aren't true."

"Ouch."

"I've been seeing you for months now, so I'm gonna say this with confidence. Unless you initiate a small-scale change in your brain chemistry, you'll remain incapable of developing the kind of healthy behavioral patterns that will get you out of this place you're stuck in."

"I love my house."

"You live in a ghost town full of snakes."

"People are stupid about snakes. And ghosts."

"Maybe so, but neither make very good friends."

"It's beautiful out there. Especially the stars . . . at night, I mean. They're incredible."

"I wouldn't know."

"Maybe I'll ask you to drop by sometime."

"I doubt it."

"Is that a no?"

"Does it matter? You'll never ask."

"Sorry."

"You're not."

Why is he smiling? Shouldn't he be pissed? She just stares at him.

"You're not sorry, Charley, and that's a good thing. You want to know why? Because it means you're a fighter."

"If I'm a fighter, then how come I can't leave my house?"

"We've covered this. You can leave. You just don't want to. And the more you give in to that urge, the more you'll come to believe the lies you're telling yourself about what you are and aren't capable of. It's a cycle, Charley. It's a self-reinforcing cycle of mistaken thinking. And we have to come up with a way for you to break it once and for all."

Even if it involves pills, she thinks.

Maybe if she weren't so damn tired, this would be it, the moment she stormed out of his office and never came back. But she is tired.

So tired she wasn't sure she was in shape to make the drive to town, a drive that's practically a straight shot across open desert on a flat, two-lane blacktop.

He's mentioned drugs at least once a session. In the beginning she'd figured this was just his way of reminding her he's an actual psychiatrist who can prescribe stuff. That he isn't just some touchy-feely psychologist with a degree he earned online.

But he's never let up on it. And he hasn't now even though she told him how her father tried to medicate her into silence when she was ten.

And she's tired.

She likes these sessions, she needs them, and the sense that he's getting impatient with her, it's affecting her more than she wants it to. Maybe more than she thinks it should.

Or I'm feeling worn down because he's right, she considers. *Not just because he went to Harvard, or because he looks like all the actors who've ever played Superman run together.*

What's that's AA saying she's always liked?

Keep it simple, stupid.

And so what's the simplest question and the simplest answer here?

Do I need sleep?

Yes. Hell yes. Dear God, yes.

"What do you have in mind?" she hears herself say. "Some kind of sleeping pill?"

He lowers his right leg from where he's braced the ankle on top of his left knee, setting aside the legal pad on which he's not taken a single note since they started. "No," he answers. "Not a sleeping pill."

He gets to his feet, turns to his desk, and opens the drawer. She expects him to pull out a prescription pad. Instead he removes a square of white cardboard, six bright-orange pills encased inside little plastic bubbles.

"What is that?"

"It's called Zypraxon." He takes a seat on the edge of his chair and holds the pill packet in between his thumb and forefinger. He's gazing into her eyes now, the talk therapist replaced by the medical doctor. "And I think it's going to be just perfect for you."

5

The first gun is under the sink.

A Beretta M9 in a holster attached to the cabinet's ceiling, within easy reach of anyone doing dishes or moving about the compact, tidy kitchen.

Jason slides his backpack off one shoulder and digs out the plastic bags.

He removes the gun's magazine and strips it with one hand, punching the bullets one after the other into the Ziploc he holds open with his other hand. Once the magazine is empty, he seals the bag and drops it inside his backpack. Then he inspects the chamber to make sure he didn't leave a bullet sitting inside.

He inserts the empty magazine and returns the gun to its hidden holster.

Dark is falling. He needs to work quickly. But the temptation to study his surroundings is almost overwhelming.

The house has two bedrooms along a short, narrow tiled hallway. At the end of the hallway is the door to the small garage. Both bedrooms have only a thin band of clerestory windows; probably to protect them from the heat. The bulletproof glass they're made of doesn't have anything to do with the temperature outside. The living room has a wall of floor-to-ceiling windows that look out onto the small courtyard. The glass here is also bulletproof, and he's willing to bet it replaced what was once a sliding glass door. Now the only entrance to the courtyard is the house's front door.

It's the lawsuit against her father that financed this place. He's sure of this.

The lawsuit was the last time she'd appeared in the press.

Jason kept all the clippings.

In the last interview Trina ever gave, she'd asserted she was asking for only enough money to start a new life for herself, something that didn't involve profiting off the memories of the Bannings' victims.

The message boards devoted to her and the killings had exploded with rage. She was a liar who didn't give a whit about the victims, they'd claimed. And her lawsuit was just another form of self-promotion.

Under a string of aliases, Jason had tried to defend her, to blame Lowell Pierce for caring only about money and filling her head with junk science and never allowing her to tell her own story. But the other posters assailed him. They claimed his statements implied a personal relationship with Trina he couldn't prove. And when he told them he would prove them all wrong someday, they'd banned him for violating some policy around threats that wasn't in the forum's guidelines. He could barely bring himself to care. He wasn't like the rest of them. They pretended to weep for the victims so they could pore over the crime scene photos. They pretended to hate the Bannings because, like him, they aspired to their purity and greatness; they just couldn't admit it.

And now he's here, inside her house.

So fuck those hypocrites.

He's hard-pressed to call the front room a living room because it looks more like a comfortable office than a place to relax. The desk and giant computer monitors—three of them, all wide-screen, fanned out across an L-shaped desk so that they almost surround whoever's sitting at it—look like Hollywood's idea of a NASA workstation. Her desk chair is coated in worn but soft-looking padding that suggests she spends more time there than anywhere else around the house.

It's the bedrooms that are calling him, but what's the sense in going through her belongings if he's going to burn them all anyway?

She's going to burn them, he corrects himself, once he manages to convince her of their future together.

Because by then she'll get it. By then they'll have had plenty of time out here alone together without the distractions of crowds, birth fathers, or restraining orders.

But for now he's got the other guns to empty.

One down, two to go.

6

She stood up the minute Dylan handed her the pill.

It was a reflexive move on her part, and she's not sure why she did it.

Seconds before, Dylan had been leaning toward her, through the several feet of space between his chair and hers. Maybe their proximity became too much for her, or maybe now that she has the pill in hand she wants to run from the office and swallow it in private before she loses her nerve.

At any rate, the fact that she's now on her feet has left Dylan staring up at her awkwardly. Worse, it suggests she wants to end this meeting, when the truth is quite the opposite. The bright-orange pill burns a hole in her palm, it seems, and she's full of questions about it.

"A what?" she asks.

"It's a derivative of a benzodiazepine."

"What's that? An antidepressant?"

"No. It's a very mild central nervous system depressant. It's designed to be fast acting, but it's also timed release, so it should remain relatively constant in your bloodstream for the next twenty-four hours. I want you to come back around this time tomorrow so we can assess."

"Assess what?"

"How you respond to the drug. We can pull you off it right away if you don't like the side effects."

"OK. And the positive effects are supposed to be what exactly?"

"A rapid reduction in anxiety and fear-based thinking without the sedation effect of a heavier benzo or Valium. It doesn't sound like you're suffering from clinical insomnia, just a sleep disruption caused by conditional anxiety. This will attack the anxiety directly but in a measured and hopefully consistent way."

"It's new?"

"Excuse me?"

"This drug. Zyprox . . ."

"Zypraxon, yes. It's brand-new actually. They're just rolling it out now. I've got enough samples for us to have a little trial run before you decide if a prescription will work for you."

"OK. When should I take it?"

"Now."

"*Now?* I need to be able to drive home."

"It shouldn't impair your ability to drive or work or anything like that. A lot of central nervous system depressants—Xanax and others—produce a single, powerful tranquilizing effect that becomes addictive. Zypraxon is designed to attack persistent anxiety at a lower dose released consistently throughout the day."

She's staring at the pill, and she still hasn't been able to force herself to sit.

"Look, Charley, there's stronger stuff out there we can talk about. This is not a wonder cure, by any stretch. But I think it's well suited for you."

"And you want me to take it right now?" she asks.

"To be frank, that doesn't sound like a question for me."

Is he losing patience with her?

Will he stop seeing her if she doesn't take the pill?

Is she doing exactly what he just accused her of doing by asking herself these questions—pretending the real issue is how someone else perceives her and not what she needs for herself? After all she's been through, why is this so scary? It's a pill, and she can be pulled off it at any time. And while she's certainly no expert in antidepressants or central nervous system depressants or whatever other class of drugs they give people to stabilize their moods these days, it sounds pretty mild.

And it's him—Dylan.

Dr. Thorpe, when he's asked her to do something she doesn't want to.

How many hours have they spent together in this tiny office, talking about her and only her? Too many to count offhand; that's for sure. And he's listened to her the way no one else has since her grandmother died. More important, he's told her the truth about herself even when it might sound unkind. Only a few people have done that for her before. Her grandmother, now gone, and her grandmother's boyfriend, Marty, whom she can barely bring herself to call these days because the sound of his voice brings back a flood of once-joyful memories.

"Water," she hears herself say.

Dylan reaches for an unopened bottle of water on his desk. He uncaps it for her.

One swig and she's swallowed the pill.

"That took strength, Charley," he says, rising slowly to his feet.

His hands grip her shoulders; it's the most intimate touch they've ever shared. "Making a new decision, breaking an old habit. It takes strength. And believe me"—he kisses her gently on the forehead—"you are stronger than you know."

It's the first time she's been touched, the first time she's been kissed in even a quick and chaste way, in years, and it makes her dizzy.

She wants to cry again, but she can't blame the pill. No way could it have gone to work this fast. She can blame her sleeplessness, for sure.

While she's at it, she can also stop searching Dylan's face for some evidence that the kiss was more than just a doctor getting carried away by enthusiasm. Dylan makes that easier for her when he turns to his desk and picks up a small notebook.

"For the next twenty-four hours I want you to keep a log of everything you go through. Anything that feels strange or off. Anything that might be a side effect. Write it down in this." He taps the notebook, then presses it into her hand. He opens the office door and steers her through it. After the sudden, unexplained kiss, the feel of his hand against the small of her back makes her skin tingle. "Then I want to see you back here same time tomorrow so we can assess."

By the time she's reached the foot of the stairs, Dylan's closed his office door again, which makes her feel unmoored and adrift.

The AA meeting will break up soon, and if she lingers here, some of the regulars might ask a bunch of prying questions about why she stopped attending.

She steps outside into the evening dark.

She hurries to her car, reminds herself with each step of Dylan's promise that whatever this damn drug is, it won't affect her ability to drive home.

Only once she's behind the wheel does it sink in that there's a strange new substance in her body, and for a second, she feels as if she's been violated.

My choice, she reminds herself. *It will be different this time because it was my choice.* She repeats these words in her head like a mantra as Scarlet shrinks in her rearview mirror.

7

When the motorcycle almost runs her off the road, Charlotte's tempted to blame the medication. How else could she have missed its approach? It's got no mufflers.

The roar that swallows her Ford Escape now sends pure, raw fear shooting through her from head to toe.

For a second she's blinded by its headlight; then it swings to the left before swerving in front of her SUV.

All right, Zypraxon. Do your thing!

Two more motorcycles appear on either side of her.

Her heart races. Her palms are so sweaty she fears they might slip from the steering wheel if she doesn't hold on for dear life.

What the hell is this? She's seen these guys before, mostly pulling in and out of the old bus sheds they've turned into their unincorporated hangout. It's where they're all headed now, she assumes—she hopes—but they've never tried to overtake her on the road like this. Was she weaving? Is this their way of punishing her? Fencing her in, drowning her in horrible sound?

Staring straight ahead seems like the best plan, but there's almost nothing for her to stare at except desert dark and the biker in the lead. At least the guy in front is allowing more distance now between the tail of his bike and the nose of her SUV.

There's faint purple in the western sky, but it's mostly dark out now. In fact, there aren't even lights to mark the spot where she knows their hideout stands. *And that's bad,* she thinks. *That means the place isn't just a hideout—it's some kind of storehouse, and they don't want anyone to know about it.*

Up until a few weeks ago, she was alone out here, which is exactly how she likes it. When the bikers first showed up, she hadn't given them a second thought. Criminals who just want to do their own thing—a change of pace from the monsters in her past. Let them cook or deal their meth in peace, she'd thought. She wants to be left alone, and so do they.

But now they're taking an interest in her. A really loud, scary interest. And up close she can see the telltale signs of hard-core outlaws.

A guy named Benny used to come to the meetings at the center all the time and share about his Hells Angels past. The other alcoholics got tired of him after a while, maybe because his shares had less to do with recovery than bragging about his criminal cred. But Charlotte was riveted every time he spoke, and now, thanks to Benny, she knows the sleeveless denim shirts these guys are wearing are called cuts; the patches on the back are signs they're full-fledged members of the gang in question. The word *Vapados* fills the center patch on each guy's back. She's not sure what it means. Is it the name of their biker gang?

Benny's shares always made it sound as if Arizona belonged to the Hells Angels. So where did these guys come from?

Only a few more minutes until they'd pass their hideout. If they still had her fenced in by then, it might be time to take the Beretta out of the glove compartment. But what good would that do?

Charlotte puts in several hours a week of practice on the thing, but she's never tried getting off a good shot at sixty-five miles an hour. If they work together, the bikers could run her off the road before she manages to fire. Then where would she be?

They're close to their hangout now, close enough that she might have to make a decision in the next minute.

She looks to one side.

Sure enough, the biker to her left is staring at her. His helmet, yellow-tinted glasses, and wind-rippling beard steal most of the definition from his face. But he's big. Thor big. He stares at her with a leisurely confidence. When she sees the tattoo of a pistol on the side of his neck, and the sleeves of ornate carnage inked down his arms, her spine feels like piano keys being walked on by a cat. "Fuck," she whispers.

He smiles. He's read her lips and he's amused.

Then he aims a trigger finger in her direction and peels away suddenly. His buddies follow suit; their headlights bounce across the roadside and briefly illuminate the old sheds they've made their own.

She welcomes the darkness that closes in all around her now, even though the absence of the deafening motorcycles leaves her with the haggard sound of her own breathing.

At least she's got her first journal entry. *Thirty minutes after initial dose, biker gang manages to scare ever-living shit out of me. Got anything stronger, Dylan?*

Should she kill her headlights when she gets close to her house?

Or do they already know she lives out here? Maybe that's why they were slowing down and checking her out. But the message of that trigger finger was clear—don't come back. She sometimes goes two weeks without leaving the house. That must be why it took them a while to pick up on the fact that she's passed them more than once today.

There's got to be some way to send a message that she could give two shits what they're doing in those sheds. Or what they're hiding.

Maybe if they knew I was Burning Girl . . .

Just thinking the nickname turns her stomach.

Or maybe that's the aftereffect of almost being run off the road.

Or maybe it's the Zypraxon.

Or maybe, and this thought makes her dizzy as well as nauseated, it's the realization that she barely noticed the bikers' approach because she was still thinking about Dylan's kiss. Dylan's quick but somehow furtive and totally inappropriate kiss.

She hates that she let her guard down on a mostly empty road because she was obsessing over her psychiatrist like some love-struck teenager.

But that's not quite it, she realizes.

Yes, there'd been a moment right when his lips touched her skin when she'd felt something open inside her. Some hunger for intimate connection she'd assumed she'd locked away. It was instinctive, this response. But now, with a little distance between her and the center, it wasn't just the kiss that bothered her. It was the way he'd touched her after. The way he'd guided her out of his office, one hand against the small of her back. As if, because she'd finally broken down and consented to taking the pill, he now saw her as firmly under his control.

Touchy. Confident yet strangely hurried.

An odd combination of words to describe his behavior, but an accurate one. And one she never would have applied to him before.

You're overthinking this, she tells herself. *You're feeling guilty and weak because you took the pill, and now you're reading too much into his behavior.*

Behavior that included a kiss.

She drives past her own house.

Maybe that's for the best. If the bikers are following her, which she doubts, this gives her a chance to kill her headlights and double back. She's made her way from the edge of the highway to her place in the dark plenty of times when she thought someone might be trailing her. Once her eyes adjust, it's fairly easy. The line of mountains on the distant horizon is jagged enough that it's often discernible against even the night sky, especially when there's still a faint fringe of purple as there is now.

When the shadow of her house rises up out of the desert floor, she hits the garage door opener attached to her key ring. The light comes on inside, and she uses its bright glow to guide herself the rest of the way in. The garage isn't covered by the security system, but any attempt to break in through the metal door would be more than visible in her headlights. Still, the minute it takes to get from her car to the alarm keypad next to the back door always leaves her feeling exposed.

Her Escape crosses the threshold. She turns on the headlights and hits the key fob. The garage door begins to descend.

Before stepping out, she scans the cement floors just to make sure no desert critters followed her in. She's had enough contact with rattlers to know they just want to be left the hell alone. Unless you step on them. If you step on them, you're screwed. If there's one inside the garage with her, it's because the tires dragged it in by mistake, in which case, it's probably dying or in pieces.

There's nothing in the garage with her. Just the ticking sounds of her cooling vehicle and the rattle and whine of the steel door descending behind her.

She's home.

Safe.

And, man, does she have to pee. It's either a result of her brush with the Sons of Anarchy or a side effect of the medication.

There's a half bath right before the main hallway's entrance to the kitchen. As soon as she sits down on the toilet, she realizes something feels wrong. It's her pants. Their weight seems off. Something's missing from the pockets.

Her phone. She hasn't carried a purse in years, and she rarely visits town in anything other than blue jeans, so she usually tucks her phone in her front pocket to avoid sitting on it. But it's not there. Her jeans feel light, and they slid too easily over her knees.

Did she leave it in the car?

She can't remember having it since she wandered into Dylan's office. She must have put it down on his desk. When she'd thought she heard it during their session, Dylan had told her the noise came from his and she needed to focus . . .

She's not sure how to describe what she hears next.

Creak isn't right, but it's too half-hearted to be a footstep.

Movement.

There is movement somewhere inside her house, just outside the bathroom door she didn't bother to lock.

And I don't have my phone, she thinks. *The same phone that would display an alert if someone messed with my alarm or, God forbid, managed to turn it off while I was gone.*

Miraculously, she manages to finish peeing. But when she reaches for the toilet paper, her hand is shaking.

It feels as if a ghost has closed its fingers around the back of her neck. And she realizes that while she lives in a state of perpetual anxiety, and sometimes flat-out dread, it's been a long time since she has been truly afraid. Not just afraid—terrified. And it's physical, this feeling. A series of pulses traveling through her body. Like she can feel her heartbeat in her hands and feet.

The sound repeats. And the silence on either side of it is unmistakable—a silence that suggests restraint, human restraint. An effort to stay as quiet as possible. *One of the bikers? Impossible.* Even if they'd killed their headlights, there's no way they could have followed her into the garage without her seeing them. Or hearing them.

But these sounds, they're coming from the direction of the garage. Or one of the bedrooms between the bathroom and the garage.

Both her arms are tingling the same way her leg does when it goes to sleep. And yet some instinct is kicking in. Some instinct that tells her it's best to pretend she hasn't heard anything. Best to act as if nothing's amiss. Then, as if she's about to begin preparing dinner, she'll make a beeline for the kitchen and the gun under the sink.

Everything is fine, she tells herself as she washes her hands. Her trembling hands.

She's had physical responses to fear before, but never this strong. The tingling in her arms is almost painful now. Her hands shake as if there's some disturbance inside the bones of her wrists.

Everything is fine, she tells herself again.

She opens the bathroom door, head bowed, as if she has no urge at all to look in either direction, as if all she wants to do is stroll into the kitchen and fix herself something to eat.

Everything is not fine, but you're going to pretend it is until you can put a bullet in this bastard. Then things will be fine again.

It takes all the effort she has, but she forces herself to go to the fridge and take out a Diet Coke, because women who are afraid they're about to be murdered don't get themselves a Diet Coke. They don't stand over the sink, taking a leisurely sip of their favorite soft drink while secretly gauging how many seconds it will take to pull their Beretta from under the cabinet at their legs. And this charade, she hopes, will give her an element of surprise.

She hears the footsteps behind her only because she's listening for them. They're soft enough that she would have missed them otherwise.

And then she realizes she's made a critical mistake.

She forgot to turn on the light in the kitchen, and now she's standing in almost total darkness over the sink, which looks about as natural as if she'd just hit the linoleum in a downward dog.

In the window above the sink, she sees his shadow. She sees his curls. Just their silhouette, backlit by the garage light.

Jason Briffel's curls.

Her hands have stopped shaking, but the tingling has moved from her arms, across her back, and up the back of her neck. It's even touching the sides of her face.

One shot, she tells herself. *Shoot him and make a break for the living room and the front door. No talk. No negotiation. He's in my fucking house. If he wants to die here, he made that choice when he broke in. I moved to a Stand Your Ground state for a reason.*

She imagines herself doing it before she's done it. Imagines pulling the gun from the holster attached to the cabinet's ceiling, turning, and firing off as many shots as it takes to drop him. She imagines it so clearly, she doesn't realize she's just tried it.

And nothing happened.

She's pulled the trigger twice and the only sounds in the kitchen are their combined breaths. Jason has raised his hands, not in surrender but to calm her. He approaches her slowly, as if she's a hysterical woman, and he's broken into her house in the middle of nowhere because he's the only one in the universe who can reason with her.

How how how how how, she thinks, the word like a mad bird's cawing in her brain. *How did he get here? How did he get in my house?*

Her new name's not even on the deed. Kayla helped her set up a trust after they won the case against her dad. No one else knows she's out here. No one except . . .

"Put the gun down, Trina."

"That's not my name."

"It *is* your name. It will always be your name. Now enough of this game playing. Enough of the denial. We're grown-ups now, and it's time for us to talk about grown-up things."

From the back waistband of his pants, he pulls a gun. One of her guns. No doubt this one's fully loaded. It's the one from her bedroom or under her desk in the living room. It has to be. But he keeps it pointed at the ceiling. The gesture says he doesn't want to use it on her, but he will if he has to, which seems as sick and condescending as the words he just spoke with oily certainty.

"You need to leave," she hears herself say. "You need to leave my house."

"This isn't a house, Trina. This is a shack, a prison. I hate to sound so judgmental, but it's pathetic. I mean, you're out here in the middle of nowhere. It's not safe."

She wants to believe he's taunting her, but he isn't. He genuinely believes the things he's saying. And he's lost a considerable amount of weight. That fact terrifies her almost as much as his presence here. When she last saw him, there was something infantlike about his portliness. Now he's lean and ready to pounce, and this suggests he's been preparing for this moment, transforming himself into a more efficient predator.

He aspires to be a serial killer. She's known this from the moment she read his letters. But his behavior has always been more stalker than murderer. Can she appeal to the former side of him? Can she soothe and seduce him?

"You scared me, Jason. The things you did . . . they scared me."

Feed his ego. Make him feel as if he's the center of my world.

"Well, that's ridiculous, Trina," he says, with a great pained smile that almost looks like a grimace. "I'd never hurt you."

"Then why are you here?"

"To bring you *back*," he says. "To bring you back to your life, your real life. Your destiny."

"With you," she says. She tries to keep her voice as neutral as she can, to not betray her disgust at these words, and apparently she's successful because he nods fiercely as he takes another step toward her.

"You made the first step yourself, and that's good. You cut yourself off from your birth father and got him out of your life. And that was the best thing you could have done. And then . . . well, the universe stepped in and handled the rest."

"The rest?"

"Your grandmother."

"What about my grandmother?" A mistake to ask this; there's a tremor in her voice now.

"It was for the best. She was in your way, too. I know you were sad when she died, but it was the only way for you to be free."

"Did you hurt my grandmother, Jason?"

"No!" he whines. He sounds like a child. And he's so genuinely wounded she knows he's telling the truth. "I can't cause heart attacks. I'm not God. But if there is a God, he took her away when he did because she wasn't your real family, Trina. Abigail is. *I* am."

She runs for it.

There's a few feet of space between the sink and the door to the living room. As soon as she bounds in that direction, she hears him erupt. "No, no, no, no, no," he says like a man whose dog has just jumped from the back seat of his car.

He crashes into her from behind, arms around her waist suddenly. He still holds the gun in one hand, which is stupid. Stupid and untrained. The two of them careen into her desk, and at any moment he could fire wildly by accident.

Her head slams into one of the computer monitors, then the solid wall behind it. She feels no pain. None of the bone-rattling, stomach-churning agony that should follow such a double blow. It's shock; it has to be. But even as she tumbles amid the wreckage of her desk, the tingling she felt earlier is all over her body, along with another sensation. It's utterly foreign, utterly without precedent in her experience. The words that leap to her mind to describe it are just as strange: *bone music*. It feels like the bass line of some song is being played inside her very bones.

The desk gives way beneath them as they struggle. Her arms flail. She feels her fingers close around the stand of one of the wide-screen monitors as it falls along with her.

What happens next takes place with the very ease, grace, and speed with which she tried to shoot him moments ago.

She is standing now, facing the living room, and Jason is on his knees. Somehow she is holding one of the wide-screen monitors in one hand. The same monitor it took both hands to get out of the box when she first installed it. The same monitor that was so top heavy she was afraid of dropping the thing before she managed to lower it to her desk for the first time. Now she's holding it one hand, her fingers gripping the open O in its A-shaped stand, as if the whole thing weighs no more than a flyswatter, and that's exactly how she's just used the thing on Jason's head.

Jason sways back and forth, his eyes wide and unblinking. Blood spurts from his right temple. In another second he'll be spitting it from his lips. Or drinking it, because his jaw is slack and the way he's swaying looks like he can't tell up from down, as if he might keel over at any moment.

"Don't get up," she says.

He doesn't listen. He throws one leg out in front of him, knee bent, foot steady on the floor.

So she hits him again.

This time she's fully present while she does it. The miracle of it leaves her in a daze. It truly feels as if the monitor weighs almost nothing. Its impact with his skull causes only the slightest recoil in her arm. To accomplish all of this, she needed only a few short breaths. And now that she's done it, she needs only a few more, and then she feels fully recovered. And she's still holding the thing in one hand like it's a costume shield.

This is impossible, she thinks. But how else can she explain the fact that Jason Briffel is now sprawled on his back, looking as if he's just been dropped from a great height? He doesn't even stir as she picks up the gun he dropped, keeping it aimed at him as she grabs for the nearest phone, the one that wasn't pulled to the floor by their collision with her desk.

Her landline is hooked to a satellite Internet connection, and he's cut the line between the base and the wall. Cell phone service out here is passable, thanks to the three signal boosters she installed on the roof. But her phone's probably back at Dylan's office, if she didn't leave it in the car.

And Jason might not be alone.

Gun raised, she cases each room, the way she taught herself to do after watching countless YouTube videos posted by retired cops. She's never been so grateful to have such a small house with so few hiding places.

In her bedroom closet, she finds his backpack. But when she reaches for it with one hand, it seems to take flight into the air behind her.

Adrenaline, she tells herself. *Just adrenaline. It won't last.*

But the tingling's still there. The bone music is still there. And there's no denying that by reaching for the bag with what she thought was a minimal amount of effort, she'd somehow ended up throwing it into the air behind her.

Breathe, she tells herself. *Shrink!*

She almost laughs at this second command. But that's exactly what she has to do. Whatever crazy hormonal event is taking place inside her system, the only way she can think to counteract it so she can function normally is to shrink every action, her every move.

She bends down. Gently gripping the zipper's pull between a thumb and forefinger, she slowly and carefully opens the bag. And even with all that deliberate restraint, the bag ends up opening like some horny dude's jeans.

When she sees the rope and the rolls of duct tape and the Ziploc bags full of her bullets, all thoughts of shrinking are forgotten.

Jason's still dead to the world when she returns to the living room.

He might actually be dead, but she doesn't give a shit. The only thing that matters to her is that he stays exactly where he is so she can bring the cops back here and show them how he broke in. How he violated her space.

She'll tell them everything. She's got nothing to hide. By then this crazy adrenaline rush will have subsided, she's sure. He can't get away. That's all that matters to her now. No way will she let him slip away into the shadows so he can lie in wait for the right moment to shatter her sanity and sense of safety again.

First she wraps his head in tape, making a muzzle across his mouth; then she binds his wrists, his ankles. When she starts binding his ankles to his wrists, she realizes she's hog-tying him just like Daniel and Abigail used to bind their victims, but she banishes the thought before it can take hold. She's trying not to beat him up, but she still can't control her own strength entirely. Her tugs and pulls knock his head against the floor with sickening whacks.

Gun drawn, she backs out of the living room.

"I'll be right back, fucker."

Amazing, the confidence with which she's issued this proclamation, the steadiness. Like her voice has recognized the magnitude of her newfound strength even as her mind refuses.

With the lightest touch she can manage, she hits a button on her key fob and opens the trunk of her Escape. With just as much care and restraint, she roots through the plastic bags from the office supply store. No sign of her phone.

Carefully, so as not to pull it off its hinges, she opens the door to the back seat, scans the floor. No sign there, either.

She slides behind the wheel like someone easing into frigid water.

She places the gun in the cup holder, barrel down, within easy reach, positioned to aim right through the windshield if she needs to. Ever so slowly, she reaches for the glove compartment, pops it open with three times less effort than she might ordinarily use. The phone's not there, either, which means it has to be in Dylan's office. Which means she's got to drive to the nearest police station herself.

Just then she realizes there's one place she hasn't checked for accomplices.

Outside.

She hits the key fob. The garage door starts to open. Gun raised, she approaches the growing square of dark. It takes a few minutes for her eyes to adjust. By then she's swept the opening. By then she can see there are no lurking shadows of cars hiding with their headlights turned off. The ground is flat. The nearest hiding place is an arroyo a good fifteen-minute walk away, the same place she does target practice with the Berettas. Besides, Jason has always worked alone.

Jason has always wanted her all to himself.

But how did he get my code?

She's got no time to speculate. She's confirmed that there are no vehicles waiting to ram her as soon as she leaves the garage. And that means she's free to go.

As she slides behind the wheel of her Escape and places her Beretta back in the cup holder, she sees that her fingers have left indentations in the metal handle of her gun.

Not just adrenaline, she thinks. *This can't be just adrenaline.*

8

The bikers roar out of the darkness, headlights winking on the minute their tires hit the road.

When Charlotte first met up with the highway, she went to give the pedal the usual amount of pressure and ended up marrying it to the floor, which sent the Escape rocketing through the night at more than a hundred miles an hour.

She's been soft pedaling it since then. It's kept the Escape close to eighty. That's what she's doing now as they cage her in.

They've been waiting for her, she realizes, maybe since they heard her approach. No doubt her third trip past their hideout in one day has them convinced she's casing the place.

Thor's next to her again, gesturing for her to pull over.

Her refusal to comply causes his mouth to contort into a snarl. The sight of his anger awakens something in her, a recognition that she's been impossibly changed. And not changed like that guy, possibly an urban legend, who was able to lift a car in one hand to free an accident victim pinned beneath it. *This is ongoing, whatever this is. It's sustained. My body knows it. My mind's starting to accept it. And that's why Thor's pissed—he doesn't see any fear in my eyes.*

He hollers something unintelligible over the wind, raises a fist in the direction of his buddies.

Watching Thor has distracted her. Her foot drifts down on the accelerator, defaulting to habit.

The Escape rockets up to ninety right as one of Thor's buddies swerves to cut her off.

Almost gracefully, the man's body flies upward onto the hood, then crashes into her windshield, leaving a mosaic of cracks. When he flips up and away, going over the roof with a sound like tumbling boulders, she sees the blacktop has been replaced by open desert. She tries to regain control, but the steering wheel's been pulled almost entirely apart, the ring cracked on top and bottom. A bulge of wires protrudes from a mouthlike fold where the horn should be.

No way could the biker's impact have done this.

She did it while holding on to the thing for dear life during the collision.

The Escape slams into a saguaro cactus with such force, the hood flips up and turns into something that looks like a wadded-up napkin. Only then does she realize she never put her seat belt on. But it doesn't matter. She experiences the impact like a kid being jostled by her friends in a bouncy house. She can see everything with the slow-motion clarity of shock—the shattering windshield, the Beretta going airborne and disappearing out the passenger-side window—and then it all comes to an end.

Even though she should be either unconscious or dead, she's sitting upright behind the wheel, her breathing rapid but barely strained.

There's a loud thud. The Escape's roof gives her scalp a sudden kiss. The top half of the giant cactus has fallen onto her hissing SUV.

She feels as if she's belly flopped into a swimming pool. The car crash has left her with a rash of tingles across her flesh and dull aches here and there. But it should be worse. Much worse given the state of the car and the fact she was bounced around like a rag doll. The music in her bones has grown more intense, as if the trauma of the accident kicked up the tempo. Whatever this thing is that's happening to her, it's hooked to adrenaline. But that can't be the only explanation.

She gives the door a push, and the entire thing comes free of its hinges and falls to the sand.

As they roar toward her through the darkness, the two remaining bikers make hairpin turns around rocks, bushes, and other knee-high obstructions. They're coming with predatory fury.

Thor pulls around to her right; his friend dismounts at her left and draws a sawed-off shotgun from his back.

Her ears still ring from the crash. But she can hear some of their shouts. They're gesturing to their feet, gesturing for her to get down, either to her knees or her stomach—they don't seem to care which. The words *bitch* and *cunt* jump out at her from their threats like hot pebbles glancing across her cheeks.

She feels as though she's observing herself from a distance, and she's astonished to watch herself sink to her knees. Just as her foot defaulted back to its normal pressure on the gas pedal moments before, she now defaults to fear and submission.

But it's a big shotgun, and she doesn't know if this altered state renders her impervious to buckshot.

Then she sees the flex-cuffs in Thor's left hand.

In his right, he's got a gun, boxy enough to be a Canik TP9, but she's not sure. She is sure that he's aiming at her, lowering it only slightly as he approaches. He's going to cuff her out here in the middle of nowhere. She thinks she can break the cuffs. Still, the ease and confidence with which he approaches her ignites a fire deep in her belly.

". . . fucking gave you an order, bitch," Thor's saying. "Clear as fucking day, I gave you an order to pull over, and what did you fucking do? *What did you fucking do, huh, bitch?*"

The Daniel and Abigail Bannings of the world are few and far between, thank God. But men like this one, men who will run you off the road because they have cast you in their paranoid fantasies, are far more common. And the tyranny of their appetites is so woven through every woman's world that imagining life without it is the same as imagining life without ground underfoot.

"Don't you fucking move—got it, bitch?" Thor snarls. There's about a foot of space between them now. He's going to step behind her to cuff her wrists. His friend raises his shotgun. "We can either have a nice long conversation about what the hell you're doing all the way out here, or Axel can put a load of buckshot in you and save us all the trouble."

Axel is a silhouette backlit by the headlight from his bike. But his aim looks steady. Thor is behind her now.

"I live out here." Her voice sounds vacant, numb.

"Oh yeah? Are you a snake?" He grabs the back of her hair and pulls it like a leash. It should hurt. He wants it to hurt. But it doesn't. *"I said, are you a fucking snake, bitch?"*

"Get off me," she says.

"What?"

"I said get off me."

"You don't give me orders, you stupid fucking cu—"

A few seconds later, he's careening toward his friend like a drunken idiot trying to dance at a wedding reception. It wasn't the most complex of moves on her part. Just a pull of his arm and a thrust really. But the strength she put behind it is otherworldly; it's like a blast of air has sent him hurtling through the dark toward Axel's shotgun. There was no preparing for it.

Axel, it turns out, is too prepared.

There's an explosion of light and a deafening boom. Drifts of torn denim snowflake through the air in front of her. Over the ringing in her ears, she hears Axel bellowing as he realizes he's just blown a hole in his friend.

Thor's drop is decisive and sudden.

Before Axel can raise the shotgun again, she runs for him, hands out, gives him what would have been a light shove just hours before.

He hurtles backward into the bars of his Harley-Davidson. The impact of his spine cracks the headlight. The shotgun hits the dirt. He and the bike fall over to one side together, their dark silhouette like a time-lapse of melting snow.

The ringing in her ears drowns out the sounds he's making now, but if his spread arms, trembling hands, and shaking head are any indication, they're probably stomach churning, and she's willing to bet he'll never walk again.

There's a cold caress around her ankles. Her stopping power punched shallow holes in the ground. When she steps out of them, the holes widen, chunks of caked desert earth tumbling off her sneakers.

There should be regret, she knows. Somewhere within her there should be some primal remorse.

But the music in her bones is at a fever pitch now, and so vivid are the nightmare images of what these two men might have done to her out here, they white out all her other thoughts. And there was a glimpse of something, just a glimpse in Axel's eyes before he cracked the bike's headlight with his spine, a glimpse of something that satisfied a thirst in her she didn't know she possessed—fear.

There's no sign of the biker she hit with her car. Did they leave him for dead, or is he crawling back to their hideout to get help? How many of them are there?

The darkness seems to close in around her now.

The thought of digging in their pockets for their phones sends a rush of revulsion through her that makes her feel suddenly ordinary again. Do they have satellite phones? They're well outside the boosters at her house that could provide decent service.

The police station's too far away to head for on foot, especially if the guy who destroyed her windshield has called for help. She had good luck against two of these guys. Against four or five? She'd need more than this impossible strength.

There's only one place she can go right now. Home. If more bikers are on the way, better to face them from behind her security system, with her guns and with some chance of repairing her phone line. Besides, maybe they'll never find her house.

In the emergency kit in her Escape she finds a flashlight.

On the other side of the wrecked car she finds the Beretta.

Home is the only place she can go, she realizes.

A few minutes after she reaches the road, her flashlight beam finds the other biker's legs. Once she runs it up his body, she sees his waist is twisted at a grotesque angle from the rest of him, his head a mound of gore. No way did he manage to call for help. The desert's ghostly quiet.

She starts in the direction of her house. After a few seconds, she begins to run. She's afraid too much exertion might flush from her system whatever insane combination of hormones is giving her this strength. But she'd rather take that risk than meet more bikers out here in the dark.

9

As the door descends behind her, Charlotte uses the keypad inside the garage to search her security system's recent history.

Somehow Jason managed to crack her code. The proof's right in front of her.

SYSTEM ENTRY 5:36 p.m.

Automatic reengagement happened three minutes after.

Next comes her arrival, two hours later, followed by her departure twenty minutes after that.

Twenty minutes. Jason's attack, overpowering him, binding him—was that really all it took?

She draws her Beretta. The metal depresses under her grip before she softens her hand.

Bedrooms, closets, bathrooms—all empty.

Not the kitchen.

Jason's still trussed up like a pig, but he's managed to squirm away from the debris left by their struggle in the living room. Exhaustion or pain from his injuries has overtaken him. He's rag-doll limp. But he's definitely alive. When he sees her coming down the hallway, his eyes widen, then narrow when he realizes she's alone.

Something uncurls in her at the sight of him. Something hungry and feral and ready to strike.

When she's a few steps away from him, he whines into the duct tape across his mouth, starts wiggling backward in a desperate attempt to escape. He seems to be remembering what she's capable of. It's good to be reminded, because there were a few moments during the strange, silent trek back to her house when she thought her night so far might have been one giant hallucination.

And what causes hallucinations?

Drugs.

Drugs like the one she's on now, the one Dylan gave her.

But Jason's fear is too real to be a hallucination. If this truly is all some giant drug reaction, it sure as hell isn't the kind they warn you about on TV commercials.

She reminds herself what she came here to do. *A phone. I need a phone.*

She checks to make sure the base station for her phone system is in its usual spot, on a table in the hallway, just by the entrance to the kitchen. It is. There's even a handset in the cradle. But when she traces the cord down to the outlet, she sees that it's dangling inches from a new hole in the wall.

Jason removed the entire socket. Even if she could find it, she'd need a technician to plug it back in and rewire it. He didn't just cut the cord. He didn't just unplug the phone. He made sure there was no way she could easily reconnect if a struggle went in her favor. And if the landline's out, that means no using the alarm's panic button to summon Scarlet PD, who are forty minutes away at best. She checks the outlet in her bedroom. It's in the exact same condition.

Her pulse roars in her ears.

She's afraid again, but for entirely different reasons. What scares her now is that the pathetic sounds Jason's making when she returns to the kitchen don't inspire revulsion, much less pity. Instead they seem like information. The way a caribou's limp is information to a hungry wolf.

Is this the drug, too? she thinks. *Is it giving me more than just strength? Is it silencing my soul, removing my remorse? Or does remorse always leave once you have the power to indulge your worst instincts with impunity?*

As gently as she can, she grips him by one shoulder and pulls him away from the cabinet until he's lying flat on the floor.

She gazes into his eyes. Studies the fear there.

She's savoring it. There's no other word for it. And he can see this, and it terrifies him more.

For the first time in months, she tries to summon memories of her grandmother. Her grief made the effort too painful before. But in this moment, it's Luanne's voice she needs more than any other. She needs some of the wisdom the woman acquired during the years she spent not knowing what had become of her daughter and grand-daughter. Without Luanne's moral clarity, Charlotte might do some-thing terrible. Something that can't be reversed. Something that will haunt her long after she finds a way to understand just what the fuck is happening to her body right now.

When we hurt people just to punish them, Luanne used to say, *we create a darkness that will live on long after our reasons for giving birth to it have faded.*

A phone, she reminds herself. *What I need is a phone. I don't need to see Jason Briffel suffer. I just need a goddamn phone.*

In each hand, she gently grips the tops of his front pockets. Then, with almost no effort, she peels the flaps away from their stitching until both pockets have been butterflied. As the stitches rip, tears sprout from Jason's eyes. There's nothing painful about the process; it's the sound of it, she figures. Maybe it makes him imagine his flesh being flayed from his bones.

Poor baby.

His key ring slides out from one opened pocket. The chunky fob for a Honda hits the floor with a light thud. But no cell phone.

She reaches for the tape across his mouth, pokes through the middle of it with one thumb. A tiny gesture, but it makes a pop like smacking gum. Suddenly Jason's breath starts whistling through the fresh hole. Slowly and carefully dragging both index fingers in opposite directions, she turns the hole into a slit. Under normal circumstances this would have required a knife. Right now she barely has to exert any pressure at all.

Where's your phone, asshole? she wants to say. But what comes out of her mouth is, "What were you going to do to me, Jason?"

"Please . . ."

"Please, what? What did you come here for?"

His phone, she thinks. *Just get his phone.*

"I told you," he whispers. "I came to set you free."

"With rope and duct tape and my guns? You really believe that? You really think I'll be your Abigail? That I'll find you women to rape and then murder them for you?"

"Why is it so hard for you to see that people care about you, Trina?"

"That is not my fucking name anymore, you sick, crazy shit." At first she thinks he's crying out because he's afraid, or because she's brought her nose to his and rage quaked in every syllable she just snarled. Then she feels something crunch in her hand. It's his right shoulder. She grabbed it without realizing it. She's broken it.

The sounds he makes now are more barking dog than sniveling child.

Her hand feels hot. Shame clogs her throat. Before she can stop herself, she's skittering backward until she slams into the wall behind her. For a second she thinks she paralyzed herself. Then she realizes the back of her skull punched into the wall on impact. It takes her a few seconds to pull it free. When she steps forward, plaster chips tumble down her back.

Why? How could she watch what happened to those bikers as if it were just a movie but the sound of Jason's agony threatens to send her into a panic?

What brought her remorse back now?

Maybe it's because Jason isn't holding a sawed-off shotgun and calling her a cunt. Yes, he came to do her harm, but he's not capable of it right now, and she just broke his shoulder in the blink of an eye. Without meaning to. And that means it wasn't self-defense.

It was torture. And how will torture save her from this night? What will it do other than take her back to the Bannings' farm in her mind?

So her soul isn't dead. Whatever's happening inside her body, she's still human. She can feel shame and revulsion even moments after savoring his fear. This is a good thing, she realizes.

Then, for the first time, she notices the slender gold chain around Jason's neck. Inside the tiny medallion attached are the stylized, painterly outlines of several flames. *Flames for Burning Girl,* she thinks. It's a goddamn token celebrating the fact that together she and Abigail Banning burned the belongings of a dozen raped and murdered women, and this fucker wears it on his neck. To see her. Suddenly his agonized wails don't make her feel so ashamed anymore.

"Where's your phone?" she asks.

He answers with sobs.

Slowly, she lifts one foot and hovers it over the center of his chest. *It's justified,* she thinks. It's justified because she needs information. She needs help.

"Where is your goddamn cell phone?"

"M-my car. I-it's in my car. In the a-a-a-arroyo."

About fifteen minutes later, after grabbing a holster for her Beretta and attaching it to her hip, her flashlight beam finds the edge of the arroyo, then glints off a windshield at its bottom. She hits the key fob. Headlights flash and a car horn bleats—a combo that seems both absurd and somehow hopeless out here in the desolate darkness. It's a Honda Civic, black, the doors caked in sand from days of desert driving.

She's about to descend the slope when she hears a sound like buzz saws approaching through the night. They're coming from the north, from the direction of Fisher Pit. On the horizon, headlights widen like bioluminescent fish emerging from the deep.

Motorcycles, eight of them in all.

There's no chance these new bikers can see her way out here; the house sits between her and the highway. Still, she doesn't want to risk being spotted, so she gets down on all fours and slides backward until most of her body is hidden. She can still see across the cactus-studded earth.

One after the other, the bikers zip past the house, headed south, toward the scene of bloodshed she'd left behind earlier. Did one of those guys manage to get off a distress call before he became cheeseburger? Or is the rest of their crew checking in on schedule? What will they do once they find those bodies? Fan out in search of anyone in the area? Will that bring them to her door?

There's not much inside Jason's car, but she does find a cell phone sitting inside the cup holder next to the gearshift. He probably left it because he didn't want to run the risk of it ringing or buzzing or lighting up while he was lying in wait for her. It's a cheap disposable. It's got plenty of juice.

She turns it over in her hands slowly and delicately, as if it were made of crystal. After several deep breaths, she starts searching its menu options with the gentlest of button presses.

The contact book is empty. So's the call history. There's only one text thread, and it's between Jason and an unidentified phone number.

The day before, Jason texted: Hi Savior, it's J. New phone. Leaving now.

The response: E-mail when you reach Flagstaff.

Jason: Can't e-mail. Switched to a disposable phone. Only text and call.

The response: Smart. Text when you reach Flagstaff. No calls.

He'd done exactly that at about eleven o'clock the night before.

Then, that morning, he'd texted again.

Getting ready for the last leg. All good?

The response: Everything's good. Will let you know if her schedule changes.

Her heart hammers. So whoever this Savior person is, they've been watching her throughout the day. Longer than that, if they knew she was out here.

Where were they now? Why hadn't they come to Jason's rescue?

The next text turns her stomach. It's from Jason.

Code is 1986474. Thanks for the tips.

What could that even mean, *thanks for the tips*, aside from the fact whoever this fucker is, he's got the alarm code to her house now, too?

Call the police, she tells herself. But just thinking these words reminds her of her one trip to the Scarlet police station to register her alarm system: two deputies, a dispatch officer, and a weary-looking sheriff, none of whom seemed ready for a short jog, much less a biker gun battle.

And whoever's helping Jason, their phone number's right here.

If they come out now, maybe she'll be able to deal with them as effectively as she's dealt with Jason. Whoever they are, they've lost the element of surprise.

Jason texted once more. I hope I'll make you proud.

"Jesus," she whispers.

Proud. What could Jason have planned to do to her in her own house that would make this monster proud?

Later, around evening time, the Savior texted, She's on her way back.

The text was sent at almost the exact time she left Dylan. She scans her memory for any lurkers outside his office. The bikers, maybe. Were the bikers a part of Jason's plan? Did that even make sense?

She dials the number.

There's an answer after three rings.

"I said no calls."

The breath doesn't leave her; instead it's as if the air inside her lungs simply ceases to exist. Like the last breath she took was some childish idea she was foolish to put faith in. She wants to say his name, but now she wonders if it even is his name. If anything he's told her about himself is true. If a single word he shared in that cramped second-floor office that smelled of coffee from the AA meetings downstairs was anything more than a prelude to this night.

"You're the Savior," she hears herself say.

"Charley?"

"You told Jason where I lived. You helped him break into my house."

"Charley, I need you to listen to—"

"Go to hell."

"I need you to tell me how you're feeling."

"Are you kidding? Are you *fucking* kidding me? You're gonna try to be my therapist *now*?"

Cool as ice, Dylan says, "No. I want you to describe what you're feeling physically. I don't know if you've been injured, but my guess is that if you're alive, you haven't been. So please, Charley, tell me how you're—"

"You drugged me. You gave me a goddamn Valium and sent me home to be raped in my own house by that sick fuck."

"No. No, Charley. I didn't. That's not what Zypraxon does."

"Who are you?"

"Just take a deep breath and tell me what you've done, Charley. Tell me if you can *believe* what you've done with your own two hands."

At first she thinks he's accusing her of something, but there's wonder in his tone, as if the fact that they're talking to each other at all in this moment is a magical thing. Nothing about him sounds guilty or even hostile. Instead he sounds animated by a higher purpose.

He *knows*. He knows that she's capable of crushing metal in one hand, that she can throw a grown man several feet in the air. That she can snap bone without meaning to.

"What did you give me?" she asks. "What the fuck are these pills?"

"A miracle. *You* on Zypraxon is a miracle. I saw what you did to those two bikers, Charley. You're the first person it's ever worked on." *Those two bikers.* How long has he been following her? "Trust me. I didn't want it to happen this way, but—"

"You helped Jason find me and break into my house. What was the point of our sessions? Just to figure out what kind of security I had?"

"You needed a trigger. Charley. Please. Listen to me. I'll take care of Jason, and I'll explain everything. But you have to trust me. This is *bigger* than you."

"A *trigger*? What the hell does that mean? Are you completely insane? *What* did you give me?"

"I took the power you try to derive from your guns and your security system and your walls, and I put it in your bare hands. I put it in your bones. That's what I *gave* you, Charlotte Rowe." There's a confidence she's never heard in his voice before. "That's what Zypraxon is. It literally converts your fear into strength. Into survival. That's what you did tonight, Charley. You *survived*. And no matter what happened with Jason inside that house, you have nothing to be ashamed of. There is never shame in surviving."

She's still searching for a response when she hears a strangely familiar sound. Familiar because she heard it only minutes before, but now it's coming through the phone at her ear. The bikers.

"Shit," Dylan whispers. He sounds annoyed. Irritated. He doesn't sound like a normal man would if a gang of outlaw bikers were suddenly bearing down on him as he stood over the gory corpses of their slain brethren. "Charley, I know it's hard to trust me right now, but believe me when I say this was not my plan. Our biker friends are . . . an added complication I didn't expect. But I need you to listen to me, and I need you to do what I say."

"Go to hell," she whispers.

"You're angry. I understand." His condescension infuriates her. She has to remind herself to keep her hand relaxed so she doesn't crush her only connection to him. "But know this. You're not going to the police, and you're not going to the FBI, and you're not going to *Rolling Stone* magazine. The people I work for will make sure they never believe what you say and never act on it if they do. And you don't need their help, so why bother?"

"You're threatening me?"

"How many are there, Charley? The bikers. This new crew. They must have driven by your place first. How many are there?"

"A lot."

"OK. One more thing. Do not under any circumstances give Zypraxon to anyone else."

"What? Why?"

"Because you're the first person to take it and live."

"You son of a bitch. You *crazy* son of a bitch. I didn't know what I was really taking!"

"I know, I know. It's a lot. Don't try to process it all right now. We'll have time, I promise."

There's that tone again. That steady, confident tone. The bikers are getting closer, and he sounds cool as a cucumber even as he reveals the extent to which he's placed her life at risk.

Did he actually just sigh?

"Charley, I have to go and take care of these guys, but there's something I need for you to do for me first."

"What?"

"Run."

He hangs up.

She tries calling him back. Once, twice. Three times. He doesn't answer.

It's a miracle. That's what's coursing through her veins now. A miracle, and it wasn't just put there by someone pretending to be a therapist. It was put there by something . . . *bigger than her*. Months. That's how long she and Dylan spent together in that office. Months. He's had months to plan for this night. For all she knows, he played a hand in bringing the *Savage Woods* films to the local movie house to trigger her anxiety and create a pretext for forcing the drug on her. And then there's the kiss. The strange, last-minute, and inappropriate kiss he gave her right before she left the office. So she would be distracted on the drive home.

Because he took *my cell phone*, she realizes. *He took my phone so I wouldn't know someone had disarmed my alarm system. And now he knows my code, so I'm not safe from him if I go back in the house. If the phone and Internet are still out, I won't be able to reset the password because it won't be able to connect to the security company's network.*

But this is only the half of it, she knows. If she goes back in the house and if he tries to come for her, even if he just tries to explain his crazy again, something far worse will happen.

She'll kill him. She's sure of it.

The sense of betrayal sings through her over and over again like lashes from a whip, far more painful and infuriating than her revulsion at being face-to-face with Jason's dangerous delusions. If she looks into those eyes right now, those same eyes that held her in a consistent and steady gaze meant to earn her confidence, she just might use whatever this strength is to tear them out of his head. Maybe he knows this. Maybe it's why he told her to run.

So maybe she shouldn't. Maybe, if he manages to escape the latest onslaught of bikers, she should let the son of a bitch pay her a visit so he can feel the full force of whatever he drugged her with. But Jason's agonized wails still play in her ears. What kind of awful music would tearing Dylan Whoeverthefuckheis limb from limb leave on a constant playback in her mind?

Amid this din of rage and confusion is another, clearer thought that rises above the clamor.

Drugs don't last forever.

She starts the Civic's engine, angles it up and out of the arroyo, kills the headlights so she can slowly roll toward the highway under the cover of darkness. But when she reaches the edge of the blacktop, she freezes.

South is Scarlet and the Scarlet police station with its four employees, none of whom seem capable of protecting her from anything bigger than a bobcat. South is also the scene of whatever fight's about to break out between a supposed Harvard-educated psychiatrist and a bunch of cranked-up outlaw bikers.

He's not just a psychiatrist, she thinks. *The guy he pretended to be would not look at a gang of bikers barreling toward him and say, "I have to go and take care of these guys," like he was getting ready to feed a parking meter. And he said he'd take care of Jason, too. What's he going to do? Break Jason's other shoulder? Or break his neck? Do I care which? The rope, remember. The rope and the tape. It was all for me.*

North, on the other hand, is a whole lot of nothing until Interstate 40, which will give her a new choice: East or west?

She tells herself she's waiting to make a decision because more bikers might come flying past. But there's no sign of anything on the northern horizon. She's waiting because she's paralyzed. Amazing to realize that despite her incredible strength, her muscles can still be seized by self-doubt.

She hears what comes next before she sees it. A crack that sounds small and thunderous at the same time—two things that contradict each other. When she looks south, she sees a column of white flame shooting up into the night sky. It's a good distance away. About as far, she guesses, as the scene where the bikers ran her off the road. Whatever its source, the explosion is a single event. It's precise. It's big. And even though she's very far away, she can see pieces of debris inside it.

She lets her foot off the brake, turns the Civic north, and gives it as much gas as she can without destroying the pedal.

North.

It's the only thought she can manage. *Go north.* And then possibly west, toward California, the only state she's ever really called home. But when she tries to think any further ahead than that, her breaths grow shallow and her vision starts to shrink, so she just keeps saying it to herself over and over again. *North, north, north.*

A daze comes over her. She thinks it might be shock, but it doesn't seem to affect her ability to drive, so what does it matter really? She's not sure exactly how much time has passed when she realizes she's forgotten to keep her grip on the steering wheel featherlight. Her knuckles look white in the dashboard's glow, but the steering wheel's intact. Slowly she eases her foot down onto the brake, pulls over to the side of the empty road.

She steps from the car, walks into the headlights, and picks up a jagged rock that's about the size of a newborn baby. It's heavy and lifting it hurts her arm. Which, in a normal world, is how it should be. When she tries to throw it with one hand, it slips and crashes to the asphalt. Her wrist sings with pain from the effort.

Whatever Dylan's miracle provided, it's over now.

The strength is gone.

And now, with the fears of an ordinary woman, she's looking out into the vast emptiness where the shadows of jagged rocks and cacti are slowly resolving underneath a star-crazed sky.

She doesn't have to be careful now as she reaches into her pocket and removes the cardboard packet. Two of the remaining pills have been reduced to orange powder inside their plastic bubbles. Another's been cracked in half. The fourth and fifth are intact.

You're the first one to take it and live.

She places the pills back inside her pocket and slides behind the wheel.

The Beretta's on the seat next to her.

Facts, figures. Short-term goals. These are her salvation right now.

She checks the phone.

Three hours. That's about how much time has elapsed between her first fight with Jason, the emergence of her miraculous strength, and this moment when it left her abruptly and without fanfare.

How could it have been only three hours? It feels like a lifetime.

She starts the car, eases back onto the highway. *North,* she tells herself again, just as the tears start. *North,* she tells herself as her hands start to shake in a way that's all too human. All too normal. All too frightened.

Then she remembers she's got five pills left, and the fear gradually starts to recede until her hands go still.

10

Before she reaches I-40, Charlotte pulls over to the side of the road and makes a call she should have made hours before. A call that will determine in which direction she heads now—east or west. Kayla answers after one ring. The same woman Dylan dismissed as being undeserving of the title of Charlotte's only friend, despite the fact that she won the case against Charlotte's dad and routinely battles wealthy wife beaters and corporations that poison entire communities.

The minute Kayla says her name, not her birth name but the name she chose for herself, Charlotte feels a sudden, hot sheen of tears in her eyes.

She speaks through a lump in her throat. "I need to meet. Someplace safe. Outside San Francisco. Wherever it is, make sure you're not being followed."

"Media?" Kayla asks.

"No."

"Your dad?"

"I don't think so."

"Jason Briffel."

"Yeah," Charlotte answers. "It's bad."

The incompleteness of the answer feels like a lie.

"Where are you?" Kayla asks.

"Nowhere. Making a decision where to go next."

"Whose number is this?"

"Don't ask."

"Whatever's happening, you know you can trust me, right?" Kayla says.

"Why do you think I called? The problem is, I don't actually know what's happening."

"All right, where are you now?"

"Near Flagstaff."

"Are you in your car?"

"No."

"But you have *a* car?"

"Yes."

"Come to California. Once you hit the 5, go north like you're going to San Francisco. You're gonna meet me in Patterson. It's south of the 580 split. When you get there, go east on Del Puerto Canyon Road, and in about two blocks, you'll see a giant Amazon fulfillment center. I'll meet you in the parking lot. Describe the car you're driving."

She does.

"OK. Pretty nondescript."

"I'll come in slow so you don't miss me."

"No, I'm glad it's nondescript, 'cause you're gonna leave it there and come with me."

"I don't want to go into the city right now."

"I understand. That's why I'm taking you to one of our safe houses. We put high-value witnesses who get threats there if law enforcement won't step up."

"Good. That's real good. Thank you. I can't th-tha . . ."

"Charley, drive now. Feelings later. OK? I'll see you in a few hours."

Drive now, feelings later, she says to herself as she hangs up the phone.

II

11

"Can we maybe do something about the glare?"

Cole Graydon isn't sure who asked this question.

He's one of seven people seated around the executive conference room's frosted-glass table. The others include three members of his company's legal team, the director of marketing, the chairman of his board, and Dr. Nora Suvari, head of gastrointestinal treatments for Graydon Pharmaceuticals.

It had to have been Nora, he realizes. She's the only one looking at him and not the eighty-inch LCD screen at the front of the room.

Up until a few seconds ago, she was doing a pretty good job of pretending to watch the final edit of this idiotic video they've gathered to approve.

A better job than he was; that's for sure.

For most of the presentation he's been looking out the window at a group of kayakers down in La Jolla Bay. Their tiny yellow oars wink in the sun. Their kayaks are bright red, making them look like bits of shark bait determined to avoid their fate. Will they manage a full loop around the bay before the video ends?

That this is the question occupying his mind on the eve of their biggest drug launch in three years—well, it won't be the first secret he's kept since taking the reins of his late father's company.

But Nora's question, and her vacant stare, makes it clear he's not the only one bored stiff. The glare to which she just referred is falling across the screen of her iPad, not the screen at the front of the room. When she catches him looking, she closes a Pinterest page and quickly replaces it with the first projection spreadsheet she can open.

He fights the urge to cackle. Instead he hits a button on the remote control next to his laptop. The wall of glass to his left darkens. The view's still there, but now it looks shadowy and slightly unreal.

He owes his life to that view.

Maybe not his life—maybe just his sanity. The compact skyline of La Jolla's village and the flower garland of mansions that crown the bluffs overlooking the bay have offered him countless mental escapes from the soul-crushing responsibilities of running this company, most of which bear down on him in this gleaming, glass-filled room.

He should chide Nora; he knows it. Call her out for pinning wedding dresses when they should be perfecting every detail of one of the most expensive launches in their company's history. He's pretty sure that's why the chairman of the board, Tucker Albright, is giving him a long look now.

If Cole stays silent, Tucker will no doubt report this exchange to Cole's mother, who may well see it as cause to hop in her hired car and be chauffeured down from her horse ranch in Rancho Santa Fe, just to see how Cole is handling everything. Which, after some prodding, she'll admit is code for, *I'm here to find out whether or not you're about to run our family's company into the ground again.*

He's not going to upbraid Nora. Not now, not later. She's a Harvard PhD who came to Graydon with dreams of eradicating stomach-eating parasites in developing nations. Today she's responsible for a piece-of-shit heartburn drug they're about to market as the only thing that will keep America's stomachs from exploding.

I know, Nora, he thinks. *I had big dreams, too.*

Tucker Albright, on the other hand, is one of the country's wealthiest beef distributors, whose only qualification for running Graydon's board is that he's chummy with Cole's mother.

But he's still studying Cole with icy focus, so Cole gives the man a warm smile.

Tucker nods and returns his attention to the giant television screen.

Caught, Cole has no choice but to watch the video.

Again.

For the hundredth time.

On-screen, an actress whose last big role involved getting devoured by man-eating slugs in a gas station bathroom sits under dramatic lighting that would better serve an interview with a Syrian refugee. The music is like Chopin on laudanum. The actress is describing, in a tone more appropriate to the recounting of a violent sexual assault, how heartburn has taken over her life. How she no longer enjoys food. How eating became a source of constant fear and worry. There's a shot of her standing outside the window of a New York deli, staring at the sandwiches inside like an orphan watching a happy family enjoy Christmas dinner.

The video is one of several that will post to a website scheduled to launch next week, www.EnjoyFoodAgain.com. While the site will be scrubbed of any obvious clues it's owned and operated by Graydon Pharmaceuticals, more than half of the visitors who flock to it, the ones sharing the most dramatic stories of heartburn-related trauma, will be those hired by a marketing firm with one explicit goal: to convince the people who end up there by chance that they're suffering from a completely bullshit condition that was invented by Graydon's marketing department.

RID. Recurrent Intestinal Disrupt.

Meanwhile, drug reps for the company, most of them so good looking they could model swimwear for a living, have already fanned out to doctor's offices all over the country, manipulating every FDA loophole possible to present their new drug, Sunatrex, as a revolution in heartburn treatment, even though there's no evidence to suggest it's any better than Nexium, which anyone who reads a newspaper knows isn't much better than Prilosec.

So far the process has unfolded without a hitch, in meetings much like this one, while Cole stares out the sea-facing glass wall, wondering what's become of his ambitions and his father's legacy, a legacy that includes inventing a drug that revolutionized the treatment of HIV throughout the world.

He's killed the sound on his phone, so when the e-mail arrives, it sends a text alert to the lock screen.

Once he's sure Tucker isn't watching him, he unlocks it.

He doesn't recognize the address. There's a video attached, so he's about to send it to his junk folder. Then he sees the subject line:

Dream big or die in your sleep.

This parody of one of his father's favorite, and most obnoxious, personal expressions—*Dream big or go home*—is an inside joke. A very inside joke. And the man he shares this joke with hasn't contacted him in almost three years. Reading it now makes his stomach feel like he just swallowed a mouthful of ice in one gulp.

He checks once again to make sure the sound's off; then he downloads the video.

At first he's not clear what he's watching. The contrast between the depressing piano music from the Sunatrex video and the frenzied images on his phone makes him seasick. Dust, tires, the outline of a speeding SUV. Whatever this is, it's footage taken by a small camera, probably a GoPro, mounted to the front of a motorcycle.

He thinks it's a motorcycle. Because the other two vehicles in the frame are motorcycles; their combined headlights light the scene with startling clarity.

When the SUV takes out one of them, sending the driver flying over its roof, Cole jumps in his seat. It draws Nora's attention but not Tucker's, thank God, and she gives him a sympathetic smile. The SUV careens into open desert. One of the other bikers pursues it ahead of the camera-mounted one. The SUV's lost to darkness for a few seconds, then the bike's headlight finds it just as it slams into a giant saguaro, an impact that crushes its nose, dents its hood.

Then the door falls off.

No, that's not right, he realizes.

The driver-side door seems to *float* off. Which is impossible. But that's how it looks. The driver pushed the door directly out from the side of the SUV with one hand, as if it weighed nothing, then dropped it to the rock-strewn dirt.

The guy driving the bike the camera's mounted to enters the frame, the angle going suddenly still now that he's parked. He pulls a sawed-off shotgun from his back, while his hulking, blond-haired friend approaches the driver with a pair of plastic flex-cuffs in hand.

The driver is a woman, Cole sees, average-looking, with straw-colored hair and a face made youthful by curves. And even though her face betrays no fear, she is sinking to her knees. Without sound, it's impossible to tell what the blond guy is shouting at her. But when he grabs her by the hair, Cole sees the woman's expression for the first time.

She's not afraid.

He's so riveted by what happens next, he forgets he's not alone. The stuttering groan that comes from him when the big biker gets a hole blown through his chest draws the attention of everyone in the conference room. Only then does he realize the video's held him in such thrall he's risen from his seat and turned his back on all of them.

They've stopped the commercial, and their expressions range from puzzled to annoyed.

"I need to step out for a minute, folks," he hears himself say.

There's a grumbled objection from Tucker, an envious expression from Nora, and silence from the three lawyers, whose names he's already forgotten. His head of marketing is refilling his coffee from the station in the corner. Cole doesn't notice their reactions as he strides out of the room, then down the hall toward his office.

His employees part before him. Maybe it's the expression on his face, or maybe it's that he's their boss. By then he's read the line of text above the video, the one he missed in his rush to open the file, and his heart has started hammering.

> New trial going well. When can we discuss the pre-
> liminary results? —D

12

The last time Charlotte saw Kayla LeBlanc in person, her hair was a shiny bob, as corporate looking as the pantsuits she always wore to the office and to court. Now she sports a classic high bun with a twist, and while it's clear she's tried to dress casual, her jeans look like they cost more than Charlotte earns in six months.

Maybe she's been springing for pricier duds ever since the California Association of Black Lawyers named her lawyer of the year. Whatever the reason, she looks way more out of place in this so-called safe house than Charlotte does. Charlotte finds that comforting. It's a sign neither of them really belongs here, which is a sign they won't have to stay for very long.

They sit across from each other at the tiny kitchen table. They got there just before dawn after ditching Jason's car at the Amazon fulfillment center, and even though she hasn't slept and is subsisting on instant coffee, the only thing in the safe house's kitchen cabinet, Charlotte doesn't feel remotely tired.

Outside, peeling paint and a rusty chain-link fence allow the one-story tract home to blend in with its neighbors. Inside, it's scrubbed spotless, barely lived in, and studded with clean, anonymous-looking furniture that belongs in the lobby of a Holiday Inn Express.

Charlotte's lost count of how many times she's told the story.

Each time through, Kayla has stopped her at various intervals to ask prodding, detail-oriented questions, the same way she'd prep one of her own witnesses to testify.

Kayla holds Charlotte's upturned right hand in both of hers, studying the light bruising along her wrist. A result of the car accident, Charlotte's sure. But maybe it came from her fight with Jason.

"How many days ago did you get this?" Kayla asks.

"It's a few *hours* old," Charlotte answers. "And it looked ten times worse right before I met you."

Kayla goes rigid. Looks up from Charlotte's hand with an expression that combines fear and disbelief.

"You don't believe me," Charlotte finally says.

"I wouldn't say that."

"What would you say?"

"I definitely think you were drugged."

"So you think I hallucinated everything?"

"Part of it, maybe. I mean, the bikers . . . there's nothing on the news about an explosion."

"It's only been a few hours. Almost no one drives that road. That's why I lived out there. There's no regular truck traffic; the mine's been closed for years. There's no reason anyone would find it right away."

"So you think the guy with the shotgun called for backup before they drove you off the road, and that's who came from the direction of the mine. And that's who this Dylan character met up with before . . . boom."

"Something like that. Yeah."

"Describe the explosion again."

"I don't . . . I'm not an explosives expert, but it wasn't *messy*, if that makes sense. Whatever it was, I think Dylan set it. It wasn't the result of a gunfight. It happened too quickly for that. The other thing, though. It was the way he said it . . ."

"Said what?"

"'I need to take care of these guys.' Like it was nothing. Outlaw bikers. Riding straight for him. Hopped-up on God knows what. And he's cool as ice. He said he'd take care of Jason, too."

"And what do we think that means?"

"Well, he killed all those bikers for getting in the way of his plan. How's he going to treat someone who's no longer useful to him? Someone he manipulated into doing his bidding?"

"You're sure he was out there when you called him? I mean, how do you know he was right where those bikers drove you off the road?"

"I could hear the second group through the phone. They were driving toward him. They must have been going to check on their hideout, and he was there."

"So he follows you, he watches what happens with these guys who drove you off the road, and then he just . . . stays out there?"

"Maybe he was cleaning up."

"The bodies, you mean."

"Yeah."

"Why would he do that?"

"Kayla, don't you get it? I'm his test subject. He set the whole thing up. The clearest thing about this drug is that it turns my fear into strength. In order to see if it worked on me, he had to scare the shit out of me. And what better way to do that than to show Jason Briffel how to get inside my house?"

"Jesus. Who *is* this guy?" Kayla whispers.

"So you don't think I was hallucinating him, at least."

"I don't think you hallucinated most of it, Charley. I think Dylan's real. I think he lured Jason out there so you'd have a run-in with him. I even think, to some degree, the bikers are real. I think this guy gave you *something* that made you believe you were doing these terrible things. But—"

"Terrible?" Charlotte asks.

"Come on. You know what I mean."

"Jason was probably going to rape me in my own house. And those bikers, they were gonna do worse. A lot worse."

"I understand."

"But you think what I did was terrible? No, wait. Moot point. You don't really think I did it."

"I think your perception was altered. Chemically. Look, you're absolutely a victim here, but—"

"So you don't believe me? You don't believe anything I've told you?"

"I said I think it's more complicated than what either of us can see. Look, I want you to get some sleep." Kayla gets to her feet. "I'm here for you all day. All night, if need be. I'm not going anywhere. But you need to get some rest."

"I'm not tired."

"You're exhausted. Your mind just doesn't know it."

Kayla takes her by the hand and pulls her out of her chair. "Come on." She leads her toward the hallway.

"No," Charley says. "No bedroom. Sofa. I don't want to be alone."

"Fine. Compromises are good so long as you at least pretend to sleep." With one arm around her shoulders, she guides Charley to the sofa. "I'm gonna make some calls, and I'm gonna do it in the other room. But I won't let you out of my sight. I'm not going anywhere. I promise."

"Calls?" As soon as she stretches out, the sofa envelops her in its cushions. It's hardly the most comfortable sofa she's ever experienced. But it feels delicious. As delicious as a mediocre meal might feel after you've starved yourself all day. "Who are you going to call?"

"I'm going to try to find out who this guy is, for one. And then—"

"You aren't going to believe me until something about those bikers hits the news, are you?"

"There you go. Eyes already drifting shut. See? Told ya you were tired."

Kayla's right. But Charlotte still has enough energy to reach out and grab her hand before she can withdraw. "Kayla. Be careful."

"I'm not going anywhere."

"No. When you check out Dylan. He said whatever this is, it's bigger than us. Whatever the hell that means."

"Charley, my firm takes on some of the most powerful corporations in the world. You can trust our research department. I promise you."

Kayla pats her forehead gently, and Charlotte feels it as if she's wrapped in gauze. Before Kayla's footsteps enter the kitchen, sleep rises to consume her in a great, dark tide. Then she shifts to one side, and something painful jabs her leg.

She sits up and pulls the packet of pills from her pocket.

From the kitchen door, Kayla watches her with frightened intensity.

Charlotte studies them. "You know," she says, "there is one way to prove that I wasn't hallucinating."

Before she can elaborate, Kayla's plucked the packet out of her hand. "Sleep. *Now.* These are staying in the kitchen with me."

13

As Luke Prescott drives west on State Mountain Road 293, he thinks of all the times he traveled this route with his younger brother after their mom got sick.

Before their mother's diagnosis—glioblastoma, stage four, inoperable, a year at best—he and Bailey had perfected the fine art of pretending the other didn't exist, which wasn't hard. Luke was aggressive and athletic back then; Bailey was computer addicted and completely uninterested in girls.

After the doctor's visit that changed their lives, the differences between the two of them seemed to fall away, and most afternoons before sunset, if one of their mother's friends was able to drive her to chemo, Luke would find Bailey sneaking a smoke in the field behind their house and ask him if he wanted to go for a ride. Bailey would grunt in the affirmative, and a few minutes later they'd be winding their way through the mountains in the family truck.

After a while the Pacific would open before them, roiling and vast. Sometimes blue and sun streaked, sometimes slate gray and belching fog. But the mountains always looked the same, their formidable, lightly forested slopes plunging toward the surf with a determination and strength both boys were trying to muster inside themselves.

The mountains look the same as Luke reaches them now—the sea, sparkling and riven by angry waves fueled by the cold autumn winds.

While his grief for his mother is like a fine layer of silt over his heart, evenly spread, no part of it thick enough to stop the flow of blood, with Bailey, the anger's still laced all through his system.

Maybe because Bailey's still alive. Out there somewhere, possibly on the other side of this very ocean, hiding from the consequences of a crime Luke still doesn't fully understand.

But it's rumors of a far less significant crime that have brought Luke to the Pacific Coast Highway today.

A right turn sends him in the direction of the vertigo-inducing staircase that leads to Altamira's only real beach. The lumpy obelisk of stone just offshore, Bayard Rock, is listed in a lot of guidebooks, but most folks drive right past it without realizing it. That, or their stomachs revolt when they get a good look at the stairs you have to take to get there. The beach is where he and Bailey would usually end up on those long-ago afternoon drives. Once there, he'd let the guy stroll away from him because he knew his brother wanted to be alone while he cried into the wind. Luke did, too, for that matter. The only time they cried side by side was when they scattered their mother's ashes there after she died.

Coming home wasn't going to be easy; he knew this. But he didn't expect the ghosts to be quite this vivid. Foolish of him to think a new badge and uniform would keep them at bay.

When he sees Martin Cahill's pickup parked at the picnic area up ahead, Luke's almost relieved. He knows it means there's a possible conflict in his immediate future, but he'd welcome anything to relieve him of the memories that besieged him on the drive here.

He pulls the Altamira Sheriff's Jeep into the turnout slowly, so as not to indicate any aggression that might set Marty and his crew on edge. Then, with a bowed head and his best attempt at a sheepish smile, he walks toward the spread of picnic benches tucked against the rocky slope.

The men study his approach without slowing their chewing.

Martin Cahill's a lot older than when Luke last saw him, but he doesn't look it. His hair's white now, but it's tied back in a lustrous ponytail. His complexion's good, especially the parts of it that aren't covered in tattoos. *So he's still not drinking,* Luke thinks. *That's a good sign.* Some of the guys with him are former alkies, Luke's sure. Maybe lost souls he's hired from the meetinghouse on the east side of town.

The shitty pickup truck is the same, though. He's willing to bet the thing's guts are as jerry-rigged as Frankenstein's monster by now. Marty could use about two more layers of storage drawers than he's got in the cargo bay; the one he has installed is covered by a maelstrom of tools, some of them sticking out of the cargo cover's missing back window.

Just a regular bunch of working guys breaking for lunch. Their lunch spot just happens to be one of the most beautiful places on the edge of the world. When they're done eating, they'll head over to Sally Witcomb's place and put in some more work on her new guest bathroom, or maybe they'll drive back to the center of town and help those Buddhists from San Francisco refinish the floor of their new teahouse on Center Street, which apparently Marty's doing for a big discount because he's into Buddhism now.

Or if Luke's initial suspicion is correct, they *were* headed over to the ruins of the old resort, and it was only when they saw Luke tailing them that they decided to pretend like they just drove all the way out to the Pacific Coast Highway for lunch.

"Well, well, well, the prodigal son returns," Marty says, then goes quiet when he realizes maybe that isn't the best opening line to use with a guy whose mother died of brain cancer and whose father's whereabouts have been unknown for most of his life.

"Marty," Luke says. "Gentlemen," he adds, tipping his hat to the rest of them. Only one or two offer even a nod in return.

"Great view, ain't it?" Marty asks.

"Always has been."

"You forget? It's been a while."

"Seven years."

"That's a while. Guess you planned on it being longer, though, if what I hear's correct."

Don't take the bait, he thinks. *You've got a job to do.*

"I'd invite you to join us," Marty says, "but it doesn't look like you got a lunch. So I guess that means you're not here for lunch."

"Not unless one of you's got extra," Luke says with a smile.

"We don't," one of the men answers, then falls silent when Marty gives him a look.

Just a warning, Luke reminds himself. *I'm just supposed to give them a warning. Anything else is not how I planned to start my first week on the job.*

"Did Laura Penny reopen her costume store?" Marty asks. "Or maybe Target's selling sheriff's uniforms now."

"It'd be a deputy's uniform. Until I'm sheriff. And, no, it didn't come from Target."

"Expecting a promotion already, huh? Admire your confidence, kid. 'Course, what I hear, even sheriff of this town would be a demotion from what you had planned."

"Yeah, well, don't believe everything you hear."

"Figure I might end up saying the same once I find out what this little visit's about."

"Marty, I'm here to remind you that the grounds of the old lodge are still private property, and anything you find there still technically belongs to Silver Shore Investments."

"*Old* lodge? You say that like the thing ever opened. Like they ever gave out a single one of the jobs they promised."

"I'm aware of the issues that stopped the project, Marty, and along those lines, it's also my responsibility to inform you that it's dangerous for anyone to access the premises."

Marty looks over one shoulder.

The unfinished remains of the Altamira Lodge are perched atop a rocky, wooded headland a short distance north. It looks like a crazy cross between a Cold War–era military fort and a billionaire game hunter's private paradise. Wind-gnarled cypresses conceal most of the buildings from view, but a few pointed rooftops are visible above the tree line. The way the sun hits it now, Luke can make out some of the giant glassless windows of the main lodge, like open mouths waiting for prey to stumble in.

Luke vividly remembers the renderings that held the town in thrall: the oversize log cabin detailing, the soaring walls of uninterrupted plate glass meant to maximize sunset views from its dining room. The wooded nature trail snaking through the row of private guest cabins behind the main lodge. All of it's an overgrown, wind-battered little ghost town now, and Luke has no trouble imagining the entire place tumbling into the sea in a shower of rock one day.

"You want to know what scares me, kid?"

"My name's not kid, Marty. It's Luke. Deputy Prescott if you want to be particular about it."

Marty looks back at him, his half smile tugging down at the corners. "Excuse me, *Deputy Prescott.*"

"It's a warning, Marty. That's all. Let's not make this more than it needs to be."

"All right, then." Marty wipes his hands with a napkin, wads it up, and gets to his feet.

Luke stiffens, feels an urge to reach for his gun. He's probably one of the best shots in the area. But carrying a gun on your hip all day comes with its own set of challenges, most of them temptations, and he's only been contending with those for less than a week.

There's also the fact that Marty's got a past. Something must have brought him to AA all those years ago. But whatever it is, it's two decades ago, and he's been an upstanding citizen since then, so there's no reason Luke can't keep control of this.

"Here's my warning." Marty's paint-splotched boots crunch the gravel underfoot. "And it's not necessarily for you, *Deputy* Prescott, so please don't take it as a threat. And it's not for the sheriff or the town council or the governor of our great state of California. Maybe it's just for all those investors who spent their money to get a . . . well, let's call it a *cozy* relationship with our governor and our town council."

"I don't exactly have their ear, *Marty*."

"Still, ambitious young man like you, you might one day. You see, it's real simple. There's a couple miles of copper wire out there, along with about six AC condensers, too many sheets of drywall to count, and enough uninstalled insulation to line most of the road back to town. And if they leave it out there, it's gonna rot before I can install it in the women's shelter over in King City, or the recovery center down in McKittrick, or a bunch of other places that actually help people who don't have rich and powerful friends."

"I see. So you're a social justice looter."

"Your words, kid," Marty says with a smile. "Not mine."

Luke should walk now. The warning's been given. He can tell the sheriff he handled his first uncomfortable duty of his first week on the job. But he doesn't. Instead he looks Marty dead in the eye and says, "You steal any more stuff from up there, you're gonna get arrested. I don't care if you install it at the Vatican. And I'll run all your men, too. See how colorful their pasts were before you taught them the Serenity Prayer."

When the brittle sarcasm starts to leave Marty's expression, Luke turns his back on the man.

"This isn't the way to do this, Luke."

"Don't tell me how to do my job, Mr. Cahill."

"I'm not talking about your job," he says. "I'm talking about your homecoming. We remember who Luke was, even if Deputy Prescott would like us to forget."

"What the hell's that supposed to mean?"

Against his will, Luke turns. His fingers get cold, and he realizes he's resting his hand limply on the door handle.

"It means you were a bully is what it means. And you were a bully before your mother died, so don't go blaming it on that, either." There must be something in Luke's expression that suggests outrage, because Marty nods and continues with more force. "I remember what you put Luanne's granddaughter through. Never letting anyone in school forget where she came from, what happened to her. Everyone remembers. So pardon us for being a little on guard now that someone like you's got a gun and a badge."

Whatever reaction Marty was expecting, it's not the one he's getting. His stance softens, and he cocks his head as if he can't believe Luke isn't going to take a swing at him. And maybe Luke should. Maybe it's weakness not to.

But just the mention of Luanne's granddaughter, Trina Pierce—*Burning Girl,* he thinks, the words freezing his gut briefly—and the memory of the baffled, wounded expression on her face that day in class when he'd decided to go after her, has hollowed him out suddenly.

"Just don't call me kid," Luke manages. "Call me whatever else you want, Marty. Just don't call me kid—that's all."

Before he says something even more pathetic, Luke gets in his cruiser and spins out onto PCH.

His gun and badge suddenly feel as insubstantial as the napkin Marty used to clean his hands, his decision to return home the worst mistake he's ever made in his life.

When he reaches the spot on 293 where cell service comes back, he calls his new boss, Sheriff Mona Sanchez.

Any embarrassing incident requiring him to reference locals by their full names should be kept off the radio. She gave him this order first day on the job. Word on the street is Dan Soto, the guy who runs the Gold Mine Tavern, got a scanner from his daughter for Christmas. And because police activity is so rare in Altamira, he just leaves it on in the background whenever he has friends over to play cards.

"I don't know what he thinks is gonna happen," Mona had added. "Maybe he's waiting for some of the McGregors' horses to get loose again. I guess that'd be fun to listen to."

Altamira's recently elected sheriff is an old friend of Luke's mother. The two women met at Fort Doyle down valley, where his mom was working as a secretary and Mona was an enlisted woman a few short months away from leaving the military for a career in law enforcement.

In the past few days, he's learned more about his mom's old friend than he had in all those years of her dropping by for dinner or helping take care of his mom after she got sick.

For starters, she's not a lesbian, as he'd always assumed. In fact, she's had the same boyfriend for ten years. Like her, the guy's half Chumash, and he's spent the last few years working on the legal team defending their tribe's casino in Santa Ynez from a never-ending series of legal challenges brought by its neighbors.

"Yep," she answers the phone.

"It's done," Luke says.

"You realize I told you to warn him, not kill him, right?"

"Just trying to take my job seriously is all."

"Maybe a little too serious."

"Is it my tone?" he asks.

"That and the wording, yeah."

"Sorry."

"No need. So did he cop to it?"

"In a manner of speaking."

"Give you any grief?" she asks.

"In a manner of speaking."

Mona falls silent. Over the past few days, he's learned that when Mona falls silent, it's his job to fill the silence.

He's descending toward town now—a small grid of sloping rooftops in the midst of a Mediterranean-looking valley, protected from cold Pacific winds by the mountains he's just passed through.

To the east the hills are low, rolling, and golden, and on either side of the road the scrubby coastal woods give way to more golden grasslands dotted by stately lone oaks. It's the kind of landscape they like to use in car commercials, and if his hometown was a smidge closer to either Los Angeles or San Francisco, it'd probably be overrun with tourists. But most of the road trippers coming up from the south don't feel the need to go much farther than San Simeon and Lake Nacimiento.

The Lodge, perched at the tip of Altamira's lone finger to the sea, was supposed to change all that, of course. The investors were even in talks to widen 293 in hopes of bringing more folks to town. But it wasn't to be, and now most people in Altamira feel the place is hemorrhaging promise, thanks to the wounds inflicted by shady investors and an ever-shrinking army fort to the south.

"Luke?" Mona asks.

"You could say he got a little personal."

"How so?"

"Brought up something from my past. That's all."

"I see . . . but things didn't escalate?" Mona asks.

"Not really, no."

"Define 'not really,' Luke. This is Altamira."

"He claimed the moral high ground. Said he was installing the stuff he stole in women's shelters and recovery homes. I said if I caught him, I'd arrest him and run all the guys in his crew."

Mona takes a sip of something. "I see. Anything else?"

"I asked him not to call me kid."

"Small town. There's gonna be a lot of that."

"A lot of what?" he asks.

"You had a mouth on you, Luke."

"So I was a prick is what you're saying."

"Yeah. Pretty much."

"And you hired me anyway?"

"Sometimes pricks do well in law enforcement."

"Do we?"

"If you put yourself on the right side of things. Absolutely."

"Well, OK then."

"Was he right?"

"Excuse me?"

"Martin Cahill. Whatever he brought up, this thing out of your past, was he in the right?"

Burning Girl, he thinks again, remembering how he'd used the words as a kind of whispered slur.

"Yes," he answers.

"Well, you got some clarity about it, at least."

"You don't even know what he brought up," he says.

"Do I need to?"

"Did you even care that Marty and his crew are looting the Lodge?"

"Hell, no. Fuck those Silver Shore assholes. I got five businesses on Center Street closed this month because of the mess they left this town in. Bastards went all over the state, drawing new businesses here, the whole time they knew their funding was all spit and vinegar. They want to protect all the stuff they left out there like trash? Let 'em hire private security with the money they never had. Marty's crew can strip that place to the studs for all I care. I just wanted us to look like we're doing our job. And you needed something to do," she tells him.

"Well, all right then."

"Sounds like you're far away."

"I actually just pulled up to the station."

"No, I mean in your head."

"Oh, well. There's that."

The sheriff's station is a small redbrick building on the corner of a block containing some of the empty frontage left by the ruined businesses Mona's still angry about. On the opposite corner, a couple of army girls from the fort sit at the cast-iron tables out front of Katy's Coffee, sunning their bare arms.

The sight of them stirs something in him, but it feels more like acid indigestion.

It's been a while since he's been with a woman. Nothing since that drunken bar hookup a few nights after the disaster that was his final FBI interview. He can't even remember the girl's name now. Only that she worked in tech, seemed a little less drunk than him, and appeared as disinterested in chitchat as he was. *Wham, bam, don't bother leaving your number, ma'am.* That's never been his style, so thinking of it now makes him feel creepy. Some of the guys he went to SF State with, they could do that kind of stuff every week. But he's a bigger fan of actually getting to know a woman, and relieving himself with porn until the time's right to hop into bed with her.

But even a date now seems like an insurmountable task. Like something only a younger, more vigorous version of himself would be capable of.

Which is nuts because he's twenty-five.

"Hey. Look up."

He follows the sheriff's order, sees his boss waving at him from her office window. She's a stout woman, but much of it's solid, the kind of body former gymnasts get as they age, although in her case, she's got the rigors of her military service to thank. Today, as always, she wears her jet-black hair in a tight bun against the back of her neck.

"Put the Jeep in park," she says.

He thought he had.

"I'm just going to say this. Every day at four o'clock, Marty has a slice of pie at the Copper Pot before he heads over to the AA meeting at the clubhouse."

"Why are you telling me this?"

"Because you know he was right, so I figure you'll keep it civilized. You know, when you go and apologize for whatever it is you did. In the *past*. But four o'clock's a couple hours away, and I got plenty of paperwork for you to do until then. So turn the Jeep off and come inside."

He does as instructed, because sometimes that's the only thing you can do.

His mom used to love the name of Altamira's most popular diner.

She'd been a big fan of that TV movie they made about Martha Stewart, the one where Cybill Shepherd played her like a fire-breathing dragon. There's a scene where Cybill Shepherd chases her business partner down the front walk of her house just so she can hurl a piece of cookware at her before screaming, "Every good cook deserves a copper pot!" It's a nasty repeat of words she had said to the same woman earlier in the movie when they were first becoming friends, and every time his mother watched the scene again, she howled with laughter.

And even though the movie hadn't been released when Abe and Dinah Crane first opened the place, his mother repeated the line, complete with a mimed pot toss, every time she set foot inside.

Luke can hear her saying it even now as he scans the mostly empty booths along the street-facing windows.

It's the lull between the lunch and dinner rush, a time when the other three restaurants on Center Street lock their doors and mop the floors. But the Copper Pot's pie case is so popular customers dribble in throughout the day. Customers like Marty, who's sitting by himself in the farthest booth, talking into his cell phone in a voice so low as to be inaudible.

He's changed clothes and showered. He looks ready for a nice night on the town. But if Mona's correct, only his sober friends will be treated to the sight of his pressed long-sleeve denim shirt and his snowy mane, which he's brushed out over his back and shoulders like some knight from a medieval fantasy epic.

Nothing in Luke's life at present feels worth dressing up for the way Martin Cahill's dressed for his AA meeting, and this realization stabs him with envy.

Finally, Marty sees him lingering inside the front door.

When Luke points to the empty bench seat across from him, the man ends his call, then gestures for Luke to come over. Changing out of his uniform was probably the right call, Luke thinks. Otherwise Marty might've shot out of his booth and demanded they talk outside.

"You here to arrest me?" he asks once Luke sits. There's no edge to his tone, and Luke feels as if he's being parented all of a sudden. And it's not such a bad feeling.

"You just make up that stuff about the women's shelter and the recovery home?"

"We on the record?" Marty asks.

"Record's for journalists. But I'm off duty, if that answers your question."

"You wearing a wire?"

"Over a bunch of AC units left behind by some jackasses who took the whole town for a ride? Hardly."

"Silver Shore's got powerful friends."

"Altamira Sheriff's doesn't have *wires*, Marty."

"Good to know. What are you doing here, Luke?"

"I'm here to apologize."

"For what?"

Fat chance Marty's letting him off the hook, more like asking him to put it in his own words.

"I might have come down a little too hard on you today," Luke says.

"Maybe so."

"*Maybe* so?"

"I don't know. If you thought I was stealing . . ." Marty sips his coffee, stares out the window. The elm tree on the corner sends stained-glass windows of dusky-orange sunlight across the sidewalk. Altamira's version of rush hour consists of a pickup, a minivan, and a PT Cruiser taking their time deciding whose turn it is at the four-way stop that marks the intersection of Center Street and Apple Avenue.

"Threatening to run your crew—that was out of line," Luke says.

This gets Marty's attention. He'd like to think the guy's impressed, but he can't be sure.

"You've always done good work. Always helped people. Everyone round here knows that, same way they all know I . . ."

His heart races. Should he slow down, try to do this in stages? He'd sure like to get it over with, but what he's trying to do is bigger than this one conversation, and he knows it, so what's the damn rush?

"Well," Marty says quietly, "maybe it was out of line to bring your mother up the way I did."

"Maybe."

"That look you gave me, though."

"What look?"

"Before you drove away, I just . . . it felt like I'd shoved an old lady or something."

"You calling me an old lady?"

"You know what I mean."

"Not sure I do."

"The fight had gonna out of you. Not sure what it means exactly, or if it's good or bad. But I could see it in your eyes . . . you aren't that little jerk I wanted to strangle when you were in high school. Or at least you've lost hold of him for now."

"Thanks. I guess."

"None of it's a load off my back, Deputy Prescott. But it might be helpful information for you."

"Thanks . . . I guess."

"Mona tell you to come over here and make this right?"

"She didn't have to."

"Would she say the same?" Marty asks.

"No. Probably not."

"There's a reason she's sheriff."

"Yep."

"And there's a reason you're one of her deputies now and not working for the FBI, from what I hear."

Well, that was a turn, Luke thinks.

"Oof. Got you there, didn't I?" Marty asks.

"I got to go to some kind of class for my face."

"A class for your *face*?"

"So I can keep it from giving everything away."

"I imagine that's probably important for a career in law enforcement. Even if it's not the career you planned."

"You're good, man. Real good. Those drunks aren't gonna get anything by you."

"Takes one to know one."

"I'm not a drunk."

"I wasn't talking about you," Marty says.

"So what'd you hear?"

"About what?"

"About my career, or lack thereof?"

Marty's jaw tightens. "Heard you rolled all your chips on a job with the FBI. Even got yourself fluent in a couple different foreign languages 'cause you heard all they want is linguists now. But it didn't work out, apparently."

"Is that all?"

"Is it?"

"Is that all you *heard*?" Luke asks.

"Yes."

"You lying?" Luke asks.

"You gonna take me in if I am?" Marty asks.

"I told you I'm off duty. Don't even have my cuffs."

"You might be able to take me bare-handed if you tried real hard."

"Fight's gone outta me. Remember?"

"Yeah, it's all I heard. It's not like you kept in touch with anyone from here. Up until you called Mona asking for a job. But, you know, thanks for letting me know there's more to the story."

Luke grabs for the first thing he can think of to change the subject.

"Trina," he says. Her name comes out sounding like a grunt. "Trina Pierce."

"What about her?"

"How is she?"

Now Marty's the one struggling to hide his reaction. He brings his coffee mug to his lips, looks out the window as if he's suddenly planning the route he's going to take to the recovery house. "She's fine."

"I'd like to talk to her."

"Why?" Marty's full-on pissed now.

"Call me crazy, but I'm pretty sure if I apologize to you for what I did to Trina, you're just gonna tell me it doesn't mean anything unless I say it to her face. So I'm trying to save us both some time. Is she still around? I mean, I know Luanne's store is gone but . . ."

So much of this day has been about Marty having the upper hand on him; Luke is stunned to see the man so visibly thrown off his game.

"She's all right, isn't she? I mean . . . she's alive, right?"

"And why would you care?"

"I just told you why, Marty."

"All right, well, let me tell you something. Apologies aren't worth shit. Apologies are a string of words people put together so they can off-load their guilt in five minutes."

"You didn't have a problem accepting the one I gave you."

"That's still pending. You go back to being the little son of a bitch I remember, it won't be worth horse dung."

"OK, well, maybe Trina should have that opportunity, too. Horse dung and all."

"She doesn't want it!"

It's not exactly a shout, but it's loud enough to draw the attention of the waitress, and it embarrasses Marty enough to turn his face red and make him reach for his fork even though his plate's only got bits of pie crust on it.

"Look," Marty says, once he's caught his breath. "I appreciate you coming over and—" The man's cell phone rings, and Luke figures he'll ignore it. But maybe that's not a luxury you can afford when your vocation is talking fragile drunks away from the bottle. Whatever number Marty sees flashing on the caller ID, it drains some of the recent color from his face.

He looks up at Luke, confusion in his eyes. It's like he thinks Luke might have something to do with whoever's calling.

"I gotta take this," Marty says.

"You want me to go?" Luke asks.

Marty shakes his head, slides out of the booth, and gets to his feet. He takes the call and brings the phone to his ear. "Give me a second," he says to the person on the other end. Luke watches as he peels a twenty out of his wallet and drops it on the table.

He's a few steps from the table when he seems to realize he's left Luke sitting there without much of an explanation. He turns.

"Later, Deputy Prescott," he says.

14

The last time Charlotte slept this deeply, anesthesia was involved, and she'd woken up with her wisdom teeth removed. The shrill beeping that calls her out of slumber now is almost as unpleasant as regaining consciousness with bloody gauze in her mouth.

Almost.

The shades are drawn, but around their edges, she can see it's almost dark outside. As Kayla walks toward the front door, she looks just as put together as she did that morning, which makes Charlotte feel like a drunk emerging from a blackout.

"Don't be mad," Kayla says, as if the prospect barely frightens her. An electronic peephole viewer is attached to the wall next to the door frame, about sixty bucks from an appliance store. Charlotte priced them out for her house before she found a system that came with cameras included.

Kayla studies the small monitor, sees whatever she'd hoped to see, and sends a text in response. Whoever this visitor is, she doesn't want him to just walk up to the front door and ring the bell. Or she's told him she won't open the door for anyone who doesn't also have her phone number.

A minute or two later, Kayla turns the knob.

Charlotte gets to her feet. She's not sure whom she's preparing herself for, but she's sure she should be prepared.

When he steps inside the house, Charlotte's breath leaves her with a startled grunt, the kind of sound you make when you almost knock over a water glass. Maybe it's just the sight of him that does her in. Maybe it's the smell of his Old Spice aftershave, familiar and nostalgic at the same time, wrapping her in a cocoon of such vivid, comforting memories she feels like it might keep her standing even if she let her knees go out from under her.

They're fragmented, but her earliest memories of him are still vivid.

The memory of his face among the many others in that dull conference room where the psychiatrists brought her a few weeks after her rescue. The way he'd stood behind her grandmother's chair with one hand resting firmly on her shoulder as Luanne cried softly into a Kleenex. They'd both tried to let her father lead the conversation, even though it was clear, even then, that her father was treating her like an alien being, a creature irreparably changed by her time on the Bannings' farm.

The way he'd taken her hand and walked her down the stairs to the beach in Altamira during those first early visits to her grandmother's after she was rescued.

Had there ever been a man in her life she could trust more than Martin Cahill, her grandmother's on-again, off-again boyfriend? And what had she done? Turned her back on him because her love for him reminded her too much of her grandmother. Practically banished all thoughts of him because they summoned her grief. Now the sight of him, his snow-white hair brushed out over his back, his denim shirt perfectly pressed, his smile warm and welcoming and eager, it's exactly what she needs to break the hard shell of shock that's grown around her over the past twenty-four hours.

"Heya, Charley," he says softly.

That he can manage to say her new name with such warmth, it makes her vision wobble.

At last her knees buckle. And when she tries to say, *Hi, Uncle Marty* in response, all that comes out is a deep, wrenching sob. With an arm around her waist, he guides her back to the sofa.

Kayla follows from a short distance. Before Charlotte collapses against Marty's chest, she glimpses Kayla watching them from the doorway, her expression grave but relaxed, as if Charlotte's breakdown is proof that calling Marty was the right choice.

15

"Arizona?" Marty asks. "What the hell's in Arizona?"

"It's beautiful," Charlotte answers.

"Yeah, if you want to live on Mars."

"Never been so I can't compare."

"Seriously, though. Arizona?"

Marty shakes his head, sips from the coffee Kayla just brought him before disappearing into the kitchen.

"I thought it'd be safe out there," she says.

"From what? We took care of the Briffel kid the one time he showed up, didn't we?"

Not well enough, she wants to say, but she knows that's unfair. Jason never would have found her again without Dylan's help. Marty and his buddies deserve credit for scaring him off her scent for a good long while.

"There are other Jasons out there. Message boards, websites about the Bannings. All kinds of stuff."

"Tell me you're not reading that crap."

"How much did Kayla tell you?" Charlotte asks.

"That Jason paid you a visit. That it didn't end well. That's all."

"I should have called you."

"Well, it's not like I would have been able to make it to Arizona in time."

"No, sooner. I mean, in general. I should have . . ."

She'd managed to peel herself off his chest a few minutes before, but there's only about a foot of distance between them on the sofa now. He reaches across it to smooth her bangs back from her forehead.

"You don't owe me anything, kiddo. That's not how it works."

"How what works?"

"Family."

Real family, is what he seems to be saying, *unlike your father, who didn't treat you like family.*

"Maybe not, but I shouldn't treat family that way."

Marty shrugs. He agrees with her, but he doesn't want to rub it in. Not when she's like this.

And he came as soon as Kayla called. That means more to her than anything in the world.

She'd had lots of plans when she started her self-imposed exile: to get an online degree, to work up the courage to live in a big city again. Or maybe even to move back to Altamira once her grief for Luanne lost some of its darkness. All she needed was time, she'd thought. Time to gather confidence. Time to let her new name sink in and her terrible fame dissipate.

On some days she'd thought it would be as simple as letting herself age to the point where no one recognized her anymore, when the resemblance she bore to the young woman her father used to trot in front of crowds was a passing one. But would that come at a price? With each year it took to gather confidence and anonymity, would it become even harder to bring Marty or Luanne's other friends, or anyone from Altamira, back into her life again?

After she'd fled to the desert, these questions tormented her. Now the answer seems clear. Marty's right here beside her, and he came at a moment's notice.

"How's everyone?" she asks.

"Same. Pissed, though. Some developers said they were gonna open a big lodge out on PCH. Turned out to be bullshit. Couple folks went under because of it. Mona Sanchez is sheriff now."

"That's good. I liked her."

"Copper Pot's still going strong. Still got the best pie in California. What else?"

Marty focuses on the blank white wall behind her. She figures he's debating whether or not to share some other piece of hometown trivia, something she might find troubling.

"What?" she asks.

"Nothing. So you want to tell me what got you to leave Arizona?"

Kayla appears in the doorway with a suddenness that suggests she's been eavesdropping.

It's not going to be easy, telling the story again now that she knows Kayla doesn't believe a big chunk of it. But at least her lawyer isn't trying to bias Marty one way or the other. Instead she rests one shoulder against the door frame and studies Charlotte intently.

Charlotte looks at the floor and starts to talk.

Occasionally she glances up at Marty to find he's gone as still as a statue, his eyes saucer-wide, his mouth set in a grim line. He's a smart man with no patience for the bullshit he believes defines most human interactions. But he can also spend a solid hour explaining how alien infiltration has taken place at the highest levels of the American government, and he can do it with the conviction of Kayla arguing a case before the Supreme Court of California. So maybe Marty's having less trouble believing all this than another person might.

By the time she finishes, he's gone pale.

"You believe me?" Charlotte asks. "Kayla doesn't."

Kayla walks toward her, holding her mobile phone out in one hand. It takes Charlotte a second to realize she wants her to look at what's on the screen.

It's from the website of the Phoenix-based NBC affiliate. The accompanying photograph is a helicopter shot of sheet-draped bodies lying in the middle of nowhere. The bus sheds have been obliterated, leaving her to wonder if they were the source of the explosion.

The headline: BLAST AT OUTLAW BIKER WEAPONS STOREHOUSE KILLS 11

It's a rush TV news article, short on details, designed mostly to support the slide show of helicopter shots capturing the scene. Eleven killed, speculation it might be related to the takedown of a Vapados storehouse in California the week before, which had forced some members of the gang to relocate into rival territory. A possible battle between Hells Angels and Vapados suggested but not confirmed. No mention of a victim who seems to be out of place. A victim like Dylan Thorpe.

"He did it," Charlotte says.

"This Dylan guy?" Marty asks.

"Or the guy who calls himself Dylan," Kayla says. "Did you read all the way to the end?"

"No."

"Read all the way to the end."

She does. That's where she finds the quote from an anonymous law enforcement source speculating that not all the bikers were killed by the blast; several were found with close-range gunshots to the head.

Marty gestures for the phone. She hands it to him, then gets to her feet.

It seems rude, but she turns her back on them anyway, closes her eyes, tries to imagine the man she talked to month after month going from biker to biker, putting bullets between their wide, terrified eyes. Using his powers of manipulation to lure Jason to her house, to convince her to take his crazy drug—those talents belong to one skill set, close-range executions to another. Was that the point of the explosion? Not to provide cover for his escape, but to incapacitate those bastards so he could execute them one by one?

And when it comes to executing outlaw bikers, is she in any position to judge? But she was defending herself. Defending herself with the power of a drug she'd been tricked into taking. A shot between the eyes—that's a different story.

That takes a very special kind of person.

A person who's been trained to kill.

"You believe her now?" Marty asks.

"Look, I never said I didn't believe she'd been drugged or that this Dylan guy's a class-A psychopath."

"But you think she was hallucinating everything else?" Marty asks.

"Possibly, yes."

"Fifteen years I've been in AA, I've seen folks detox from all kinds of shit. Guys so nuts they'll meet you for lunch and apologize for the warlock who followed them into the restaurant. None of those folks had it as together as she does right now."

"Charley," Kayla says, "we've got a more pressing issue to discuss."

"What in Christ's name could *that* be?" Marty asks.

"Your car, Charley. The SUV you were driving when the bikers ran you off the road. If it's close to this crime scene, then—"

"Maybe he got rid of it," Charlotte answers.

"How?"

"I don't know. He blew up their damn storehouse. Maybe he threw my car on the pile. I don't even know who this guy really is, much less what he's capable of."

"You really think this guy was just carrying around the kind of explosives that could trigger a blast like that?"

"Or he used whatever he found on-site. Maybe he found something with all those weapons that he used as an explosive."

"You think he has that kind of training?" Marty asks.

"He said he was going to take care of eight bikers. Take care of them. On his own. And he said it like it was nothing. And it looks like he did."

"And the Briffel kid?" Marty asks, a catch in his voice.

They fall silent. She wonders if, like her, they're both imagining Jason dying of thirst on the floor of her kitchen.

"There's no way," Charlotte says.

"No way what?" Kayla asks.

"There's no way Dylan did that to those bikers and just left Jason there."

"Maybe he threw Jason on the pile along with your car," Marty offers.

"That's a big maybe," Kayla whispers.

"He said he'd take care of him. No maybe about it."

Charley could be imagining it, but Kayla's expression seems to have changed, softened a bit, become less skeptical. She wonders if that's going to be the key; that with each passing minute she doesn't change her story, or lose her grip on the details, or do any of the other things that suggest someone suffering from a delusion or advancing a lie, Kayla will come to believe her.

"I want you to see a doctor," Kayla says. "If you won't come into the city, I'll find one in Modesto or Fresno. But you need to—"

"I'm not crazy."

"I'm not talking about a psychiatrist, Charley. I'm talking about an internist. You were given a strange drug. You need to have blood work done. Get your vitals checked. Everything."

"I don't feel sick."

"You don't know what you are because you don't know what's in these pills! It might not be a good thing that your bruises from the car wreck are healing so fast. There could be something wrong with your blood. Maybe it's not clotting properly. There's just too much you don't know about this drug right now, and the only way to learn is to put yourself at this psycho's mercy again."

"What's some random doctor going to be able to tell me about the effects of a drug that shouldn't exist? Unless I tell them about the drug. Which would be reckless."

"So you're not interested in finding out how this drug really works?" Kayla asks.

"Oh, I am," she says.

Marty stiffens, studies her closely.

"In the field," Charlotte says.

"I'm sorry." Kayla's voice is a strained whisper. "The *field*?"

"A test. Look at it this way. You'll get to find out if I'm delusional or not."

"And how exactly are you going to conduct this *test*?"

"Jason was a trigger. That's how Dylan described him. Zypraxon is a drug that converts fear into strength, but it needs a trigger. A strong one."

"It converts *your* fear into strength," Kayla adds. "If we believe this story that you're the only one to take it and live."

"Right. So to do another test, I need another trigger."

She thinks back to those terrifying moments before the drug took effect. Knowing someone else was in the house wasn't enough. Otherwise she would've torn the toilet paper dispenser off the wall while she was peeing. Knowing someone was approaching her from behind wasn't enough, either. Otherwise the Diet Coke can she'd been holding as she stood at the sink would've exploded in her grip. Was it the stark terror of finding herself face-to-face with Jason? Or was it being attacked?

Maybe it was all of it in combination—a destination she can reach after mounting a staircase of increasing fear. There's only one way to find out for sure.

Marty clears his throat. "Why don't I just try to run over you with my car and see if you end up tearing the grill off with one hand?"

"I'm open. But the first time the bikers surrounded me during the drive home, it wasn't enough to trigger me. It was Jason breaking into my house and attacking me when I tried to run that did it. So I'm thinking we'll need to find something . . . similarly terrifying."

"Are you in favor of this, Marty?"

"Guess that depends on what kind of trigger we're talking about."

"Nobody has to get hurt," Charlotte says. "Now that I know what I can do while I'm on it, that'll be easier. Did you bring a gun, Marty?"

"Yep."

"Kayla?"

"As a lifelong member of the Democratic Party who supports sensible gun control I refuse to answer that question. And I don't like where this is headed."

"Why?" Charlotte asks. "We're not going to commit any crimes. We're just gonna find a way to stop someone from committing a crime against me."

"What's happening to you, Charley?" Kayla asks.

"I told you what happened to me, and you still don't believe me, so I'm trying to get you to understand that this is real. That a man who stalked me for most of my life, a man who idolizes serial killers for Christ's sake, broke into my house, and I was able to bring him down in thirty seconds with my bare hands even though it's been five years since I've gone for a jog."

"Don't make this about me. You were administered a drug without your knowledge and without your consent by someone who lied about who he was to get you to take it. Someone who may in fact be a trained killer. That's the story here, Charlotte. We need to find out who the players are before we do anything else."

"It's not the whole story, and you will see that if we do a test."

Without meaning to, she's cornered her. If Kayla admits to being afraid Charlotte might snap someone's neck by accident, then she's admitting to believing more than she's letting on about Dylan's magic pills.

But there's something else in her lawyer's eyes now. The fire of curiosity. The gradual acceptance that if this pill is truly what Charlotte says it is, its implications are more than this tiny safe house can contain. But Kayla's fighting it.

"There could be a corpse in your house right now," Kayla says. "The corpse of the guy you filed a restraining order against years ago. And when Dylan told you to run, he might have done it so that he'd have evidence against you. We need to deal with that, Charley."

"I've got a cell phone with an extended text thread between him and Jason planning a break-in of my house."

"And you haven't gone to the police with it."

"Is that really what you recommend? Going to the police with *this* story? When Dylan, a man I don't know, a man I can't trust, might be in possession of all the evidence?"

"I recommend a change of focus here."

"Marty, you've pulled drunks out of some of the worst bars in the Central Valley. Take us to the worst one."

"Charley!" Kayla snaps.

"I'm not going to hurt anyone, Kayla. I'm just going to show you what this stuff does."

"All right, well, if you're doing this on my account, forget it! I don't want to know."

"Yes, you do. You want to know for every woman who has to walk home alone at night. Just like I want to know for every victim of the Bannings, including my mother, all of whom would be alive today if they'd had something like this in their system."

"Apparently not, because it only works in you, according to Dr. Nutjob."

"Well, I guess that means I have a responsibility then."

"No, no, *no*! You do not have a responsibility to this insane man."

"I have a responsibility to *them*!" She's spent so much of the past year alone she can't remember how long it's been since she raised her voice like this. Kayla flinches as if she's been slapped. Marty's still as a statue and trying to keep whatever he's really feeling out of his expression. They know who she's talking about when she says *them*. Maybe, like her, they've memorized the faces in the photo collage of the Bannings' victims the media uses whenever Abigail makes some wacko new statement from behind bars.

"Maybe he's dead, Kayla. Maybe he didn't take care of those guys. Maybe he's one of the eleven bodies out there, and these pills, they're all that's left of whatever it was he was trying to do. He's got the number to Jason's cell phone, but he hasn't called. So maybe these pills are mine now, and it's up to me to figure out if they can ever help anyone the way they helped me last night."

"You were not *helped* last night. You were violated. Charley, you've spent most of your life afraid. I understand that. And your fears were justified. But don't let yourself become a victim of this guy's crazy schemes just because you've—"

"Kayla, don't patronize me, and don't force me to be alone with what this really is. There is a *science* to this. A science to what happened to me last night. And that's bigger than Dylan Thorpe or whatever his real name is. It's bigger than me. It's bigger than all of us. You'll see that if you let me show you."

"And maybe *this* was his real plan!" Kayla gestures to Charley.

"What?"

"Getting you addicted to his drug. Getting you so amped about what it can do you're going to ignore the real threat against you."

"Which is what exactly? The Scarlet Police Department?"

"Try the FBI or the ATF. That's who's investigating this biker massacre."

"Dylan says this is bigger than them."

"So he mentioned them specifically?"

"No, but since neither of those agencies has a drug that provides superhuman strength, I'm going to assume it is."

"Oh, I get it."

"Get what?"

"You're trying to figure out how to use this drug so you can fight off law enforcement if they come for you?"

"I'm done with this conversation, Kayla. I'm sorry I brought you into this. You're free to leave. I won't hold it against you. I promise. But seriously. Enough."

"I'm not going anywhere."

"Good. Then knock it off! I'm glad that you feel you have a frame of reference when grade-A sci-fi crazy is thrust into the middle of your life. But I *don't*, OK? And I've had one of the craziest lives of anyone I know.

"I'm doing the best I can with this. But you're going to have to forgive me for thinking we're in uncharted waters here and that a lot of the old rules don't apply anymore. This drug, wherever it came from, it was given to me by a man with crazy black ops skills who assumed a cover identity for three months so he could earn my trust. If you think I'm going to try to fight off a man like that with the FBI, who didn't capture the Bannings for over a decade, by the way, you're the one who's not thinking clearly. I want to know how this pill works, and I can't exactly walk into a CVS and ask the pharmacist, OK? But if me trying to get some knowledge here freaks you out, fine. I'll clear out of here and figure out my next move, and you can forget we ever met up today."

Kayla swallows, but Charley can tell what she'd really like to do is roll her eyes and groan. But she doesn't do either. Instead she turns to Marty and says, "Why aren't you helping me here?"

"I don't know you that well, to be frank," he says. "It's Charley I'm here to help. And seems to me if this Dylan guy was such a threat to her, he wouldn't have given her a bunch of pills that make it easy for her to rip his face off."

"People can do a lot of harm from a distance," Kayla whispers. "Especially powerful people. We need to find out how powerful this particular guy is."

"Sure. But if he were all that powerful, what the hell does he need Charley for?" Marty asks. "I mean, no offense, darling. I'm crazy about you, but you're not exactly the leader of the free world."

It's a damn good point, she thinks for the first time. Things have moved so fast these past few hours she hasn't stopped to ask the most important question. *Why me?*

"Look," Marty says. "Charley's right. There's no frame of reference for this stuff. I'd rather see her do something than worry herself into crazy by speculating about who this asshole is when she could be figuring out what he gave her. If she wants to try to make the most of a colossally shitty situation, I'm in. I've got a gun in my truck, and I know my way around some really sketchy places."

Kayla's chest rises and falls.

"Fine," she finally says. "I've got a gun, too."

16

The bar looks like the dirt beside the irrigation canal burped up an old trailer it couldn't swallow.

There's no sign, just a smattering of decrepit cars and pickup trucks that suggests most of the clientele inside is more meth than man.

According to Marty, it's the kind of dive where the regulars find their favorite stool by noon, are singing along to every song on the jukebox by three, and then by dinnertime are lecturing anyone who'll listen about how the world's done them wrong their whole miserable lives. By eleven they're ready for a fight. Or something worse, if they've managed to score a pick-me-up from one of the resident dealers, who may or may not also be the bartender.

It's ten to eleven now. She's showered and brushed her hair out, and she's wearing a fresh outfit Kayla picked up for her at the nearest Walmart. Jeans and a baggy powder-blue T-shirt. She looks like a lot of women do when they go grocery shopping, but in this hellhole she's bound to draw attention just because her clothes don't stink of spilled beer.

Attention is exactly what she gets when she pushes the door open.

A blast of stale beer along with something more acrid and unidentifiable hits her with enough force to make her eyes water.

There's a pool table off to her left. At first she thinks the men gathered around it are in the midst of some verbal altercation that's about to turn physical. Two of them are nose to nose; one's shouting into the face of the other in a high-pitched, barking voice. And he's using lots of hand gestures while he does it. It takes her a second to realize the man's aggression is reserved for the asshole supervisor he's describing in his shrill tale of workplace woe. His volume and his movements are probably the result of whatever's got him hopped-up, and the guy he's talking to doesn't put distance between them because he's too drunk to be bothered. The most unnerving thing about this little scene is that no one, not his friends and not the bartender, is asking him to quiet the hell down.

Heads turn as she passes. She feels the men's stares like pinpricks on her skin. Each look almost slides past her, then catches on the sight of her bare arms and braless chest and youthful features, and locks in like motion-activated security cameras finding an intruder.

She counts two other women in the place.

One's passed out at one end of the bar; the other's sandwiched in a corner booth in between two hulking guys who look like bikers. Her glazed eyes focus on nothing in particular while the men talk across her. Occasionally they slam the table with the sides of their fists to make a point. The impacts are strong enough to jostle their beer bottles, but the woman, who wears an outfit slightly more revealing than Charlotte's, doesn't even flinch. She's somewhere far away from this place. Maybe someplace with blue sky and birds and men who acknowledge her presence.

Charlotte takes a seat at the bar.

The pill's been in her system for an hour. That's about the same amount of time it took her to get from Dylan's office to her house.

To distract herself from the looks she's getting, she makes a mental checklist of the symptoms she's on the lookout for. The shaking hands, the throbbing in her bones—the phenomenon she's nicknamed bone music. The former, she thinks, is a sign the drug's about to kick in, the second that it's in full bloom throughout her body. But these are just guesses. There's a lot she's still not sure of. Not yet. That's what tonight's about.

The nearest bartender glares at her, but he doesn't come over. His glare seems both a warning and a dismissal.

When she hears the bar's door open, she fights the urge to look over her shoulder. But she's sure it's Marty. He's changed into a baseball cap and some paint-splattered clothes from his truck that conceal the gun he's now carrying on his hip. The plan is he'll keep her within sight at all times while he tries to hang back.

Marty only told her one story about this place. It was general, but it was enough.

One of his AA sponsees had to make a serious amends for something he'd done here. An amends that involved him turning himself in to the police and pleading guilty to a charge that got him ten years in Folsom. And the reason he'd had to turn himself in is because no one in this place reported what he and two of his buddies did to a woman in the corner while everyone else drank beer and played pool. Not even the woman, even though she'd lost most of her teeth during it.

Outside, Kayla has parked her car a short walk from the bar's entrance, next to the tall, spiked steel fence designed to keep drunks from driving into the water supply for the nearby farms. If all goes as planned, she'll have a front-row seat to Dylan Thorpe's magic show. And so will Marty. And so will whoever makes the mistake of following Charlotte out of this place.

"Can I get a drink?" she asks.

It's not that she's rude; it's that she doesn't keep her eyes averted or soften her tone. She doesn't ask the question the way these men believe a visitor, especially a female one, should. She doesn't address them in a way that says, *You're in charge, big boy, and I remain here at the pleasure of your bad attitude.* The wording alone calls attention to how brazenly the bartender's been ignoring her and sends a ripple of tension through the two men seated at the bar next to her. They rouse like coiling snakes. One of them runs fingers over his sweating beer bottle; the other taps out a frenetic rhythm on his. Both study her, their jaws working, as if the five words she just spoke have awakened a predatory energy inside them.

The bartender comes over, stands in front of her. This isn't the type of place where a napkin precedes a drink order.

"Diet Coke," she says, staring him in the eye.

"You want a lemon in that?" the bartender asks.

"Sure."

"There's a Save Mart about ten minutes from here. I hear they got 'em on sale."

The bartender departs. The guy closest to her at the bar cackles, punches his friend lightly in the elbow.

Charlotte locks eyes with him.

For a second she worries that her gaze is too steady, too intimidating. That her knowledge of what she might be able to do to him if he tries to harm her has given her a confidence that might frighten the guy into submission.

She's wrong.

His mouth curls into a sneer. It's a similar reaction to the one Thor the biker gave her when she refused to pull over on his command; only now she's seeing it up close.

His baseball cap is on backward, giving her a full view of his bloodshot, rheumy eyes, his bulbous drinker's nose. He's stocky and about her age, but years of hard living make him look ten years older, and she's not sure how much of his bulk is muscle or just beer fat.

His buddy is watching her, too, only his baseball cap is turned forward, hiding his face in shadow. He's slouched forward on the bar, staring at her. Either he's the more focused of the two or the more drunk.

She tries to imagine both men crying out in pain the way Jason did the night before when she broke his shoulder. It feels like a version of that old mental trick people recommend when you have to speak in front of a large group. Just imagine everyone in their underwear. But the trick backfires. It doesn't make the men glowering at her now seem more human or less threatening. It doesn't, in her mind's eye, at least, dim the flames of their evident hostility toward her.

"You a cop?" Backward Cap asks.

"You a criminal?" she asks.

"Cops wear bras," Forward Cap says, his voice just above a growl.

"The lady ones do at least," his friend adds.

"I wouldn't know," Charlotte says.

She turns her attention to the television above the bar.

Both men fall silent, but she can feel their stares.

She's here to attract a criminal, not create one. But for this to work, the line between incitement and entrapment will be thin. And right now she doesn't see a lot of other options.

Marty had insisted on his ridiculous test on the way over, and it had been a total flop.

Right after she'd taken the pill, he asked her to start slowly walking toward the nose of the car, into the glare of the headlights so she couldn't see what he was doing behind the wheel. Then he'd tried startling her with bleats of the horn to see if he could trigger the drug. When that didn't work, he'd put his foot on the gas and accelerated toward her, slamming on the brakes at the last possible second. It had scared the crap out of her and almost caused Kayla to put a bullet in him. But it wasn't enough. It didn't re-create the raw, primal fear of being attacked by Jason in her own home. And neither, apparently, does sitting in this bar, surrounded by guys who look like they want to eat her alive.

When the bartender delivers her Diet Coke—which he's poured, without ice, into a grimy-looking glass—she grips it gently, realizes she's in no danger of breaking it, and takes a sip from it like an ordinary person.

The shitty presentation of her drink sends a message. *Hit the road.* Maybe the guy's pissed because she asked to be treated the same as his male patrons. Or maybe he thinks she's in real danger and doesn't want to deal with the resulting mess if she sticks around.

She pulls out the money clip Marty lent her. The one Kayla gave her a hundred dollars in twenties for. She flashes the bills conspicuously. If her words, attitude, and outfit don't end up making her a target for a bastard, maybe the money will. The bartender watches her as she pushes a twenty across the bar; then he picks it up, pockets it, and says, "I'll start you a tab."

She's been only pretending to watch the television over the bar, but now the images on-screen capture her full attention. They also take her back to two different places at once, which makes her head spin. Her house, when she'd come across the story of the first murder—*The first face,* she corrects herself—online a few weeks ago, and Dylan's office the day before. A lifetime ago.

Even though she'd played coy with him, the truth is she did keep to their agreement. She didn't even know there'd been a second killing.

Now she does, thanks to an eleven o'clock newscast out of San Francisco.

It's not a live shot. The helicopter footage of closed-down, traffic-snarled streets in Santa Monica has a subheading that says, LAST WEEK, and the streets are bathed in early-morning light. The chyron at the bottom of the screen says, NEW VIDEO RELEASED IN "MASK MAKER" KILLINGS.

"Can you turn that up please?" she hears herself ask.

The bartender appears in front of her.

"This isn't a sports bar, girlie."

"Does that look like sports to you, *boyo*?"

Forward and Backward Baseball Cap don't whoop or whistle or make sarcastic sounds of encouragement over her retort. They glare at her instead. On any other night that'd be a bad sign. Tonight it's a good one. The bartender, however, has followed her gaze. When he sees the footage of flaring police lights followed by a cheap black-and-white headshot of the Mask Maker's first victim in happier days, Charlotte's words shame him.

He grabs the remote, raises the volume until the voices of the newscasters are barely audible.

". . . identified as Kelley Sumter, who'd recently moved to Los Angeles to pursue acting ambitions and had changed her name to Harley Grey. But aside from the gruesome early-morning discovery that shut down many Santa Monica streets late last week, the rest of twenty-four-year-old Sumter's remains have not been found. Just her face. And now in this surveillance video, which we must warn you many will find disturbing, we see the man police believe to be Sumter's killer, the Mask Maker. In it, he stages the horrifying scene that brought a city to a standstill just last week."

The video's grainy and black and white, but she recognizes the statue from a visit she'd made to LA with Luanne before she died. It stands at the spot where Wilshire Boulevard dead-ends into Palisades Park, a long, palm-tree-studded pedestrian thoroughfare that sits on a bluff high above Pacific Coast Highway and Santa Monica Bay.

If the image were clearer, she might be able to make out waves in the dark ocean behind the statue. As it is, the statue's a shock of bright white amid a jungle of shadows.

The video's star is a quick-moving figure who appears out of the right side of the frame like an apparition. Quick, stealthy, athletic, and based on what he does next, incredibly strong. He scales half the statue, slides his backpack to one side by dropping one strap from one shoulder; then he fastens something around the statue's head like a mask. The newscast cuts away before Charlotte, or anyone else watching at home, can linger on the details of the surgically removed human face.

"While there are few identifying features on the video to help law enforcement, detectives are still hoping something about these images will lead to the capture of this killer . . ."

The newscast cuts to a police detective, identified as Manuel Ramirez, in front of a phalanx of microphones. He's a wall of a man, with salt-and-pepper hair. Charlotte can't tell if his eyes are sad or tired. "At this point, based on the video, we cannot assume the gender or ethnicity of the suspect. But what we can be sure of is that this person, even if not responsible for the murder itself, is most certainly an accessory. And we are doing everything we can to find them."

Questions erupt from the reporters. But the newscaster's narration takes over again.

Just as Charlotte fears, the report cuts to the cell phone footage that horrified her, and the rest of the country, when it hit the Internet. "So far no official statement on whether or not this killing has been linked by forensic evidence to a similar and equally gruesome discovery almost a month ago now at Griffith Observatory. That discovery involved the partial remains of twenty-six-year-old West Hollywood fitness instructor Sarah Pratt."

It's just as she remembered it. Jerky footage from someone walking toward the iconic observatory in bright morning sunlight. An entire group has just disembarked from a large tourist bus, which can be heard humming in the background beneath the excited chatter of its passengers.

The man doing the shooting is still getting his bearings, capturing mostly the backs of heads in front of him as he tries to pan up to the observatory's domed roof. There's a series of high-pitched cries off to his right. As if they're unsure whether the cries are of warning or pleas for help, the crowd starts moving in that direction, and the cameraman goes with them. That's when he captures the James Dean memorial—a bronze bust of the famous actor sitting on a white column of stone emblazoned with his name. The footage freezes at the first glimpse of the ill-fitting, grotesque mask of human skin that's been stretched across the bronze face underneath. But the audio continues uninterrupted, screams spreading throughout the crowd. The combination of the gruesomely defaced statue and the escalating panic of the crowd terrifies Charlotte as much as it had the first time. It's worse, maybe, than a gratuitous close-up of the ghostly face itself.

But it's not enough to trigger the drug in her system. It's a different kind of horror, a revulsion she can feel in her gut. The killer's cruelty is the same kind that led Abigail Banning to whisper, "You are now nothing," into the ears of her victims before she cut their throats.

The report cuts back to Detective Ramirez, who says, "The staging, the manner of death, obviously those speak to a connection between these two crimes. But further forensic analysis is needed before we can make any other statements."

From the crowd, a reporter shouts, "Are you not willing to call these crimes murders or are you gonna wait until the bodies are found?"

The detective stiffens. "After consulting with forensic pathologists, we are reasonably sure it's not possible for these victims to have survived what was done to them."

The explosion of laughter startles her so badly she almost falls off her stool. It's Backward Cap. He's doubled over the bar and is slapping it with one palm. "Can you fucking imagine?" he wheezes. "Can you fucking imagine? What, like, you're there for some kid's fucking birthday, and there's a fucking face on one of the fucking statues! I'd be like, 'Did we pay extra for this bitch, 'cause maybe I would have liked to have a selection to choose from, you know?'"

Forward Cap says, "You think they'd charge more depending on how hot she was?"

Backward Cap laughs harder. "Or how big of a bitch she was. Hell, I'd pay, depending on the woman. Beats looking at a bunch of telescopes any day."

"What?" his buddy asks. "Are you on a game show? I'll take the face for five hundred, Pat."

"Alex," Charlotte says.

Both men fall silent. At the sound of her voice, the bartender picks up the remote, kills the volume, and changes the channel. To sports. Even though this isn't a sports bar.

"What was that, Diet Coke?" Forward Cap asks. He laughs less than his friend, and the long, studious looks he's been giving her since she sat down suggest that if he's not quicker to violence, he's better at planning it.

"Alex Trebek is the host of *Jeopardy!*; Pat Sajak is the host of *Wheel of Fortune.*"

They just stare at her. Will this work? She hopes so. She's pretty sure she can provoke these guys. But throwing a drink in their faces to do it seems cheap. Almost like entrapment. On the other hand, she's never met an arrogant ignoramus who didn't fly off the handle when corrected by the facts. Especially from a woman.

"The game show you were referring to, the one where you pick a category and a dollar amount, that's *Jeopardy!*"

"What's your problem, Loose Tits?" Backward Cap asks.

"Two women were murdered. Horribly. And you guys think it's funny. I'd say the problem is yours, and it's in your brains."

Everything gets darker suddenly. The bartender is standing right over her, his formidable bulk blocking out the flickering television.

"It might be time for you to head back to San Francisco. Maybe get your kicks on Market Street. I hear that's a better place for girls with opinions."

Charlotte looks to the guys at her left. They're almost to the point of ignition, but they're not quite there yet. And if she lets their hero bartender put her in her place, then she might have lost them for good.

"Soon as I finish my drink, *sir,*" she says.

"The second you do," the bartender says.

She nods. He moves away, but he's lingering.

"Uh-oh," Backward Cap says to his friend. "Looks like we insulted a lady. A real one, too."

"No shit, huh?" Forward Cap says. "I don't know, maybe we should check those jeans. Seems like she's got a big ol' pair of balls to me."

"Huh. Well, you know what my dad always said 'bout men and women."

"What'd he say?"

"Come on. You know his old joke."

"Which one?"

"Why'd God give women vaginas?"

"So men would talk to 'em."

Charlotte lifts her glass to her mouth and drains the rest of her Diet Coke. Then she slams it down hard enough to suggest she's offended. She is, but in an abstract way. Mostly she's relieved they've set up her next line of attack so nicely. She stands, takes a step toward them.

"You losers have about as much chance of being able to see what's in my pants as you do of finding a word in the dictionary."

It's like she's thrown ice water in their faces. Maybe it's the insult, or maybe it's the confidence with which she hurled it.

Either way it's time for her to get moving.

When she passes Marty's table, she locks eyes with him. He holds her gaze briefly, letting her know he's ready to follow.

She's outside and headed along the irrigation canal when she hears the door open.

She expects another verbal volley, maybe some shouted taunts or another disgusting joke about women. When she hears their footsteps punching gravel, she realizes this is escalating more quickly than she anticipated.

The realization that they're only feet behind her now sends a familiar shiver through her entire body. Her hands begin to shake.

It's a moment in which powerlessness and outrage collide and fight for prominence, producing several seconds of terrified paralysis, and it feels like it's enough to unleash the drug's power.

They slam her into the fence from behind—a maelstrom of whiskey breath and wheezing grunts. Just as she'd planned, she reaches out and grabs two of the steel spokes. She forces herself to go limp so they think they've got her.

One's got his arms around her from behind and is grinding his groin against her ass; the other grips the back of her neck with so much pressure it should hurt like hell but doesn't. His hot breath bathes her ear. They're laughing because they think they got her, and she's saying nothing because the bone music is back. This time it feels pleasurable, delicious even. Maybe because she knows what's really causing it.

"I got an idea how we're gonna get in those pants, you mouthy little bitch." It's the one who has her by the neck. He's growling right into her ear. Forward Cap.

Backward Cap says, "What're we gonna do with whatever we find there?"

"Well, if we like it, we help ourselves to a piece. If we don't, we'll cut it off."

Slowly, hoping they won't notice the motion right away, she begins to pull on both spikes. The resulting sound reminds her of train cars coming to a slow, tortured stop. The sound of steel being bent by a constant and steady force.

"Fuck," Forward Cap whispers. He releases her neck. *"Fuck!"* There's no malice in his voice now, just a kind of dumbstruck horror.

They're both stumbling away from her. She's bent the spokes at almost ninety-degree angles. Finally, the one in her right hand snaps free with a sound like a giant guitar string being flicked by a giant finger. A tug and the one in her left hand comes free as well. When she turns, Forward Cap stumbles backward over his own feet.

"Who likes hand jobs?" Charlotte asks.

They run.

A few seconds later, Kayla emerges out of the darkness, lowering the gun she's drawn. Staring at the steel spikes in Charlotte's hand. Her jaw's slack; her eyes are wide. She's shaking her head back and forth. From the other direction comes Marty. No drawn gun, probably because he had faith the drug would work. But he seems as awestruck as Kayla. And, like her, he seems unwilling to get too close.

"Talk to us," Kayla says. She sounds winded. "Describe what you're feeling."

"What are *you* feeling?" Charlotte asks.

"Like I'm gonna wet myself. But don't answer a question with a question. It's annoying."

"Bone music," Charlotte answers.

"What?" Marty asks.

"It's like there's music playing inside my bones. Or a beat, at least."

"Like a waltz beat or a samba beat or a rave beat?"

"Is that a serious question?" Charlotte asks.

"Is it painful, is what I mean?"

"No," Charlotte says, "it's like I can't feel pain. And I'd go with samba if I had to pick."

She throws the spike in her left hand at the dirt with one downward thrust. It lands like a perfectly aimed spear.

Kayla gasps. Then Charlotte takes the jagged end of the other spear and drives it slowly into her left palm. The pain is a dull, muffled thing. The skin should break, but it doesn't. Instead it develops an instant dark bruise that comes on too fast, then seems to vanish the second she withdraws the steel. Like her body's trying to assert its usual response to being stabbed, but the drug suppresses it.

Kayla and Marty flank her now. "Keep talking, Charlotte," Kayla says.

"OK. What do you want to know?"

"Just keep describing what you're feeling. Altered vision? Mood changes?"

"I'm not about to turn Incredible Hulk on either of you if that's what you're afraid of."

"Hey, Charley," Marty says. "Just a suggestion—maybe hold the sarcasm until our entire sense of reality isn't being turned on its head."

"Sorry, but this is just the kind of moment sarcasm was made for, Uncle Marty."

"Your heart rate," Kayla says. "Is it elevated?"

"It doesn't feel like it. It's like I said. The feeling in my bones and what you saw me do. It's pretty simple."

"This is *not* simple," Kayla whispers. "This is not simple, but this is . . ."

For a second Charlotte thinks Kayla has literally lost her mind. How else do you explain it when a grown woman starts suddenly jumping up and down and clapping her hands together and cackling like a hyena? "Oh my God! Oh my God!" Kayla cries over and over again.

She looks like she just won the lottery. But even in the midst of her joy, she doesn't allow anything less than five feet of space between herself and Charlotte. Now it's clear why Kayla had such a hard time believing her story; she wanted it to be true so much she didn't trust herself. She wanted it to be true the way we want fairy tales and romance novels and Santa Claus to be true. And now that she has undeniable proof, it's like she's a child again.

Charlotte laughs, then feels awestruck that she can laugh. That even as the drug courses through her, making the impossible possible, she has all her human emotions within reach.

"Women," Marty mutters. Charlotte makes a fake grab for his throat, and he goes skittering backward so quickly he ends up on his ass, which only makes Kayla laugh louder, which only makes Charlotte laugh louder.

"If it's anything like last night, we've got three hours," Charlotte says once she catches her breath. "Let's play."

17

"Again," Marty says to Kayla.

"I've circled twice, Marty. Nobody's here."

"Third time's the charm."

"For you and the eye doctor, maybe," she grumbles.

Kayla's right, the place does look abandoned. The warehouse has meteor-size holes in its walls. Weeds grow in the broken asphalt of its empty loading docks. The chain-link fence looks relatively new, like someone threw it up for protection after the last tenant left, but even it's collapsing in sections.

By the time her companions start arguing over which particular nest of shadows will conceal the car best, Charlotte's managed to thread her hair into a ponytail without tearing out large chunks by the roots. Together with the fact that she hasn't torn a hole in any part of Kayla's back seat, this accomplishment makes her feel pretty damn proud of herself.

Inside, they find almost nothing Charlotte cannot bend to the point of breaking.

She's most impressed with what the drug does to her aim. After snapping some rebar with her bare hands, she's able to throw pieces of it through the air with enough force to spear the wall from what would amount to two car lengths away, a trick similar to what she did outside the bar when she sent the steel spike into the ground. To overcome gravity like this from this distance, an ordinary human would require impeccable aim. For her it's not an issue because of the insane amount of propulsion that comes from even the lightest flick of her wrist.

With each successful hit, she takes another step back. Eventually she discovers the point at which distance overcomes her enhanced strength. At about three car lengths between her and the wall, the rebar starts to fall short.

"We need to film this," Charlotte says.

"You sure about that?" Kayla asks.

"I'm sure I've only got one pack of pills, and if I run out and nobody believes me, there's gonna be no way to prove we're not all crazy."

"You planning to tell the world about this?" Marty asks.

"I don't know yet. I don't know anything yet. But if we have to tell someone, I want to be believed."

Charlotte begins rubbing two pieces of rebar together to see how long it takes her to make sparks. The answer—ten seconds. They light up the vast, shadowy interior of the warehouse, making it clear how much her eyes have adjusted to the darkness.

"I'm not trying to be a pain in the ass," Marty says. "I just don't think it's a good idea to have any of this on film. Not yet."

"I understand you feel that way, and I'm not asking you to store it on your phone for longer than it takes to transfer it to some kind of portable hard drive. And I don't want either of you on camera. I'll keep you out of it as best I can—I promise. But I've got to have some kind of record that this is actually happening."

Marty's staring at her, wide-eyed and frightened. It takes her a few seconds to realize it's not the prospect of putting all this on film that's got him scared. Not in this moment, at least. It's that she just gave him an order in a firm tone of voice, and right now, when she's capable of breaking steel, her orders mean more than they did an hour ago.

"You've got the pills, Charley," Kayla says. "That's your proof."

"Yeah, and we saw how easy it was to prove they work. All I have to do is set myself up to be raped and murdered. You can't trick this drug, guys. If I know the threat's not real, nothing happens. I mean, come on. Imagine I'm in police custody, trying to get them to believe my story, but the only way to prove it is to get them to drop me in the worst neighborhood in town, where I might end up breaking some guy's neck or, you know, destroying private property. Do you really see that going well for me?"

It's dark again inside the warehouse, but she can tell from the shapes of their bowed heads they're studying the shadows at their feet, considering her words.

"Also, there's another reason we need the film," she says.

"What's that?" Marty asks.

"It might be all you guys have if something happens to me."

"All right now," Marty says, closing the distance between them. He seems to have forgotten what she's capable of until he's curled an arm around her back. By then it's too late to pull away without being insultingly obvious about it. But he does stiffen briefly before he begins walking her toward the ruined entrance. "Nothing's gonna happen to you, Charley. Come on. Let's go do your little movie shoot. We've only got two hours left."

They'd agreed to do the shoot back at the safe house. When they'd first rolled up, and Kayla and Marty asked her to hang back while they cased the place, she'd had to remind them she was the one capable of breaking someone's spine with a light shove, so why not have her go in first? With bowed heads, they'd complied. The house had turned out to be as empty as they'd left it.

Now, the shoot complete, she's in the shower, washing off the grime of that awful bar, scrubbing her ear of the sticky film left by her assailant's hot whiskey breath.

The strength left her a few minutes ago. Three hours after being triggered, just as she'd expected. And even though she feels newly vulnerable, there's a comfort to knowing the pill keeps a regular schedule. That parts of it are knowable, quantifiable. It makes it seem a little less frightening than it was the night before.

Under the spray, she studies the mottled skin on her hand. She'd spent several minutes passing it back and forth through the stove's open flame while Marty filmed. The skin should be badly discolored, but instead it looks like it's been drawn on with a red marker and the ink has already started to fade. The effect was similar to when she pressed the spike against her palm: a riot of sudden bruising accompanied by dull pain that was mostly pressure. There's probably some threshold, some intensity level at which the heat and the flames become unbearable. But if the first test is any indicator, it's more than can be produced by a single stove.

Recounting her story for the unbiased lens on Marty's phone felt therapeutic, more cathartic than repeating it to Kayla and Marty, maybe because she didn't feel like she had to make anyone believe her. The proof was right there in her hands, in the way the flames kissed her skin. For good measure, she also bent several pieces of rebar they'd brought from the warehouse, and cracked some chunks of concrete, the latter of which Kayla and Marty convinced her to carry in from the car with the two of them flanking her like Secret Service agents so nosy neighbors couldn't observe her impossible strength.

There'd been one other endurance test she'd wanted to try, but when she asked them to head out to the backyard with her, they just glared at her.

Good call, she thinks now. *Maybe I'm not ready to try taking a bullet, either.*

But there was another test they had agreed to help with.

Once they'd finished making the video, Kayla drove to a gas station and came back with a box of wine and two bottles of vodka. Charlotte has always been a lightweight—one glass of wine usually makes her powerfully dizzy. And the hard stuff makes her sick to her stomach after a few swallows. Given her past, and her grandmother's genes, she's always figured this for a blessing. Her weak stomach and delicate sense of balance are probably what kept her from self-medicating over the years. But they also ruled out evening libations as potential sleep aids, which made her more vulnerable to Dylan's plot, so maybe she shouldn't be so grateful for these metabolic quirks. Not yet anyway.

But with Zypraxon thundering through her system, she was able to drink two glasses of straight vodka without so much as a wince. Same story with the wine. As Marty and Kayla looked on in astonishment, she metabolized both bottles like they were iced water with lemon. The pill doesn't give her just strength but a kind of temporary imperviousness to any physical limitation.

Except flying, she thinks, laughing under her breath. *But maybe if I ran fast enough to get started . . .*

There's a knock on the door. It's Marty, checking to make sure she's OK.

A few minutes later, she's toweling off, realizing she's got no idea where she's headed next and wondering if she should have been giving more thought to that than to Dylan's deceptions and magic pills.

Is she spending the night here? The choice makes her feel suddenly exhausted, in the way everything she did while on the drug should have made her feel but didn't.

What would the AA folks say?

One step at a time.

Which in this particular instance means it's a better idea to change into a real outfit and not pajamas.

Kayla and Marty are waiting for her in the living room. They've got steaming cups of coffee, which they're taking absent sips from as they watch Jason's disposable phone do absolutely nothing on the coffee table between them. They'd bought a charger for the thing when they bought Charlotte's change of clothes.

Neither of them looks the slightest bit tired, even though it's after two in the morning.

"I don't mean to be blunt," Marty says, "but should you really be carrying around the cell phone of a guy who tried to rape you?"

"It's a disposable," Kayla said. "I looked it up online. It sells for about twenty bucks."

"Guess that's why it looks a decade old," Charley says. "He probably bought it for cash. And it's Dylan's only way of getting in touch with me."

"Which he hasn't done," Marty says. "Which is strange."

"He seems like a pretty resourceful bastard psychopath asshole," Kayla says. "Something tells me he'd find a way to get in touch with you even if he lost the number to Briffel's burner."

"We'll get you a new phone on the way to Altamira," Marty says.

"Altamira?" Kayla says. "Hiding out in her former hometown? That sounds like a good plan to you?"

"She doesn't even know who she's hiding from. How's she gonna figure out the best place to hide? He might know where she is right now. I don't know."

"He knows everything," Charlotte says quietly. "He knows *everything* about me. For three months, I met him once a week, and I told him everything. He knows how I lost my virginity. He knows everything I'm afraid of. He knows what my favorite movies are, my favorite books. There's no hiding from him. There's no hiding from what I told him."

"You're not just saying this because you want to go home again?" Kayla asks.

"What am I going to do? Change my name again? Go off the grid *again*? Look how well it worked out the first time. I mean, here we are in the middle of . . . whatever the fuck this is. He found me before. He'll find me again."

"Now, wait a minute," Kayla says. "We don't have any evidence he targeted you because of your background. He could have been stalking that health center for anybody he thought was right for this plan of his. Any damaged, frightened woman who walked through the door. And with your background, you just turned out to be the supercharged version of what he was already looking for."

"Which explains why he put in three months of work on you," Marty offers.

"Maybe," Charlotte says.

"Or maybe not," Marty adds quietly. "Look, all I'm saying is, there's no perfect decision here, so she might as well make the one that's best for her."

"And you think that's going back to Altamira? With you?"

Kayla's not giving in easily, but there's less bite in her tone, and it feels to Charlotte like she's transitioned into a cooler, analytical mode.

"The one time that Briffel asshole tried to make trouble for her in Altamira, we showed him to the freeway, and he never came back. A lot of the guys that helped me that night, they're still there, they're still sober, and they still do what I say."

"Charley?" Kayla asks. "What do you want to do?"

"One thing, though, if you do decide to come back," Marty says. "There's something I need to take care of first."

"Oh, Lord," Kayla says. "What does that mean?"

Shaking his head, Marty says, "Just something weird I gotta figure out."

"Weirder than everything else that's happened tonight?" Kayla asks.

"I just gotta find out if it's a coincidence or not." To Charlotte he says, "You remember a guy named Luke Prescott?"

"Luke Prescott." The name comes out like an involuntary grunt. Hearing it now, in the midst of all this, is like waking from a coma to be told your dog tore apart the living room.

Luke Prescott. The guy who'd treated her like she was some dark force invading their pristine small-town high school, all because she got called on more in class than he did, which was because she knew the right answer a lot more often than he did. He was a slick bastard, even at seventeen. Sometimes his strategy against her worked; other times it got his ass called to the carpet. By constantly accusing her of trying to work her past for sympathy, he was able to hang that past around her neck like a scarlet letter. Years ago she would have called him a bully. Now she thinks back on his bullshit and just finds it competitive and desperate. Luke tried to be smarter and better at everything than anyone. With her, he had just had big, obvious targets to use.

Whatever his motives, Luke was the primary reason her life in Altamira didn't turn out to be quite as normal or pristine as she would have liked it to be. As Luanne would have liked it to be. The guy made it his job to constantly remind everyone of what had happened to her and where she'd come from, and always in a way that hinted she might have been perverted by the darkness she'd been exposed to at such a young age.

"Why are we talking about Luke Prescott right now?" Charlotte asks.

"He's back in town," Marty answers. "And the circumstances of his return are a little weird. And they sound a lot weirder now in light of all this."

"Slow down. You think Luke Prescott is working with Dylan? I thought that guy would be some asshole lawyer by now."

"Hey," Kayla whispers.

"For the bad guys. You work for the good guys. Marty, what are you talking about?"

"Prescott's one of Mona's deputies now."

"*What?*"

"Yeah. Apparently, he went up to San Francisco State, learned a couple different foreign languages, graduated with honors, got an MBA. Was all prepped to ace his interview for the FBI. Then for some reason he doesn't get past the front door, and he's back in Altamira, hanging his head and asking Mona for a job."

"Nothing against Altamira, but that's a pretty long fall," Kayla says.

"Exactly," Marty says. "And it's suspicious."

"You don't think he interviewed with the FBI?" Charlotte asks.

"No, I think he did. What if the FBI's involved in this somehow? What if he's working for them?"

"That's a reach, Marty," Kayla says.

"You want to know where I was when you called me? I was at the Copper Pot with Luke. Who was asking me for your contact information so he could apologize. When'd you say this Dylan guy first approached you? About three months ago, right?"

Charlotte nods.

"That's around when Luke first got in touch with Mona. She had a deputy set to retire, Bill Poindexter, so Luke had to wait until early this month to start."

"That's still a reach," Kayla says.

"About twelve hours ago, this would have all seemed like a reach, Kayla."

"Still," she says, "guy comes crawling home with egg on his face. Knows he's going to be seeing folks he was a dick to back in the day. Makes sense he would try to make amends."

"Look, I knew Prescott. Charley knew Prescott. That kid thought he might run the FBI someday. Now there's only two ways an arrogant know-it-all like that's going to come crawling back home on his hands and knees. One, he knows he's never got a shot in hell at a government job. Or two, he's made some kind of backroom deal that guarantees him one if he does something else first."

"I need a nap," Kayla says. "This is making my head hurt."

"And," Charlotte says, "I should add that Marty also believes that space aliens have infiltrated our government at the highest levels."

"My personal beliefs about our country's strained relationship with extraterrestrial life is a complicated conversation for another evening," Marty says. "The point here is that I need to make sure Luke isn't trying to set some kind of trap with this apology business."

"No," Charlotte says, "I do."

"You going to take one of your pills before you do it?" Kayla asks.

The lawyer's penetrating glare is on her now and not Marty.

"I don't know," she says, averting her eyes. "I'm almost out."

"And you've got big plans for the ones you have left?" Kayla asks.

"Let's take this one step at a time," Charlotte says, forcing herself to look into Kayla's eyes again.

"Uh-oh," her lawyer says with a half smile. "Looks like someone's been bit by the superhero bug."

"You believe me, Charley?" Marty asks.

"I believe you're right—we have to be sure. And even if it's bullshit, I won't mind hearing an apology out of Luke Prescott's mouth. The guy was a real jerk."

"Still, try not to break his neck or throw him into a tree."

"I won't be able to if he doesn't attack me," Charlotte says.

Marty stands.

"Now?" Kayla asks. "You're gonna head out now?"

"Better to arrive in the dark, when most of the town's asleep," he says. "As for me, I probably won't be sleeping for the next five years anyway, so . . . You ready, Charley?"

She hadn't thought it all the way through, but she's relieved to have an objective, a direction. And after the dislocation of the past twenty-four hours, the prospect of some kind of homecoming, a return to the familiar, slows her heart rate some, makes her feel as if she's coming to rest on something soft.

So she stands, too.

And then Kayla stands, and suddenly the three of them are staring at each other as if they all feel like they've forgotten some important piece of business. But Charlotte can tell the desire to keep moving is strong in all of them, driven in no small part, she fears, by a desire to leave all the dread that seems to radiate from this little prison of a house.

"All right," Kayla says, clearing her throat. "I guess I'll head back to the city. See if whoever's investigating the biker blast has made any noise about your house."

"Thank you. Seriously, Kayla, I can't thank you enough for what you've done."

"Well, when you see my bill, maybe you'll feel differently."

"Jesus Christ," Marty grumbles. "Really?"

"No. Not really." Kayla rolls her eyes. "But don't thank me yet. I'm not done. None of us are."

She hugs Charlotte quickly but firmly, as if she fears committing to the embrace fully will unleash some storm of further emotion that will do them all in. She offers a smile. She's halfway out the door when Charlotte says, "Call me when you get home safe."

"On what?" Kayla asks. "Jason's burner? No, thanks. I don't call dead people."

"Call me," Marty says. "I'm listed."

"Let's not move too fast, Marty." As Kayla pulls the door shut behind her, she points to the electronic peephole viewer on the wall next to her. Marty steps forward, makes sure the door closes all the way, and watches as she makes her way to her BMW.

"You two would make a cute couple," Charlotte says.

"Yeah, we're a regular Mothra and Godzilla."

18

"This is a mistake, Cole."

Cole looks at the paper cup of coffee trembling in the armrest next to him. He's pretty wired already, so maybe his director of security is right. Maybe he should lay off the caffeine. But surely that's not what Ed means. The man wouldn't care if Cole were guzzling whiskey on the way to this meeting.

It's the meeting he objects to.

And he's probably also a little pissed Cole refused to let several well-armed members of their private security team travel alongside them in the leather-upholstered passenger compartment of this spacious helicopter. But he'd never say so directly. Ed's nothing if not loyal, one of the only holdovers from his father's era who's never treated Cole with anything less than respect.

He's a giant of a man, a former deputy chief for the LAPD who headed up their counterterrorism and special operations bureaus before entering the far more lucrative world of private security. His shiny bald dome reflects the morning sunlight streaming through the panoramic windows with such intensity Cole's afraid to remove his sunglasses. Because the man's mouth rarely changes from a thin, determined line, Cole's left with no choice but to view the slight grimace Ed's worn since they took off as a sign the man's truly afraid of what Dylan might be capable of.

"Are they in place?" Cole asks.

"We'll have snipers north and south."

"Not east and west?"

"West of the site's mostly flat wash with a slight downhill grade until you get to the freeway. Nearest mountains are way too far from the site to have any good perches. Same situation to the east. Also, never a good idea to have snipers staring right into the sun. And given that it's Arizona, the nearest tree is probably in Flagstaff."

"Or Sedona. Strike team?"

"Fifteen minutes out. Best we could do given the absence of cover. Which I imagine might be why he picked the place. He's got a Special Forces background aside from being a mad genius, right? Might explain some of what's in here."

He pulls a stack of pages from his canvas briefcase. It's held together with a giant paper clip, which tells Cole it was printed out just before they took off from downtown San Diego. Whatever's in it, his security director didn't want to share it over e-mail.

Good call, he thinks as soon as he starts reading.

It's confidential information about the biker massacre in the middle of the Arizona desert. There are some initial police reports from the first investigators to arrive on scene; reports pulled off law enforcement servers the public would like to think are a lot more secure than they actually are. They're followed by a transcript made up of a series of fragmented conversations. The name of the person speaking is provided wherever possible, but in most cases, the hackers made educated guesses, such as Officer 1, Possible ATF Agent, as they dipped in and out of the mobile devices being carried by the investigators on scene, eavesdropping for as long as they could before the cyberdefenses of whatever telecommunications company they'd penetrated got wise to their presence.

This is one of only a few instances in which Cole's ordered the off-the-books digital services team of their private security contractor to hack into the mobile phones of strangers. He doesn't even know the company's name, and Ed insists they keep it that way. Plausible deniability and all that. But in those other instances, he'd been out to disprove rumors that former employees had stolen proprietary science. And he had, sparing the targets a great deal of trouble and jail time and God knows what other ruin the board would have elected to unleash on them. In other words, he'd used evil for good. Now he's using it because lives have been lost.

Ed's highlighted chunks of the transcript in green.

Cole holds up a page marked by four different highlights so Ed can see it. "What's the theme?"

"Officers and agents on scene speculating bikers couldn't have pulled it off. They used words like *mercenary, Special Forces. Special ops. Trained killer.* All words that could be associated with Dylan Cody's background. The explosion knocked most of the guys flat, broke some bones on the others, but only killed a few of them. The rest of the work was close-range gunshots."

"But there's no mention of Dylan."

"Unless you consider rapid-fire, close-range gunshots delivered minutes after a C-4 explosion to be part of his skill set."

"It is. Any ID on the bikers in the video he sent?"

"One of 'em. The one who got a shotgun blast through his middle did fifteen years for aggravated rape. He has a long-standing relationship to the crystal meth community in the American Southwest."

"Huge surprise. And the girl?"

"We think it's an alias."

"An alias?"

"We matched her image to an Arizona driver's license photo for a woman named Charlotte Rowe, but Charlotte Rowe only popped into existence about a year ago. I want them to keep looking before I show you anything."

"I could still use a preliminary report."

"They do better work when they think you're waiting. And losing patience."

"All right, I trust you."

Ed nods. It's the closest they'll ever have to a tender moment.

"I want the strike team rolling in when we land."

"Cole—"

"I don't want them to *strike*, Ed. I just want a show of force."

"You want them rolling in right as we set down next to the building he's sheltering in? That could be chaos, Cole."

"Pageantry, Ed. The word is *pageantry*."

"Fine. You're the one who knows what this guy's capable of."

Ed's baiting him.

He doesn't bite.

Ed begins tapping instructions into his mobile phone.

"So wherever this place is," Cole asks, "it's not exactly the middle of nowhere?"

"It's close," Ed answers. "Just a little ways north of Tucson."

"I imagine Tucson would object to being depicted as the middle of nowhere."

"I don't know. I've got an aunt there, and she says that's exactly the appeal. Any idea why he picked this place?"

"Quick escape from this mess he caused with the bikers."

"Seems like he'd want to get farther away. He's certainly had enough time. What do you think?"

"About what?" Cole asks.

"I'm just saying, you know him a lot better than I do. What's your guess?"

More bait. Again he doesn't bite.

He needs Ed. Badly. And if Ed wants to take this moment to express some disapproval of the tortured path Cole and Dylan have walked together, the man's allowed. There are only a few of Graydon's dark secrets Ed doesn't know, and the ones he doesn't, Dylan knows all too well. Cole can't afford to make an enemy out of Ed or anyone else. Not now, not today.

"Symbolism," he answers.

"Symbolism?"

"The location's going to have some kind of symbolism. That's all I can figure."

"Symbolism related to what?" Ed asks.

"His beliefs."

"Beliefs? The guy's a scientist and a soldier, not a preacher."

"Actually he manages to combine the worst of all three," he says.

"I see," Ed says. "Well, you'd know."

"Ed?"

"Yes."

"Why don't you just ask me what you want to know?"

"Fine. Is there some kind of involvement between you two that might be clouding your judgment here? If that video's real, a meeting like this . . . We're talking a week of prep, negotiations. At least. This could be an ambush, Cole, and we're flying right into it."

"My involvement with Dylan's work is exactly why I'm obligated to take this meeting."

"You know what I'm asking."

"You want to know if he took me out to the Hotel del Coronado and did things to me that made me forget my own name? Is that it?"

Ed just stares at him. The man's no homophobe. His reticence probably has more to do with an aversion to discussing his employer's personal life. If Cole's mother were in this seat, Ed would be just as demure on the topic. But can Ed hear what he's really asking? If Cole's judgment around Dylan is warped by libido now, that means it was warped by libido two years ago. And two years ago, he did a lot worse than rush into an ill-advised, last-minute meeting in the middle of Arizona with a man who might be capable of bending steel with his bare hands.

Ed seems to realize this. He slouches back and turns his attention to the view.

The Airbus H155 is supposed to be one of the quietest helicopters millions can buy, but Cole can feel every thump of its rotary blades in his bones. From this altitude the desert looks like a vast sea whose sandy bottom has been churned up by a global apocalypse. A place without borders or habitation, even though they crossed the California state line only minutes ago. It's not hard to imagine Dylan living out here like some hermit.

Correction. It's *easy* to imagine Dylan living out here like some hermit.

Easier than accepting Cole should have been keeping better tabs on the guy. And that he didn't because the mere thought of Dylan hurt him in ways that suggest Ed Baker's right; his judgment when it comes to Dylan has been clouded.

It wasn't the Hotel del Coronado.

It was the Montage in Laguna. Not as historic, but just as luxurious.

And, yes, on more than one occasion during their visits there, Dylan did make him forget his own name. But Cole had been foolish enough to think theirs was a passion bred by the secrecy of what they'd embarked on together, a fleeting, if white-hot, intimacy their special project had produced in them both. If it had occurred to him that Dylan was, quite literally, playing him like an instrument, such thoughts took a back seat to the shared intensity of their ambitions. Or that's where he tried to shove them so he could justify letting Dylan shatter him in the bedroom.

And the great, miserable irony is that Cole's never been one for relationships.

He still balks at his mother's insistence that he find some handsome young banker or lawyer to marry. When he was in college, before gay marriage became the law of the land, he'd delighted in his freedom from the conventions and rituals that seemed poised to doom the ambitions of his fellow Stanford overachievers; his freedom from the reality of some wife's biological clock or her bewildering emotional needs weighing down his potential life's work. Back then the road ahead had seemed clear of obstructions, an endless stream of professional accomplishment and occasional release at the hands of gorgeous, skilled professionals who made regular appearances on his favorite porn websites.

But now he's thinking of that journal his father left for him, the one that mentioned Dylan.

To hear his mother tell it, stories of departing presidents leaving behind private letters in the Oval Office for their successors had inspired Cole's father to leave him a series of journals that were essentially long letters addressed to him, solely about the running of his company. Today they fill several thick, leather-bound books Cole keeps in a locked cabinet in his home office. It was in those journals, just days after Dylan's disappearance, that he found a description of Dylan Cody that couldn't have been more accurate.

He is as well versed in the chemical reactions that govern the mind as he is in how the mind can be shaped and manipulated by external factors. He sees the brain not as a flawed, damage-prone instrument, meant to be healed, but as something to be maximized, the first phase of a computer application desperately in need of overdue updates.

After he finished reading those words, Cole blamed exhaustion and Project Bluebird's humiliating end for the tears he'd shed.

Now he's not so sure.

19

His face pressed to the cabin's window, Cole watches the abandoned restaurant grow in size as they come in for a landing. Thanks to the Internet, Cole knows that the rest stop formerly known as Jackie's is popular now with outdoor explorers, the kind of people who love to take GoPro videos inside empty missile silos flooded with rainwater and post them to YouTube.

The old sign must be fifty feet tall. It rises out of the sand like a monolith, as if it's still desperately trying to grab the attention of motorists on a freeway that ended up moving miles to the east, too far away to supply the place with enough customers to survive. A few of the old neon letters are visible—**J A C**—but most of the sign's been gnawed away by the unobstructed winds.

The chopper's runners extend from either side of the fuselage with a slight whine. Meanwhile, the strike team pulls into place; four shiny black SUVs moving Secret Service–like over the expanse of brown. They kick up rooster tails of dust before fanning out on either side of the restaurant. Three in front, one in back. Although given the place's state of disrepair, the terms *front* and *back* seem relative. Only one SUV parked behind the place. That tells Cole the back wall's still largely intact, offering limited means of escape.

What strikes Cole the most as they land is the absence of any other vehicle. Which means Dylan got here on foot. Which is a reminder of all the things Dylan's been trained to do. Imagining those skills married to Dylan's wonder drug makes Cole's stomach lurch.

Yeah, now that you're not sleeping with him anymore, it doesn't seem like such a great idea, does it?

Once they've touched down, Ed slides the passenger compartment door open and goes to step out first. Cole stops him with one hand.

When his feet hit the concrete of the old parking lot, he counts the black-clad members of his security team who've drawn their weapons and aimed them across the hoods of the SUVs. Six in all, each brandishing a fully loaded Glock. It's the show of force he asked for.

Now he plans to offset it a little.

Gripping his phone in one hand, he walks in front of them toward the shattered windows and crumbling facade. If the team takes a shot, they'll probably end up hitting Cole first.

Dylan emerges from the whale's mouth that used to be the restaurant's front door. He's assembled some ordinary civilian clothes into an effective if more monochromatic version of desert camouflage. His shirt and pants are sand lashed, but he's wiped down his face and hair.

Technically they're out of the security team's earshot, but the recording device under Cole's shirt is also transmitting to a tiny earpiece in Ed's left ear.

Cole braces himself.

Dylan sinks to his knees and laces his fingers behind his head, as if preparing to be arrested. Cole's fine with the pose. For now.

"Where is she?" Cole asks.

"Not here."

"Who is she?"

"You don't already know?"

"I know everything about her seems like an alias. What's her background? Is she one of your old Special Forces friends?"

"There're no women SEALs. Yet." The implication is clear: his drug could change all that; Project Bluebird could have changed all that, if Cole hadn't pulled the plug.

166

"Who is she, Dylan?"

"Keep digging. You'll get to it. It's more obvious than you think."

"Where is she now?"

"Out in the world. Making the most of my gift. Just as I'd hoped."

"Your *gift*? Are you serious? Your gift is proprietary science that doesn't belong to you."

Dylan's gentle laughter is as condescending as a pat on the head. "What are you going to do? Turn me in? Give the Justice Department a tour of your little island lab? Open up your books so everyone can see who was funding us? Did Project Bluebird even *have* books? Honestly! Let's not waste our time on this petty nonsense. We have far more important things to discuss."

Cole surprises himself with the speed of what he does next. He hurls his phone in Dylan's direction. Dylan lashes out with one arm and catches it just in time. The phone doesn't come apart in his hands. No burst of superhuman strength. When Dylan realizes the goal of this gesture, he smiles.

"Clever," Dylan says, "but I haven't made that much progress. You want your phone back?"

"I have other phones."

Dylan hurls it at him anyway.

Cole catches it but with both hands.

When he looks over one shoulder, he sees even Ed has his gun drawn now. The rest of the security team are standing with Glocks aimed at Dylan, rather than braced across the hoods of their vehicles. Cole gestures for them to stand down. They all comply. Except for Ed. He doesn't move an inch.

"Why here?" Cole asks.

"Think."

There's no hint of malice in Dylan's expression. Not even a hint of challenge. But there never is. He's smart enough to make someone believe personal destruction is in their best interests.

"I'm not an Arizona historian, Dylan."

"But you know history is the reason we're here. Which means you know me. So think. Why would I pick this place?"

Think back on our relationship, is what he's saying. *Think back on all the conversations we had, all the private movements we shared together, moments I was willing to throw away completely as soon as you cut off my funding so more volunteers wouldn't die.*

Luckily Cole doesn't have to. He knew the answer after a brief web search. He knew the answer when Ed asked him the question on the flight, but to say so would have meant admitting to a level of intimacy he wasn't ready to reveal to Ed just yet.

Still, he scans their surroundings to see if there's some clue that might suggest his first guess is wrong.

Just behind Dylan great shafts of dusty sunlight stream through the restaurant's ruined ceiling, falling across the scattered rows of booths inside. Stacked against the hole-filled walls are piles of rotting chairs and sun-bleached cushions pulled from the booths. The booths were red leather once, Cole assumes; now most of them are bone white. The preservative effects of the dry desert air have done a steady battle with the wind and whatever other forces have passed through this place, taking bites along the way.

To the east is the slight downhill grade Ed mentioned. The freeway is so far away it's almost impossible to see the sunlight winking off the roofs of passing cars. But if the map he studied before he left is to be believed, somewhere down there is Aravaipa Creek.

"Grant's massacre," Cole says.

Dylan smiles. He gets to his feet slowly, brushing the sand from his knees. "One hundred forty Apache women murdered and scalped by a coalition of Natives, Anglos, and Mexicans. Mutilated. Another testament to mankind's bewildering appetite for inflicting suffering."

"There were political reasons for the attack."

"There is never a political reason for *mutilating* anyone."

"The federal government was reducing the money they provided to ensure peace between merchants and the Natives, especially the Apache. The merchants were afraid they wouldn't have the goods to pacify the tribes. It set the stage for the attack. I'm not saying it justifies it."

"Nonsense. Women and children scalped and mutilated in their beds. It was sexual sadism. No different from this Mask Maker in Los Angeles. They just didn't have the word for it yet."

"Do you have other women?" Cole asks.

Dylan cocks his head to one side, as if he's waiting for Cole to finish this question.

"Out in the field, I mean," Cole adds, "enjoying your gift."

"Just one. The one you saw."

"Did you test it on any others?"

"Yes."

"How many?"

"One."

"Not Charlotte Rowe, the girl I saw on the tape."

"No."

"Did you sleep with them?"

"The first girl, yes. Not Charlotte."

Cole regrets asking the question as much as he regrets the blush Dylan's answer brings to his cheeks.

"I told you," Dylan says. "I don't adhere to popular labels in that area."

"There is no popular label for someone whose sexual identity is entirely professional ambition. Well, there is. But they don't give them out at Harvard."

"What are you accusing me of, Cole?"

"The first girl. The one it didn't work on. Is she dead?"

"Yes."

Cole feels his pulse beating in the side of his face. Amazing that *this* news, amid the rest of it, makes him feel like he's breathing through a straw. Dylan's expression is blank. He studies Cole as if whatever emotional reaction Cole will have to this information is a tiresome but necessary inconvenience. But Cole isn't seeing Dylan anymore. He's seeing video footage he long since destroyed; footage of a decorated war hero chewing on his right arm after he'd torn it from his body and beaten himself with it until one of his legs broke.

My money, he thinks. *My money funded all that bloodshed, all those scenes I can't erase from my nightmares. All of it, thanks to my money. My* father's *money.*

They'd come up with a phrase for it, for the swift orgy of relentless, cannibalistic self-destruction that consumed all four test subjects within minutes of their trigger events. *Going lycan.* If only they had truly become something else in those final moments, another creature, not a wide-eyed howling human suddenly programmed to quite literally tear itself apart in a frenzied rage.

Did it matter that they were willing volunteers? That they knew the risks? That the last two had actually watched videos of what had happened to the first two and still agreed to take the drug? These facts had comforted him some back then. Back then he thought he'd put a stop to it by shutting the project down. He never thought Dylan capable of taking the nightmares they'd seen in that lab out into the world.

"Do you need to sit?" Dylan asks.

"Fuck you," Cole whispers.

Dylan nods and looks away, waiting, it seems, for Cole to collect himself.

"So this first girl," Cole asks, "she went lycan?"

"She knew the risks. I told her I wouldn't let her suffer. I kept my promise."

"So you were wrong. It had nothing to do with the gender of the subjects. And even though I forbade you to test it on women, you went out and did it anyway."

"You forbade me to test it on women because you're a sexist and you have Mommy issues."

"I put a stop to it because I was tired of watching people tear themselves apart."

"I see, so it was just an excuse then. So you could fire me because you'd finally panicked. Give me a break. You didn't care about those volunteers. You cared about exposure."

"I didn't fire you. I cut the funding for a project that ended in disaster, and if you remember correctly, it wasn't just my call to make."

"Don't worry. I remember our partners quite well."

"You were one of our most brilliant scientists, Dylan. I could have put you on something else the next day."

"Oh, on what? Some antianxiety drug that's just going to tranq people into functional oblivion? I was trying to create survivors, not blissed-out drones."

"But you didn't."

"Until now."

"And you killed a woman to do it, which makes you a monster."

"And you, as always, are a revolutionary pretending to be a shill. The conflict will drive you mad, Cole. I guarantee it."

"Because I'm not willing to kill any more people in the name of your research?"

"You don't have to." He extends his arms and gives Cole a bright smile. "You have a successful test subject."

"And she's already killed someone."

"I'd say that's an unfair reading of what happened on that video, wouldn't you? She was protecting herself from two thugs who were probably going to rape her and leave her for dead in the middle of the desert. Forgive the absence of tears."

"Where is she, Dylan?"

"She won't be that hard for you to find if you reactivate The Consortium."

Cole's barely been able to say this name aloud to himself in the two years since Project Bluebird ended. It's easier to remember those horrifying videos of their test subjects than it is to recall the weight of responsibility these secret partners brought to bear on him. The idea that Dylan could so casually call for its *reactivation* is as offensive as everything else he's said and done these past few days. Maybe even more so.

"Are you out of your fucking mind? You want me to call up five defense contractors, all of whom still lie awake at night worrying the results of your project will come back to haunt them, by the way, and . . . what? Invite them to brunch? Tell them you've set a success-ful test subject loose in the world with your drug? How exactly do you think they'll respond?"

"Managing The Consortium has always been your responsibility. I'd prefer to stick to the science. Our relationship works better that way."

"We are not in a relationship."

"I understand that you're hurting, Cole. I understand that I caused some of that pain when I left so quickly. But deep down you know I truly don't give a single red fuck. That I consider your pain to be an inconvenience and a distraction from a goal far more important than anything your heart might think it wants. And if there's anyone who should know the importance of prioritizing objectives over feel-ings, it's the head of Graydon Pharmaceuticals."

"If you think for one second that my contempt for you in this moment has anything to do with the fact that you got me to bottom in a couple of hotel rooms, you are even more of a delusional narcissist than I thought. What you have done is irresponsible and reprehen-sible, and it might bring a show of force down upon your head that not even I can stop."

"A show of force worse than this?" Dylan asks, gesturing to the phalanx of guns.

"A lot worse."

Dylan nods sagely, as if Cole were offering up this information as part of a deal point, and not a warning, and he's decided to accept.

"Gender might not have anything to do with it," Dylan begins, ignoring the bitter laughter that comes from Cole when he realizes Dylan has reverted to a scientific lecture. "With Charlotte, I pursued another theory, and it looks like it's paid off."

Dylan checks to make sure Cole is still listening; then he slowly walks around behind him, turning his back to the security team. He's making himself a better target, but he's also concealing his hands and any weapon he might draw and blocking Cole from the strike team's view while he does it. It's a test, Cole's sure, to see how willing he is to hear more about the science of Dylan's latest experiment. Cole turns.

Dylan continues. "You see, with our male volunteers, what we thought was their strength turned out to be their liability. Their combat experience. The trauma of it reshaped their amygdalae in ways too subtle to detect on an MRI. That's where the aggression, the self-destruction, came from. My first female subject, she had a similar trauma in her past and most likely similar amygdalar deformation.

"But Charlotte's different. Charlotte grew up in proximity to great physical trauma, but it was never directly inflicted upon her. Her wounds . . . they're psychological. All of this will make more sense once you dig in to her past. Which I'm confident you'll do despite your protests. But my point is that Charlotte Rowe is exactly the type of subject the current version of the drug works on. A vigilante spirit without the actual physical wounds that it usually takes to create a vigilante.

"Her mind and her past set the stage for exactly what we've always been shooting for. A panic response from the primitive brain that *doesn't* shut down the frontal cortex. You've seen the tape. She doesn't tunnel. She doesn't freeze or go into quiescence, but her fear is real. The drug's done exactly what it's supposed to do; it's harnessed the power of her fear to almost perfect mental acuity, and the by-product is the same level of physical strength we saw in our old subjects, only without the self-destruction. Now the challenge is figuring out exactly how it works in her and duplicating the results in a wider variety of subjects."

"What about her blood? Are there traces of paradrenaline?"

"I'll find out."

"You haven't taken her blood?"

"A lot's happened very quickly."

Is he being coy, or has he lost access to this woman?

Dylan had performed early animal tests himself, videos of which he'd brought to Cole to snare his interest. In those first nonhuman subjects, the ones who hadn't torn themselves to shreds, the drug had somehow tricked the adrenal glands into making a variant of adrenaline never before documented in an organic life-form. It was the most astonishing and otherworldly aspect of Zypraxon; that its functioning in the brain somehow keyed the body into synthesizing an entirely new hormone, a hormone that produced bursts of superhuman strength, especially when you considered that unleashing superhuman strength in the body had never been Dylan's intention. He'd set out to increase mental functioning during moments of extreme terror, and only as a means of preventing panic or paralysis. But in the end, it was like he'd created something akin to an antidepressant that had the unexpected side effect of allowing people who took it to grow wings and fly several miles.

Paradrenaline was their name for this new, previously undocumented hormone, and while there'd been traces of it in the bodies of the human subjects who had torn themselves apart, the samples had degraded too rapidly after the subjects' deaths to be preserved in a lab. Worse, the samples taken from animal test subjects had produced no effect in humans. The idea that there was someone out there now whose system might be flush with it made Cole's head spin with genuine excitement for the first time since the helicopter had touched down.

Zypraxon aside, there was no telling what paradrenaline might be able to do under the right circumstances—what it might be able to power, to heal.

"On that tape, she's running from you, isn't she?" Cole asks.

Dylan looks as if he's been slapped. Cole tries to suppress a smile and fails.

"That camera," Cole continues, "it wasn't yours. You stole it from those bikers on the tape, didn't you? And my guess is she was running from *you* when she ran into them, wasn't she?"

Dylan swallows. Cole's never seen the man so thrown off his game, and he allows himself a second or two to take pleasure in it.

"The situation was more complex than that," Dylan whispers.

"This wasn't your *plan*, to send her out into the world like this. You lost her, and now you want us to get her back."

"There were unexpected variables. But, no, I did not *lose* her. And I don't need you to get her back. She won't be that hard to find once you activate The Consortium. She needs to be constantly monitored to see what she'll do. The results will be beneficial to us all."

"Why was she running?" Cole asks.

"As I said, there were unexpected varia—"

"Why was she running away from you, Dylan? What did you do? Lie to her? Trick her into taking the drug because you couldn't bring yourself to tell her what had happened to your last subjects? What did you do to this woman?"

"I put the power of gods in her hands." Cole's never seen the man's passion take this angry a form. "That's what I did to her. Charlotte Rowe is now patient zero for a benevolent virus that could wipe out sexual sadism, rape, and domestic violence, and if you don't make every effort to watch everything she does with what I've given her, you will be missing out on the scientific breakthrough of the century.

"You think that video is my endgame? I want this drug perfected, balanced, made available to the world. Just like I did when we started. And I can't do that without you or Graydon or The Consortium. And you can't come within an inch of matching your father's legacy if you don't make a breakthrough like this, and you know it. It's why you're here. But if you don't help me, I'll destroy every pill I have left. In fact, if you decide to keep me here now, all the pills I have left and all the documentation of every adjustment I've made to the formula since I left you will be incinerated before you can get to them—trust me."

If only I could read minds, Cole thinks, *but even if I could, I'd still have trouble reading his. So many distractions. So many memories.*

Is he lying about making adjustments to the drug post–Project Bluebird?

Maybe. Is he really capable of testing the same drug that had caused three subjects to go lycan on another human being without making at least some small adjustments to the formula? If the answer's no, then there's still some vestige of the man Cole gave his body to so recklessly and frequently.

If the answer's yes, then he's a straight-up monster and Cole should have him shot down where he stands.

Yeah, but Zypraxon, though. If it's working now . . .

"I don't trust you," is all Cole can manage.

"On this particular matter, you should. I never would have asked for this meeting if I didn't have something to hold over you, and you know it."

"When did you adjust the formula?"

"After I left."

"And after you killed your first *woman*?"

Dylan just stares at him.

"You didn't make any adjustments before you tested it on Charlotte Rowe?"

"Like I said, I had a different theory."

"You were counting on her to have a different brain?"

Dylan just stares at him.

Shoot him, Cole thinks. *Shoot him right now. Anyone who could give that pill to an unsuspecting person after watching someone tear themselves apart—*

"It *works*, Cole," Dylan whispers, as if he can read Cole's thoughts. "I was right. It works. And whether you can admit or not, you want to know why. You *have* to know. We both do."

After a deep but quiet breath, Dylan continues. "No amount of social progress will ever change the average difference in physical strength between the genders. It *must* be leveled with biochemistry. And until it is, the most persistent and insidious crimes in our society will continue day in and day out, across the globe."

"And your mother will still be dead," Cole says.

"Yes, and cheap pop psychology will still be incapable of distracting me from my goals."

"We're in agreement there."

"Activate The Consortium, Cole. Enlist their surveillance technologies. Hell, they could use it as a chance to test something new of theirs. But if you tell them the truth, if you tell them everything I've told you and you show them the video, they'll see the potential. They'll see we can't miss a minute of this. This is everything we've been working toward."

Is this all aging is? Cole wonders. The discovery that a lapse in judgment like the one he showed with Dylan could have a lasting ripple effect?

Or is he just blaming Dylan for the fact there's a part of him that doesn't want to give up on Project Bluebird, either?

These are private thoughts. Not to be even mulled over in Dylan's presence. God knows, the man's smart enough to detect them and use them to his advantage, no matter how silent Cole remains.

Cole starts to leave.

"My guess is she's in a town called Altamira," Dylan says, "just south of Big Sur, west of the 101 freeway in the adjacent valley."

This news stops Cole in his tracks, which he's pretty sure was Dylan's intention. "So you don't need us to find her."

"She'll use Zypraxon again. Mark my words. And when she does, that's when we convince her to come in for testing, and that's when you get those vials of paradrenaline you've always been after."

"And if I just bring her in now and get whatever I want from her?"

"You won't."

"Why not?"

"Because you're not me."

"Is that a compliment or an insult?"

"She's had one successful run. On the third or fourth, she could go lycan, just like the others. There's no telling. Better to hang back and see how she performs. See if she's worth tipping your hand to. Because if she's not and you bring her in and reveal everything we've done, there's only one way to be rid of her, and you're not very good at letting people die."

"Some people call it murder."

Dylan doesn't answer.

Cole can feel surrender in his bones, can feel it relaxing his limbs and his posture, and possibly his face, before he can stop it, which gives him no choice but to continue past Dylan and start for the helicopter. The engine chugs as the rotary blades begin to spin.

"Cole?"

He turns.

"It's good to be working with you again," Dylan says.

"Suck my dick," Cole answers with a smile. "Again."

Then he heads for the helicopter with Ed on his heels.

They've just flown back over the state line into California when Ed lets out a startled grunt. Since they've boarded, he's been listening to his recording of Cole and Dylan's conversation with noise-canceling headphones.

A few minutes ago, something inspired him to start a web search on his phone, and now he's eager for Cole to see the results.

Cole takes the phone.

Instantly he recognizes the face that accompanies the article. It's like seeing an old college classmate, someone who was familiar to him on a daily basis for a short period of his past but has since vanished from his life entirely. This isn't one of his Stanford classmates, however.

Her hair's completely different now, her face longer and more adult. But she's the girl in the video. "It's Burning Girl."

"That explains everything," Ed says.

"Not everything," Cole answers.

And Ed says nothing, maybe because he knows Cole's right.

20

When Luke was in college, he didn't know the meaning of a day off.

Days off were for other people. People who didn't have life plans. People who didn't use wipe-off pens to turn one window of their dorm rooms into a running list of both daily and weekly tasks and objectives.

If he didn't have class, he was studying or working one of two jobs, or he was in the gym. Holidays, especially the long ones, were spent doing prep work for whatever classes he was planning to take the following semester. It always gave him a thrill to walk into a language course already fluent in basic conversational phrases.

Yeah, how'd that work out for you, hotshot? You're really wowing Mona with your Mandarin, aren't you?

He's not too crazy about days off now, either. Especially since his job feels like a monotonous grind that only uses a third of his available mental energy. When he shelves his badge after a long week, he doesn't feel the kind of bone-deep exhaustion and satisfaction he associates with hard work.

Instead he feels restless and bored.

A slug of Heineken should help.

When his cell phone rings, he jumps, spilling beer down the front of his shirt. He grabs for it, expecting to see Mona's name on the caller ID, but he doesn't recognize the number.

"Howdy, hometown hero," Marty says when Luke answers.

"OK. We can go with that, I guess."

"Still want to see Trina?"

Luke stands, brushing beer foam from the front of his T-shirt.

"I'd like to be in touch with her, yeah. But I didn't say I could—"

"You're renting the old Hickman place, right?"

"Yeah, but—"

"We'll be there in twenty minutes."

"Wait. *Now?*"

"No, not now. Twenty minutes."

"Yeah, I'm not really ready to receive visitors."

"Ah, just brush off the Cheetos dust and put the porn away. She's not expecting high tea, for Christ's sake."

"I'm not watching porn."

"And it's not gonna be *visitors* plural. Just her. I'm gonna wait outside in case you start wailing on each other." For some reason, Marty cracks up like this is the funniest joke anyone's ever made.

"Yeah, or maybe this evening I can meet her in town or something, and we can grab a cup of coffee or a—"

"What's your problem, Jack? Do you want to make this right or not?" Marty barks. "She's in town, she doesn't have much time, and she's willing to see you. Isn't this what you wanted?"

"Why doesn't she have much time?"

"Ask her yourself. In twenty minutes."

"Marty—"

"Oh, and by the way, she changed her name. Goes by Charley now."

"OK."

"You know, probably because of people like you."

Marty hangs up.

Luke reaches for his beer and downs the remainder of it. *Whoever said you can't go home again was just engaging in a bunch of wishful thinking.*

As Marty drives, Charlotte studies the pill in her palm.

Up close and in broad daylight, she can see the wrongness of it, the lumpiness that suggests it didn't come off a factory assembly line. In Dylan's office, she'd been distracted by too many things to notice the strangeness of the pills or the cheapness of their packaging.

"Take it," Marty says. "Soothe an old man's nerves."

"You're not that old," she says.

"Come on, Charley. You don't want me busting in on your old high school bully with guns blazing, do you?"

"I don't want to waste a pill over something that's probably not true."

"What? You got big plans for the rest?"

"We've been over this."

"Not really. I mean, I get it. It's important. What they can do. Maybe they could help people in the right hands. Only problem is, the hand that gave it to you doesn't seem like one of those hands."

"I'm having a hard time believing Luke Prescott is in on this, Marty."

"You had no idea Dylan was in on it, did you? And you still don't really have any idea what *it* even is."

Ouch.

"Fine."

She swallows the pill as if it were an Advil and turns her attention to the road.

They'd arrived in darkness early that morning, after which she'd slept until noon, occasionally roused by the sounds of Marty moving about the house, having low conversations with guys who'd dropped by throughout the morning, other sober men he'd enlisted to help protect her. "I've kept their secrets. It's not asking much of them to return the favor," Marty told her. Each time she woke, this thought comforted her enough to send her back to sleep.

By the time she'd woken up for good, the only one in the kitchen was Marty, hiding his sleeplessness behind a cup of coffee and a warm smile.

It's just the two of them now as they drive the winding road from Marty's property to the valley floor. To call his house a mobile home wouldn't do it justice. It always looks freshly painted, and he long ago added redwood decks on all sides, a vegetable garden, and a row of poplar trees around the perimeter that give a watery luminescence to the dry, grassy hills surrounding his property.

"Marty, I don't want it to sound like I don't appreciate what you're doing."

"It doesn't. Now that you took the pill." He gives her a cockeyed grin.

"No matter what happens, you don't have to put your life in danger for me."

"I know. I don't have to do any of the shit I do. Except, you know, shit. And eat. And sleep. And drink water. I do stuff 'cause I want to. 'Cause it matters to me."

Because *you* matter to me, is what he's saying. She reaches across the gearshift and squeezes his knee briefly to let him know he matters to her, too.

The Hickman place is in the opposite side of the valley from Marty's, on Lowell Drive, a serpentine street that branches off from State Mountain Road 293. It hugs the inland base of the mountains that stretch all the way to PCH, so there are more trees here than around Marty's place, and they dapple the large, unfenced lots and their tiny houses with deep pools of shadow. In another hour or so, the sun will disappear behind the Santa Lucia Mountains even though there's hours to go before dusk.

The old Hickman place, a ranch-style house with a gently sloping roof and a front room that juts out onto its unkempt front lawn, is a ghost of its former self. It used to be one of the nicest homes in town, built and owned for as long as she could remember by the family who started the local drugstore on Center Street. But the store's gone and so are the Hickmans, including their daughter, Emily, who'd made it a point to invite Charlotte to all the pool parties she had in high school, parties where Charlotte remembers feeling fairly welcome and not too openly stared at. Probably because Luke wasn't there drumming up contempt for her among the other guests. While the oak tree out back is just as impressive as it used to be, and the view beyond just as beautiful, the aboveground pool is long gone, and so's the tall cast-iron fence to which the family used to tie strings of blue-and-pink balloons.

At first she assumes the man who appears on the stoop can't be Luke Prescott. He's too tall, too broad. But of course, she's comparing him to the high school version, which is nuts.

He's got the same military-grade buzz cut that makes his sandy-blond hair look like it's painted on his skull. But his face is wider now, his features more evenly balanced. That constant squinting expression, which always made him look like he was getting ready to say something biting and sarcastic even on those rare occasions he wasn't, is gone now, and she can't help but wonder if there were other things she read into his personality based on ephemeral aspects of his physical appearance.

Or you're cutting him too much slack because this new body of his is something to see. And how'd things go the last time you got distracted by a man's looks?

Luke gives them a stiff wave and an even stiffer, more awkward smile.

Marty rolls the window down.

"You sure you don't want come in, Marty?" Luke asks.

"Sure as Sam."

"Who's Sam?" he asks.

"It's just an expression."

"It is?" Luke asks.

"No," Charlotte says, stepping from the truck. "It isn't."

Marty shoots her an angry look, but it shows her how nervous he is. He really does believe Luke might be some sort of threat, and he's not sure this is the best way to handle it.

"We'll be fine," Charlotte whispers, then gives him a peck on the cheek.

It was a deliberate strategy, surprising Luke in the middle of the day at home like this. Marty insisted on it. And it's clear Luke is bothered by her sudden arrival. But who wouldn't be? It's the inside of his house that'll tell her the most.

How lived in is it? Is this stay, this new job, temporary?

Like all crazy conspiracy theories, there's no surefire way to disprove Marty's idea that Luke might be some sort of secret agent, part of a vast conspiracy that includes Dylan Thorpe and the pills. But the state of Luke's life might offer up some helpful bits of evidence.

"Charley," he says with a respectful nod, avoiding her stare.

"Luke," she answers. "Place looks different."

"You and Emily were friends?"

"She invited me to some of her parties. We weren't besties or anything."

"I see."

"Believe it or not," she adds, "I actually got invited places back then."

She never believes people when they claim their angry words just slipped out. But in this instance, these angry words did, in fact, just slip out. But she managed to hold back the punch line, which would have been something along the lines of *Despite your best efforts, you jerk.*

"We didn't have any parties," he says, but he's looking at her feet, and his flaring nostrils suggest embarrassment and nervousness.

"That's not what I meant. I wasn't talking about your family, I . . ."

"I know what you meant."

A bird cries somewhere in the distance. A San Francisco–bound jetliner has begun its descent over the valley, and she'd rather stare at it for the remainder of the day than spend another awkward moment on this scraggly front lawn.

"So Marty says you didn't have much time to see me. What, are you just passing through or something?" Luke finally asks.

"Something like that."

"You got time for a beer?"

"I got time for a Diet Coke."

"You always were big on Diet Coke."

This feels like bait, and she's not willing to take it. What's he trying to do? Sell her on the idea that he was always sweet on her and his constant bullying was just his way of dealing with the fact that he liked her? Does anyone really believe that crap anymore? Even if it's true, how's she supposed to feel about it now? Grateful for the attention, no matter how negative it was? And if he was paying enough attention to her to know her favorite beverage, could he not see how much his constant insults hurt her?

Somewhere out there, she thinks, *there must be a man who wasn't raised to believe his every cough in a woman's presence is somehow a gift to her.*

If Marty hadn't sent her here with a clear objective, she might be giving voice to these thoughts, but instead she's chewing her bottom lip in an effort to keep her expression neutral.

"I don't have any Diet Coke," he says.

"OK."

"I mean, I don't drink it. If I'd known you were coming, I'd have run out and bought some."

"I get it. We surprised you."

"No, that's fine. I mean, if you're only in town for a short while, I'm glad you came by."

"Let's go inside, Luke."

His cheeks are ablaze. The sight pleases her, for many reasons, some of them too complicated for her to sort through in this moment.

He gestures to the front door. She follows him into the house.

21

The inside of the house, like the yard, has a hollowed-out feeling that makes memories of those long-ago parties ring in her mind.

The place is mostly empty except for the den, which looks as if a bachelor pad apartment has been slid through the front door intact and then wedged into this one room. There's a flat-screen TV resting on top of a chest of drawers that looks like it belongs in a dorm. The bookshelves on either side are too small. The hunter-green curtains don't match the yellow walls, and she doesn't see the color anywhere else in the house.

Across the entry hall, in the dining room, cardboard boxes are shoved neatly against one wall, three rows deep. There's no real mess, but it's clear most of Luke's belongings are still inside and he just moves between them to retrieve his essentials. In one corner of the room there's a mostly empty desk and a desktop computer; its wide-screen monitor pulses with a succession of high-definition images. Snowy mountains, sparkling lakes, the peaks of the Scottish Highlands.

When she turns and sees the new alarm panel on the wall behind her, she remembers her own back in Arizona, and the sting of betrayal threatens to distract her.

Luke's surroundings don't fit with either of the two scenarios she was on the lookout for: the eruptive mess of someone who's hit a brick wall in life or the too immaculate, too orderly domicile of someone who hasn't fully committed to their new home, maybe because they don't plan to stay for very long.

What she sees is something in between the two: order and a lack of commitment and an awkward marriage of his grad school life and his new, uncertain one. But who is she to try to analyze this house and his stuff in this way? She's not a detective, for Christ's sake. This thought gives her a second or two of relief before she remembers that if she's going to survive the mess she's currently in, she better acquire the skills of a detective, and quick.

"You like Sprite?" he asks.

"Sure. As long as it's diet."

Luke nods and ducks into the kitchen. She doesn't follow, but she's got a good vantage point from where she's standing. Almost nothing on the counters. No blender, no toaster. Just a coffee maker and a stack of mail. The butcher-block table's too small, just like everything in the house is too small.

He didn't plan to live here, she thinks. *That's all I can figure.*

Luke returns with an open can of Sprite Zero and nothing for himself, which makes her feel awkward and like she shouldn't take a sip. But he wasn't out of her sight for more than a second, and would he really drug her with Marty outside? If he did, would she be as immune as she'd been to the vodka and wine she'd guzzled the night before? Or is that something that only happens after Dylan's wonder drug has been triggered? There's still a part of her that wants to refer to the drug as Zypraxon, but she'd like to know if the name, like much of what Dylan told her, is complete bullshit.

"So what brought this on?" she asks, gesturing to the room around her.

"I needed a place to live. It's cheap, believe it or not. Silver Shore was renting it out for some of their foremen on the resort project, but when that fell through, they broke their lease, and Emily was desperate to fill the place. Her dad's been gone awhile."

"No, I mean, asking to see me like this."

"Marty didn't tell you?"

"He said you were with the sheriff's department now; that's all," she lies.

Luke nods.

This is not a secret agent, she realizes, *or if he is, he's super bad at it, because right now I could cut his discomfort with a knife. And he might thank me if I did.*

Then she sees the stack of books on the shelf, the guides to criminal profiling and crime scene investigation. On top of them is a file folder, its thick stack of pages perilously close to sliding free, which suggests he shoved them in their current spot quickly. The top page sports a blaring headline. She can't see the whole thing, but two of the words she can see make her stomach go cold—*Mask Maker.*

Tell me he's not writing a book about serial killers, she thinks. *Please, God, tell me he didn't ask me here for some kind of interview.*

"So is Altamira Sheriff's consulting on the Mask Maker killings?"

"Oh, that. No. That's just a little weekend reading."

"Weekend reading?"

"Something to keep my head busy."

"A little amateur detective work?"

"Yeah." He stares at the floor. Swallows as if it's painful. "I guess that's what I am now. An *amateur* detective." He says these last two words with such venom, she's surprised he doesn't finish them off by spitting on the floor. Whatever his reasons for getting rejected by the FBI, he's not exactly repressing his feelings about them.

"Figure you're here because Marty and I had some words yesterday," Luke says.

"About me?"

"About a lot of things, but you came up."

"And so he guilted you into this?" she asks.

"Into what?"

"Apologizing," she says. "You are going to apologize, right?"

"Should I?"

"Yes, you should," she says and takes a sip of Sprite.

"I didn't expect this to be this hard."

"Well, maybe it should be."

"You're not going to make this easy, are you?" he asks.

"I'm here, aren't I?"

"You sure you don't want a beer?" he asks.

"Do you?"

"Yes," he says.

He ducks into the kitchen and reappears with a bottle of Heineken, wiping the evidence of his first sip from his lips with one forearm.

"You're enjoying this?" he asks.

"What?"

"You're smiling," he says.

"I am?"

Luke nods and takes another sip of beer.

"Sorry," she says. "It's been a crazy few days."

"Is that what the name change is about?" he asks.

"The name change is a year old." *And even that's more than you should say to him right now.*

"I'm gonna do this, Charley."

"Do what? Apologize?"

"Yeah. I'm just . . ."

"You're just what?" she asks. "Working up the nerve?"

"Marty, he . . ."

"He what?"

"I don't know; he told me apologies are all bullshit. That they're just things we say to make ourselves feel better, and so I guess I'm trying for more here."

"OK. You know what might make this easier? For you, I mean."

"What?"

"You could ask me what I think you should apologize for," she says.

Luke stares at her as if she's an oncoming train. He swallows. "OK."

But he says nothing, and the silence between them extends.

"Are you going to ask me, Luke?"

"What would you like me to apologize for, Tr—Charley?"

"Can I sit down?"

"Of course," he says.

She takes a seat on the sofa's edge, her eyes level with the file on the Mask Maker.

"Here's the thing," she says. She's not measuring her words, and this makes her wonder if the drug's giving her confidence. Not through its chemistry but through the knowledge that it's there, waiting to deploy if she's attacked. "There was like a day or two, when I first got here, after school started, where I thought things might be normal. I think some of it was 'cause I was older and I looked different from the girl on the book covers. It'd been a year since I'd done an appearance or an interview or anything like that. And I thought, wow. Maybe, just maybe, for these last two years of high school, I'm going to get a taste. A taste of what everyone else has gotten. A taste of normal.

"And then you started up. European History. Last period. I got called on and you didn't. Then you tried to jump in on me. But you didn't know the answer, and so Ms. Stockton told you to be quiet, and you got embarrassed. And that's when it all began. Every day, every time we were together. Every chance you got. Nobody in that school called me Burning Girl until you did, and once you started, they never stopped. And I guess what I want to know is why?"

He's staring into his beer bottle, circling the rim with one finger. His breaths are labored things that make his chest rise and fall, but it sounds like he's drawing them through his nose. Right now his jaw's entirely too tense for him to breathe through his mouth.

"I was afraid of you," he finally says.

"Jesus. Really?"

"No, I didn't think you were some serial killer. I could tell you were a good person."

"Oh. OK."

"Look, this is going to sound . . . ridiculous."

"Ridiculous?"

"Lame. It's gonna sound lame, all right? And it's going to sound like an excuse and I don't want it to but . . ."

"Just say it, Luke."

"My mother, before she got sick, she didn't want me to leave. She wanted me to stay here and take care of her. My brother, we all knew he wasn't the caretaker type. You have to actually care about things that don't have circuit boards. Anyway, he was already on his way to . . . I don't know what. The point is, there was only one way my mother was going to let me get out of Altamira, and that was if I was the best fucking student at Los Pasos High. Ever. And I was. Until you showed up. It was like, whatever you'd been through, it just made you more grown-up. I could memorize anything, but you had this ability to reason through stuff the rest of us didn't have."

"I didn't stop you from getting good grades, Luke."

"No, you didn't. But that was just half of it. I needed everyone at that school to think I was the smartest one in the room. I needed the guidance counselor to lean on my mother *every day* and tell her to let me go. To let me get out of here and make a life for myself. To tell her to stop falling apart every time I talked about going off to a school that wasn't right down the highway. And then . . ."

"She died," Charlotte says, as gently as she can.

"Yeah, and part of me thought I was being punished."

"Punished?"

"For the way I'd treated you."

"That's crazy."

"Yeah, well, for a while there after my mother died, that's what I was. Crazy."

She's not sure what she expected him to say, but it sure as hell isn't this. These are the words of someone who's been through the pressure cooker of grief and come out irreparably changed. *Someone like me.*

"How's your brother?"

She didn't mean to strike a blow, but that's how Luke seems to receive the question. His previous admission rendered him vulnerable, and now he doesn't have the energy to put his guard back up. He's staring into space, like he's forgotten about his beer, even though he's gripping the bottle by the base with both hands.

"Luke?"

"I'm sorry."

She's not sure if he's apologizing for drifting off or for the way he once treated her. And for a while, it seems like he's not sure, either, because he just keeps staring at nothing.

There's a part of her that's hungry for any apology he's willing to give, but this reaction to the mention of his brother is so startling she can't imagine leaving this house before she's made some sense of it. If she can get some actual facts out of Luke, maybe she can convince Marty to let this whole thing go, and they can focus on whatever's next.

"Luke?"

"I'm sorry for the way I treated you back then. I'm sorry for the type of person I was. And I'm sorry . . ."

"What?"

"Nothing."

"No, tell me."

"I was gonna say I'm sorry the type of person I was then made me end up where I am now. But that's making it about me, isn't it? I mean, that's selfish. And I really did want this to be about you."

He forces a smile, looks up from his feet.

When their eyes meet, his smile fades as if the sudden shock of meeting her gaze has produced the same electrical charge in him that it just did within her. She hates the thought that she's enjoying his pain, his humility, his brokenness, even though she's sure all those things stem from more than this meeting and their pained history together. Still, God forbid she be attracted to the idea of any kind of suffering, in anyone. She plans to hold on to that moment when she recoiled from Jason's broken shoulder, the shoulder *she* broke, for as long as she can.

But who wouldn't want to hear this kind of stuff out of one of their former bullies?

He was never violent with her, never threatened her physically. But he did create an atmosphere of hostility and suspicion that dogged her every step for two years. By itself, his behavior seemed insignificant, so if she ever complained, people would tell her to get over it. They were just comments. Just words. But when you're forced to hear the words almost every day, don't they add up to something bigger? A sort of crime unto itself? Death by a thousand cuts, as some people like to say.

Now, against her will, she's thinking of Dylan.

Of a conversation they'd had in his office weeks before, about how people who've been through serious, violent trauma often tend to discount the smaller abuses they face. Dylan compared this to people who literally can't feel physical pain. It sounds like a blessing until you remember that pain is designed to protect, to save your skin from the flame, your bone from the pose that might snap it, and once it's gone, you can do fatal damage to yourself without realizing it. He saw this as a metaphor for how people who'd been through extreme instances of abuse sometimes lost the ability to detect the smaller abuses, the signs that someone wasn't truly loving or a good match. It's why it could be so hard for them to build lives better than what they'd been through. So hard for them to move on.

By that logic, refusing to sweep Luke's past behavior under the rug was a good thing. A healthy thing.

A good thing according to Dylan, she thinks. *And who is Dylan again exactly?*

The thought makes her jump. Luke flinches at the sight of it.

Maybe he wasn't a real psychiatrist. Maybe he was able to deceive her because he spoke with the authority of someone who understood darkness; not because he had studied it, but because he'd lived through it himself.

She closes her eyes.

Too much. It's too much to think about Dylan right now.

"Hey," Luke says softly.

It's a mistake, looking into his eyes. A mistake to wonder if his pain, his contrition, is making him even more attractive to her. And it's true now, she realizes, that his insults, his bullying, hurt more than they would have if they'd been inflicted on her by someone who had seemed less confident and less comfortable in his own skin, despite his recent admission to the contrary.

"I didn't kill anyone on that farm." Her vision mists. She'd hoped a good night's sleep would help keep her emotions in check, but no such luck. "I was seven. I never even saw any of the victims."

Luke nods. "I know," he says quietly, "and I'm sorry if I ever made anyone think otherwise."

It's exactly what she needed to hear. It's exactly what she's always wanted to hear from him.

She's on the verge of asking for a tissue, but when she blinks a few times, the tears don't spill.

"And if there's anything I can do," Luke says, and it's clear he's rehearsed this part, "to make up for it, let me know."

"Tell me what's going on with your brother," she says. "You looked like you got hit by a truck when I asked about him."

"It's messy," he says slowly, then takes a slug of beer.

"And the rest of this isn't?" She smiles, hoping it'll take some of the edge off her words. It does, apparently, because he smiles back and studies her for a second or two with an expression she'd describe as almost wistful.

"My brother hacks computer systems the way some of us have too much to drink on Saturday nights," he says. "You know that, right?"

"I remember some . . . antics, yes."

"Yeah, everyone remembers that prank he pulled, hacking the Copper Pot's phone lines and sending calls to that manure store, but since then he's graduated to bigger stuff."

That's not all of it, or else Luke wouldn't be clearing his throat and studying the wall behind her and shifting his weight from one foot to the other as though the whole story's trying to worm its way out of his stomach like bad gas.

Charlotte says, "So is that really all there is—"

"He was taking classes at a small community college down in LA. Night classes, mostly. Business administration, that kind of thing. I guess the idea was he was going to go do something with computers, but legit, you know? Like start his own consulting business or something. Anyway, one day the dean of the school up and disappears, and he takes most of the tuition money with him. School's so broke they have to shut down. I mean, it wasn't a big operation to begin with, but it was what Bailey could afford. It was the best most of the students could afford. Cheap enough that they didn't have to take out loans, but expensive enough that they had to work a bunch of jobs first and save. But the whole thing turned out to be a racket, and the dean was planning it for years.

"When Bailey called he was furious, angrier than I'd ever heard him. It was like he'd made this attempt to be an honest, upstanding person and this asshole fucked him over, along with all the other students who'd already paid for the year. I tried to calm him down. Told him he could come up to San Francisco and crash with me for a while, just until he figured things out. And he did come up for a visit. But he only stayed for a day and it was . . . Well, now I see it was kind of his way of saying goodbye."

"Goodbye?" Charlotte asks.

"He said he was going to do some traveling, try to figure out what he was going to do next. That I probably wouldn't hear from him for a while. The last time I got on his ass about hacking, I didn't hear from him for months, so this time I held my tongue, told him to do what he needed to do. A few weeks later, they found the dean of that school living under an alias in Australia. I didn't connect the two until . . ."

"Until what?"

"My final FBI interview."

She was starting to put the pieces together, but she didn't want to put words in Luke's mouth, so she kept silent, nodding to indicate her understanding.

"So my first interview goes well, I think. I mean, why shouldn't it? I'm crazy qualified. And I'm exactly what they need. Someone proficient in multiple languages. I figure I'm a lock. But then this agent I've never seen before walks into the room and orders everyone else out. Agent Rohm. That was his name. Big guy. Deep voice. Southern accent. Kinda like Foghorn Leghorn. He tells me I've only got a thirty percent chance of making it to the academy at Quantico, but there's a real easy way for me to make it ninety percent. Or he thought it was easy, at least."

Charlotte just nods.

"He said I could inform on my brother, who was now one of the most wanted cybercriminals in the United States."

"The dean . . ." Charlotte says.

"Yeah. Bailey's the one who found the dean. And the stolen money. Even though law enforcement was taking all the credit. Bailey shipped them everything they needed to find the guy; then he fled the country. Meanwhile, the feds took the credit for the arrest, and now they want to put my brother in handcuffs because he hacked, like, a dozen different companies to do it. But I think it was the satellite company that probably put him over the top."

"Your brother hacked a *satellite*?"

Luke nods and takes a slug of beer.

"Did he tell the FBI it was him when he sent them the evidence?" Charlotte asks.

"No. But he slipped up, apparently, because something was traceable back to him. Rohm wouldn't tell me what it was. Could've been powers of deduction. Like they looked at the list of students who got ripped off, and there was only one or two who were real good at computers. And then there was one who was *real* good at computers, and that was Bailey. I wasn't in much of a position to ask questions. The only thing Agent Rohm would tell me is that my only shot at the FBI would be if I ratted out my brother."

"And what did you say?"

Luke meets her gaze. "I told him to go fuck himself with an umbrella."

"Literally?"

"Word for word. If I'd had an umbrella I would have given it to him, but it was sunny out that day."

Charlotte smiles. "And what did he say to that?"

"He said I'd never get a job in government or any law enforcement agency outside of some rinky-dink small-town police department for as long as I lived. Those were his exact words, by the way. *Rinky-dink.*"

"And so you went and got a job at the first rinky-dink small-town police department you could find."

"Yep," he says, and his smile seems genuine. "I showed him, right?"

For some reason, this story means so much more than his apology. It's proof, she realizes, that he's a changed man; that he was willing to give up his lifelong dream rather than betray his family—his *only* family. That's not the Luke Prescott she knew in high school. But it's the Luke Prescott standing before her now, a man dealing head-on with the sacrifices loyalty entails.

"What?" he asks suddenly.

"What do you mean?" she asks.

"Your face . . . I don't know. Your expression, I'm just . . ."

"Just what?"

"I can't read it."

"I'm impressed."

He stares at her for a while, and then his entire frame seems to relax, and she wonders if this is the first time he's talked about this with anyone. If her words are the first nice thing anyone's said about the sacrifice he made for his brother. Only then does it dawn on her how truly alone he is. A few days earlier she would have described herself as alone. Not lonely. But alone. And by choice. But when she needed help, she had no trouble drawing people around her who cared about her. Kayla, and then Marty, and now Marty's posse of 12-steppers.

And now Luke? she asks herself.

No, that's crazy. Luke is just a down-on-his-luck guy looking to make some kind of amends that will smooth his homecoming. But that thing he said, though.

If there's anything I can do to make up for it, let me know.

Would it be so bad having a cop on her side right now? Especially a smart, highly educated one, who reads textbooks on profiling and crime scene investigation?

Or a hacker who can find people living off the grid on the other side of the world? Could the same hacker tell her everything she wanted to know about someone who had lied to her about who he was?

"Where'd you go?" Luke asks.

"Excuse me?"

"It's like I lost you there for a second."

"You did. Kinda."

"Can I ask a question now?" he says.

"Shoot."

"You don't live around here anymore, do you?"

She doesn't answer.

"And you're back, but Marty says you don't have much time. And you changed your name . . . so . . . what's going on?"

"It's been a busy couple of days."

Luke nods, but he's clearly disappointed in her answer.

"My turn," she says.

"Yeah, OK. I guess we can pretend that was quid pro quo."

"You said if there was anything you can do to help, to let you know. How serious were you?"

"Serious, but—"

"When was the last time you heard from your brother?" she asks.

Luke takes a careful sip of beer, staring at her while he does so.

"Why?" he asks once he swallows.

"Because I need his help."

The struggle inside him is almost painful to see: the war between his desire to make good on his word to her and his desire to guard his family's secret.

"I need to find someone. And if your brother can hack a satellite, he can find anyone, right?"

Luke's mouth opens to protest.

Just then the alarm panel next to the front door releases a shrill series of beeps. It doesn't sound like any alarm or warning she's ever heard; it's almost musical. A two-tone pattern that repeats again and again, more mischievous than threatening.

Luke dives into the kitchen and returns with his gun drawn. That's when she sees the computer monitor in the front room flashing black and white in a rhythm that matches the alarm's maddening song.

Luke advances on the panel, gun drawn, then lowers it when he reads whatever's on the display. A second version of the chirping tune starts up somewhere close by, accompanied by the familiar sound of a cell phone vibrating against a wooden table. In any other circumstance, it would be intolerably rude of her to pick up Luke's phone and read the display, but this is a special circumstance for sure.

The words she sees flashing across the screen are the same that are now flashing across the monitor. And when she joins Luke in the foyer, she sees the same words scrolling across the alarm panel's display.

YES I CAN YES I CAN YES I CAN YES I CAN
YES I CAN YES I CAN.

22

Luke's musical tastes don't get any harder than classic rock, so he's not surprised the alarm's shrill song makes him want to cover his ears with both hands. But damn if he's actually going to do that in front of Charley. He couldn't if he wanted to because he's still got his gun in hand.

"What the fu—hell?" he cries.

"I'm a grown-up," Charley says. "You can curse."

She turns from the alarm panel and advances on his computer; he follows.

"Last time you saw your brother, did you go to the bathroom at all?" Charley cries over the racket.

"My brother and I don't go to the bathroom together!"

"That's not what I'm asking," she shouts.

"I can't think with this damn noise!"

"Stop it, Bailey!" she shouts.

And just like that, the music stops.

The message on the computer screen freezes, the words blaring YES I CAN.

A glance over his shoulder confirms the burglar alarm's display panel holds the same freeze-frame.

Luke places the gun on its side next to the keyboard, muzzle pointed at the wall. He's not sure what's startled him more—the fact that the crazy music just stopped, or that Charley was so confident his brother was the composer.

"Your phone," Charley says, but she's scanning their surroundings now.

"What about it?"

"Did you leave it alone with your brother the last time you saw him?"

"I don't . . . maybe. I don't know."

"He probably put some kind of malware on it so he could spy on you. Then he used it to hack your Wi-Fi here at the house."

In response, three quick beeps come from the alarm system. The message on the computer screen is quickly replaced with one that says, BINGO!

"You know about this stuff?" he asks.

"I'm not an expert like your brother, but we used to get hacked a bunch when I lived with my dad. There were a lot of ass wipes on the Internet who thought I was lying about not killing anyone on the farm. I had to learn how to protect myself."

He keeps his mouth shut. She probably doesn't mean it as a dig, but he's embarrassed nonetheless. How many times back in high school did he vaguely imply she might have been *changed* by her time with the Bannings? More than once, that's for sure. And this is who that bullshit put him in league with. Hackers.

Focus, he tells himself. As if his brain wasn't already overloaded from Trina's—*Charley, Charley, Charley,* he corrects himself—visit, the knowledge that Bailey's been watching his every move makes his pulse roar and his head spin, which seems to him like a good combination for a heart attack.

"Spy on me," Luke whispers. "He was spying . . ." He turns to the computer and the tiny camera embedded in the top of the monitor. "You were *spying* on me?"

The message on-screen is replaced by a series of Zs emerging from the bottom of the screen, increasing in size as they drift upward—the universal sign for snoring.

"Obviously you all don't have the same taste in TV shows," Charley says.

"You couldn't tell me you were alive, but you were spying on me the whole time? That's awesome, dude. That's just fucking awesome."

"Luke . . ."

"What? You told me I could curse."

"It's the volume. Marty's outside."

Just then a crude outline of a clock appears on the screen. A red line slashes through it. All of this happens on a black background that seems to have wiped all personal touches from the computer monitor. Luke somehow finds that more unnerving than having his privacy invaded.

There should be relief in here somewhere. Relief that Bailey's alive and safe. But where's the apology? He's not seeing the emoji for one slide across the screen, so he figures he's got the right to be pissed. For now.

"No time," Charlotte says. "He's saying no time. No time for what?"

The clock with the red line through it is replaced by a cartoon of a woman with thick-framed cat-eye glasses and a bun on her head. She grows in size until she's revealed to be pushing a rack full of books.

"Librarian?" Luke asks.

"He doesn't want us to keep talking to him on your computer," Charlotte says. "He wants us on a public server. Best place would be a library. Hence, the librarian."

Three beeps from the alarm system again.

"Where's the nearest library?" she asks.

"Paso Robles. I'm going to ask you again how you know so much about this stuff."

"Change your identity and you learn a few things. Wait," Charley says, with enough volume to suggest she's talking to Bailey directly.

The screen goes black.

"My question," she says, "the one about you being able to find anyone. Was that what you were answering?"

YES, comes the flashing response.

"OK," Charley answers, "so you're offering to help me?"

The word on-screen stays solid but a red stream moves through each individual letter, almost like neon coming to life.

"Why?" she asks. "We barely know each other."

There's a second or two of silence. Amid his anger, Luke feels a twinge of sadness over the thought that his sudden connection with Bailey might have just been severed.

As he's about to call out to his brother, new words appear on the screen, letter by letter; the font is even typewriter-style.

```
Anyone who can make my brother apolo-
gize for something is fine by me.
```

Charley's laughter dies when she sees Luke's glare.

The message vanishes. It's replaced by WWW.CHATEEUR.RO.

"Pen," Charlotte says.

Luke reaches into the drawer and hands her one, along with a Post-it note, but no way is he writing down the URL himself. So what if his refusal to do so makes him feel like a stubborn eight-year-old. He's got a right to be pissed, doesn't he? And it's got nothing to do with Agent Rohm or the FBI or anything Bailey might have done in the past. It's the silence since. It's the fact that Bailey never let him know he was OK.

The URL vanishes.

It's replaced by the words:

```
Go in hot.
```

Then the computer screen returns to normal, a spray of icons over a shot of AT&T Park mid–Giants game. The alarm system even lets out a weak, strained chirp, like whatever Bailey's done is the equivalent of a stopper being pulled from a drain.

Charley tears the Post-it note from the pad, folds it neatly in half. She appears gripped by excitement, but when their eyes meet, she blushes in a way he'd find undeniably cute in any other circumstance.

"Go in hot?" Luke asks. "What does that mean?"

"Pick a screen name that's got something to do with fire. Or Burning Girl, I guess. I assume you're gonna come with me."

"Uh, yeah. I am."

"OK, well, let me just tell—"

When she turns from him, he grabs her by the shoulder. Not thinking. Too hard. She spins. Her eyes lock on the hand he's gripping her shoulder with. He removes it quickly, even manages to spread his fingers in a silent gesture of apology. But he's not sorry he stopped her hasty escape from the house. And she seems more fascinated by his sudden grab than angered by it. Which is odd.

But all of this is odd.

"Look, you may not think I'm in a position to ask a lot from you right now, but he's my brother. Marty *cannot* know about this. Like at all."

He can see a flash of some kind of struggle in her expression, but she hides it quickly under a tense mask, looks to the hardwood floor between them, her fist closing around the folded-over Post-it note.

"Charley, it's obvious you're in some kind of trouble, and I can tell he's watching out for you. And that's great. But he doesn't like me, and we've already been at each other's throats once this week and . . . I just . . . He can't. He can't know about this. Please."

"What if he follows us to the library but doesn't go inside? And I don't tell him what we're doing there?"

"You really think he'll think we went there to check out some books? He'll know we're there for the computers, and he'll probably connect it up with that thing my brother did with the manure store in high school."

"You're being paranoid, Luke."

"My brother's wanted by the FBI, and he's been secretly watching me move around my house for months."

"But *Marty* doesn't have anything to do with that."

"I know, and I want to keep it that way."

She stares at him. Not aggressive or fearful—calculating. Whether she's assessing him or the situation, he's not sure.

"What kind of trouble are you in, Charley?"

"The big kind."

"And you honestly think Bailey can help?"

"Maybe, yeah."

"Can I?"

"I don't know. Can you?"

He's not sure exactly what she means, but he's surprised by how quickly he made the offer. Big trouble usually means trouble with the law. Only once she turned his question around on him did he wonder if that might be the nature of her dilemma. If she's on the run for something she's done, as opposed to from someone who wants to hurt her. He has a badge now. Not the government-issued one he'd always dreamed of having, but it's still a badge. But in this moment it feels no more meaningful to him than a child's toy. Did Agent Rohm leave him that angry and jaded, with that little respect for the law, for the system?

The answer comes out of him before he can stop it. "I can try. If you let me."

"So you're saying I should milk this apology thing for all it's worth."

"Something like that, yeah," he answers.

"OK. Fine. No Marty."

With that, she turns and heads for the door. When she realizes he hasn't followed, she looks back, sees him in the kitchen strapping on the holster for his gun. The expression she gives the weapon in his hand is almost wistful, like she thinks he's cute for bringing it along.

"A date?" Marty asks. "Really? Right now?"

"It's not a date," Charlotte hisses. "And if you say that one more time, I will reach through this—"

"You're going off alone with him. You won't say where. What the hell else could it be except for a date?"

She grips the edge of the truck's open window, glances back to where Luke is sliding behind the wheel of his black Jeep Wrangler. Avoiding, on purpose, she assumes, her pointed glares. How could he put her in this position?

Simple, she thinks. *Because it's his brother; that's how.*

"If I follow, what's he gonna do?" Marty asks. "Have me arrested?"

"Probably not."

"Then I'm following."

"He'll probably take me in for questioning."

"For *what*? How much did you tell him?"

"Marty, just . . . please. I need you to trust me on this one."

He lets out a long hissing breath between clenched teeth, shakes his head.

"When we get back, maybe we can all sit down and have a meal together, and you two can bury the hatchet or something. Or, you know, do what men do when they've been bumping chests so much their backs are starting to get sore. Like yoga."

"My back's fine," Marty says, voice low and growl adjacent, "and this isn't about me."

"It is, though. Whatever words you guys had the other day, they've got you confused."

Got you confusing your ego with your brains, she wants to say.

"So you trust him? You don't think he's part of this?"

I think he's about to become part of this if his brother turns out to be helpful. But you can't know that. Yet. Instead she says, "Maybe. We'll see. I'm still figuring it out."

Marty shakes his head and stares out the windshield.

"Besides," Charlotte says, "it's not like I won't be able to protect myself if I'm wrong."

"Pill's been sitting in your system for how long now? For all we know it might wear off if you don't, you know, activate it in time. There's too damn much we don't know about this stuff."

"I agree," she says.

"Yeah, sure you do."

"Marty."

He checks the dashboard clock. It's almost 1:00 p.m. She feels an ultimatum coming.

"If you all aren't back by six this evening, I'm gonna consider you a missing person and make sure Mona believes it, too. And I'll be damn sure to let her know you were last seen with her shiny new deputy."

"Fine."

"And I'm gonna take that video we made last night to the FBI and tell them everything you told me."

"No, you're not."

"Excuse me?"

"You're not because you can't. I've got the thumb drive we put it on this morning."

"You didn't . . . but the . . . Crap, you deleted the original off my phone when I wasn't looking. Slick, girlie. Real slick."

"*Girlie?* Really?"

He glares straight ahead, hands tensing and untensing at ten and two on the steering wheel.

"I'm starting to feel unappreciated," he says quietly.

"Feel something else."

"What?"

"Spared."

He looks her in the eye, expression doleful. "Maybe I don't want to be spared all this."

She leans in, kisses him on the cheek. He's clearing his throat, preparing to say something else maudlin but kind, she's sure. But just then she reaches across him and pulls Jason Briffel's disposable cell from the armrest. His eyes widen and his jaw gapes when he realizes she's just swiped his last possible bargaining chip.

"Six o'clock," he calls after her. "First part of what I said still stands. If you're not back by six, I—"

"Six o'clock," she calls back.

When Luke starts the Jeep's engine, Marty fires up his truck a second later. For a minute or two, it seems as if the men's vehicles are conducting a little battle of the bands over her; then Marty peels off down the street, making the biggest show of not following her that he can.

"How'd it go?" Luke asks when she climbs inside his Jeep.

"Not well," she answers.

He nods and backs out of the driveway.

"Well, I appreciate it," he says a few minutes later as if no time has passed between her comment and his response, a sure sign he's measuring his words carefully. Would he be measuring them this carefully if his brother hadn't decided to make a surprise appearance during their reunion?

"What's that?" he asks, eyes on the phone resting in her lap.

"It's a phone."

"I know that."

"I'm expecting a call on it. At some point . . . I think."

"OK."

Up ahead, Marty takes a sharp left into the middle of town. She can't help but watch his truck as they fly past. Maybe she's afraid he's going to double back and land on their tail, or maybe she feels a stab of guilt at having left his protection against his wishes, especially after he dropped everything for her.

"He's a good guy, isn't he?" Luke asks.

She's startled he's read her thoughts, until she realizes it's not that hard for him to tell what she's looking at. No doubt her expression's far from serene.

"He is," she says. "But it sounds like you didn't think so yesterday."

"We had a . . . thing."

"What kind of thing?"

"What's it matter? It's the reason you and I got to talk today, and that means it's ultimately a good thing, right?"

"Is it?"

He blushes. It looks good on him. Again. But she's always been attracted to any small sign of vulnerability in a man who works hard to look strong. Her kryptonite would be a calendar of nothing but shirtless firemen cooing over kittens. But she's got more experience with calendars of men than actual men, which is why the thought of playfully drawing attention to the bands of pink on his right cheek and jaw makes her both dizzy and nauseated at the same time.

"Well," he finally says, "you're the reason my brother decided to break radio silence after a year, so I guess that's good for me, right?"

"Yeah, that's gotta sting a little."

"More than a little, but I appreciate your understanding."

"Sure. So which way are you gonna go?"

"The 101."

"I wish you wouldn't," she says.

"Really?"

"Can you take Bennett Road around the fort? That should get us there, right?"

"And it'll add about forty-five minutes to the trip."

"The library's open till five, right?"

As he slows and shifts lanes to avoid leaving the valley, he gives her a long, stony look. Scans her from head to toe, it seems. Only then does she remember she's got the URL for the chat room where they're supposed to meet Bailey written on a Post-it note in her pocket, and unless Luke memorized the thing when she wrote it down, the note's the only connection he has to his brother. She didn't set it up that way, but it's how things are. For now.

A few minutes later, they're heading south on Bennett Road, past horse farms and spreading oaks and golden fields.

"You couldn't have traveled back-road and surface streets the whole way here," he says.

"Says who? You don't know where I was coming from. But, you know, nice try trying to get me to tell you."

His tongue makes a lump under his upper lip, and it's clear he's trying not to smile.

"You really afraid of freeways right now?" he asks after a brief silence.

"I'm limiting my use. Not the same thing. You know, it's like the option on the GPS. Avoid freeway usage, or whatever."

"I've heard of it. But most people don't use it to run from the cops."

"I'm not, either." *I think.*

"Good thing, 'cause you're riding with one."

"Yeah, and he didn't stop to ask me what kind of trouble I was in before he got in the car with me," she says.

"I did, though."

"Did not."

"Did. I asked what kind, and you said big," he says.

"And that was good enough for you?" she asks.

"I'm here, aren't I?"

She looks at him until he feels the force of her stare and glances in her direction.

"What?" he asks.

"Are you just gonna keep asking me random, rhetorical questions until I give you the information you want?"

"They're not random. And only one was rhetorical."

"The last one."

"Right. The last one."

She looks out the window, amazed suddenly to be back in this familiar valley. It's like the past couple of days have blown the newer layers of sand and grit from her life, leaving only the rocky fundamentals underneath. Or some crazy rearrangement of them.

Her grandmother's on-again, off-again boyfriend is now her temperamental bodyguard. Her former bully blushes in her presence when she teases him. While chauffeuring her places.

Maybe this is what growing up feels like for people whose lives aren't marred by serial killers and stalkers. Things shift underfoot only slightly. Some people remain but change roles.

And maybe this is exactly what Dylan wanted, she thinks. *For me to go home again, back to Altamira. Why?*

"Charley?"

"Yeah."

"You don't have to tell me who's after you, but tell me this."

He waits until she turns her attention to him.

"Is it who you're going to ask my brother to find?"

"Something like that, yeah."

Luke nods. If he's about to say anything else, it's cut off by the chirping sound that suddenly fills the Jeep.

Jason's phone is ringing.

"Pull over," she says.

23

"Charlotte?"

She walks slowly toward the shade offered by the nearest oak tree. Her heart's pounding from the sound of Dylan's voice. It's filled her with all the feelings his drug relieved her of the night before, and the night before that. Made her feel weak, flushed, and powerless.

Will a simple conversation with Dylan be enough to set her recent dose of Zypraxon, almost an hour old by now, loose in her system?

As if any conversation between her and Dylan will ever be simple again.

They never were.

Once inside the tree's umbrella of shade, she turns. Sees Luke standing in front of his Jeep. Steadily he looks back and forth in both directions along the empty two-lane blacktop, his hand resting against his gun hip protectively. Protecting *her*, it seems. That's a comfort, at least.

"Charlotte?" Dylan says.

"I'm here."

"Looks like you're building some sort of team. Are you sure you can trust them?"

She scans the empty fields, the mountains on either side of the valley. They're in the middle of someone's definition of nowhere, but he can see her.

"Trust is important," she manages.

"In certain situations, yes."

"But not in ours?"

"I'm here for you, Charley. I've always been here for you."

"Always?"

"From the beginning of our relationship, I mean."

"You call this a relationship?" she asks.

"Of course it is. Not all relationships are sexual."

"I'm asking about your relationship to the concept of trust," she says.

"Ah, I see."

"Do you? Do you see me right now? Is that how you know I'm not alone?"

"I thought Altamira would be your last choice, to be frank. But I guess it makes sense. So what did it come down to? The choice between San Francisco or your old hometown, or the choice between Kayla and Marty?"

This is a safe guess based on what he knows about her, the fact that she'd call Kayla or Marty for help. Maybe she's overreacting.

"So where are you headed now? An overnight in Cambria? Maybe a nice little bed-and-breakfast close to the beach with your handsome new friend? You might want to give him permission to relieve himself. He's looking a little shifty, if you get my drift."

Sure enough, Luke is pacing slowly on the road side of the Jeep. He must be wondering what the hell he's gotten himself into. But from a distance he probably looks exactly like someone who needs to pee.

Jesus Christ . . .

The wind knocked out of her, she looks to the sky, to the fibrous strands of clouds threaded across the dome of blue. She's thinking of satellites and drones and all the other so-called technological marvels shrinking the world down to a screen. Somehow Dylan has access to such tools.

But then she realizes what he doesn't seem to know. Like the fact that she and Luke are headed for a library in Paso Robles. Or what they talked about with Bailey before they left. Or who Luke even is. Or maybe he does and he's holding it back to see how much she'll tell him. Or worse, he'll learn those things in time now that he's caught up to her.

"*Trust* is one of those words that's lost its meaning—don't you think?" he says. "It used to mean the ability to keep a secret when someone asked you to. Now it's an unreasonable request we make of people we're trying to control, a demand that they buy into our illusions of who we are. That they never question our fantasies. That they never introduce anything into our world that upsets us, changes us. Educates us."

"You're a sociopath."

"Maybe. But I get a lot done."

"Who are you?"

"You can tell Kayla to stop digging in to my past. She won't find much. Not the juicy stuff anyway. And as I'm sure you know, the best cover stories are as close to the truth as you can make them. I only told you one real lie, Charley. My last name. The rest? Well, they were sins of omission mostly. And let's just say none of the work I did on behalf of Uncle Sam is sitting on a server waiting for a diligent lawyer to find it."

"Is that who helped you track me to the middle of an empty field? The military?"

His laughter is gentle. "Oh, no. I've traded up from the military. Way up."

"But you're still afraid to confront me face-to-face. And so are they, apparently, whoever the hell they are. What with my ability to break their arms and all."

"I see. So you've taken it again, have you? Is that what you did last night? Break some arms? Did they deserve it at least?"

"Wouldn't you know if I had?"

Silence. She just scored a point without meaning to.

He *doesn't* know. So whatever the net of surveillance he's thrown around her, and Kayla and Luke and Marty, it's got gaps. Limits. Or maybe there was a delay. Maybe he didn't pick her up until she reached Altamira.

"A penny for your thoughts," Dylan says.

"I've given you more of my thoughts than you had any right to."

"We're not out to hurt you, Charley. Not me. Not the people I'm working with."

"Safe to say you and I have very different definitions of the word *hurt*. And maybe every other word in the dictionary."

"Perhaps, but you're too valuable to us now. Jason Briffel, on the other hand, he *was* out to hurt you, and I took care of him. As promised."

"I never made you promise to kill him. I never even wanted to lay eyes on him again."

"I know," he says quietly, "but I killed him anyway. Don't worry. I didn't leave a mess. Nice work on his shoulder, by the way."

And there it is, she thinks, the breath going out of her as if she's being gradually squeezed by a giant hand. She figured he'd kept his word, but she'd done everything she could not to linger on the possible details of how.

Shouldn't she be flooded with relief to hear that Jason's corpse isn't still lying on her kitchen floor? Well, she isn't. If anything, this seems to have joined her fate to Dylan's.

"And now you've replaced him," she says.

"That's nonsense. You're still in shock."

"He said my house was a prison, and he was going to set me free. He thought I was valuable, too."

"Interesting. I wouldn't have called it a prison. I'd say it was a cocoon, and you were ready to hatch. Where Jason and I disagreed was on what you should become once you were hatched, and whether or not he should live to see it."

"So has Abigail Banning handpicked you to fill his shoes?" she asks.

She assumes his long silence means he's simply lost patience for their back-and-forth, but when he speaks again, his voice sounds reedy, weak, as if, for the first time, she's managed to knock the wind out of him, and not the other way around. "You are better than this," he growls.

"Better than what? You?"

"Better than these . . . *base* insults. I am not . . ." His attempt to clear his throat actually forces him to cough. "I am not a serial killer," he finally whispers.

"Prove it."

"How?"

"Tell me who you really are."

"I'm a scientist and a soldier, and perhaps a bit of a crusader. A revolutionary, even. And, yes, you are my test subject, and, yes, I have very high hopes for you."

He's off balance and his tongue's gone loose. Was it comparing him to a serial killer that did it? Or just the Bannings? He seems to have no real compunction about murder, and Abigail Banning is about as far from being a Harvard graduate as you can get. Maybe the real Dylan Whoever is a classist asshole above all else, and she's just discovered his sore point.

"So you're a scientist who just happens to have an army of drones or spy satellites or hackers at his disposal, or are you working with someone who does? Are they *scientists*, too?"

"They're one of the wealthiest corporations on the planet. When they put their eyes on you, they cannot be outrun. So don't even try."

"And why does this powerful company have its *eye* on me, Dylan?"

"Would you like to know my final diagnosis of your situation, Charley?"

"I'd like to know what you've signed me up for. *Again*. Without my knowledge."

"You were waiting. That's what you were doing in that house, with a gun in every room. You were waiting for someone to come after you. That house wasn't a fortress. It was a trap. For *them*. For whoever came first. That's what was truly plaguing you out there in the desert. Not terror. Not dread. Not nightmares of your past. But your desire for revenge."

Maybe, she thinks. Maybe she went down to that arroyo every evening not just to fine-tune her defensive skills but to practice for an eventual, gratifying kill. People spend their whole lives, their whole professional careers, trying to put a thumbtack through the precise moment fear turns into aggression. No way in hell can she let Dylan distract her with such a vain pursuit now.

"Whatever helps you sleep at night, dude."

He laughs.

"Why did you call me, Dylan?"

"Because it's time for you to get to work. Enough with the hometown reunion. I didn't give you those pills to watch you dawdle in Altamira, trying to make an army out of your uncle Marty's former drunks. And . . ." She hears papers shuffling, the creak of a desk chair. He's either been handed something or is reading something. "Really?" he says. "Luke Prescott? The asshole from high school? I thought you hated him. He's grown up to be quite a looker; I'll say that much."

Why does this get to her worse than all the other things he's said? This suggestion that his surveillance of her, of *them*, is being updated and expanded even as they speak. Are they all being watched 24-7 now? Kayla, Marty, Luke, and maybe his brother, too, if they continue their road trip south. What good will come of having Bailey look into Dylan when the guy seems to be five steps ahead of them and armed with the same tools as the NSA? That could only get Bailey and Luke in more trouble than they already are.

Focus, she tells herself. *Focus and remember who you're dealing with—a liar and a murderer.*

"What do you mean," she finally says, "get to work? What is *work?*"

"The world is full of bad men, Charlotte. Go find some. Show them what you can do."

"Show *you* what I can do," she says. "You and whoever you're working for."

"*With.* Working with. Try not to kill anyone. Although if you do, don't worry. We'll clean it up. Just make sure they're worth killing."

"I've only got three pills left." She says these words without thinking, and he laughs gently. Laughs, she figures, because he thinks he hears a craving for more Zypraxon in her voice. Really she's just trying to throw up a last-minute hurdle, grasping for any complication she could find. Or maybe not. Maybe it is a craving.

Or maybe Dylan's in my head and I need him to get the fuck out right now.

"I'll fix that soon enough," he says. "And I'll be in touch when we need you to come in."

"Come in where?"

"You'll see."

"Yeah, well, maybe when you come for me in person, I'll have a surprise for you."

"Charley, the company I'm working with had over twenty-five billion dollars in revenue last year alone. They employ private security contractors who have removed dictators from power. I'm watching an image of you right now that's giving me heat signatures of every living thing in the field you're standing in. There's a small animal twenty feet away from you, probably a gopher, and some deer nosing through the woods at the base of the mountains to the west. And your new friend Luke is still bouncing on his heels. Trust me—from here on out, there is nothing you can do to surprise me. Happy hunting."

Silence.

Just silence. Just the wind rustling the tall grass around her.

Just rage.

She tries to crush the phone in one hand.

It doesn't work.

So just wanting to pound Dylan into the dirt isn't enough to turn me into the Incredible Hulk, she thinks. *Bummer.*

24

When Luke sees her approaching, he goes still. She figures his tight, uncomfortable-looking smile is meant to mask his concern.

"Do you need to go to the bathroom?" she asks.

"Um . . . no, not really. Why?"

"Can you get behind the wheel?"

"What?" he asks.

"Just get behind the wheel."

"OK. But are you . . ."

When she walks to the back of the Jeep, he throws up his hands and gives in to her command.

She places Jason's disposable phone behind the passenger-side tire.

"Start the engine!" she calls to him.

"Are you getting in?" he asks through the open window.

"In a minute. Just start the engine."

"And then what?"

"Back up a few feet."

He does. At first it looks like the phone's going to get spit out from under the advancing tire, but then the tire catches just enough of its bottom section to crush it with a loud crunch.

"Again!" she says.

Luke rolls the Jeep forward a few feet, then repeats the action. There's a series of soft pops as the interior of the phone gives way. When Luke pulls forward again, the tire leaves behind a spray of broken pieces that are close to being unrecognizable. She kicks them into the dirt beside the road with one foot.

Then, before she can think twice about it, she raises both hands and gives a double middle-finger salute to the empty field, the tree she stood under, and the sky overhead. She spins in place, hands up, birds out, until she finds herself standing next to the Jeep's passenger-side door. Luke stares at her.

"So I guess the call didn't go well?" he asks.

Forcing breath into her lungs, she slides into the passenger seat. She wants to meet Luke's joke with one of her own, wants to look him in the eye and return his sheepish smile. But she can't. She can't because the world seems too small all of a sudden. Because her life, once again, has been reduced to a thin stream moving through a channel carved by psychopaths.

Before she can reconsider, she reaches into her pocket and pulls out the Post-it note with Bailey's URL on it. She extends it to Luke. He doesn't take it.

"What's that?" he asks.

"Your brother. It's the URL he gave us. For when you go talk to him."

"Aren't we both going to talk to him?" he asks.

"No. You should leave me here."

"*Leave* you here. What? That's crazy. It's like a forty-five-minute walk back to town. I'm not—"

"I'll have Marty come pick me up."

"Well, do you have another phone with you? 'Cause the last one's kinda roadkill now."

"No, I don't. Maybe you could call him after you—"

"OK, you know what? Let's just stick with the original plan and—" She grabs his hand when he reaches for the gearshift.

"Luke, if Bailey talks to me, he could end up in more trouble than he's already in."

"My brother's hiding out from the FBI. Probably in a foreign country."

"I know."

"I'm just saying you'd be hard-pressed to make things any more difficult for him."

"I know," she says. "And given the situation I'm in, it's still possible."

His smile fades, but she's not seeing surrender in his eyes. She's seeing determination, calculation, an unwillingness to give in to her fear. Is it too soon to call it loyalty?

"OK. Then let me just ask this. And I promise you—no, I *swear* to you—your answer will never leave this car."

She nods.

"Did you kill someone?" he asks.

Her mind flashes to the biker somersaulting down her windshield. Would the guy be dead if he hadn't tried to run her off the road? *Nope.*

"No."

Although, she thinks, *given who Dylan claims to be working for, he could probably make it look like I did.*

"Did you rob someone?" he asks.

"No."

"But someone's after you?"

"Yes. This is more than one question, Luke."

"And you made time to drop in on *me* during all this?"

"You would have made a really good FBI agent."

"I know. So . . . your drop-in?"

She studies his face; his expression's blank. Another sign he's switched into investigator mode.

"I thought you might be in on it," she says.

His eyes light up with surprise.

"Correction. *Marty* thought you might be in on it. This . . . *thing* . . . It's big, and, uh, when I told Marty about it, he said you showed up in town after interviewing with the FBI and maybe . . ."

"Maybe what?"

"Maybe you were trying to find me. Or watch me. I don't know—he just thought you might be part of it."

Luke's barking laughter fills the Jeep. It sounds genuine, and it leaves him breathless, doubled over, and gripping the top of the steering wheel with both hands. "That's *awesome*," he finally manages.

"Awesome?" she asks.

"No, it's just that . . . I mean, if you had any idea how completely lame my life was right now, the fact that you'd think I'm involved in some sort of massive conspiracy . . . It's pretty funny, Charley. I'm sorry. I'm not trying to make light of your situation. But seriously, all I do is drive around a town I never wanted to see again, getting into fights with guys like Marty even as I try to convince them I'm not the giant prick I used to be, and then I go home to my mostly empty house, watch free porn and fall asleep, usually after the third beer and a frozen dinner. But honestly, I like your version of my life better. It's way more exciting."

"Well, if you want excitement, I can definitely give you some of that."

"Sounds like it."

"And it wasn't my version; it was more Marty's version," she says.

His laughter proves so infectious, she finds herself smiling despite herself. After a few deep breaths, their eyes meet. He's looking at her in a way she's not used to being looked at. With a mixture of eagerness, concern, and longing. Maybe not for her specifically. But for the chance to be part of something.

"Is that what you're looking for, Luke? Some excitement?"

"I told you what I was looking for," he says quietly.

"Remind me."

225

"A chance to do right by you."

"You already did that when you told me the truth about Bailey."

"I'm not leaving you out here, Charley."

"I'll give you points just for driving me this far."

"Not enough. I mean, I'll do whatever you want. But I won't feel like my job is done if you cut me loose now."

All right, buddy, she thinks. *You asked for it.*

"I was seeing a psychiatrist where I was living in Arizona. I confided everything in him, everything I'd been through with the Bannings. Afterward. We talked for months. Then he convinced me to take this antianxiety drug. He said it just came on the market, and he gave me a sample."

She has his full attention now, can feel his gaze heating up one side of her face. But if she looks him in the eyes, she'll lose her nerve.

"What I didn't know is that he'd contacted one of my worst stalkers and given him enough info to break into my house that night. The same night I took the pill. But when he attacked me . . . the drug. It wasn't just an antianxiety drug. It was something else. It made me strong."

"How strong?"

"Very strong."

"OK."

There's fear in his expression. She can see it. But at least there isn't *You're fucking nuts, lady* in his eyes. She knows damn well what that looks like, and there's no sign of it. Still, he could have his own idea about what *very strong* means, and it's probably not even close to reality. If she shows him the video, though . . .

"Are you on it now?" he asks.

"I took another dose before I saw you. In case you were . . ."

"*Oh.*" He nods, eyes wide. "Oh, OK. Wow. All right. So I shouldn't piss you off, I guess. I mean, is that how it works?"

"No. That's not how it works."

"How does it work?"

"You would have to terrify me. You'd have to make me believe my life was in danger. That level of fear, that's what kicks the drug into action."

"And you thought your life would be in danger if you came over to my house?"

"I just wanted to prepare for the possibility. That's all. It's not like I dosed up so I could come over and kick your ass, all right?"

"Of course not." But he struggles to swallow, and his voice sounds weak.

"Are you gonna be all right? You look pale."

"It would be easier if I didn't believe you. But I do. And so I'm freaking out a little right now. Right? I can admit that. I mean, I'm still a man if I admit that, right?"

She laughs, nods. It eases his tension a bit.

"Keep going. So the stalker . . . Is he . . ."

"I didn't kill him, but I came close. Then I left to get the police. It was adrenaline, I thought. But once I got on the road and I ran into the bikers, I realized it had to be the drug."

"Bikers," Luke says flatly. "Bikers . . . in Arizona. *Holeee* . . . that story on the news? That was *you*?"

"No. Not entirely."

"What's *not entirely* mean when a biker gang is slaughtered?"

"This isn't going how I thought it would. Telling you all this."

"Just ignore me," he says. "Just keep going. I'm sorry. Keep going. So the bikers?"

"Dylan got the rest."

"Who's Dylan?"

"The psychiatrist. My psychiatrist. Or so I thought."

"A psychiatrist who kills biker gangs."

"Uh-huh."

"And the stalker guy? What happened to him?"

"Dylan killed him."

"I'm gonna go out on a limb here and guess that Dylan isn't just a psychiatrist."

"No. He isn't. He's a scientist with some sort of military background. When he just called me to find out why I wasn't out in the world using the other pills he gave me, he described the heat signature of every living thing in this field. Including you."

"I see."

"He also identified you by name."

"Probably from my license plate," he says calmly.

"I figured that part of the story would freak you out more than all the others, but instead it's knowing I might be able to trounce you that's got you sweating."

"I'm not sweating. Am I sweating?" He angles the rearview mirror to look at himself. "Yeah. OK. Well, male privilege being called into question. Whatever. I went to college. I get it."

"I'm not sure it's your license plate that did it. He says he's working with a company that made twenty-five billion dollars last year, and they hire the best private security firms in the world. I wouldn't put it past them to have some kind of facial-recognition software."

He grunts, nods, and looks at the empty road. But she's more taken with what he doesn't do. He doesn't jump from the car and run for the nearest cover. He doesn't even look to the sky for the tiny blip of a drone that might have been circling overhead this whole time. Instead he's processing. Absorbing all she's told him.

He's into this, she realizes.

Maybe because he doesn't know the half of it. Wait until he watches the footage. Right now he's probably imagining her doling out superpowered high kicks and crippling uppercuts, not bending metal with her bare hands.

"Twenty-five billion dollars a year," he finally says. "What kind of company makes twenty-five billion dollars a year?"

"I feel like this is a rhetorical question."

"I can think of two kinds off the bat. Defense contractors and pharmaceutical companies. One's good at surveillance; the other makes antianxiety drugs."

"I didn't realize drug companies made that much money," she says.

"It's one of the most profitable businesses in the world."

"Is there one that does both?"

"Not that I know of. Not that anyone knows about. But nobody knew about this drug, right?"

And the fact that you could see that right off the bat is part of why I need your help right now. But she doesn't say it. Because he's smiling.

Why is he smiling?

"Why are you smiling?" she asks.

"Because my brother is going to have *so* much fun fucking with these people."

"Wait. What? No!"

"Well, that's what you're gonna ask him to do, right?"

"No. I . . . I was going to ask him to get background on Dylan so that I had some idea of who he was and why he was doing it. But I don't need it now because I know what I'm up against, and it's fucking terrifying."

"You didn't even know their names."

"I know they can see us from *space.* That's enough to know I shouldn't send your brother after them."

"I think you're underestimating my brother."

"We're not talking about the dean of a corrupt community college."

"I know. That's why I think Bailey's gonna be pumped."

"Luke, you are being completely insane right now."

"You just brought me a story about a drug that gives you enough strength to pound biker gangs into the pavement. Maybe slow your roll when it comes to handing out the crazy label. Just sayin'."

"OK. I guess that's fair. But, seriously, I can't—"

"Look, I still want to help. What do you want to do, Charley?"

When she doesn't answer, he says nothing for several minutes, allows her to gaze out at the empty field, the lone oak, the mountains that should be beautiful and awe inspiring. Instead they feel like looming barricades between her and any bright future.

"Whatever you want to do," he says, "I'll help. I'll make Bailey help, if I can."

"You could lose your job."

"Boo-hoo," he says.

He allows her another long silence.

The sight of the dashboard clock puts her back inside her body: 2:20 p.m.

"I guess I could try to disappear. But he says there's no outrunning them."

"Bailey could give you some pointers on that, I'm sure."

"Maybe," she says, "but I don't want to. This is my name. The name I picked for myself. I don't want to give it up."

"I understand."

Another silence.

"You thirsty?" he asks.

She's so startled by his question, she locks eyes with him.

"I keep an ice chest in the back with some bottled water. You want one?"

Why is she blinking back tears all of a sudden? How is it that this simple offer has exposed the chink in her armor? Is she really about to break down over a bottle of water?

It's not that, she realizes.

It's what he's not doing. He's not turning the car around. He's not ordering her off onto the side of the road. He's not recoiling from her history, from her terrible burdens, from the darkness that's dogged her every step. Instead he's settling in, making plans with her, starting with a bottle of water.

"Hey." His whisper makes the brusque little word sound gentle, soothing.

She holds up one hand and turns her face to the window again so she can deep-breathe the threat of tears away.

"Hey," he whispers again. His hand comes to rest on the gearshift. Not touching her, but maybe getting ready to the minute she gives him the OK.

Once she's steadied her breath, she reaches over and pats his hand gently. "Hey," she whispers back.

He nods, watching her closely, and for a second there's the tension of wondering whether he'll grip her shoulder or her knee, or try to comfort her in some other physical way that might spin quickly out of control given the emotions already roiling inside her. And this tension, however unpleasant, is a delicious contrast to everything she was feeling just moments before.

"So, um, no on the water?" he asks with a smile.

"I really appreciate the offer," she whispers.

"It still stands whenever you're ready. Or thirsty."

"Luke?"

"Yeah."

"What did you do?"

"What do you mean?"

"When you walked out of that meeting with . . . What was his name? The agent who tried to—"

"Rohm. Agent Rohm."

"What did you do when you walked out of that meeting? I mean, you must have felt like your life was over, right? The life you'd *planned* anyway . . . How did you keep from . . . I don't know . . . giving up?"

"I made the choice in the middle," he says.

"The choice in the middle? Is that like a Buddhist thing?"

"Maybe. I wouldn't know. What I know is moments like that suck because you feel like there are only two choices, and they're both horrible. On the right, you go after the person who's kicked your teeth out until you've destroyed your life trying to destroy them. And on the left, you give up completely. Find some cheap-ass apartment and some bullshit punch-the-clock job, and drink your feelings away in your spare time. Or smoke weed, if that's your thing."

"Is it your thing?"

"No. Hate the smell."

"So Altamira Sheriff's. That was the choice in the middle?"

"Yeah. I mean, it's not complete surrender. But it's not exactly revenge, either."

She nods. She likes his logic, and she likes the phrase.

The choice in the middle . . .

When the idea comes to her, she flushes from head to toe, and for a second or two, she wonders if the drug has kicked into gear, if the accumulation of stress has triggered it in some new, residual way. But when she grips the door handle next to her, it doesn't crack or bend or warp. This really is just adrenaline. The adrenaline rush of someone who's just seen a narrow band of light resolve at the end of a long, dark tunnel.

"Drive," she says.

"Where to?"

"The library. Like we planned."

Luke starts the Jeep.

She stares at the road ahead. Just a glance into Luke's eyes might turn her sudden burst of confidence to dust. It's crazy, this idea. It's absolutely crazy, but it's got something else wrapped through it, something that felt entirely elusive just seconds before. Hope. Not for complete freedom, but for some version of it. Hope that she might be able to disrupt Dylan's plan to send her out into the world as his guinea pig, if not spin it to her advantage. To someone's advantage.

She's not sure how much time has passed when Luke says, "Are you gonna tell me what—"

"No. Not till we get there. I may have reconsidered by then anyway."

"OK."

"We'll still talk to Bailey no matter what, but . . . I just need to think for a little bit."

"I got it. I'll just drive. I love driving." But he doesn't sound like someone who loves driving. He sounds like someone holding in a belch with every muscle in his body.

Golden fields. Rolling hills. Glimpses of sparkling lakes. It's beautiful country, but the last leg of their little road trip feels interminable all of a sudden, and she's shifting in her seat by the time they're coming down out of the hills and into Paso Robles, Altamira's classier big sister. This is where they came to see first-run movies in a nice, comfy theater when Charley was a girl—when Trina was a girl—the place they'd drive to for dinners so fancy she and Luanne would have to wear sundresses and sandals. Ah, California!

On the outside, the library looks modern and immaculate; sandstone walls banded with strips of red brick. The roof's a cluster of pyramids covered in a kind of weathered green metal that reminds her of statues from ancient Rome. After her time in the sterile safe house and the seemingly endless twenty minutes she spent inside that repulsive roadside bar, the library's clean, hushed interior feels like an oasis of comfort and safety.

She'd expected doubt to set in by now. Instead she feels the opposite. Her confidence builds with every step they take toward the computer lab, a double-sided row of private carrels in the middle of a shelf-filled book room, which, to her relief, is almost devoid of other people.

Luke allows her to take a seat at a carrel on the end, then pulls a chair up behind her.

If he's losing patience with her silence, he's managed not to show it.

The chat room welcomes her with a bare-bones layout; yellow bands on each side and dialogue flowing in languages she doesn't recognize. Most of them Eastern European, she's sure. She clicks on the tab that allows her to set up an instant free profile.

"Go in hot," Luke whispers. "Remember?"

"Burning Girl isn't exactly anonymous," she whispers back. "Especially given current circumstances."

"I agree. But I figure whatever name you pick, it's gotta stand out. This thing has private messaging, right? I don't figure he's gonna want to hash this out in the main chat room."

"Nah, he probably won't."

In the entry blank for her username she types, flamingmanureguylover.

Luke's attempt to control his laughter turns into a little eruption of huffing breaths.

"It's hot and it's partly about him," she whispers, "so I figure'll it get his attention."

Second later, an invite to a private chat pops up from msstocktonpresents666.

"Ms. Stockton?" Luke whispers. "What does that mean?"

"Our European history teacher. Remember? We talked about it back at your place."

"Wow. He really was listening to everything."

She accepts the invite, and a private chat room opens.

U have a good memory, Bailey writes.

She lifts her fingers to the keyboard.

It was a pretty good joke. Looks like you've graduated to bigger stuff now, she types.

Next to her, Luke gives off the energy of a coiled snake.

Big bro with you?

Yes, she types.

Tell him I'm sorry.

She lets these words sit on the screen.

Tell him he should have taken Rohm's deal. Tell him there was never anything he could have given feds on me. I wouldn't have put him in that position.

The breath leaves Luke so quickly she's afraid it's the first sign of a groan that might draw the attention of the librarian at the nearby information desk. He growls under his breath, runs his hands back through his hair.

"Tell him to go to hell," he whispers.

"Really?" she asks.

"No."

Guess that didn't go over well, comes the response.

"Ask him if he's somewhere safe," Luke whispers.

She complies.

Yes, comes the response, very far away, safer for you if you don't know where.

"Tell him that's the truth because when I see him again, I'm gonna wring his neck," Luke says.

"Really?"

"He's better with that kind of thing than actual concern. Actual concern makes him feel . . . confined."

Charlotte types in the response exactly as Luke worded it.

The response comes without a pause. ;)

"See?" Luke asks.

> What's your story, Burning Girl? Sounds like you're in big trouble, too.

A minute later, her hands are still resting on her lap, and she hasn't typed anything in response.

"Charley?" Luke whispers. "Are you going to tell him?"

??? appears on-screen a few seconds later.

Still here, she types, just give me a sec.

"He won't believe me," she finally says.

"I believed you."

"You could see me. He can't. He can't look into my eyes and know I'm telling the truth."

And you still haven't seen it in action, she thinks. *So you don't really understand, either.*

"Is that really it?" Luke asks.

She looks back at him, takes advantage of the connection she has with him that she can't establish with his brother. "Not entirely, no," she whispers. "Even if I ask him not to, he'll probably go after them, won't he?"

"Given his history, yeah."

"I don't want that. Not yet."

"Even if he just gets information?"

"They're expecting that. Kayla's already run some kind of background check on Dylan, and he knows about it somehow. And there was something else he said . . ."

"What, Charley?"

236

"He said there was no way for me to surprise him," she says, "now that they can see everything I'm doing."

"Sounds about right," Luke responds, and for the first time since she asked for silence on the drive there, she hears doubt creeping back into his voice.

"It isn't right, though." The words give her the confidence to lift her hands to the keyboard again. "It's wrong. I know exactly how to surprise him."

Still need you to find someone, she types.

Listening, comes the response.

"If they're gonna make me do this, whoever *they* are," she whispers, "I'm doing it on my terms."

I need you to find the Mask Maker, she types.

25

"Whoa," Luke whispers.

The serial killer in LA? Bailey answers.

"Whoa, Charley."

She holds up a hand to silence him, then types, Yes.

She braces herself for a flood of questions about her motives, her plan.

On it, comes the response.

And that's it.

"Wait," she says.

"Yeah, yeah," Luke whispers, glancing over his shoulder to see if anyone is watching them. "That sounds right. Let's wait a minute here and just—"

Again, she holds up one hand to silence him, then types, You can find him?

> I can do my best. I'll be in touch.
> That's it???

A few seconds later, Bailey's response: I'm like the Secret Service. I don't discuss procedure. Better for everyone that way. Take care of my brother, i.e., don't take any of his shit.

After a minute of radio silence, she types a string of question marks, gets nothing in response. Behind her Luke's gathering anger takes the form of heavy breathing and the occasional unnecessary throat clearing.

Bailey's gone. For now.

"Let's talk," Luke says.

"You say that like we've haven't been talking all day."

"Seriously, Charley."

"Outside."

His footsteps are so heavy she can hear them scraping the soft carpeting behind her. Is he that pissed, or has a rush of adrenaline made her hypersensitive to his close pursuit, to the glances from the librarians they walk past at the information desk? Is it from the nagging fear that some trace of her chat with Bailey might actually be left on that computer back there, even though she closed out every screen and Bailey picked the chat room because nothing about it was permanent?

Once they're on the sidewalk and a good distance from the library entrance, Luke grabs her by one shoulder. A mistake, he seems to realize too late. By then their eyes have locked, and he remembers everything she told him on the ride there and holds his hands up in a gesture of surrender.

"Look, I gave you an out," she says.

"A serial killer?" Luke hisses. "You're actually going to go after a serial killer?"

"'The world is full of bad men, Charlotte. Go find some. Show them what you can do.' That's what Dylan just said to me. Your brother locates criminals, so I'm just asking him to do what he's good at. That's all."

"I'm not worried about my brother. I'm worried about you."

"I appreciate that, but it was your advice, remember?"

"Go after a serial killer with a drug you don't understand? When did I give that advice?"

"I made the choice in the middle."

"How is that—I mean, what are you even talking about? Charley, you have to go to the authorities."

"I'm sorry. What authorities? Do you have a direct line to the president I don't know about? Twenty-five billion dollars a year. Aerial surveillance technology. Private security contractors that take out dictators. That's what I'm up against, Luke, and the only thing that can stop people like that is a thermonuclear warhead or the threat of one. You have any lying around?"

"You're not a killer, Charley. Trina Pierce was not a killer. Everyone knew it no matter what they said. No matter what *I* said. Don't do something crazy just 'cause you think you still have to prove that to the world."

"The world? I don't want the *world* to know about any of this. I want the world to leave me alone for the first time in my life. To stop treating me like my mother being raped and murdered by those monsters makes *me* special. Because when the world does that, they make Abigail Banning feel special. Jesus Christ, Luke. My entire life I've been forced to indulge sick freaks on the Internet who want to turn that woman into their own Hannibal Lecter, and the minute I finally got free of them, Dylan Fucking Thorpe shows up and throws me headfirst into this nightmare. So if I'm really stuck here, I'm doing things my way."

"I appreciate your anger, Charley. You—"

"Oh, don't patronize me. You don't—"

"Then stop talking about your damn feelings and start talking about the facts. I spend my weekends reading about this guy. For starters, they don't know if he is just one guy. But he's on his way to being one of the most proficient, if not *the* most proficient, serial killer in American history. I mean, do you even know the first thing about him? What this guy does requires months of planning on top of some sort of medical expertise. And he's managed to abduct both his victims from public places without popping up on a single security camera."

"That's not true. They've got him in Santa Monica last week."

"Because he wanted them to. He's never been caught on camera when he didn't want to be, Charley. The guy makes the Bannings look like amateurs."

"The Bannings killed for nine years before a deliveryman recognized me from an age-progression photo. They were not amateurs, Luke."

"His abductions are not on camera. They haven't even pinpointed the abduction sites. Do you realize the kind of skill and patience that takes in this day and age?"

"Ten bucks says they've got him on tape, and we just don't know about it because they're holding it back so they can eliminate false confessions. The cops did the same thing with five different pieces of evidence in the Banning case."

"Oh my God. Is that what you just sent Bailey to do? Hack LAPD and the FBI?"

"Well, you could ask your brother, but he doesn't discuss procedure, remember?"

"This is insane," Luke whispers.

"You're right, and it's been insane for forty-eight hours, and I gave you an out, and I didn't have to tell you about any of it, so screw you for judging how I'm handling it."

"I'm not judging you. I'm trying to keep you from destroying what life you have left."

"I made the choice in the middle. Just like you said. And when I'm done, there's a very good chance the Mask Maker won't be killing women anymore."

"You are . . ." Luke begins, shaking his head. But instead of finishing he pulls out his phone. "Nuts," he says as he starts dialing. "You are completely nuts, Charley. And I wouldn't be doing right by you if I let you . . . I mean, this just . . . this has to stop right now."

"What the hell are you doing?"

"I'm calling Mona, and I'm telling her everything. We'll figure something out. We'll get you some kind of help. Aerial surveillance technology, my ass. Dylan Psychofuck is probably a lying psychopath who's following us in a truck with some binoculars. He could be lying about everything."

"Put the phone away, Luke."

Instead he turns his back on her and puts several feet of distance between them.

She closes her eyes, grits her teeth, tries once more to turn anger into a trigger event. She won't crush his face. Just his phone, and then hopefully, by proxy, some of his massive crusader's ego. But it doesn't work. Anger's not enough. Rage is not enough. She needs stark terror.

Should she attack him right now? Make him fight back in a way that will trigger her? But is that worth the risk? If he does go through with this call, she can just deny everything and make Luke look like the crazy one. A betrayal, sure, but isn't that what he's doing to her right now?

And then the light changes and the traffic starts streaming past the library, and she sees a giant refrigerator truck with the cheerful logo of some produce company on its side round the distant corner. The driver accelerates when he sees a green light waiting for him a half block ahead.

"Hey, Phil, is Mona on duty?" Luke says into the phone.

Charlotte walks to the edge of the curb.

"Tell her it's urgent. Is she on her cell? . . . How far? . . . No, I mean how long has it been going to voice mail?"

The truck approaches, engine bellowing, huffing exhaust.

This time it will work. Because this time it's not a car being driven by a loved one who's practically family. This time it's a truck driven by a stranger. A huge truck. And maybe the driver's late for a delivery or a pickup or a hot date or who knows what else; what she knows is he's sitting about seven or eight feet off the ground and won't see her if she steps in front of him at just the right moment.

The truck's only a few yards away now. And as she studies that grill, visualizes herself stepping in front of it, she feels the tingling in her hands, the slowly accelerating drumbeat of bone music. The onset of terror.

Maybe she'll need to break a bone. Maybe the truck will have to tear into her before the Zypraxon in her system blooms. But surely an attack from a giant, moving wall of metal will be perceived the same way an attack from a rageful human would.

Why would the terror be any different, any less effective? And maybe she'll find out what kind of miracles Zypraxon can work on a freshly broken femur.

"Tell her I need to talk to her right away," Luke says. "She needs to call me on my—"

"*Luke!*"

He spins, looks her in the eye.

"Watch this!"

She steps off the curb and thrusts one arm out in front of her.

Luke's terrified shouts and the truck's squealing brakes deafen her.

Despite her best efforts to keep them open, she screws her eyes shut. She's rocked back on her heels as if from a sudden, strong wind and in the same moment it feels as if her arm has exploded into flame. Then she tilts forward onto the balls of her feet again, and her lips kiss the steel grill.

The truck didn't stop just in time.

She stopped the truck just in time. With one arm.

When she opens her eyes again, she's dwarfed by the truck's grill, and her arm's buried deep inside it, in a fresh gash that looks custom designed just for her. The pain, in its Zypraxon-muffled form, ricochets up her forearm, sings through her shoulder, then arcs across her upper back before it leaves behind a dull, throbbing ache she'd normally associate with lifting something heavy. The entire process feels as if the pain searched for a place in her body where it could perform its expected, agonizing work, but it kept getting denied entry, so it decided to give up and evaporate altogether.

The truck shudders, as if its very carriage is coming to terms with the miraculous strength that just brought it to a halt, a force that was not just sudden and powerful enough to stop it but impossibly precise.

Slowly, she removes her arm from the hole.

She's bleeding from a dozen different scratches. The bruising is fierce and terrible. In her fist, she holds on to a chunk of metal from the grill. She passes it to her left hand, then twiddles all of the fingers on her right. They work perfectly. No additional spike of pain shoots up her arm. Nothing's broken. The skin's a mess, but the bones are intact.

With her left hand, she slowly crushes the chunk of metal and lets it drop to the concrete.

Then, a few feet away, Luke makes a sound like a bird that doesn't know if it's dawn, dusk, or feeding time. She's never seen someone who literally looked as if he were about to jump out of his skin before, but that's how Luke looks. He's in a half crouch, his arms spread on either side of him, as if preparing to dive through the air to knock her out of the truck's path. He's frozen in midcrouch, his mouth agape and his eyes wide. Without meaning to, he tossed his phone. It lies on the pavement a few feet away.

The driver's screams come to a sudden, choked halt when he sees her. Reflexively, she hides her not-injured-enough arm against her chest and covers it with the other. "I'm OK," she cries. "I'm OK."

Just as the truck driver drops from his cab to the sidewalk, she hops up onto the pavement as if the entire event were nothing more than a brief stumble. At the sight of this, the driver lets out a moan so full of relief it sounds almost sexual. He clasps one hand to his chest, forcing breath back into his lungs.

"I'm so sorry," she says. "It's not your fault. You totally stopped in time. I'm such an idiot. I'm so sorry. Thank you. We were just . . . my husband and I, we were fighting, you see, and I got distracted because he was being such a huge dick."

The driver stares at her in a daze, whispering words under his breath, too quietly for her to make them out, but she's willing to bet every other one is profane. Hands braced on his knees, he bends forward, mouth agape. His baseball cap falls to the sidewalk, revealing his sweat-soaked rat's nest of wiry black hair.

She bends down and picks up Luke's cell phone, slides it into her pocket with a sliver of the force she'd normally use for such a task.

Luke hasn't moved, but his heaving chest makes it clear he's still breathing. She's about to wrap one arm around his waist before she realizes it's the bruised and bleeding one, the one that should be broken, if not torn from her body entirely, and isn't. She goes to wrap her good arm around his waist and remembers that if she pulls too hard she might detach his torso from his hips.

"Thank you, sir," she tells the driver.

The driver just stares after her. Still bent over in a crouch. "Thank you," she says. "I owe you my life. Honey, we should go. We'll be late to get the baby."

"What fucking baby?" Luke whispers.

"*Now*, sweetheart," she hisses.

He takes a step, then another and another. He lags behind, his expression making him look like he's the one who just stopped a speeding truck with one arm. He's swallowing over and over again, sucking in half breaths through his nostrils, staring dead ahead as if he's being marched toward the gallows. But they're making decent enough time. Within a minute or two, they round the corner, putting the still stunned driver out of sight.

"You OK?" she asks.

"I'm fine," he croaks; then he stumbles a few steps to his right, grabs a public trash can by the rim, and empties the contents of his stomach into it.

III

26

The woman he might kill next is doing a lousy job of stretching her quads. She's bracing herself against the cargo door of her RAV4 with one hand, but her form's still off. And when she pulls back on the ankle of her bent left leg with her other hand, her hips wobble and she bites her lower lip.

So she's an inexperienced jogger. That's good. She's also doing her stretches out here in the parking lot on Portola Parkway and not closer to the trailhead, where there's more space, which says she doesn't have much experience with Whiting Ranch Wilderness Park, either. Another very good sign. When she does take to the trail, she'll be self-conscious and insecure, preoccupied with how she looks to the other hikers and bicyclists and, more important, not very aware of her woodsy surroundings.

He's made it a point to get to the park an hour before dusk. If everything goes well, he'll need the cover of night to work under. But he figured the late hour would also introduce him to a woman so eager to get a run in before the park closes she'll be too distracted to notice she's being stalked. Self-conscious and insecure are even better than rushed, however, and it's a great sign, he thinks, that he's stumbled across such a promising target within minutes of his arrival.

Changing his method of abduction with each new patient hasn't been easy, but it's been an essential component of his success so far. Otherwise, the cops might have linked the first and second disappearances before he managed to complete his work. Before the masks were placed. And the masks are key. They're the only reason he does this. No matter what becomes of him, no matter who eventually steps up and tries to tell his story, it's all about the masks. If they get that part wrong, then it means even his biographers haven't taken the time to get to know him, and that means no one ever will.

This is the first time he's tried to claim a patient out in the wild— or a contained and lightly trafficked version of the wild. If tonight goes well, it will be as a result of all the extra steps he added to his process: an interim hiding space for the patient, a judicious use of the thick brush that lines the lower section of the Borrego Canyon Trail, a ball gag to quiet her in those brief moments before the sedatives take effect, or in the event that they somehow manage to wear off before he gets her in his trunk. So, yes, insecure and nervous are great signs in a potential new patient, but with this particular patient, the key factor is really weight. A few extra pounds means no core strength to fight him off. Too many and he won't be able to drag her off the trail undetected in whatever time fate gives him to do the job.

He studies the woman's meaty thighs, notes the slight roll poking over the waistband of her bike shorts. Soft and thick. Not bulky and bottom heavy. *Perfect.*

He imagines her enjoying fruity tropical drinks with a group of her girlfriends at some noxious chain restaurant, the kind that serves desserts the size of babies.

He imagines her swirling her straw as she listens to one of her prettier, slimmer friends go on and on about the trendy new fitness class she's taking and how it's supposedly changing her life.

Imagines her pacing her apartment later that night, listening to Taylor Swift but hearing only her pretty friend's boasts, knowing she'll never have the confidence to walk into a gym or some new class full of glistening little Southern California fitness nuts, but realizing that she has to do something, has to make some attempt to lose the weight that's probably dogged her since her teens, even if it's the last-minute, hastily planned run she's preparing for now, in a pair of New Balance shoes that aren't right for this or any trail.

In about ten years, if somehow she'd managed to marry well, she could become the type of woman who ends up in his office, expecting his scalpel to add ten more honeymoons to her failing marriage. There's no ring on her finger now, and come sunset, if he does his job right, she'll never marry. But when he's finally done with her, her life will have meant something. Or her face will have meant something, at least, once he's separated it from her pettiness, from her weakness.

First she has to fail his test.

Slowly, he starts to approach her, forcing himself to take short steps, which isn't easy given he's six foot three. But the short steps make his running pants whisk together, a repetitive sound that alerts her to his approach at just the right moment.

She's down on one knee, double-knotting her right shoe, when she notices him. At first she seems stricken by the sight of his legs. They're muscled tree trunks that make formidable impressions even inside his baggy pants, and they encourage her to glance up at his torso. Later he'll don his black windbreaker, but for now it's tied around his waist, so his tank top can offer her an expansive view of his bulging shoulders, his biceps like goose eggs, the Michelangelo-carved veins along his powerful forearms. Something like desire and hope lights up her expression, as if, for an instant, she thinks he might be *the* one. And then she gets a good look at his face. The light goes out of her eyes almost instantly.

There's no telling which feature of his she focuses on first, but whichever one it is, it repels her. Maybe it's his offensively long mouth, which despite its size still doesn't manage to close entirely over his fat tongue. Together these attributes conspire to make him always look slightly winded, a cruel injustice given that he's spent his entire adult life in peak physical condition. Maybe it's his forehead, which rises like a wall toward the sudden flat top of his skull, too flat for his latest hair implants to distract from its startling angularity. And then there are his eyes. They crowd the bridge of his nose so closely, there's no making them look evenly spaced, no matter how much he has his nose sanded down. And it's been sanded down plenty, to the point that it now looks both perfect and perfectly out of place, like a piece of statue designed to plug a congenital hole in the center of his face. Maybe she sees only one or two of these things. Maybe she notices all of them at once. It doesn't matter. What matters is that she gives him the brusque, dismissive smile he's come to expect from women all his life, then returns her attention to her shoe.

She's failed the test.

She's his now.

They used to fill him with paralytic rage, these moments, these split-second exchanges in which a lifetime's worth of accomplishments, from his medical degree to the hours he spends in the gym to the millions he's amassed in savings, are rendered worthless by a series of genetic attributes. Of course, if he put some effort into it, he could big-talk her past her initial reaction. Make it clear how rich and successful he is until she was leaning on his every word. Because once she knew enough details about his life, a chunky, entitled little bitch like her would realize she should be grateful for any attention from a man like him. But none of that would erase the wretchedness of that first moment, of that flash of truth in her eyes when she saw for the first time the face he's never been able to escape.

During medical school, he watched students with half his skill earn twice the respect of their professors because their big, perfectly balanced eyes and tiny, sculpted chins invoked a parental tenderness in just about everyone they met. Since then, he's watched rival doctors bring in twice the number of patients solely because the strong jawlines and proud Roman noses they exhibit in their professional headshots suggest a confidence and skill they do not truly possess. You had to be the relentless victim of these constant injustices to see how prevalent they were. He calls it the tyranny of faces, a tyranny so pervasive, so woven through the fabric of society, that it goes well beyond the deferential treatment granted the exceedingly beautiful. This injustice is made up of the millions of unearned gifts bestowed on those whose faces are merely balanced or proportional, who possess random, genetically determined arrangements of features that just happen to trigger primal, but positive, emotional cues in those around them, cues that bear no real connection to who they are as people. To what they actually say. To what they actually do.

Why is he the only one who can see this—that our faces are masks, rendering our personalities, our behaviors, our true accomplishments, utterly irrelevant, and yet we seem to have utter, idiotic faith in them as indicators of what's in the soul?

With each face he removes and places on public display, he comes another step closer to revealing this injustice to the world.

It took only a few seconds for this woman, this total stranger, to dismiss him, as so many have done before. But the rage has left him entirely in the short time it takes him to reach the circle of benches and concrete next to the trail's entrance. Now it's been replaced by a giddy sense of anticipation that sends a pulse of heat to his balls. The base of his cock thickens.

He turns his back to the woman, dons his windbreaker, and props one leg against the bench in front of him; then he bends forward slowly to stretch out his hamstring.

A group of mountain bikers flies out of the tunnel of branches that mark the trailhead, slowing as they near their parked cars.

There are other parks he could have picked. Bigger parks with more room to hide. Smaller parks he could slip in and out of more quickly after nightfall. But many of them were scorched by recent wildfires that devoured their mature trees. What's brought him to Whiting Ranch is the densely wooded first stretch of the Borrego Canyon Trail, a little finger of wilderness passing through typical

Orange County subdivisions, the kind where the red-tile-roof houses all look the same and the streets are gently curved to distract from the fact that the entire neighborhood was laid out on a single sheet of drafting paper. Beyond the first stretch, the houses fall away and the trail rises into the drier hills beyond. If all goes well, his new patient will never get that far.

He hears her footfalls behind him, sluggish slaps against the concrete, turning crunchy when they hit the dirt.

He keeps his back to her as she passes, makes sure his baseball cap is secure. He's taken care to pull most of the threads from the logo on the cap's brim—a logo for some medical supply company whose name he can't even remember, a giveaway he got at some conference years before. Now the brim bears a few loose loops of blue thread, confusing enough to throw off a potential witness should they try to describe it later. Every minute said witness spends wondering what sports team the hat promoted is another minute he gets to work in peace, without distractions.

As tempting as it is to check the contents of his fanny pack, he can't do that now, not out in the open like this. Instead he grips the outside and gives it a little shake, as if he's just making sure the thing's secured to his hip. It allows him to feel the lumps made by the ball gag and the ten-milliliter syringe containing his special blend of ketamine, Versed, and propofol.

He's locked and loaded and ready to go.

After a few minutes on the trail, he spots her.

She's already losing steam, probably because she took off too fast. Her chocolate-brown ponytail is swaying when it should be bouncing, and she's glistening with sweat. He's never run up behind a patient in this way, and he's pleasantly surprised by the delicious tensions inherent in the act. By the multiple contrasts. Waiting and the exertion, simultaneous assessments of the trail ahead and behind, of the thickness of the brush on either side, of his speed, which must stay steady without giving away that he's slowly gaining on her. He feels like a wolf and a snake in one. Or a snake riding on the back of a wolf, waiting for the right moment to strike. A ridiculous image, even if it is a fitting metaphor. He has to hold back laughter.

When you become this good at something, he thinks, *that's a sign it's exactly what you should be doing.*

It's time. He can feel it. His cock can feel it. He's desperately hard.

The light is fading, lacing the shade from the branches overhead with threads of true darkness. The brush on either side of the trail is as thick as he needs it to be. And it's quiet, save for their twin, interposed footfalls. Another minute or two and she'll notice him.

Another few minutes after that and the trail will rise, and the brush will thin out.

It's now or never. Or more accurately, it's now or start over. And he doesn't want to start over. He can't start over.

She failed the test. It's decided.

After a deep, steadying breath, the man they call the Mask Maker accelerates.

He pulls the Talon air-weight baton from the thigh holster hidden underneath his running pants.

With the press of a button, he extends the baton to its full length.

Before she notices him inches behind her, he brings it down across the woman's upper back with enough force to send her face-first into the dirt, her breath coming out of her in a desperate, ineffectual wheeze that sounds nothing like a scream.

27

When Julia Crispin was nineteen years old, she was raped at knife-point inside her parked car after leaving a bonfire party on Mission Bay. It was the summer before her sophomore year at Yale, and when she returned to school a few months later, she brought with her a long, slender scar that snakes along her jugular vein to a spot an inch or two beneath her collarbone on her left side.

Julia is fifty-seven now and the CEO of Crispin Corp, one of the most successful surveillance technology companies in the world. Like Cole, she inherited her business from her father. Unlike Cole, she has considerably more experience in the CEO position, a fact of which she never fails to remind him. She's a handsome woman with a long, fine-boned face, pale, freckled skin, deep-set blue eyes, and dark eyebrows that always make her appear as if she's finishing up a frown. For as long as Cole's known her, she's worn her hair in a platinum Jackie-O bob. The scar's still with her, and it has a tendency to peek above the collars of the lustrous silk blouses she favors. She's never made an effort to conceal it with makeup. It's like she's daring people to ask her about it. Or better yet, reminding them of what she's survived.

Cole can see the top half of it now, and he'd rather focus on it than the stoic expression on her face as she watches the microdrone surveillance footage of Charlotte Rowe and Luke Prescott taken that afternoon.

She's watching the footage on a tablet he brought her, which his tech team assured him was air gapped, meaning never connected to the Internet. It's also been stripped of any drive or device that could support a cellular or Wi-Fi connection. They transferred the footage onto it the old-fashioned way, with a portable hard drive.

Julia's office is carved out of the earth underneath her sprawling glass-and-steel mansion in Rancho Santa Fe, which means it offers no view of the horses she keeps in the stable or the snaking front drive lined with willows and precisely placed beds of wildflowers. Down here, an ignorant visitor might assume the glass walls are designed simply to make the banks of television screens behind them disappear once they're turned off. But the glass hides more than the televisions; behind them is another set of walls, steel encased, with enough electromagnetic shielding to deflect the surveillance efforts of the NSA.

It saddens him a bit that Julia's office bears no photographic evidence of her accomplishments. No framed photos of her shaking hands with presidents or other CEOs. Just dark-glass walls; recessed, pinpoint track lights that can be made bright enough to simulate sunlight; spindly steel-and-glass furniture like the uncomfortable chair he's sitting in now; and the persistent flicker of CNN, FOX, MSNBC, and Bloomberg News. But when your life's work is developing cameras and recording devices that are all but invisible, maybe it's bad form to broadcast your accomplishments.

"Is that a tree?" Julia asks without looking up from the tablet.

"Yes," Cole answers.

"She's kicking over a tree. With one foot."

"It's not a very big tree."

"I can see how big it is. And the man watching her?"

"A police officer with the Altamira Sheriff's Department. His name's Luke Prescott. They were high school classmates."

"And she's showing him what she can do," Julia says. "Lovely."

When she reaches the end of the video, she sets the tablet down faceup. A tiny gesture, but one that seems to challenge the veracity, or at least the importance, of what she's just seen.

"Microdrones took these?" she asks.

"Yes."

"Not ours, I presume."

"If they were yours, I wouldn't have lost four of them when the wind picked up, and I'd still be able to see her after dark."

"I'm flattered. It is hard to find good help these days, isn't it?"

"Why do you think I'm here?"

"Better microdrones?"

"Let's talk about the footage."

"I'm supposed to believe this woman is on Zypraxon?"

"I think it's worth taking a closer look. Don't you?"

"Where's Dylan now?"

"He's got a hideout in Arizona. A little tract house outside Tucson. I'm sure the neighbors don't know who he is or what he's done."

"And the reason we're not busting the doors down and stealing the pill from him?"

"He says he'll destroy it if we try. When I met with him, he said he'd set up some sort of incinerator that would burn the supply he had as well as all his research if he didn't get back to wherever he'd hidden them by a certain time."

"So he's modified Zypraxon's formula since you shut down Project Bluebird?"

"Since *we* shut down Project Bluebird, yes," Cole reminds her.

"He's not using the formula we have. So if we want to wash our hands of this, we'd also have to wash our hands of any chance of seeing this drug work, and then we'd be left to deal with this Charlotte Rowe on our own. Which means we might have to wash our hands of her as well. If we have the stomach for it."

"Suddenly it's *we* again."

"Yes, well, *we* disagreed on how Dylan should have been dealt with when he walked away overnight. This safe house. Is he refining the pills there?"

"It doesn't look like it. I think he's got a lab or a storehouse somewhere, but he's stayed put since making contact with us. Wherever the place is, I'm guessing somewhere in Arizona. When he goes for it, we'll follow him."

"But he hasn't gone for it?"

Cole shakes his head.

"Why am I not looking at video of him, by the way?" Julia asks.

"Because he can't kick over a tree with one foot."

"That we know about. So you had him followed after your meeting?"

"I did. And we spoke again after, and he agreed to download a tracker to his phone. It was my condition."

"Your condition for what?"

"I'm not proposing a relaunch of Project Bluebird, Julia."

"Not yet anyway. What are you proposing?"

"A closer look. That's all."

"So is this just a friendly warning that you've been seduced by Dylan again?"

If she's not willing to play around, there's no reason he should, either.

"I need TruGlass."

Julia stiffens, carefully removes her glasses. Maybe it's a subconscious gesture, triggered by the mention of her most potentially revolutionary invention, or maybe the gesture's simply designed to maximize the impact of her sudden glare.

"TruGlass is a prototype, Cole."

"You expect me to believe it's been a prototype for seven years?"

"You have spies inside my company?"

"I had my father in your bed every other weekend until he died."

"Well, isn't that charming. I didn't realize he was working for you."

"What's charming? Your affair or my candor?"

"You mobilized millions in capital to finance the crazy experiments of a handsome Navy SEAL who fucked you three ways from Sunday."

"You willingly contributed your millions when I showed you a rat tearing the head off a python in ten seconds."

Julia sits back in her chair and smiles at her lap. Cole can't tell if it's humility or anger that's inspired these gestures.

"I'm not judging you for what happened between you and my dad. Over and over and over again. In fact, I find it kind of comforting."

"How's that exactly?"

"It's a testament to Dad's character, really. That he married the bimbo but screwed around with a woman of substance and accomplishment on the side."

"That's a helluva way to talk about your mother."

"Standing up for my mother's integrity has never been your job, Julia. But again, I'm not judging you."

"Then what are you doing?"

"When you try to dismiss your genuine interest in Zypraxon as solely the result of some deception I foisted upon you because I was cock-whipped by Dylan Cody, you leave me no other choice." This doesn't seem to faze her, so he crosses his arms and lets the fingers on his left hand come to rest atop the spot where her scar resides. He taps three fingers along his collarbone several times to make his point. If she gets it, she doesn't let on.

"You realize we all have our contingency plans, right?" she says. "Should any of this ever come back to bite us in the ass."

"As do I."

"I have satellites on that island 24-7. Any ship gets within two hundred nautical miles of it, I get detailed manifest information in twenty minutes."

"We all need friends with satellites."

"I'm serious, Cole."

"I know, and I feel bad for you because it sounds boring. And repetitive. Get a hobby, Julia. There's nothing left on that island for anyone to find."

"But there might be again soon is what you're saying, isn't it? Provided you like what you see once you get a closer look at this Charlotte Rowe and whatever Dylan's convinced her to do."

"Provided *we* like what we see."

"We?"

"You, me, Stephen, and Philip."

"Right. But you're *not* suggesting a relaunch of The Consortium."

"Not yet. No."

"Not until I give you TruGlass."

"It will help me make a determination about the potential next steps. How's that?"

"The problem, Cole, is that I'm not just giving it to you. I'm giving it to Charlotte Rowe, about whom I know nothing other than she can stop a truck with one arm and kick over a small tree with one foot."

"I brought you a file. It's interesting reading."

"I'm sure, but will any of it tell me whether or not she can be trusted with my most valuable piece of technology?"

"No."

"Then the answer's no."

"Four willing test subjects failed miserably. And apparently another one Dylan tested on his own, a woman. So gender isn't the deciding factor. But for some reason, it's working like clockwork in Charlotte Rowe, and we're not sure why."

"Dylan knows. Why did he pick her?"

"He has a theory, but that's all. And he's got some clear biases around her that will become evident once you read her file. We need a closer look, Julia."

"Bring her in."

"If we bring her in, we take ownership of her. We take ownership of Dylan's problems and his mistakes. Right now we should watch, support, and learn."

"This isn't just about surveillance, is it?" she asks. "This is about showing her what you're capable of. You want to impress this girl with my invention."

"Dylan and I are working two different angles. He used a lot of vinegar. I plan to use more honey."

"TruGlass isn't a party favor."

"That is not the honey to which I'm referring."

"And if she takes my invention and runs to the press with it?"

"I'll stop her," Cole says. "Quickly."

She taps her fingers on the folder, as if the mere act of opening it now will constitute an unacceptable surrender to Cole's request. "This is giving me a headache. I hate headaches. I'd rather be stabbed in the stomach than have a headache."

"You'd prefer Dylan to be out in the wild on this? On his own? Honestly, I'm not just assessing how we might all benefit from this. I'm also containing it."

"There's nothing connecting any of us to what he's done with this woman. Maybe it should stay that way."

"Or maybe Zypraxon finally works. And this really is what we've been waiting for."

He's got her. He can tell from the long, unbroken stare she gives him.

"I'll give you two pairs," she finally says.

"That's generous." *And unnecessary,* he thinks, *which means there's a catch.*

"One's for her; the other's for Dylan. He's to wear it at all times. The minute he takes it off, I'll blow this whole thing apart."

He knows better than to ask what *blow this whole thing apart* means. He's already relieved she didn't propose another alternative— to wipe the slate clean.

"I'm sure that will be fine," he says.

"Make sure. So we can be confident this isn't a waste of our time."

"I will," he says.

She nods, opens the file on Charlotte Rowe, and stands.

As much as he hates being dismissed like this, his father also taught him that one of the keys to good salesmanship was also one of the keys to good negotiation. Never sell through the close.

"Cole?" Julia calls when he reaches the door.

He gives her his full attention again.

"No matter what this turns into," she says, "make sure Dylan has no exit plan this time."

28

The expansive view from the redwood deck Marty's attached to his trailer relaxes Luke a little, helps him take his first real deep breaths since the moment Charley decided to stop traffic outside the library.

There aren't a lot of houses in the grassy hills on the eastern side of the valley, so he's not used to gazing down at his hometown from this angle. The town below looks like a tiny circuit board floating in a sea of ink, and across the valley, the mountains are coal black. Their peaks, which usually appear gentle and sloping, are etched against the darkening blue of the western sky. At their base, the street he lives on now is a slender fringe of lights.

By the time Marty emerges from the front door of his trailer, promised cup of coffee in hand, Luke's reasonably confident he might be able to form a coherent sentence again. But when he takes the heavy ceramic mug from Marty's grip, his hands shake.

He drinks from it too fast to catch the odor of whatever Marty's spiked it with.

"Whiskey?" Luke asks after a few swallows. "You?"

"Always keep a bottle around to deal with newbies," Marty says. "Big Book of AA recommends it. DTs are a bitch—sometimes there's no other way. And not everyone can afford a fancy detox or rehab. Sometimes they gotta make do with Uncle Marty's sofa."

Love seat's more like it, Luke thinks. He got a glimpse inside the trailer when he used the bathroom earlier. The place is immaculate, not quite as cramped as it seemed from the outside. His own vices have never reduced him to wedging himself onto another man's love seat for a night or two or seven. Not yet anyway. But what are his vices? Anger? Regret? Arrogance? Do those even count? Or should he be more worried about his tortilla chip intake?

Marty leans against the deck rail, pops a piece of gum into his mouth. "Nicotine gum. Quit the smokes five years ago. I'll quit the gum any day now. Promise." He smiles and chews.

"Thank you," Luke says. He's not sure what he's thanking Marty for exactly—the coffee, the spot of whiskey, or for going easier on him now that he's clearly wrecked by the knowledge of what Charlotte can do.

Of what that drug can do, Luke corrects himself, *in Charlotte.*

The truck was the least of it. Watching her kick over a tree with one foot, then pull a fence post the size of a man out of the ground, all in the quiet serenity of a vast, open field and not some crazy science lab, was harder to take. He's not sure why.

He's not quite sure of anything anymore.

Except for one thing.

He's embarrassed to be this beside himself. But if it's transformed Marty from protective dad to nursemaid, that's cool, at least. Cooler than having Marty treat him like some punk out to destroy Charley's life.

He closes his eyes for a minute or two, listens to the poplar trees around the property making sounds like dry hands rubbing together.

"When she showed me what it could do . . . what *she* could do on that stuff, I whizzed myself a little," Marty says.

"I get it."

"No, I mean literally. She and Kayla, her attorney, they were jumping up and down like they're at some campus women's meeting, and I'm sitting there trying to keep more than a few drops from spilling out."

Luke just stares at him.

Marty stares back. When he realizes Marty isn't kidding, he cracks up. Then Marty cracks up, too.

The trailer's front door opens and out steps Dr. Brewerton, who introduced herself to Luke earlier with a handshake twice as strong as his own. Her hair's a salt-and-pepper pageboy cut. Her Ralph Lauren men's dress shirt hugs her stout frame.

"Something funny out here?" she asks.

"Ah-uh. Everything's serious when you're here, Doc," Marty says with a wink.

"Cute." She laces her stethoscope around her neck. "You want to tell me what she took?"

"She didn't *take* anything," Marty says. "She thinks she got slipped something."

"All right, well, I didn't see much evidence of it, to be frank. Her blood pressure's slightly elevated. Heart rate's the same, but not by much. Bruising on her arm looks to be about a week old, so I'm guessing that's not related to whatever she got slipped today?"

Try four hours old, Luke thinks. He stares at the deck floor to keep these thoughts from the good doctor's view.

"No, it's not," Marty says.

"What were her symptoms this afternoon?"

"Racing heart," Marty lies. "Feeling kinda manic, I guess. She said it was like she'd downed a whole pot of coffee in several minutes, but she hadn't had any caffeine all day."

"Exactly the words she used," Dr. Brewerton says.

"Yeah, well, they should be. I'm just quoting her."

"People usually slip women things that slow them down, not speed them up."

"I'm not in the habit of drugging women, so I wouldn't know."

"Marty," the doctor says.

"What?"

"You sponsored me through my divorce from my husband and my marriage to my first wife. You really think you can't trust me with what's going on here?"

"There's not more to this story, Marcia. She was feeling weird, and we just wanted to get her checked out is all."

"All right, well, will you convince her to let me take her blood? That injury to her arm was clearly major. It could have left her with an infection that explains some of her symptoms today."

"So you asked to take her blood and she said no?" Marty asks.

Dr. Brewerton nods.

Because she figures there's a trace of something in her blood Dylan Fuckface and his benefactors won't want the world to see.

"Then there's probably no convincing her." Marty gives the woman a sheepish smile.

With a weary frown, she looks back and forth between the two men, then sighs. "OK. You asked me to see if there was any reason she should be admitted to a hospital, and I'm not seeing one. The symptoms you describe appear to be gone, and nothing about her vitals is alarming. No restricted movement from the injury, either, or from any kind of blockage or stroke. Obviously, I can't do the kind of tests a hospital could, which is why it's always advisable to go to an ER for tachycardia or the like. But that's the best I can do in your trailer."

"Thanks, Marcia."

She nods, grunts, and steps off the porch. As soon as she crosses the bottom step, she stops and turns. "And I'll just say this, gentlemen, and don't feel like you need to say anything back. If you all are seriously worried about her, and you're not taking her to the hospital because you're afraid of whoever did that to her arm, you all are being damn fools. 'Cause there's resources. That's all I'm saying. Good night."

Marty nods. Luke nods. Then they sit there in silence as her Chevy Tahoe pulls out of the driveway and then downhill, toward town.

"How is that possible?" Luke asks.

"How's what possible?"

"Normal blood pressure and heart rate, after what I watched her do all afternoon."

"The miracle of modern pharmaceuticals, I guess." Marty smacks his gum, probably in an effort to draw out more nicotine.

Suddenly a car whisks past the Tahoe, headed in their direction. It's halfway between boxy and streamlined, with slender headlights and a shiny silver paint job, and it's way nicer than most of the vehicles Luke sees around town. By the time it pulls in to the driveway, he can make out the Audi logo on the grill. The stylishly dressed black woman who steps from behind the wheel looks vaguely familiar. Like she might have played a minor role in a TV show he used to watch as a kid.

Charlotte's lawyer. Trina's lawyer, before she became Charley.

He'd monitored the news coverage around her lawsuit, seen footage of them walking in and out of courtrooms together. She looks just as confident and put together now, even though all she's doing is mounting the front steps of Marty's trailer.

She turns her attention to Luke. "You must be the asshole from high school."

"Really?" Luke says. "Still?"

"It's only been a day," Marty says.

"Since *high school*?" Luke asks.

"You know what I mean," Marty says. "Forgive Mr. Prescott's jumpy nerves, Kayla. He got his first show of what Charley's capable of this afternoon."

"So the circle widens." Kayla glares at him. Or maybe it's not a glare. Maybe it's just how she looks at people. People she thinks are assholes.

"Or," Marty offers, "it stays wide because someone's refusing to stay away. I thought Charley called off your background check this afternoon."

"Yeah, well, I figured since I know who's behind this, I should share my thoughts, even though Charlotte's convinced we're all being tracked by drones now."

"I'm listening," Marty says.

"So am I," Luke adds.

"I found a Dylan *Cody* who served in the United States Marine Corps before becoming a Navy SEAL. He was stationed with Seal Team Three out of Coronado, but not for very long."

"Let me guess. He got lured away by something lucrative and more private," Luke says.

"Not quite. He was accepted to Harvard University, where he pursued a concentration in chemical and physical biology before graduating with honors. Then he went on to get his PhD."

"Concentration?" Marty asks. "I thought they were called majors."

"Really?" Luke asks. "That's where your focus goes right now?"

Kayla seems pleased by Luke's remark, which pleases Luke. He's not interested in trying to win somebody else over today.

"What'd he get his PhD in?" Luke asks.

"Neuroscience. Shortly thereafter he was hired by a company called Graydon Pharmaceuticals. Ever heard of them? It doesn't matter. You've probably been prescribed at least two of their drugs in your lifetime."

"I knew a drug company was behind this," Luke says.

"What'd he do there?" Marty asks.

"Nothing," Kayla says, as if she doesn't believe her own answer. "Brilliant guy. Gorgeous. Hired out of Harvard. A veteran of Special Forces. I mean, drug companies are all about marketing, and this one hires Superman in scrubs and then never lets him appear at a public function on Graydon's behalf. You'd think they would've made him the face of something."

"Or he was working on something they didn't want anyone to know about," Luke says.

269

"Sounds about right," Marty adds.

"What about before then?" Luke asks.

"Before Graydon?"

"No, before the marines."

"That's when I got called off," Kayla says. "So what do you think? You think this intel's good enough for a drop-in even though she didn't want me digging?"

"For your own safety," Marty points out.

"That's not why she called you off today," Luke says.

Kayla's eyebrows go up. Marty gives him a similar expression.

"I mean, maybe it's part of it, but it's not the only reason."

If Charley's refusing help from someone this smart and capable, maybe letting Kayla and Marty in on her plans is for her own good.

Yeah, and remember what she did the last time you tried to do something you thought was for her own good?

"I'm listening," Kayla says.

"So am I," Marty adds.

Sorry, Charley.

"She's cutting you out so she doesn't have to tell you what she's planning to do."

A little while later, they're all seated inside Marty's trailer, and Charlotte's looking at him like she wants to punch a hole through his chest the way she did that truck's grill.

Is the three-hour window thing for real, he wonders, or was she just trying to ease his rattled nerves?

At Luke's request, they've powered off their cell phones and placed them inside Marty's mailbox at the mouth of the driveway. A skilled hacker, he explained, could use their handheld devices to listen in on everything they're saying. Kayla didn't disagree, Charlotte didn't have a strong opinion since she was still without a new cell phone, and Marty, whose bookshelf includes titles like *Alien Conspiracy*, *Secrets of the Trilateral Commission*, and *Loch Ness Unchained*, already had a little piece of paper taped over the camera on his desktop computer. He still shut the thing down and powered off his Wi-Fi network as well.

"I don't get it," Marty says for the second time. He's leaning against the kitchen counter, arms crossed over his chest, nicotine gum forgotten in one corner of his mouth.

Is he acting dumb? Maybe he's just in shock. Charley couldn't have been any clearer.

"What's not to get?" Kayla asks. She's on one end of the love seat, bent elbow braced against the arm, resting her face in her open palm as if it's the only thing keeping her head from falling apart.

"The plan," Marty says. "What's the plan? I mean, it's one thing to want to go after this guy. But how are you going to find him?"

"That's your brother's job, right?" Kayla asks Luke.

"You think your brother's going to be able to find out who's killed those women with just a few keystrokes?" Marty asks.

"No, I don't," he answers.

"And why not?" He's touched ice blocks warmer than Charley's voice.

"He's good, but he's not that good."

"Says who?" Charley asks.

"Says me."

"He found a white-collar criminal living under an assumed name in Australia and he hacked a satellite to do it."

"Fundamentally, he knew who he was looking for," Luke responded, "and he exploited a back door in a telecommunications company, a back door the company has since publicly acknowledged and closed."

"Sounds pretty skilled to me," Kayla says.

"Everything about this is different. Back then, he had his target's height, weight, everything about his mannerisms, physical appearance, and tics. It may sound irrelevant, but that's all pivotal in a hack because it allows you to predict what passwords they pick, how they might try to move money. Possible aliases."

"Who's the expert in hacking again?" Marty asks.

"I looked into it some because I wanted to know how my brother had destroyed his life."

"You don't know he's destroyed his life," Marty says. "He could be in Tahiti covered in swimsuit models right now."

"Yeah, 'cause he was always a big hit with swimsuit models. The point is, the only way Bailey's been able to pull off something like this is when he had a body of knowledge about a specific individual. He doesn't have that here. He's got a ghost, just like the cops. Whatever methods he does use to try to find the Mask Maker, there's no reason to believe they'll be any better than what LAPD's using right now."

"They could be faster," Kayla says, "given that he won't have to deal with warrants and all."

"The best he'll be able to do is hack LAPD and get you as much of the case file as he can. Maybe the BSU profile on the guy if there is one."

"Well, that's super illegal," Kayla mutters, but she's staring at the floor vacantly, as if strict concepts of legality don't mean as much to her as they did the day before but she's still obligated to reference them now and then.

"BSU?" Marty asks.

"Behavioral Science Unit of the FBI," Kayla says. "They deal with serial killers."

"They *try* to deal with serial killers," Charley says.

"What does that mean?" Luke asks.

"It means two agents from BSU probably flew to LA on the taxpayer's dime and spent a few days in their hotel rooms using trendy pop psychology to write some superficial 'profile'"—she mimes air quotes—"based on a shallow reading of the crime scenes. Now the local cops are leaning on that profile instead of doing their jobs, which is actually investigating the evidence they have. In the process, they'll eliminate way too many potential suspects so they can trim their workload and the 'profile'"—she fires off another set of air quotes—"will give them permission to do it."

"That's a lot of air quotes there, Trigger," Marty says.

"And a pretty rash dismissal of an esteemed unit of the FBI," Luke says.

"Really?" Charley asks. "*You're* going to start defending the FBI?"

"Look, I get it. You're mad at me for telling them you want to—"

"No, I'm sick of people getting tingly over BSU because of Clarice Starling, OK? Have any of you ever read the FBI profile of the Bannings? A crystal ball would have been more help."

"I heard they used those, too," Kayla says.

"Charley," Luke says, "FBI profiling is a very valid—"

"The profile ruled out all women, for Christ's sake. It was a female serial killer."

"To be fair, she was working in conjunction with a male sexual predator, who connected up with many of the points made in the profile," Luke says.

"And he wasn't committing the murders. *She* was. And by ruling out all women, the profile blinded the local cops to something they should have seen before."

"Which was what?" Kayla asks.

"There were no signs of struggle at most of the abduction sites because the victims, mostly women traveling alone, trusted their abductor. More than they would have trusted any lone man traveling on a back road or hiking through the woods. And they trusted him because he had a *woman* with him. If the profile had been right, and Daniel Banning, or some sick freak just like him, was acting alone, there's a chance my mother never would have rolled down her car window so fast."

"You don't know that, Charley," Marty says. "Come on. She had a flat tire in the middle of nowhere, and she was with a baby. She needed any help she could get."

"And what about the two girls they beat in their motel room?" Kayla asks.

"Yeah, you mean the ones who didn't think twice about telling the Bannings which cabin they were staying in because a woman was asking?"

Luke thinks Charley might be fighting tears, but he can't tell. She's like a different person now, and it's been that way ever since she showed him what she could do. Surly and embarrassed, as if he's seen her naked and she didn't want him to.

She didn't *want you to see what she could do, genius. You forced her to show you when you tried to call Mona.*

"The Bannings were an exceptional case," he says. "By any standards."

"So's the Mask Maker," Charley says. "And I don't need an FBI profile to find him."

"Well, good, because I think it's the best Bailey's gonna be able to do. That and the case files from LAPD."

"Fine," she says.

Luke knows he should take a breath. Maybe a few. At his house. With a beer. But instead he hears himself say, "What do you mean, *fine*? I mean, what does that even mean here?" He sounds like he used to when he was eight years old and his mother told him he couldn't have a third Coca-Cola.

Only when he sees the way everyone's staring at him does he realize he's shot to his feet.

"Yes, Luke. Fine. If that's all Bailey can get, I will find the guy on my own. Alone, if I have to."

"And then what?" Marty asks. "You gonna burst through the walls of his house like the Kool-Aid Man, or Kool-Aid Girl, or whatever?"

Kayla says, "Shut up, Marty."

"It's a good question," Luke says.

"I don't disagree," Kayla responds.

"She just likes telling me to shut up," Marty says.

"The answer's no," Charley says. "I am not going to burst through his walls like the Kool-Aid Man."

"What are you going to do?" Luke asks.

"I'm going to make sure he never kills again."

"How?" Luke says with such anger in his voice it makes something wild dance in Charley's eyes.

So she has a plan, he realizes. She's not flying blind, with desperation as her driving wind. She knows exactly what she wants to do; she doesn't think he can handle it.

"Oh my God," Kayla says softly. "You're gonna do it just like the bar, aren't you? You're gonna bait the guy. You're gonna try to get him to take you, just like one of his victims."

Charley's answer is in her silence.

"You're out of your fucking mind," Luke says.

"And you're free to go at any time."

"Oh yeah? Now that you've got my brother working for you."

"Give me a break. He agreed to help me because he wanted to. You didn't talk him into anything."

"And you could be sending him after these people, not using him to work with them."

"I am not working *with* these people. And if you really think your brother, by himself, is going to be able to take on a corporation the size of Graydon Pharmaceuticals and whoever they can afford to hire, you're the crazy one."

She gets to her feet and moves into the tiny kitchen. Marty steps out of her way, riveted, it seems, by the confrontation building before him.

"This is just crazy, and desperate. You've got no idea what you're doing or why you're doing it."

"Oh, really? I thought you knew exactly what I was doing. I'm out to prove to the world I'm not a serial killer. Still! Wasn't that what you said back at the library?"

"That's not what I—"

"It *is* what you said. It's exactly what you said. And if you didn't mean it, maybe you're the desperate one right now. What happened to the guy who wanted to help me no matter what?"

"He's still trying."

"Oh, bullshit. You're freaking out because you can't handle what I can do. I never should have told you or shown you any of it."

"You're not doing anything, Charlotte. The drug is doing it. *Dylan's* drug is doing it. And you're choosing to take it again for reasons that are certifiably insane. Am I the only who feels the need to weigh in here?"

"*Weighing in* is what we're calling this?" Kayla asks.

"All right, fine, so it's gonna be all about my tone then! Or how I'm not saying it in the right way."

Charley answers by turning her back on him and opening the refrigerator door. Is she actually looking for something inside or is it just an act?

"So tell me, Charley. Trina. Whatever it is. Tell me why you're going after the Mask Maker."

She slams the refrigerator door shut with enough force to shake the trailer. Luke can feel the pulse of terror that moves through all three of them, the fear that maybe the drug isn't out of her system, or maybe this is some new episode. Charley either doesn't notice or she doesn't care.

"Because I want to. That's why. Because if these people are going to force me to be their guinea pig, then by God, I'm going to use what they've given me the way I want. I'm gonna find the man who did that to those women, and I'm gonna look right into his eyes when he realizes that I am the end of him. And I will not spend another second justifying that to some prick who's on an apology tour because his life has hit the skids and he's just now realizing he's too big of an asshole to make any friends."

Marty winces.

Kayla swallows.

Her words strike a blow to his gut, and the pain that radiates outward, while phantom and fleeting, fills him with a bewildering urge. It feels almost like a craving, this acute desire to return to that moment in his Jeep when he reached for her because he thought she was about to lose it, the moment when his hand made it no farther than the gearshift before she rested hers atop it.

Why would he think of that moment now, when her words have slugged him this hard? It's like his brain's convinced there's something he can squeeze from the memory and apply to his wounds like a balm.

Oh, shit, dude, he thinks. *Oh, shit.* He's familiar with this voice in his head, the voice that warns him away from serious risks. The voice that sounds just like his freshman-year roommate, Reggie, who had a particular, steady way of pointing out when things were about to go seriously off the rails. Like when he realized the hot girl visiting their room was about to turn psycho, or the coffee they'd been drinking out of the bottom of the pot had been sitting there for days. *Oh, shit, dude. You are totally falling for—*

The words fly from him before Reggie's voice can finish his sentence.

"Well, shit. You didn't just rent Dylan a space in your head. You bought him a house there. Good luck with your treatment, Burning Girl."

"Get out."

"Works for me," he answers. But there's a tremor in his voice. Kayla cocks her head to one side, sympathy flashing in her eyes. "Don't worry. I'll keep all your crazy secrets. And if Bailey doesn't find a way to get in touch with you himself, I'll let you know. If, you know, you're not off hunting terrorists by then because it's what you *want*."

He's moving so fast he's startled by the sound of his own footsteps punching the wooden steps out front. Startled to suddenly be speeding downhill toward the valley, holding the steering wheel in a white-knuckled grip.

He keeps swallowing, but nothing gets rid of the lump in his throat. And that look Kayla gave him, the one that seemed surprised by the level of emotion in his voice, replays on a loop inside his mind.

He can feel the cold, analytical parts brushing off their spectacles and preparing to lecture him the way he just tried to lecture Charlotte. Preparing to explain away his bewildering mixture of hurt and embarrassment, his acute sense of rejection.

On the one hand, it's probably shock. Some people—*most* people—would have full-on lost their minds once they saw what that drug can do. So all things considered, maybe he's doing pretty well, thank you. And who'd be surprised to learn that one afternoon of friendly conversation and criminal conspiracy wasn't enough to put all the years of ill will between him and Charlotte at bay?

But there'd been a moment back there on the porch, after he'd managed to steady his hands, around the time he and Marty had started to shoot the shit, when he'd felt more settled inside his own skin than he'd been for weeks. Months, even. When he'd felt like a part of something. Included.

Well, that's gone now, isn't it?

Get out, she'd said to him.

Can't get any clearer than that.

Yeah, and she said it because you jumped down her throat, lectured her, and then, when she disagreed, you told her how to think.

And those final words. God, they hurt.

They hurt because she is right.

He doesn't have any friends, and he's not sure how to make any. This only became clear to him once he was separated from his ambitions. Scratch that. This only became a problem once he was separated from his ambitions.

There've been times since he returned to Altamira when his loneliness has felt like a weight on his chest. He knows it's too heavy to remove on his own, but on most days, he's too proud to ask for help. So he lies to himself and says tomorrow will be the day. Tomorrow will be the day he'll go someplace and just sit and see who talks to him first and hope that the first stirrings of chitchat with a stranger might reveal the seeds of a new life. A new life with new friends, and a new vision for his future he can be proud of.

And she could see all this, of course.

Maybe because he'd told her things about himself.

Or maybe because he wore this truth about himself like clothes.

Or maybe because she'd always been able to see these types of things about people.

Isn't that part of why he'd been such a dick to her back in high school? Why he'd fixated on her? Because what she'd been through had taught her things about the world most teenagers didn't know. Or if they did know them, the knowledge had put them in a mental hospital. The fact is, even at sixteen, Trina Pierce / Burning Girl / Charlotte Rowe had been the type of person who could see through your bullshit, your poses. And that had made her scary and threatening. And also special. Remarkable.

Back then he'd chosen fear. Fear and cruelty.

But ever since then, he'd felt himself tilting in the other direction.

Now he's wobbling back and forth between the two like a metronome, and all he wants is his own shitty sofa in his own shitty house with a less than shitty beer.

He's turning into his driveway when his old roommate's warning voice speaks up again.

Uh-oh, dude. You're totally into her, and you probably always have been.

29

After Luke leaves them in stilted silence, Marty says, "This is my fault."

"It's not your fault," Charley answers.

"If I hadn't made you go see him—"

"You didn't make me. You wanted to check him out; that's all. I'm the one who wanted to see him."

Because I thought you were full of it, she thinks.

"So," Kayla interjects, "you think he'll really be able to keep all this a secret?"

"Will you?" Charley asks.

"Attorney-client privilege." Her smile is strained.

"Seriously, though?" Charley asks.

Kayla clears her throat, studies the ceiling while she works her jaw. Charley's seen her perform this trio of movements before; it's her usual routine when she's trying to collect thoughts she doesn't like.

"Well, considering you haven't made me aware of any intention to commit a crime—"

"The hacking doesn't count?" Marty asks.

"She's not doing any hacking," Kayla answers. "She simply asked someone with a history of hacking to find someone for her. That's all."

"Not just someone." Charlotte feels guilty Kayla's resorting to verbal acrobatics to defend her. In fact, she'll feel guilty if Kayla stays here much longer.

"True," Kayla says. "So I guess what it comes down to are the specifics of what you're going to do to this guy once you find him."

"You heard her," Marty says. "She's going to stop him from killing."

"Yeah, I heard her, and it's vague."

"Well," Charley says, "maybe when it comes to you, I should keep it that way."

"Suit yourself." Kayla gets to her feet. She reaches into her brief-case and hands Charley a slender manila folder. "That's everything I found on Graydon and Dylan Cody before you told me to stop. Most of it's public. Some of it took a little digging. Do what you will with it."

She's pissed; Charley can tell.

"Kayla, there's only one person in my life who's done better by me than you, and that's my grandmother. I can't drag you into the middle of this. If you lost your career, I'd never forgive myself."

She nods, studies Charley's face for a bit, her eyes unreadable. "That's fair, I guess." She surprises Charlotte with a strong, quick hug. "You know where I am if you need me."

So do they, Charlotte thinks, the pit of her stomach going cold as Kayla pulls away.

Her lawyer's got one foot out the door when Charlotte calls to her. "Do you think I'm crazy?"

"No," she answers. "I think this whole thing's crazy, and you're just adapting. 'Night, guys."

"I'm gonna miss you, Mothra," Marty says.

It takes Charlotte a second to remember Marty's comment from the night before, the one comparing him and Kayla to Godzilla and Mothra.

"Huh?" Kayla asks.

"Ignore him," Charlotte says.

Kayla takes her advice.

A minute or two later, they're listening to her car leave the drive-way as Charlotte rifles through the contents of the file.

Her attention catches on a color printout of some magazine pro-file of Graydon's CEO, probably because it has the most photos. The man in question is seated on the edge of a sofa in a sprawling office that's all glass, steel, sunlight, and cream-colored upholstery. His blazing-blue eyes practically bore a hole in the paper. The rest of his face is a collection of bones so sharp it looks like a peck on the cheek from him could draw blood. No suit and tie for this billionaire. But he doesn't look like a scooter-riding tech mogul, either. Rather, his powder-blue dress shirt, the top three buttons undone over a hairless chest, along with his black designer jeans, make him look like a dad just home from the law firm on a network television show.

Cole Graydon's his name, and the first few paragraphs of the article make it clear he inherited the company from his late father. No mention of the fact that he looks so tightly wound his head might pop off at any second and go spinning across the floor. Maybe it's just the picture. Or maybe not. Charlotte recognizes the look; it's been hers for years.

"Luke won't blab about any of this." Marty's started reading over her shoulder. "Not with his brother in the middle of it now."

"Here's hoping."

He uses his fingertips to slide the papers she's not reading out from under the magazine article.

"And what about you?" she asks.

"What about me, darlin'?"

"Do you want out of this?"

"So your grandmother can rise up out of the grave and wring my neck? No, thanks."

"She was cremated."

"Fine. Tear me apart on the wind, then."

"Seriously, Marty."

"When'd you get this idea in your head that you're some kind of burden to me? Never mind. Don't answer that, 'cause I don't care. Let's just get it out. Let's just reach in there with whatever it takes and get that thought off your mind for good."

She studies his face, looking for signs of doubt. Instead she finds a warm, sincere smile that softens her chest. He opens his arms; she steps into them. And for a while she just leans into the embrace.

"Marty, do you think I was too hard on him?"

"He was out of line. He doesn't know you well enough to say all that shit. And when he called you Burning Girl, I almost knocked his teeth out."

"Still."

He kisses her on the forehead, takes a step back, but doesn't release her shoulders. "You got enough on your plate right now without having to worry about Luke Prescott."

"Right," she answers, but she's not sure she's convinced.

"Speaking of which . . . What do we do now, just wait for Bailey to get back to us?"

"Pretty much. And pray that Dylan and his friends let us."

He nods, turns to the fridge. "Got you a sandwich from the Copper Pot. You hungry?"

"I'll eat it later."

"OK. Try to get some rest, Charley. I know Marcia didn't find anything wrong with you, but I don't figure wearing yourself out while you're taking this stuff is gonna be a good idea."

She nods.

But she doesn't rest.

Nightmares aren't her problem. They never have been. She suffers from a different kind of nocturnal affliction.

Sometimes, like tonight, right when she's about to nod off, some horrifying image blazes big as a drive-in movie screen in her mind, and the end result leaves her feeling like she's been snatched back from the edge of sleep by a giant claw. Sometimes it's a detail from one of Abigail's murders, committed just a few yards from where she was probably filling in a coloring book with crayons at the time.

And sometimes it's Abigail, clawing her way through a window, gripping the blade of her bowie knife in her teeth, her thick golden hair fanned out around her head like a lion's mane. Other times her kidnapper waits patiently on the living room sofa, or hides behind the shower curtain, or tucks herself into the kitchen's deepest pool of shadow.

They're brief, these images, but when they come, they're powerful enough to leave her awake and pacing the house for the next few hours. What saves her from them now is Marty's trailer; it's new and unfamiliar. Nothing inside this tiny guest bedroom—a glorified train compartment, really—reminds her of old abductors or old night terrors.

Instead she keeps seeing Luke.

She sees the hurt in his eyes before he steeled himself with anger and stormed out the door. Then she remembers his parting shot, his accusation that she was caving in to Dylan's plans and not resisting them, and her anger shoots through the veins of her guilt like ice. Then, as sleep starts to tug at her again, the thaw begins, and the process repeats itself.

Hurt, rage, thaw. Hurt, rage, thaw.

Marty's right. Luke doesn't know her well enough to see inside her mind, to peek into her soul. If he's right—even if this new plan means she's giving in to Dylan's deceit—he's not the one to make that call.

Enough of this debate.

She swings her feet to the floor, pads into the kitchen, and makes short work of the sandwich Marty saved for her. He's sawing logs in his bedroom, which can mean only one thing. A peek out the nearest window confirms it. Two of Marty's buddies are standing watch. Sitting watch is more like it. They're in a dark pickup truck in the driveway. Beneath the cloudless, star-filled sky, with the town twinkling below, they look like a moody California postcard.

She pulls some sodas from the fridge, drops them in a recyclable grocery bag she finds under the sink—two diet, two regular, just in case either guy's watching his sugar intake.

When she knocks on the roof of the car, they both jump.

She's surprised to find them awake and talking. The dashboard clock says it's almost 2:00 a.m. After she shows them what's in the bag, they step from the truck, introduce themselves with wide-eyed looks and tentative handshakes, taking the sodas like they're unexpected offerings from a queen.

The wiry, balding one's named Dale. He's got dense tattoos peeking out from the sleeves of his AC/DC T-shirt. His partner, for the night at least, is named Lonnie. He's older, but at first he doesn't look it because he sports a mane of gray hair that's not quite as healthy and full as Marty's, but almost. The guy smells so strongly of cigarettes, Charlotte feels like she just took a puff of one. She knows a bunch of Marty's crew, but these guys are newbies. She's not sure if that means they're newly sober or just new to the area. The thought that Marty might feel compelled to enlist the aid of AA members who are closer to their checkered pasts than he is makes her stomach knot.

For a while they just talk in the darkness. They sip their sodas hesitantly, give her looks both wary and curious that would probably make her uncomfortable in broad daylight. It's empty chitchat, for the most part. About their lives. Where they lived before Altamira (Dale, Saint Louis; Lonnie, San Diego, Indio, and West Covina). For the most part, they don't touch on the big stuff. The heavy stuff. Like whether or not they're sober, and if they are, for how long. But the talk, idle as it is, soothes her, and the deference they show her doesn't feel half-bad, either.

By the time she's bid them good night and is heading back to the trailer, she's thinking about how many conversations she's had just like that her entire life. Conversations with folks who already know her story but are trying not to let it show. She always tries to do her best during those talks; meaning she tries not to twitch or say anything neurotic, or psychotic, or even forlorn. She always tries to look, for lack of a better word, healthy. Well. And even with everything that's going on now, she reverted right back to form with Dale and Lonnie. Big smiles, safe, polite questions. Some of it fueled by genuine curiosity, most of it driven by a desire to appear stable and sane in the eyes of two men she doesn't know.

Good luck with your treatment, Burning Girl.

The second she steps back inside, Luke's words slap her across the face. Maybe because she's standing in roughly the same place she was when he spoke them.

There's a rustling off to her left. Blinking back sleep and holding one of the biggest guns she's ever seen, Marty emerges from the bedroom, hiking up his jeans with his non-gun hand.

"You OK?" he grumbles.

"Fine. Just bringing the guys some sodas."

Marty nods, gives her a thumbs-up. Draws his bedroom door gently shut behind him, leaving her once again with other men's voices ringing in her head.

First Dylan. Now Luke.

Well, if she's being technical about it, first Luke, then Dylan, then a second version of Luke, who claimed to be better than the first Luke. But in the end, they're both men who barged their way into her head, insisting they know her better than she knows herself. Trying, she suspects, to bend her behavior to suit their own fears. She knows what makes Luke tick, or at least she's pretty sure. For now Dylan remains a mystery, and she's afraid if she learns too much, she'll start making excuses for the bastard. Because sometimes that's easier than admitting you've been betrayed.

There's only one way to keep the voices of both men from hijacking her every other thought. She has to make sure her own voice is louder. In her mind, at least. And she can think of only one way to do that right now.

In a corner of the living room, there's a compact desk Marty's turned into an office area. It's just a square piece of wood attached to the wall that folds up almost like a Murphy bed. Underneath it are some file boxes he's pushed into a crazy arrangement that must give his legs some room to move. It's more than enough for her. In the desk drawer she looks for some paper. She's pleasantly surprised to find a couple of Mead college-ruled notebooks, one of which is completely blank.

When she opens the cover to the first blank page, the impetus to turn her thoughts into ink gets lodged somewhere just above her wrist.

The reason she's never kept a journal is because she grew up terrified her father would find it and publish it somehow. By the time she moved in with Luanne, this fear had spoiled the act forever. Privacy, she was convinced, existed only inside her head. Diaries were for normal girls.

But now her need to tell her own story is stronger than it's ever been. Maybe because Luke tried to force his own definition of that story on her, and Dylan's trying to bend it to an ending he's designed.

The memories overwhelm her now.

Where does she begin?

Maybe with the road trip she took after she won the settlement from her father.

It wasn't exactly a restful vacation. After the victory, and after she'd staked out a little town in Arizona as her new home, she'd driven to the grave sites of every Banning victim who'd died on the farm while she was there, including her own mother.

If she couldn't find out what the victim's favorite flower was, she brought them white roses, and she sat with each of them for a good, long while, as if her new name, her new identity, gave her the space and the quiet to grieve them the way they deserved. They were all from the South, either tourists who'd unwittingly wandered into the Bannings' hunting ground in the Chattahoochee National Forest or, like her mother, were on their way to visit family in a nearby city or town like Atlanta, Chattanooga, or Asheville.

She started in New Orleans, with Cassie Murdoch and Jane Blaire, best friends buried together in one of those aboveground tombs so popular in the city. Cassie loved yellow roses; Jane was a big fan of peonies. She left them a little vase of each.

Then she headed due east, to Pensacola and the grave of Jennifer Albright, a flight attendant from Augusta, Georgia. If the *Dateline* special was to be believed, the fiancé Jennifer left behind ended up being a wonderful father to her two kids from her first marriage, but he didn't respond to any of Charlotte's e-mails about Jennifer's favorite flower, so she got white roses. She shouldn't have been surprised by his silence. The families of the victims had always resented her father for the *Savage Woods* films. She'd hoped the lawsuit she'd won against him might change their opinion of her, but maybe they just saw it as her own grab for profits, and not an attempt to break free and build her own life.

Next stop, Knoxville, Tennessee, and the grave of Emily Connolly, a CPA who'd decided to take the scenic route to Gainesville, Georgia, for her first meeting with a man she'd been chatting with online. When she never showed up, the man she was scheduled to meet, Zach Pike, remained a suspect in her disappearance up until her body was unearthed on the Bannings' farm. Charlotte and Zach had traded e-mails over the years—no surprise, given that in her own way she was also wrongly accused, by Hollywood, if not law enforcement—and that's how she knew Emily liked tulips.

Next stop, Atlanta. Her mother's grave, which she'd visited countless times before, but since it was on the way to her last stop, she brought her another vase of stargazer lilies.

Lilah Turlington and her boyfriend, Eddie Stevens, were the only mixed-gender couple the Bannings killed, but that's not why Charlotte saved them for last. They were both buried in Asheville, North Carolina, and unless she wanted to go out of her way by several days, the drive there would take her closer to the "Murder Farm," as the press had dubbed it, than she'd been since her rescue at age seven.

She remembers the drive now.

The mountains, low, rolling, and green, gentler and more inviting than the coastal peaks near Altamira. But within the seductive folds of their threadlike valleys, a place of nightmares had endured and thrived.

She knew the farm's main house was still standing, but the root cellar, where the victims had been held captive and raped, had been dragged from its foundation by the FBI during their search for buried bodies.

The house was a near ruin, of course, but dark-hearted hikers regularly posted pictures of it online, pictures in which they posed with serious expressions next to crumbling walls pockmarked with satanic graffiti. The owners of the neighboring pig farm bought the land after the investigation was concluded, and while they claimed publicly they were repulsed by all the attention, the rumor was they'd give you a guided hike to the place for a small, under-the-table donation. Her father had told her years before the only reason they hadn't shot the *Savage Woods* films there was because the new owners had demanded an exorbitant fee, a fact he'd relayed with a shake of the head, as if they were just bad businesspeople and not greedy profiteers.

It wasn't quite the stuff of horror movies. It was the stuff of people who, for whatever reason, thought it would be cool to live in one.

The temptation to visit the place, if only to demystify it in her mind, plagued her for most of the drive to Asheville. But she knew she wasn't up to such a visit alone. She never would be. Still, the urge was strong as thirst on a hot day.

She remembers how hard she gripped the steering wheel for that last leg of the journey. How she forced herself to stare at the winding highway ahead. How she kept the windows rolled down just a little so the wind could make a sound like a flag flapping on the prow of a speeding ship. A sound that drove out her thoughts.

Lilah Turlington's favorite flower had been the calla lily. Charlotte had no trouble finding some as soon as she got to Asheville.

When she finally reached the grave site, Lilah's story weighed more heavily on her than the others. Maybe because before her murder, Lilah Turlington, born Lisa Hilliard, had accomplished what she, Trina Pierce, now Charlotte Rowe, was just setting out to do. She had escaped her past, made a new life for herself.

The black sheep of her wealthy family, she'd changed her name after graduating from Bowdoin and moving to Asheville, probably so her new crystal-selling, Reiki-massage-practicing hippie friends wouldn't know she was descended from a family that built and managed some of the largest oil and natural gas pipelines in North and Central America. While they weren't married, she and Eddie were raising Lilah's son together; he was only two years old when they left him with friends before going camping and met the Bannings on the Appalachian Trail.

If Lilah knew the identity of her son's birth father, she never let anyone know. After her disappearance was reported, her older brother, who at that time was poised to become chief executive officer of the evil empire Lilah had fled, took custody of her son and whisked him out of the country. Either to Canada or Mexico, no one in the press was ever sure. Morton-Hilliard Corp. had projects in both countries, and a press office capable of managing far more complex scandals than a missing hippy-dippy backpacker who might have abandoned her son.

Charlotte had always envied Lilah's little boy. Envied what she saw as his fairy-tale ending: the wealthy family whisking him off to a foreign country, protecting him from the dark repercussions of the tragedy that had befallen his mother. So different from what her father had done for her.

But it wasn't until that sunny afternoon, sitting on a stone bench beneath the branches of an oak tree in an Asheville cemetery, that she'd realized it was Lilah Turlington who'd given her the idea to remake herself. That by turning toward her heart and away from her family's money all those years ago, Lilah had planted a seed of hope in the mind of Trina Pierce, and the bloom was Charlotte Rowe.

Maybe this is why she's never kept a journal. By the time she felt comfortable enough to begin, there was too much damn material to know where to start.

Now it comes to her all at once.

The sight of the pen in her frozen hand, which she's been staring at now for who knows how long, confirms it. But she hasn't wedged herself into this corner of Marty's trailer to write her memoirs, only to find her voice. She's got no plan for whatever ends up on these pages.

This is for her and only her—something between a letter and a prayer.

So she can't begin with Lilah, or that cemetery in Asheville. She has to begin with the precise moment her nightmare began.

They didn't plan to kill my mother, she writes. *She wasn't like the others, the ones they stalked and captured.*

By the time the sun starts to outline the bottom of the window shade next to her, she's still writing.

30

"Who's bored?" Mona Sanchez shouts from her office.

Luke looks up from his desk. Peter Henricks, the only other deputy at the station, is tentatively raising the hand he's not using to refill his coffee mug.

Judy Lyle, who's both reception and dispatch, swivels in her desk chair and glares at Mona's open office door as if a polka band just started up a set inside; it's an expression that doesn't quite match the Pepto-pink sweater she's tied around her neck and draped over her back like a cape. Like many of Altamira's senior residents, Judy's a woman of stark contrasts, the kind who reads syrupy-sweet romance novels before bed but curses like a drunk sailor the minute someone cuts her off in traffic. Luke's a fan.

As for Peter, his best quality, as far as Luke's concerned, is how quickly he volunteers for crappy assignments, and Luke's pretty sure that's exactly what this random question of Mona's is shaping up to be. One seriously crappy assignment.

Reach for the stars, Henricks. Come on. I'm rooting for ya!

It's not like Luke's silence is a lie. *Boredom* isn't quite the word he'd use to describe his current mood, or any of the moods he's suffered since he stormed out on Charley two days before. *Defeat. Despair. Angst.* Those are more appropriate. That said, the only real excitement in his life since then has been talking Stanley Morrison's wife out of running over his skis with her truck because she caught him texting an old girlfriend. So if they're being entirely truthful, maybe he should raise his hand, too.

But what does he know about things like honesty and truthfulness? He's just an asshole who can't make friends. According, at least, to a woman he was trying to keep from getting killed by a madman.

When nobody answers out loud, Mona appears in the doorway to her office. "Seriously, who wants to venture a guess as to why a pharmaceutical company's buying the old resort?"

"What?" Luke shoots to his feet, all eyes on him suddenly.

Well, that was smooth, hotshot.

"You have strong feelings about this, I take it?" Mona asks.

"Which one?"

"There's only one resort anywhere near here, and it's not finished."

"Which drug company?"

"Graydon. Ever heard of 'em?"

Don't answer, and don't mess yourself.

"That's crazy," he says. "I mean, why would a drug company want the resort?"

"I believe I just asked that question."

"It's still nuts."

"And you're jumping in your pants about this why? Did you have an offer in on the place?"

"How'd you find out about this?"

"Mayor's office called. Says they're working up a press release. Graydon's paid off all of Silver Shore's debt. They're gonna partner with them on the whole deal, it looks like. They're even going to retain the same lobbying firm that was trying to get the state to widen 293."

"Well, that's gonna suck." Judy Lyle swivels back to her desk. "How many trees are gonna have to die for that?"

"Says the woman with a job and health insurance," Peter Henricks grumbles.

"So I take it nobody's got an answer," Mona says. "Just a bunch of feelings, it sounds like."

"I can try to find one for you if you like."

The words are out of his mouth before he can think twice. It's a strange offer, and Mona's stare makes that clear.

"An answer, I mean," Luke adds.

"I take it Stanley Morrison isn't filing assault charges?"

"On behalf of his water skis? Give me a break."

"Well, I gave you a job actually, so I figure we're square in that department."

"Sorry. That was out of line."

He better cool it if this is going to work.

What he wants is an excuse to get out of the station.

What he wants is an excuse to talk to Charley again, and this is most certainly it.

Of course, he could always just apologize. Which he knows he'll end up doing if he goes and talks to her. But he'd like to arrive with his hat on, and then remove it at the moment of his choosing. What's the matter with feeling useful while you're being forced to eat crow?

"You're just going to talk to people around town?" Mona asks.

"Well, they're not buying it sight unseen, so they must have been poking around before now. I'll find out if anyone strange has been around recently."

"Stranger than you, you mean?" Judy asks.

He gives her a frosty look, which she returns with a coy smile.

"Maybe I'll check in with some of the folks who, uh, we thought might be paying visits to the old place. See if they've seen any other activity."

"The social justice looters, you mean? You think they'd tell you if they had?"

"I think I can get you a pretty clear picture of what's been going on out there."

"All right. Just go. I can tell you're antsy. When you're done, finish up with some patrols; then radio in."

He grabs his hat and windbreaker off his desk.

A thought strikes him at the door and he spins.

"Mona!"

"Sheriff," she says quietly when she reappears at her office door.

"Sorry. Sheriff. What are they gonna do with it?"

"Apparently Graydon's getting in to the leisure business. The company's got a venture capital arm that stashes their money in different places. But this is the first time they've done anything with a hotel. So the plan's the same as it ever was. Turn it into a resort. If it's real, it could be great for the town. So find out if it is."

He nods. As he turns to go, he hears Judy say, "Maybe they'll leave an antidepressant on everybody's pillow at turndown."

Marty's truck isn't parked in front of his trailer, but he recognizes the guy sitting on Marty's steps as one of the crew he threatened to run a few days before. With the surliness of a teenager whose parents have taken his smartphone away, the guy tells him Marty's shuttling back and forth between job sites. When Luke asks him about Charley, he goes quiet.

How much does the guy know, Luke wonders, besides the fact that Marty ordered him to watch over his home for the day?

As worry knits his expression, the guy stares past Luke, and that says his worry's got nothing to do with Luke and everything to do with the subject of the question.

"She went off on her own, didn't she? And Marty told you not to let her."

"Something like that," the guy grumbles. "She went up to the lake. Said she'd only be gone for a half hour."

"How long's it been?"

"Twenty minutes."

"What's she driving?"

"My Camaro."

Lake Patrick is a quarter of the size of Nacimiento to the south, and it's hardly a tourist destination even on the weekends, so he's not surprised to see the guy's battered white Camaro is the only car in the parking lot next to the boat launch on a Monday. And he's not surprised to see Charley walking the narrow crescent of gravelly beach, which, like the lake itself, seems to appear out of nowhere amid the tinder-dry golden hills.

At the sound of his cruiser, she looks up, drops the stick she's holding in her hand.

Only now does he realize how little real shelter his last-minute mission gives him. When their eyes meet, all the anger and embarrassment of their fight comes rushing back. She looks better, more well rested. But it also looks like her new store of energy has allowed her to retreat deeper inside herself after applying a thicker skin.

"Hey," he says.

The same thing he said to her when he almost touched her in a sudden, unplanned way.

It wasn't intentional, but she blinks and looks to the sand. Is she trying to avoid that little memory, too?

All things considered, *hey* is a pretty hard word to avoid, and if they actually end up speaking to each other again, maybe they'll have to agree to just let that little moment between them go.

Or maybe he's reading too much into this, into her. Maybe that little moment meant far more to him than it did to her.

"So I have some news," he says.

"I'm listening."

"It's not Bailey. I haven't heard anything from him yet."

"OK."

"It's Graydon. They're buying the resort."

She's so startled she seems to forget the tension between them.

"For what?" she asks.

He repeats what Mona told him moments before, putting special emphasis on the detail about the mayor's office, because that makes the whole thing seem more real.

She doesn't say anything for a while. Just stares out at the placid black water reflecting the few strands of cloud overhead. She's pondering this news in some faraway place in her head, but she hasn't asked him to leave, so maybe she'll invite him to join her there in another second or two.

"Thanks," she finally says, then turns her back to him and picks up her stick again.

"Thanks?"

"Yes. Thank you for bringing me this information. It's very helpful. I will be resuming my *treatment* now." She drags the stick through the gravel and sand at her feet.

"Oh, don't be a . . ."

"A what? A woman who can remember two days ago?"

"Did it ever occur to you I might be afraid of you getting hurt?" he asks.

"Did it occur to *you* before you said all those shitty things to me?" she asks.

There's some method to whatever she's doing with the stick in the sand.

"What are you doing?" he asks.

"None of your business. You're out, remember?"

"Look, we were both a little out of line that night."

"Oh, is that what you've decided, Dad?"

"Oh my God. I went to San Francisco State, for Christ's sake. It's not exactly a bastion of the patriarchy, all right? Can you stop talking to me like this?"

She turns, and for a second, he's afraid she might throw the stick at him. "You called me Burning Girl, asshole, after a whole day of trying to prove you weren't the guy you were in high school."

"You know, maybe, just maybe, you could stop bringing up the way I was in high school every time I do something you don't like."

"Act different and I will."

"All I did was say things you didn't want to hear."

"No, you had a meltdown. You had a meltdown because for three hours I was stronger than you were."

"Stronger than I was? You were stronger than a speeding truck! Give me a break. So I freaked out. What do you expect me to do? Ask you to rob a bunch of banks with your bare hands?"

"I gave you a break, and you were a dick."

"Well, that's not when I had a meltdown, by the way."

"So we agree it was a meltdown and not you being the voice of mansplainy reason?"

"Call it whatever you want. The point is, I didn't freak out when I saw what the drug can do. I freaked out when you said you were going after a serial killer. Because I don't want you to get hurt. And I don't want you to get hurt because I . . ."

Shut up, fool.

At least it's not Reggie's voice this time. It's his own.

His throat's closed up, and his chest's suddenly made of metal. And even though he knows on a conscious level that his arms and legs are still attached to his body, it doesn't really feel that way. Charley's just staring at him, her expression unreadable. It seems a little tense, a little wary, and a little skeptical, all at once. As if she knows what he was about to say and doesn't believe it. Or maybe she just doesn't want to.

"I just . . ."

"You just what?" she asks.

"I liked helping," he finally says. "I want to help. And I fucked up. And I'm sorry."

Before she can respond, there's a buzzing sound from her pocket. She pulls out a cheap-looking cell phone. "Prepaid. Marty bought it for me." She reads the text message, drops the stick, and walks past him.

"Where are you going?"

"Package just showed up at Marty's house. No return address. Strange delivery guy. Marty's on his way there."

He's tempted to follow her, but he's distracted by something else.

Now that she's moved out of his way, he can see a pattern to the marks she was making in the sand. They're words.

He walks closer, positions his back to the lake so he can read them clearly.

PLANNING. PLEASE BE PATIENT.

She's right next to him suddenly. When her hand comes to rest on his shoulder, he jumps, but she's too busy pointing up at the sun with her other arm to notice.

"Look," she says. "Blink a few times and let your eyes adjust and you'll see them." He follows her instructions. "They're tiny, so if they line up with the sun, the brightness hides them. But they follow me everywhere I go."

If they're drones, they're the smallest drones Luke's ever seen. And they're moving together in a strange, swarmlike pattern. Almost like they're feeding off each other. Or positioning themselves in relation to each other. They're small enough and high enough that if he'd noticed them on his own, he would have dismissed them as specks on the surface of his eyes. Or maybe a cloud of gnats.

"Hell," he whispers.

So the message in the sand is for them.

"Makes you wonder if all the crazy people in the world are really crazy, doesn't it?" she asks. She lowers her arm and her eyes, squinting and blinking the glare away. "Sure you still want to help?"

She starts for the Camaro without waiting for his answer.

31

Three hundred people are waiting for Cole in the auditorium at Graydon headquarters, most of them journalists, but he's pacing backstage, Dylan's voice tinny through the earpiece in his ear.

"Yes," Cole says, "I'm aware it could mean anything. That's why I'm asking you what it means."

"I don't know," Dylan answers.

"Guess."

"Can I see it?" Dylan asks.

"It just came in, and I'm a little busy right now."

"Where are you? It's loud."

"I'm running my company, thank you."

"Right. The stomach drug no one needs."

"You spoke with her the other day. What is she planning?"

"I told her the world was full of bad men, and she should go find some and show them what she can do."

"And now she's planning something and she wants us to be patient and you have no idea what that is."

"Well, maybe if I could see the message."

"I said I'll send it to you. Later."

"Or you could tap me into your feeds instead of sending me things on a delay."

"Not a chance. Speaking of which, you're getting a package later today. The thing that's inside it, you'll need to wear it at all times."

"A tracking device seems excessive. I'm just sitting here waiting for my subject to perform. Just like you are."

"This request didn't come from me."

"The Consortium. Good to know they're back in the game."

"Don't get ahead of yourself."

On the other side of the drop screen bearing a projection of Graydon's logo, he can hear the audience growing restless. The stage manager waves at him and points to her watch. Cole holds up a finger.

"E-mail me when the package arrives."

Before Dylan can say another word, Cole ends the call with the press of a button.

He'd thought a little clarity about Charlotte Rowe's message in the sand might focus him before he took to the stage, but talking to Dylan has only rattled his nerves.

A minute later, when he walks out into the floodlights, greeted by robust applause, he feels his performer's instincts kick in. Media presentations are one of those rare moments when he feels like something more than a pretender to the throne. Maybe because, unlike some other aspects of the job, he's incredibly good at them.

But he's halfway through his speech when he hears Dylan's voice saying, *I told her the world was full of bad men, and she should go find some and show them what she can do.* His vision seems to blur. Then he sees the puzzled faces in the front row and realizes he's fallen silent. Once he manages a deep breath and starts reading from the teleprompter again, the words he hears coming out of his mouth sound like they're being spoken by a stranger.

32

They should have made him wait outside the trailer, Charlotte realizes now.

Then, once she and Marty took the measure of both packages and realized how completely strange the contents of the bigger one were, they could have sent Luke on his way without letting him into the next level of this.

But they didn't, so he's up to date on everything. And now she feels stuck with him.

He's standing with her on Altamira's windswept beach, the whitecaps making frenzied love to Bayard Rock just offshore. Thanks to the mountains behind them, it feels like they're much farther away from Marty's trailer than they actually are.

Cell phone service out here's lousy, but apparently it's good enough for Marty's text message to reach Luke's phone.

"Clear as a bell," Luke reports.

"That's just . . ."

"Impossible?" he asks.

She nods, but she feels like a fool for saying so. In this strange new world, how can she know what is or isn't possible? How can she know the first thing about a pair of contact lenses capable of transmitting crystal clear images of everything she sees?

They looked innocent enough at first. But the note with them felt threatening.

WEAR THEM WHILE YOU WORK.

Also in the box, an eight-inch tablet that didn't bear the logo of any tech company she was familiar with; when they powered it on, an entry blank appeared in the middle of a black square. The passkey came inside a felt pouch; a digital counter containing seven digits. Every thirty seconds, the last number changed; every minute, the second. The third number took a minute and a half to change, and by the time they figured that out, they were all in agreement that every number in the sequence probably changed after a specific interval of time, so if you lost the passkey, there was no accessing the website that captured the contacts' transmission.

She has no idea how the transmission's getting from the contacts to the website, but she doubts it's something easily intercepted like Bluetooth or a cell connection. For all she knows, the damn things have a direct connection to a satellite. They'd been so dazzled by the tech, they'd almost forgotten about the second package, the one with the plastic bag full of Zypraxon.

"Let's head north," Luke suggests now.

A few minutes later they've climbed the perilous stone steps back to PCH and are headed up the coast in Luke's cruiser. She's got his cell phone in her lap so he can drive, and the texts from Marty keep coming. Little comments on everything he's seeing through her eyes while he sits in his trailer with the tablet. At least he's a good driver . . . You're coming up on one of my favorite trees . . . Looked like he got pretty close to that Camry. Is he distracted? . . . Ugh. A RAV4. Hate those. They look like a toddler's shoe with tires on it.

They're thirty minutes up the coast now.

"Any drop?" Luke finally asks.

"Nope."

"Damn," Luke whispers, "so they're definitely watching, too."

"I think that's the whole point."

"I need to head back, make a pass through town before I bring you to Marty's so Mona thinks I'm on patrol."

There's a question lurking in the way he said *bring you back to Marty's*. Should she answer it? Is she ready to decide whether she should let him back in? Maybe there's a better way. Make him earn it.

"So what's your assessment?" she asks.

"Of what?"

"Of these," she says, pointing to her eyes, and the impossible, undetectable technology they contain. "Of what they're doing with the resort."

Luke furrows his brow, chews his bottom lip, signs he's considering his answer carefully because he knows this is an audition. "You said when Dylan called you the other day he didn't seem to know what you guys did at that bar, right?"

"Correct," she answers. "Or he didn't mention it, at least."

"And why wouldn't he, if he was trying to frighten you? I mean, he had no qualms about giving you my name and telling you stuff about that field we were in."

"So you're saying he didn't know about me and those two wannabe rapists."

"That's exactly what I'm saying."

"OK. So what do you think that means?"

"Whatever his plans for you out in the desert, he wasn't prepared to put eyes on you right away. It took him a day to get the kind of surveillance in place that would scare the crap out of you. Scare you out of sending my brother after him anyway."

A little dig there, she thinks, *but I'll forgive him if he keeps coming up with strong theories.*

"Keep going," she says.

"I think whoever he's working with, he had to go to them at the last minute because his initial plan didn't go the way he wanted it to. Or maybe he was forced to go to them sooner than he wanted to."

"OK."

"And that's interesting."

"How so?"

"Because both possibilities suggest Graydon wasn't in on his original plan. Which might also mean they're not all that happy about what he's doing. Which might also mean the relationship between the two of them has . . . weaknesses."

"All right then," she says, trying to conceal how smart she thinks these deductions are. "Why is Graydon buying the resort?"

"They're investing in you."

"Or trying to show me how powerful they are."

"No," he says, shaking his head. "These people could sweep you up off the street at a moment's notice if they wanted to. I mean, the drones, the contact lenses. If it was what they wanted, you'd be in one of their labs for the rest of your life. And I don't mean to be harsh, but as of a few days ago, there wouldn't have been a lot of people missing you."

A chill goes through her, and it's not just from the ocean wind ripping through the half-open window. It's because what he said was the truth.

"So why not?" she asks. "Why not just kidnap me and treat me like a lab rat? Why bail out my hometown?"

"Well, for starters, maybe they're not total monsters."

"Like Dylan you mean?"

"Yes. And if they bring you in, you become their property, which means you become their problem. If they leave you out in the field, there's distance between them and what Dylan's done."

"OK. And the resort means what?"

"A nice gesture, perhaps. Or a peace offering from the good cop in the relationship."

"A peace offering that costs millions."

"Which is chump change to them. But not to you."

"And that means what?"

"They've watched you for days now. It's clear you're not going to the police or the press. You've shown what you can do to only a small circle of friends. So they're confident you're going to do what Dylan's asked. So now they're investing in you."

"Maybe. Or they're just flexing their muscles. Showing me I can never outrun them."

She can tell from the way he adjusts his grip on the steering wheel that he doesn't agree. But he keeps his mouth shut.

That's progress, she guesses.

"The point, Charley, is that I don't think you're being ganged up on. I think you're in the middle. And that's a better place to be."

As he does his fake patrol through town, the words *stuck in the middle* roll back and forth through her mind.

Is it really better? Of course it is. Anything that diminishes Dylan's power is a good thing. Had he gone rogue? Was that what their sessions in Scarlet were about? He was preparing to test a drug on her that wasn't even his?

Take it that chat didn't go well?

Another text from Marty; this one reminds her of the one technological limitation of her mysterious new gift—no audio. For them, it's a limitation. For her, it's a perk.

On our way back now, she answers. I no longer want to strangle him.

Marty's waiting for them on the front deck when they pull up.

She figures Luke will follow her inside if she just doesn't say anything, but when she steps from the cruiser, he doesn't unbuckle his seat belt.

"I better check in back at the station." If there were any more expectation in his stare, he'd be a kid on Christmas Eve.

"What time do you get off?" she asks.

"Seven."

"Marty's grilling."

"He any good?"

"Come back after you get off and find out."

His smile fades. "Does this mean I'm back in?"

"It means you should come eat with us."

"Fair enough," he says.

She watches him pull away.

"You got an extra steak?" she calls out to Marty, who she's pretty sure heard the whole exchange from where he's standing, hands braced against the deck rail.

"I always get extra."

"Good."

"You sure you've forgiven him, or are you inviting him to dinner because you like him in that uniform?"

"He's smart," she says as she walks up onto the deck. The cruiser's taillights round the last visible bend in the road. "And he says the reason he freaked out the other night is because he was worried about me."

"Men always say that kinda shit when they fuck up," Marty growls.

"Takes one to know one."

"Yep."

"You got a steak for him or not?" she asks.

"Sure thing."

"His uniform does nothing for me, by the way." She heads inside before he can see the lie in her eyes.

33

Once Cole's made the rounds of the postpresentation cocktail reception, smiling, nodding, chitchatting with those board members present, he slips back upstairs.

He's one of the first. The carpeted hallways are empty; most of the glass office doors are closed. It's no surprise his administrative staff is using the presentation as a chance to unwind for a bit, which, at a company like Graydon, means drinking one and a half cocktails out of plastic cups while deigning to make small talk with a coworker who might have a less advanced degree than you.

Inside his locked desk drawer is the personal laptop he's set up for what may or may not become Phase II of Project Bluebird. He pulls it out, enters his password, and blacks out his soaring windows with the press of a button.

There's an e-mail from Dylan, which surprises him. He knows the package was received at four o'clock that afternoon, but he expected the guy not to let him know out of mere defiance.

From his pocket, he pulls out the digital key Julia Crispin provided him with, uses the current code to log in to the portal for both feeds.

If one screen is black, he can use the archive link underneath it to access the most recent four hours of footage. But the screen for DC—Dylan Cody—is black and there's no link below. So Dylan received the package, but he hasn't activated his TruGlass yet. Maybe defiance is still in play.

CR's also black, but in her case, there's archived footage.

He watches her slide the lenses in, takes in the startled expressions of the men with her, the cop, Luke Prescott, and the long-haired contractor with the dishonorable discharge from the marines and the brief stint in jail for aggravated assault, Martin Cahill. If there's an odder crew out there, they're probably on a sitcom. The lack of audio is frustrating, but he's still stunned by how clear the images are. A few notches below high-definition TV.

Charlotte and the cop head outside, get into the guy's sheriff's cruiser, drive through that little town, then into the mountains.

Could they have taken off in search of a target that soon?

No way, he thinks.

When they park on the side of Pacific Coast Highway, he realizes they must be testing the thing's range. Based on their expressions, they're as impressed as he is.

The voyeurism of it all is distracting, and he finds himself enamored by the fairly ordinary sight of them descending a set of stone steps to a windswept, rugged beach below; he's so enamored, he misses Dylan's feed coming to life, until the word *live* pops up next to a green dot just underneath his screen.

At first he's not sure what's he's watching in the second panel.

Blurs of movement. Maybe it's the packaging being torn away.

A black T-shirt hits tiled floor next to bare feet.

A hand turns a shower knob.

The image seems to jerk a little.

Blinks, Cole realizes. Lots of them. Dylan must be getting used to the way the things sit in his eyes.

Suddenly Dylan's staring right back at him, through a small mirror that's about to fog. He douses his head under the shower's spray, makes a kissy face and sleepy eyes. Then he looks down, giving Cole a perfect view of the water sluicing down his muscular body as he grabs his cock and balls from below and starts soaping them like a porn star.

Cole slams the screen of his laptop shut, cursing under his breath.

When he calls Ed Baker, his director of security, the man answers after one ring.

"How's our girl?" Cole asks.

"Had to bring the microdrones down at dusk, but ground teams A and B both have eyes on Cahill's trailer."

"She inside?"

"Nope. And she's got guests."

"Outside?"

"Yep. It's a cookout."

Is Ed joking?

The sustained silence tells him that's not the case. The man's tone is certainly frostier than usual; it has been since they flew to meet Dylan in Arizona. If Ed had his way, they'd clear the warehouse of all the surveillance equipment tracking Charlotte Rowe and use the space to waterboard Dylan into revealing whether or not he's altered Zypraxon's formula.

Note to file: don't put Ed Baker and Julia Crispin in the same room together. He might have an insurrection on his hands that ends with Dylan's balls being electrocuted.

"So that's what she was planning?" Cole finally asks. "A cookout?"

"I'm gonna go out on a limb and say no."

"Then what the hell is she doing?"

"Everybody needs downtime."

"She's had two days of it. And she's the one who just told us she's planning something. Was she messing with us?"

"We need to find out more about what Dylan said to her during that call," Ed offers. "Whatever it was, it made her destroy that disposable phone."

"Dylan claims he gave us a full account of his call."

"We can't know that for sure. It's reckless, letting him talk to her."

"We've got better eyes on him now. He just activated his TruGlass."

"Yeah. About that."

"Yeah, I know. He's showering."

"Sort of. Look, we don't know how much he's told this girl, and we can't let him be the only one communicating with her."

He isn't, Cole wants to say. But he's not telling Ed about the purchase he made that afternoon, or the jobs he'll be able to bring back to Altamira after a few phone calls. He's communicating with Charlotte Rowe, all right, but in his own way. And damn if he'll run any of that by Ed, who has begun talking out of school because he hates being cooped up in warehouses overseeing outside security contractors.

"Let's bring him in," Ed says. "Have a conversation where he doesn't set the terms. Find out how much risk he's really put the company in."

"He hasn't been on the payroll for two years."

"Yeah, but he's been making choices that endanger the company for three now."

"We're watching, Ed. That's all we're doing. Watching. The minute we decide to force a conversation with either of these two parties, we take ownership of this. *I* take ownership of this. And I'm not ready for that yet. I need a verified episode of her defending herself on Zypraxon against a formidable opponent, preferably a man or several, and I need her to survive."

"You've got the biker video."

"I need it from a source I can trust. That's what *verified* means. And not edited, for Christ's sake."

"We've got her demo from the other day."

"Against a truck, a tree, and a fence post. I need her to survive a fight, Ed. A bad one. That's the whole point of this drug."

"OK. You want us to create one for her?"

"Ed—"

"For God's sake, Cole, it's crazy letting her wander around like this."

"She is the *only* human this drug has ever worked on. The only one. But if she's going to be worth anything to us, she has to be able to use it, fight on it, and survive."

After Ed clears his throat, he says, "I apologize. For my insubordination."

Insubordination is right. Another inch over the line, and Cole would have reminded him that the days of his father and Ed running secret drug trials in developing nations—on volunteers who didn't have the slightest idea what they were being given—were long over, and they weren't coming back. At least the people Project Bluebird killed had volunteered willingly, knowing the risks.

Cole's little speech has been good practice for the pitch he'll have to make to the entire Consortium to get Project Bluebird up and running again.

The other option—have Graydon provide all the funding—is unthinkable.

How would he ever explain that to his board or his mother, if she got wind of it? That's the beauty of The Consortium, despite the perils of the egos involved. By pooling their resources, each company can make financial contributions that fly just under the radar of its legal and accounting departments. And, of course, the secrecy protects all the companies involved from any opinion the Justice Department might one day have about how they collectively decide to share in the benefits of their efforts, should any ever materialize.

"Any leads on Bailey Prescott?" he asks.

"No, and the digital team's frustrated. But if the guy's wanted by the FBI, I guess it makes sense."

"We hack the FBI all the time."

"Yes, and we did it again, and it's only revealed how little they actually know about him. Are we sure that's who she was talking to at the library?"

"It's as good a guess as any."

"She could have just been researching us," Ed says.

"She meets Luke Prescott; suddenly she's on her way to the nearest computer lab, where she hangs out for fifteen minutes. I don't think so."

"All right, well, I might have something," Ed says.

"You personally?"

"Yeah, some contacts from my former life."

"LAPD?" Cole asks.

"Uh-huh. Apparently, it's not in the news, but Parker Center was hacked last night."

"As in LAPD headquarters?"

"As in Robbery Homicide, specifically."

"The department was targeted? Anything specific?"

"My source described it as broad-brush. Probably deliberately so whoever it was could hide what he was really after. But whoever did it was good. Very good. Cybersecurity didn't notice the breach until this morning, and by then the creeper was long gone. But they think he was in their network for hours. Just kinda hanging out, looking at whatever he felt like."

"And you think it was Bailey Prescott?"

"I didn't say that."

"Do *they* think it was Bailey Prescott?"

"No, my guys don't even know that name, and I didn't give it to them. It's their working theory that got me thinking."

"I'm all ears."

"They think it was journalists after info on the Mask Maker case. But, you know, what if it wasn't journalists? What if it was her?"

"Holy shit," Cole whispers.

What had Dylan told her again? *Go find some bad men. Show them what you can do.* Well, if this was true, she was on the trail of a real grade-A psycho. And given her background, her taste in bad men made a lot of sense.

"Holy shit," Cole whispers again. "You kinda buried the lede on this one."

"Could be nothing. Or it could be the beginning of quite a show."

"I'll say."

"You're sure as hell not going to bring her in now, are you?" Ed asks.

"Anything else?" he asks, trying to conceal how floored he is by this news.

"Yeah, your b—excuse me. *Cody.* He's giving us quite a show on his TruGlass."

"What does that mean?"

"I believe it's called *edging.*"

"Oh, for fuck's sake."

"How long do we have to watch?"

"Take breaks. He can't jerk off forever."

"You sure? Maybe he invented a drug for that, too."

"Take breaks, Ed. Good night."

He hangs up, just sits there for a while, disgusted by the primal, lizard-brain urge he feels to pop open his laptop and take a peek at Dylan's show.

Instead he lifts the screen and logs in to the feeds from ground teams A and B.

In seconds he's looking at two different night vision angles on Martin Cahill's trailer. There's tinny audio via parabolic microphones, distorted, watery-sounding music drifting from some stereo he can't see. Watching a creepy night vision version of something as innocuous as a friendly cookout seems comic. The green flares around each body and blazing, whited-out eyes are appropriate for fast-moving predators, crawling through brush. Not a bunch of lanky, slouching shadows hanging out around a smoking grill.

Even with the lousy sound he can recognize the song they're all listening to. "Angel of the Morning" by Juice Newton. And he can see her there on the deck, leaning on her elbows, sipping a beer, it looks like. Her eyes are pinpricks of flare. She's either staring at the group of men talking in the driveway nearby or gazing off into the night, maybe as she entertains fantasies of tearing a serial killer apart with her bare hands.

"You are something, Burning Girl. You are really something."

It takes him a few seconds to realize he whispered these thoughts aloud.

34

"Juice Newton?" Charlotte asks. "Seriously?"

Marty's iPod is hardwired to the three little speakers he's mounted on the deck rail. Besides being a few generations out of date, the poor thing looks like it's been through a ground war between rival paint manufacturers. But it's working, and that's all that matters, as Marty pointed out when she tried, in vain, to scrape some of the paint off the display with her fingernails.

"Hey. Don't make fun. Some of us enjoyed it when songs had actual lyrics."

"Not judging. Just surprised, is all."

It's a cool, breezy night, more so up here in the hills, but Marty's stripped down to shorts, tank top, and an apron and put his hair in a ponytail, all so he can withstand the heat of his grill, which looks considerably newer than his iPod.

Maybe it's the half a beer that's done it, but she feels truly relaxed for the first time in days. It doesn't hurt that Luke's there, doing his level best to make small talk with Marty's crew. The sight of him down in the driveway with the other guys, out of uniform and in what looks like one of his best dress shirts, has removed the constant replay of their last cruel words from the tape deck in her mind. Now she's calm enough to notice Marty's interesting taste in music.

She's surprised nobody else has said anything. Stevie Nicks, ABBA, even a track or two from the Go-Go's. And, of course, the song playing now. She hates to stereotype, but the last time she checked,

"Angel of the Morning" wasn't exactly a fan favorite among guys who threw up drywall for a living.

"Take it you'd've said something if he'd heard from his brother," Marty says.

"That's correct."

"And I take it you'd've said something if he got shitty with you out on PCH earlier."

"Like I said, he apologized."

The closing chords of "Angel of the Morning" are replaced by gentle piano and eventually the soft, familiar voice of John Denver. It takes her a second to recognize the specific song, "Sweet Surrender."

"All right," Charlotte says. "Where did this music come from, Marty?"

Marty sets his tongs down, wipes his hands on his apron. "Well, if you must know, this was one of your grandmother's playlists."

"Gram never had an iPod."

"That's right. She had all these on a mixtape, and I made a playlist of 'em after she died."

"Wow. How come she didn't play them for me when she was alive?"

"'Cause she didn't want to make you sad."

"Sad? Why would they make me sad?

"They were your momma's favorites. That's why she made the tape. Back when she was getting sober, she'd listen to it every night before bed. Said it calmed her heart some, especially when she was still jittery from the withdrawals."

"I see."

"Dammit. Now I made you sad. Want me to put something else on?"

"No, I'm not sad. It's nice. Leave it. I just . . ."

"Just what?"

"Do you think we didn't talk about her as much as we wanted to because we thought we'd have to talk about everything that came after?"

"Your mom, you mean?"

"Yeah."

"I take it your dad didn't talk about her much?" He flips a steak, his lack of a direct answer an answer in itself.

"Why would he? Weren't they getting divorced?"

"Meh. It wasn't the first time she'd walked out on him. They might have patched things up again. For your sake."

"Can I ask you something?"

"Shoot."

"Why didn't you marry my grandmother?"

"Luanne didn't want to get married."

"Did you?"

"Nope. It was kinda perfect. When we weren't rocking each other's world in the bedroom, we went off and did our own thing. We were married on the weekends, she liked to say. Any more than that and I would've gotten in the way of her reading."

She laughs.

He smiles at the grill. "Has there been anyone, Charley?"

"Anyone what?"

"You know, anyone intimate. Any relationships." He casts a glance at the driveway. At Luke, she realizes. Maybe he's trying to assess her vulnerabilities in the area of romance so he can keep Luke from exploiting them.

"I'm not a virgin, if that's what you're asking."

"I wasn't, but OK."

"No relationships."

From those two answers, he can probably put two and two together and figure out she lost her virginity to a man she didn't know all that well.

She can't even remember the guy's name; he'd used friendly chitchat and long, inviting stares to pick her up at a rest stop during her grave-site tour. He was handsome enough, but also nervous, a little

319

distracted, and disheveled, like he wasn't used to picking up strange women in a Denny's, or he had a life he was obligated to get back to soon, and what he was about to do with her didn't quite fit. He knew what he was doing, and he'd been patient with her, mixing plenty of casual, relaxing conversation with his slow, studied exploration of her body. More important, there'd been no ring on his finger and no tan line where he might have removed one. Of course, she'd only been able to confirm the second detail after he'd fallen asleep next to her in bed.

Only later did she realize the crazy, reckless irony of going home with a man she'd met in a Denny's, given her past and the nature of her road trip. That might have been part of why she did it; the combination of being on the road, with her new name and her new wad of cash, made her temporarily fearless. Or maybe her past was exactly why she'd felt safe enough to do it; how often does lightning strike twice in the same place?

"Where'd you go?" Marty asks.

"Sorry."

"Memories?"

"Something like that."

"Is it the music? You sure you don't want me to change it?"

"No. No, not at all."

"I guess I just thought it would be appropriate."

"How's that?"

Marty transfers three of the steaks to an empty plate. Turns to face her again. "Well, she's why you're doing it, right? Your mother, I mean. This plan of yours, it's for her, isn't it?"

"I guess you could say that."

"Don't let me put words in your mouth."

"No, I just . . . I didn't think about it that way; that's all. Is that why you're gonna help? For my mom?"

Marty eyes the guests chatting in the driveway, making sure they're out of earshot, she assumes. "Truth be told, I'm helping you because I loved your grandmother more than I loved anyone in the world. I've picked people up out of the gutter. But I've never seen someone put herself back together the way she did after she lost you two. Now I see more of her in you every day since you came back. So *my* plan, if you'd like to know, is to do whatever it takes to keep you from going away again. Even if it means hanging out while you make choices that have me messing my shorts like a baby who ate chili."

Her vision had been starting to get tear blurred right up until Marty got to that last line. Now she's laughing so hard she's coughing. She drowns it with a swallow of beer. It empties the bottle.

"Another soda?" she asks.

"Sure thing."

Inside, she's got both hands full and is headed for the door when she sees her notebook sitting on Marty's desk. Foolish of her to leave it out in the open like that, with all the company outside.

During two marathon sessions, she'd managed to pump out about sixty handwritten pages. Some of the memories came out fragmented, more like parts of an outline, and some, like the most recent ones, are crystal clear.

She sets the beer and the soda down next to the love seat, picks up the notebook, and starts scanning the trailer for a secure place to stash it.

Just then the door opens, and there's Luke.

In the trailer's harsh overhead light, his jeans look freshly ironed, and she can see she was right: it really is one of his best dress shirts. Navy blue with a red polo pony and white buttons. There's a spot, right where the top two buttons are undone, that she shouldn't focus on for too long, a spot that lets her know he keeps his chest hair trimmed to a manicured stubble.

"Howdy," he says.

"Howdy?"

"Just, you know, a common form of greeting."

And it's not hey, she thinks, *because that's what you said in the car when you almost touched my leg.*

"Howdy," she says back.

"You know, I thought those guys would be nicer to me if I was out of uniform. But it kinda took some work."

"Didn't you threaten to run all of them because you were having a fight with Marty?"

"Yeah, there's that."

"Well, whatever you did, it's fine now. Things seemed to be going all right last time I checked."

"Same strategy I always use to win people over."

"And what's that?"

"I just tell a few stories that make it clear I know I'm an asshole."

"Is that so?"

"Worked with you, didn't it?"

"No, not really."

"Ah, well. Shucks."

"Honesty. Telling me what happened with your brother. That's what worked for me. If you really want to know."

"Well, good, 'cause I do."

He looks at the notebook she's holding against her chest with both arms like it might fly away. And he doesn't ask about it, which she appreciates.

"So am I out of the doghouse yet?" he asks.

"Why? You eager to get home?"

"Not in the slightest, actually. I'm having a pretty good time, and the steaks smell great. But I'd be having a better time if I knew you and I were . . . cool."

"Cool?"

"If I knew whether or not my offer had been accepted."

"To help, you mean?"

He nods.

"What about your job, Luke?"

"Yeah, as you can tell, it really takes up all my time. I was in the station for what? A whole hour and a half today?" Apparently he doesn't like what he sees in her expression, because he bows his head. "Look, if you're not comfortable after everything, I get it. I'm not gonna force you. I just . . ."

"You just what?"

"I don't want you to string me along because you're afraid I'm gonna run to the press or the FBI or something."

"Well, you did almost call Mona when I asked you not to. That was scary, Luke."

"I know. And I apologize. And no matter what happens, no matter what you decide, I won't say a word about any of this. I promise."

She's not afraid of him blabbing. She agrees with Marty. With Bailey involved, Luke won't bring any outside attention to this.

And she's not still mad at him. Not exactly.

Instead, looking at him now, dressed in his version of decked out, his big brown eyes full of sorrow and expectation, his stare steady and penetrating even though he's downed two beers—she counted, which should tell her something—she feels something altogether different.

Something that must be attraction, but it's all tangled up in other feelings like sadness and anxiety. And because she's so rarely felt attracted to a man who isn't a character in a movie or novel, she's not sure if those are signs it's real or fleeting. It feels like there's a weight to Luke Prescott that's pulling on her, making her unsteady on her feet, but if she gives in, she's more likely to end up flat on her face than in his arms.

Part of her wants to tell him to go. To absolve him of his past sins. To tell him that when it comes to her and their shared past, the slate's clean, and he should go back to his small-town cop life and make the best of it. Because no way can she drag him through the mud ahead, even if he throws her the rope with gusto.

But that's the easy way out.

Is it better to be helped by people who actually care about you? Or is it better to be helped by someone with a self-interest that matches your own in some way? Which camp does Marty belong in? Which camp would Luke belong in, if she lets him back in?

Finally, her arms respond to this storm of thoughts before her mouth can.

She holds the notebook out to him. "I want you to read this," she hears herself say.

"What is it?" he asks in almost a whisper.

"It's my story. I mean, it's not a novel or anything. I wrote it in the past two days. But it's not my father's version, and it's not Hollywood's version. It's mine. It's actually what happened to me. And if you're gonna help me, I want you to read it."

"Deal," he says. He takes it from her grip.

Then he brushes past her, and to her shock, she realizes he's about to sit down at Marty's desk with it.

"Well, you don't have to read it *now*."

"Why not? I'm all out of cop jokes."

"OK. Well, go in the guest bedroom, where you have some privacy. I don't want the guys coming in and . . . you know. Flipping through it or something."

He nods as if this were the most normal of requests. As if everything about this exchange is normal. He's pulling the door shut behind him when she calls his name. He stops.

"I want your help. But I don't want your agenda. And I want you to listen to what I'm thinking and not tell me what I'm thinking. Can you do that?"

He nods. Then when she goes silent again, he holds up the notebook and waggles it a little, as if he's reminding her she just gave him a job to do. Then he pulls the door closed behind him with a soft click, and for a while she just stands there, wondering how something that feels so important could happen so quickly.

When he notices she's awake, Marty asks, "What's he reading in there?"

Beer plus red meat equaled a wallop of a nap as soon as she'd cleaned her plate. Now she's come to in one of the deck chairs. Most of the guys are gone, but a few stragglers remain, sitting in a circle of chairs someone brought down to the driveway after she nodded off.

"He's still reading?" she asks.

"Yep. Even came out and got his steak finally, then took it back in there so he could read some more."

Well, that's something. She'd figured he'd ask to take it home with him so he could only pretend to read the rest.

"Uh-oh," Marty says.

He moves to the deck rail like a dog perking up at the approach of a stranger. A pair of high-riding headlights swing into the driveway. A sheriff's cruiser, just like the one Luke drove her around in that day, only the deputy who steps from it is half Luke's height and twice his age.

"Whatcha need, Henricks?" Marty calls to the man.

"Luke Prescott here?"

"He's inside. Why?"

"His cell's off. We tried calling him a bunch from the station. We're getting calls from Dorothy Strickland, lives across the street from him. Says his alarm's making all kinds of racket. But it's weird. Sounds almost like music."

"Bailey," Charlotte whispers, getting to her feet.

"Go," Marty says quietly. "Get Luke and go. I'll stay here."

She slips inside as Marty says, "We'll take care of it. Thanks, Henricks."

35

The alarm's still singing when they get to Luke's house, the same two-tone chime Bailey used to get their attention the first time. This time the sound fills Charlotte with excitement instead of dread.

"Stop!" Luke calls out. "We're here."

The music stops, but there's some kind of flashing light in the living room. It strobes through the rest of the place like some effect in a cheap haunted house. It's the monitor of Luke's desktop, she realizes. It's flashing the same words over and over again. TARGET ACQUIRED.

Luke hits some light switches, but it doesn't make the words on-screen seem any less ominous. When he takes a seat at his desk, the words stop flashing. Further proof Bailey can see and hear them through the monitor's built-in camera.

New words appear on-screen, white on black. Comically large, but devoid of any ironically cheerful graphics this time.

Check your e-mail, brother.

Luke taps a few keys. The monitor doesn't respond. He throws up his hands.

Bailey does something that returns the computer to Luke's control, and a few keystrokes later, Luke's clicked through a link in a new message from the address maskssuck346@hotmail.com. They're staring at the website for a plastic surgeon named Frederick Pemberton, based in Newport Beach. The man looks like the victim of his own profession, with a sculpted nose that doesn't match his uneven features. On top of that, his headshot is so airbrushed he looks like a cartoon appearing though a cloud of fog.

Luke's hands are on his lap, but a Word document suddenly opens on-screen, partially covering the web page. Text, typed by Bailey's unseen hand, appears in the white space.

You're welcome.

"Charley." There's hesitation in Luke's voice—hesitation and warning—and it's fighting with his resolve not to give her any more fiery lectures; she can tell.

"I know," she says. "I know what you're going to say and I agree. Bailey?"

Yes.

"I can't go off just this. You need to tell me more."

Trust me. It's him.

"Bailey," Luke says suddenly. "What was Mom's nickname for the dog we had when you were in seventh grade?"

We didn't have a dog when I was in seventh grade.
We had fish, asshole.

"Probably should have done that sooner," Luke mutters. "Sorry. As you were."

And their names were Siegfried and Roy because
you thought it was funny to name fish after tigers.

Charlotte clears her throat. "Bailey, I know you don't discuss procedure, but I can't just go off a name like this."

> It's not funny, FYI. Naming fish after tigers. It doesn't even make sense.

"It's definitely him," Luke says.

"It makes even less sense because those weren't the names of the tigers," she says. "Those were the trainers."

Silence.

"Well, shit," Luke finally whispers.

> Any more talk, computer lab. New library. Same chat room.

"Why?" Charley asks. "What are you afraid of, the FBI?"

> Screw the FBI.

"Yeah, that went great," Luke says.

> Relax, brother. They only had a subpoena to look at your phone records and e-mails from more than 180 days ago, and you bored them to death, so you're fine. Not afraid of FBI.

"Bailey, who do you think is watching us?" she asks.

> Maybe it's whoever you're afraid of. They seem worse than FBI. Otherwise you wouldn't be dealing with me.

"All right," she says. "Well, don't be afraid of them."

Startled, Luke looks up from his palms.

The lack of any new text suggests Bailey's also surprised.

"What?" Charlotte says. "You think they're going to try to stop us? We're doing what they asked. We're trying to find a bad man. They should be thrilled."

"We're doing what *Dylan* asked," he says. "They might not be such a team, remember?" He looks instantly regretful. "Take the chair. Talk to him. I'll get you something to drink."

So he's trying. *That's good,* she thinks.

> If you're going to make me discuss procedure, I want to hear yours. Why are you going after this guy yourself?

"It's a long story," she answers.

> So's mine, but you seem to know it all already.

"I know the version your brother knows. That's all."

> Touché I guess.

"How sure are you this is the guy?" she asks.

> 85 percent.

She laughs.

> Let me put it this way. If you're planning to share what I tell you with the press, I'd say I'm 90 percent

sure. If you're planning on taking out a hit on this guy, I'd drop it to 75 percent.

"Well, that is certainly manipulative, Bailey Prescott."

???

"So whatever you've learned, you're willing to see the guy's life destroyed by the media, but you don't necessarily think he deserves to die. Is that it? Do either of those things have anything to do with whether or not he's a serial killer?"

White space.

Luke returns, sets two Sprite Zeros down on the desk next to the keyboard, starts reading over her shoulder.

"Did we lose him?" he asks.

"I don't know."

Answer me this.

They both perk up.

You'll do surveillance on this guy before you do whatever it is you're planning to do, right?

"Yes," she answers. "Lots."

OK. It goes like this.

Luke hurries into the kitchen and returns with a dining table chair, which he places right next to hers as the Word doc begins to fill with text.

Christopher Rice

The masks are made with a process called plastination. It's patented, and you can buy the equipment from a company in Germany. It's a great way
to make medical samples of body parts because
the process stops the decay and replaces fat and
body fluids with polymers. LAPD's tracked down
all the customers in Southern California and found
users are medical and/or legit. For the most part.
But they've got suspicions about one. The Bryant
Center in Newport Beach. Heard of it?

"That's where that exhibit is, right?" Luke asks.
"What exhibit?" she asks.
"The one with all the bodies. You know, where they're all pre-
served and posed and you can see the muscles."
"Oh yeah, I saw pictures. That's disgusting."

The exhibit is just part of it. Bryant Center is run by
multimillionaire real estate guy Denny Bryant, who
started a center for "youth sciences." Antiaging
stuff. Mostly quack medicine. But the exhibit pays
a huge chunk of the bills. It's been sold out since
it opened. Plastination is how all the bodies in the
exhibit were made.

"You didn't send us a picture of Denny Bryant," Charlotte says.
"You sent us this Pemberton guy."

Chill. I'm getting there. Robbery Homicide Division
thinks Bryant might either be their guy or he's covering for their guy. He's got a history. Charges of
spousal abuse from an ex-wife. Some shit with

hookers he got buried. Classic rich fuckhead. But he's not the killer.

"Why are you so sure?" she asks.

There's a lot that's not made it into the press about the masks . . . yet. Surgery behind them is excellent. Top-notch. Killer has to be a skilled surgeon. But there's no shortage of those in Southern California.

"But they also have to know how to . . . *plastinate*, or however you say it," Luke adds.

That part isn't as hard. It's a four-step process. You just need the space and the equipment and some practice. Real problem is they haven't found individual surgeons who have bought plastination kits and materials. Also both abductions super skilled. From different crowded areas. They think first outside nightclub in downtown LA, but not sure. Second, side street off Ventura Blvd. in Studio City. More sure, not 100 percent. No one turning up on surveillance cameras scoping out areas in advance. But abductions as methodical as surgeries. If the masks hadn't turned up, the two disappearances might never have been linked by police.

"Denny Bryant's not a surgeon, I take it," she says.

No. But they think the Mask Maker is connected to the center in some way. They think he's using their chemicals and equipment. Problem is Denny Bryant knew he'd be implicated as soon as the first mask was found. And he was smart about it. He had his lawyers go in on day one and hand over purchase records for all the center's labs so it looked like they were being cooperative.

"Isn't that cooperative?" Charlotte asks.

No. It's bullshit. He knows what they're gonna be after, and it's his employee records and security access logs. They're going to want to look at the names of anyone who had access to the chemicals and equipment. And for some reason, that's what he wants to keep secret. And a judge just agreed he had a right to.

"So the cops went after a warrant, and it was denied?" Luke asks.

Judge said it had all the makings of a fishing expedition. And apparently he shared the suspicions of Bryant's lawyers.

"Which were?" she asks.

That the warrant had less to do with the Mask Maker and more to do with the fact that the state anatomical board has raised ethics questions about where Bryant got the bodies in his exhibit. He says he's got legal paperwork for all of them, but he's never volunteered to show it to anyone, and the anatomical board doesn't have the authority to make him. Also, LAPD didn't help their case by not going after similar warrants for the personnel records of other major medical facilities that do plastination in SoCal. Made it look like Bryant was being targeted without significant probable cause. Which he was. Because he should be.

"Bailey, how do you know all this?" Luke asks.
"Maybe later, you guys could—"

Told you. I don't discuss procedure.

"Did you hack Parker Center?" Luke asks. "Call me crazy, but if I have a brother who just hacked one of the largest police departments in the country, I feel like I should know. It'll help me figure out what to buy you for Christmas."

Relax. We hack Parker Center all the time.

"Who's we?" Charlotte asks.
"Oh, fuck. Did you join Anonymous?"

Those guys are all over the place. We're more focused.

"On what? Ending up in jail?"

No. Making sure only the right people do.

"Bailey, can you get us to Pemberton?"

I got access to the Bryant Center's security access logs and payroll records since it opened. According to what I found, not a single doctor worked on the plastination for the exhibit. That's impossible. Each body would have taken fifteen hundred hours to make. Process is insanely complex. The idea that they could have done that with just the three surgical techs they have listed as employees is absurd. Nobody would ever believe it. But they still purged them from the rolls anyway. Because they're panicking.

"So you think they know the Mask Maker worked for them, and they purged all evidence of him from the rolls because . . . why? They're afraid of the scandal?"

No. I think the Mask Maker did something else for the Bryant Center, and they don't want anyone finding out what it was. And they're so eager to cover it up, they don't give a shit what other crimes he's committed.

"What could he have done for them that's that significant?" Charlotte asks.

"Get them the bodies," Luke answers.

"Jesus. You think he murdered everyone in the exhibit?"

"No," Luke says. "He just probably got them through some unethical means."

"So . . . Pemberton?" Charley asks.

His name was purged from every payroll record, except for one. They missed it, but he's marked "direct deposit." Means he wasn't a onetime indie contractor. He was a regular employee. I found another one they missed. For another doctor. Dr. Ella Stanovski. But I ruled her out.

"Because she's a woman?"

No. Because she's five two. Likely victims overpowered at some point. Pemberton is six three, has a gym membership he uses daily. He's also single. And he's got a country house near Temecula with plenty of land around it and enough square footage for an operating room. Which he bought the equipment for a year ago.

"So he's doing surgery out of his house?" Luke asks. "Is that really that weird?"

He doesn't advertise it. And there isn't enough room in his offices in Newport Beach to house the extra equipment he bought.

"He wasn't just replacing stuff?"

No insurance claims on busted or outdated equipment.

"Jesus Christ, Bailey."

I know. I'm good.

"You're thorough," Luke says. "Let's leave good and bad out of it for now."

"Did Pemberton buy any of the stuff needed for plastination?"

No.

"OK," Charley says. "So we know Pemberton was on staff at the Bryant Center, along with at least one other doctor. We know someone, possibly Denny Bryant, purged their names from the rolls. Possibly because he played some hand in getting bodies for the exhibit through unethical means—"

"Which we have no proof of," Luke says.

"True. We also know he's a skilled surgeon with the time, the means, and the literal space to commit the murders. And possibly access to equipment he could use to make the masks, which means he would have to be sneaking into the facility—"

Wait. There's more.

"What?" she asks. "I'm listening."

> Plastination requires a vacuum pump chamber that removes acetone from cadavers and forces polymer into cells. According to sales records Bryant Center showed LAPD, they purchased four. According to security camera system I hacked, they only have three on-site right now.

"Well, that's something," Charlotte says.

> It's not all. Denny Bryant called Pemberton's cell phone three times yesterday from a cell phone he usually uses for hookers, four times the day before that. I couldn't get to the voice mails, but earlier today he broke down and sent the guy a text. I got it.

"What did it say?" Luke asks.

Bring it back.

"The vacuum pump chamber," Charlotte says.
"Maybe," Luke says. "Did he answer?"

You've got mail.

Luke clicks through to his e-mail account. This time the message is from a different Hotmail address: Thetruthistruthier620@hotmail.com. Luke has attached a screen capture he took on his computer monitor of a text dialogue—no names, just phone numbers. There's Pemberton's text, just as Bailey described it. The response is a photograph, an aerial shot, probably from a helicopter, of a vast field of tin roofs on a barren, scorched plain.

"So Denny Bryant says bring it back, and Pemberton sends him a photograph of . . ." Charlotte stops so Bailey will finish. The browser minimizes, thanks to Bailey's invisible hand.

The Kakuma Refugee Camp in Kenya. The largest refugee camp in the world. Pemberton went there on a volunteer mission with a group called Global Healers two years ago. Guess who's one of their biggest donors.

"Denny Bryant," Luke answers.
"Who doesn't call or text him again after getting the picture of the refugee camp."

Correct.

"So whatever connects those two at that refugee camp, it shut Denny up, even though he's got Robbery Homicide breathing down his neck," Charlotte says.

To the screen, Luke says, "Well, you've certainly uncovered a conspiracy around how they got the bodies in that exhibit; I'll say that much."

It's more than that.

"Yeah, if you take out the rule of law and allow only the circumstantial to be your guide."

Blow me. This is good work.

Luke takes a deep breath, turns to Charley. "Can I just play devil's advocate here for a second?"

Charlotte nods. Her thoughts are clouded with images of refugee camps, bodies posed like mannequins, only with all their muscles and tendons exposed, disturbing details that take on a ghostly presence all around her now. Despite their agreement that he wouldn't lecture her on the subject of her, she'd love for Luke to shine a beam of clarifying light through this spectral fog.

"All this proves is that there's something Pemberton and Bryant got up to that they don't want exposed by a warrant. It doesn't prove either of them is the Mask Maker."

"I know that," she answers. "But whatever they've done, it's bad enough they're willing to obstruct an investigation into a serial killer to keep it hidden."

"Still."

"I get what you're saying. But it's enough to start following him—don't you think?"

Luke looks to the screen, then gets to his feet and gestures for her to follow.

Seriously???

"Shut up, Bailey. You went missing for months. I can step out for five minutes."

In the adjacent hallway, he stands as close to her as possible, drops his voice to a whisper.

"The contact lenses. Are you going to do what they say? Are you going to wear them while you work?"

"All things considered, I don't think I have a choice."

"Why's that?"

"I'm afraid of what kind of package they'll send next if their gift isn't exactly received. Know what I mean?"

Luke seems to suppress a shiver. "OK. Well, that means if we start following this guy, then Graydon's following this guy, too."

"OK."

"I'm just saying, it's something to consider in terms of possible guilt. It might be the same as leaking his name to the media."

"They want to see Zypraxon in action. They're not interested in getting involved in a criminal investigation."

"Maybe."

"Then why watch us from afar? Why not meet with me or abduct me? You're right. They want to keep their hands clean."

"I agree, but . . ."

"But what?"

"It would help me if I had some idea of what you were planning to do, Charley."

Her deep breath feels like it adds ten pounds to her frame.

Marty hadn't pressed over the past two days, and it was easier to her to believe her idea wasn't bonkers when she didn't have to discuss it out loud.

"It's like Kayla said, I'm going to bait him, just like I did those guys at the bar. That way I can be absolutely sure it's him."

"And then?"

"I'm not going to kill him, Luke. Once I'm absolutely sure he's the guy, I'm going to overpower him and restrain him and leave him there right next to undeniable proof of who he is and what he's done. Then we'll call law enforcement and let them know what's waiting for them."

There. She'd said it. And it doesn't sound crazy. Given everything she's been through these past few days, it sounds relatively simple and sane.

"Are *we* going to be waiting for them?" he asks.

"Nope."

His shoulders sag. His chest rises and falls from what looks like his first deep breath in days. She realizes their fight two days ago left him with the conviction she was out to kill the guy. How else could he have interpreted her words? She'd be the end of him; isn't that exactly what she's said?

Maybe she should have cut Luke some slack. He's certainly cutting her some now.

"So," she says.

"So," he says.

"Are you in?"

"I'm in."

"Good."

"We'll see." When she flinches, he adds, "If I'm any good at this, I mean. Not if you're—"

"I get it."

But she didn't get it until he said it, and she's glad he did.

When they return to the desk, the message waiting for them is:

Hope you used protection.

"Cute, for a ten-year-old," Luke says.

"We're going after Pemberton," Charley says. "What can you give us on him?"

Lots. But it's what I can't give you on him that's worth looking into.

"I'm listening," she says.

His house outside Temecula. It's got no Internet. No smart networks. Nothing I can even knock on to get in. It's a five-thousand-square-foot former vineyard. Does that sound normal for a guy who has five million sitting in savings?

"No," she says.

The Bannings killed in the age before wireless Internet blanketed most of the country, but the isolation of their farm was a secret to their long-term success. Sloppy, escalating serial killers already planning their celebrity jailhouse interviews murder on roadsides in fits of sadistic sexual passion. Methodical, long-running monsters have special, secure workshops where they can do their terrible deeds in peace.

"Can you go deeper on him, Bailey?" she asks.

No answer.

Luke groans. "Don't tell me you have to get permission from this hacktivist collective you're working with?"

I don't discuss procedure.

"So your friends think it's fine to go after a police department, but not a guy who might be killing women?"

Suddenly the backspace bar starts devouring everything in the Word doc until there's only whitespace left.

> TTYL. After I send pictures of Luke showering to
> the *LA Times.*

Then the document closes, and the alarm system lets out that strange blip noise that sounds like a stopper being pulled from a drain.

"Maybe it's a good thing he disappeared," Charlotte says. "I'm not sure you two could handle being in the same country together right now."

"I think you're right."

"How long has she been back?" Mona asks.

"A few days," Luke says. When he closes the door to Mona's office, Judy turns in her desk chair and gives them her version of a curious look: pursed lips, furrowed brow, flaring nostrils. Basically the way you'd look if you smelled shit. And maybe that's prophetic because what Luke's about to do inside Mona's office is shovel some serious bullshit.

"Does this have anything to do with that crazy alarm at your house last night?" she asks.

"Possibly. That's what I have to go to LA to check out," he lies.

"So this stalker of hers, you don't think he's around here anymore?"

"She says the last time he called her, he told her he was down in Orange County staying with friends and that she should come and join them so they could have a great life together killing animals on his ranch."

"Jesus. So he's *that* kind of stalker." She settles into her chair. He follows her lead, even though he'd rather stay standing so he can stare out her window and keep her from making direct contact with his lying eyes.

"All her stalkers are pretty choice."

"How many she got?" Mona asks.

"An Internet full, apparently. It's why she came back. Living out on her own was too dangerous, apparently."

Aaaand that's more than you needed to say.

"But she doesn't have restraining orders out against any of them?" Mona asks.

One, but he's dead. "What good would it do?"

"Trina Pierce. That's certainly a blast from the past. What's her new name again?"

"Charley. Charley Rowe. Short for Charlotte."

"How many days you need?"

"I don't know. Until I find something, if that's OK. It's not exactly like I'm that much use up here."

"You are, actually. It's just being useful here means doing things you hate."

"I wouldn't say that."

"I know. Because you're wanting me to let you head down to Orange County with your new friend Charley, so you're being real nice. There's no overtime here. You realize that, right?"

"I do. She wants to make a home here again, Mona. I'd like to play a part in making sure she's safe. Or at least feels that way."

"And let me guess. She's filled out real nice in the chest department."

"Mona, that's no way to talk about a woman."

"I'm talking about how men talk about women. There's a big difference."

"What happened to rehabbing my reputation?"

"In Orange County?"

"I don't know if you remember, but it's not like I was real nice to this girl in high school."

"And that's why you're making the effort now? That's the only reason?"

"Yes."

Mona clears her throat, folds her hands on the desk in front of her. Studies Luke like she's trying to figure out if he lied about his age or needs hair replacement treatment. Or both. Luke, on the other hand, is feeling surprisingly relaxed. *Funny,* he thinks, *how the events of the past few days have made it so much easier to lie.*

About what matters anyway.

"I remember," she finally says. "I remember your mother being none too happy about all the Burning Girl crap you pulled at school."

"Why didn't she say anything?"

"'Cause you were so agreeable back then."

Just take the hit, he thinks. *It means she's giving in.*

"Check in every day," she says. "Take your own car. You're not in uniform, obviously, 'cause it's way out of your jurisdiction. Whole thing is purely exploratory. And if you do find anything that requires a response, you bring it to me. I bring it to this county; they bring it to the relevant department in Orange County. It won't be a huge headache at all, which is why I'm *so* glad you're pursuing this, by the way. Point is, you're on an information-gathering mission only. Think college newspaper reporter. With social anxiety."

Luke stands. "I actually did write for the paper at SF State."

"Good, now work on the social anxiety part."

Luke opens the door before Mona's finished talking.

"I'm probably just letting you go because I'm sick of watching Judy check out your butt every five minutes."

"That's a nasty lie!" Judy shouts.

Just for good measure, Luke wiggles his butt as he passes Judy's desk. He can't help himself. He's that excited to have cleared the hurdle that is Mona Sanchez so quickly.

36

Frederick Pemberton owns two vehicles: a motorcycle and an SUV.

Within a few hours of their arrival in Newport Beach, Luke managed to plant GPS trackers on both of them; the Kawasaki the doctor drove to work and the Cadillac SRX he left in the parking garage under his condo high-rise. The high-rise is ten stories, a drab stone tower fringed with deep balconies, right at the entrance to the Lido Peninsula, a little finger of land that sticks out into Newport Bay.

According to the stats Bailey sent, Pemberton lives in 8B; a twenty-five-hundred-square-foot two-bedroom unit with a view of the harbor. But it's also got neighbors above, below, and along the eastern wall. A shitty kill house, by any measure. And the building's security is mostly for show. A guardhouse at the entry next to some aboveground visitor parking. Keypad entry to both the lobby and the subterranean garage—the kind of defenses designed to keep thieves from backing up vans and trucks to the place, not the kind favored by residents with grave secrets. As evidenced by the fact that it took Luke twenty minutes to plant the tracker on Pemberton's Caddy and make it back to the Jeep several blocks away, where Charley waited for him with her shaky hands clasped between her knees.

The parking garage at Pemberton's office tower—a fifteen-minute drive away at Newport Center, where immaculate, modern high-rises stand on a circular drive around an upscale shopping mall—was even less secure. Luke returned to the Jeep without having broken a sweat.

Now they're back at the Travelodge in Corona del Mar, waiting for the doctor to finish his workday, the contents of their recent trip to Best Buy spread out between them on one of the room's bouncy twin beds.

Luke's busy assembling stuff. Charley's busy assembling her thoughts.

Luke seems to be having more fun.

She bought four GPS trackers total out of her dwindling funds, as well as an additional tablet to monitor their signals. Luke paid for the car mounts, one for the GPS tablet, the other for the tablet that came with her *are these things real* contact lenses, which maybe she should be wearing right now because technically she's working. They both are.

But for now working means waiting for Pemberton to go on the move again. Whoever's watching the transmission from the lenses, are they really going to be that interested in seeing Luke unwrap the equipment while she scrolls through texts from Bailey on her burner phone?

She's not even reading the texts. Not really. She's got them memorized. And it gives her something Zen-like to do as she draws a map from memory in her head. Pemberton's condo is eight minutes south of their motel if they take State Road 55; twelve if they take surface streets. His office is only a few miles east, but Upper Newport Bay cuts through the land between, which will force them onto crowded PCH to the south or north onto the toll road if they have to pursue the good doctor in a hurry.

Eyes on 73.

"It's Bailey," she says. "He got into the tollbooth cameras."

"All of them?" Luke doesn't even look up from the mount he's assembling.

All three entrances? she types.

Jamboree Road, McArthur, 55 intersection.

"All of them," she says.

"Hot dog." But he's already assembling the next mount, too pre-occupied to give in to excitement.

Hot dog is right. It's a huge help. Between this and how quickly the GPS trackers got planted, she feels dangerously close to a good mood.

If Pemberton's taking a long drive, to his country house, for instance, he's got almost no choice but to use the toll road at some point. He can't get to the 405 or the 5 freeway without it. Better yet, the old pay booths are all gone. The whole thing's run by cameras that snap your license plate photo when you enter and send you a nice fat fine in the mail if you don't go online and pay the toll within five days. Cameras Bailey can now see through.

Meanwhile, about seventy-five miles south and a little ways inland, Marty, or one of the guys he's got working with him, is currently perched on a back road that snakes through the dry, boulder-strewn mountains just east of Interstate 15, and he's studying the former vineyard Pemberton's turned into his country house.

Based on what she saw online, the surrounding countryside is beautiful, but Temecula is hardly the Napa Valley of Southern California many of the locals would like it to be. It's more rugged, for one, and you can still snag a parcel of land for only several hundred thousand dollars. But a short drive south is the Pala Casino Spa Resort. That's where one of Marty's buddies has parked a motor home so the whole crew can use it as their crash pad in between watches. It's a great idea, although she won't want to smell the inside of the RV if this thing drags on for too long. But so far none of the guys is complaining.

Yesterday evening Marty gave her an excellent report on Pemberton's place.

It's a sprawling, Spanish mission–style house sitting all by itself on the side of a scrubby, boulder-studded slope that used to be terraced with vineyard fields. "Kinda like a Del Taco someone squashed and then pulled out on either end" was Marty's description of its architectural style. More important, it's hemmed in by a tall cast-iron fence and patrolled by three giant Doberman pinschers Marty says look mean enough to make Godzilla take a step back.

Some guy, not Pemberton—too short, no trace of a nose job, a battered pickup that doesn't seem like the doctor's style—stopped by yesterday afternoon just before dusk. The dogs greeted him with furious hunger and not a trace of affection. The guy hurled several raw steaks through the fence, then raced back to his truck as if he thought they might be capable of jumping the enclosure.

A local caretaker—that was Marty's guess. If he had access to the house, or even inside the fence, he had no interest in using it. Not with those hounds standing guard.

Luke agreed with Marty, and added that if you wanted people to steer clear of your place, hire a local to tell everyone how scary your dogs are.

Charley thinks there's a chance the guy's just a concerned neighbor who might be worried about the dogs. That said, why feed them steaks? Isn't that supposed to make dogs more aggressive?

She can't handle another unanswered question right now. Not for another ten minutes at least. She sucks in a deep breath, rolls over onto her back, and stares up at the motel room's cottage-cheese ceiling. She tries to inhale a few deep, steadying breaths without distracting Luke from what he's doing on the other side of the bed.

"Sleepy?" he asks.

"My brain feels like wet cement. Is that the same thing?"

"Not really. So how many?" Luke asks suddenly.

"How many what?" she asks, genuinely confused.

She doesn't have the slightest clue what he's asking about. How many dogs did Marty spot at Pemberton's vineyard? How many times had he seen the visitor drop by to feed them? How many car mounts did they buy? She's been so lost in thought she can't remember which of the facts, assessments, and plans swirling through her head they've actually had a conversation about since returning to the motel.

He's assembled both the mounts. He holds them up proudly with a boyish, endearing smile that makes something unnerving happen in her stomach. There's a suction cup on each that will allow it to stick to the dash.

"The Xanax," he asks. "How many did you take?"

"Oh, right. Ten."

She already told him, but he's probably forgotten. Lord knows they've got enough to think about.

"And they were two-milligram pills?" he asks, dumbfounded.

"Yep."

"You took twenty milligrams of Xanax, and you didn't even get drowsy?"

She nods. "Same deal as the wine and the vodka I drank the other night."

"How'd you trigger?"

"If I never have to run across another highway again in my lifetime, it'll be too soon."

"Which highway? The 101? When did you guys do this?"

"Night before last. We told you we were getting ready. People honked but none of them even grazed me this time. Probably thought I was a ghost. But it was enough to trigger; that's for sure."

"I figured you were looking up directions and stuff."

"Marty had a sponsee who went and helped a newcomer clean out his house of a bunch of prescriptions he didn't exactly need."

"Newcomer?"

"That's what they call them in AA."

"Gotcha. So Marty got his hands on a bunch of pills and thought, *Hey. Let's see if we can make Charley overdose while she's on Zypraxon.*"

"Not exactly that, no. If this guy's a medical professional and he's really pulling off these abductions in public, chances are ten to one he's using some kind of tranquilizer or anesthetic. Something to subdue his victims long enough to get them into a vehicle."

"What other pills did you try?" Luke asks.

"Well, he also had Percocet and OxyContin. Oh, and Ambien."

"How many did you take of those?"

"Ten."

"Each?"

She nods.

"And you didn't feel a thing?"

"No. It's like it just burns up in my system."

"Jesus. Not to be too blunt, but I don't understand how you can take this stuff without your heart exploding."

"Neither can the people who made it, apparently."

Luke fastens both tablets into the mounts to make sure they fit. When it's clear they do, he pulls them out again, sets them aside, huffs out a deep breath, clearly in search of another place to focus his nervous energy.

Bad news.

The text appears on both their burner phones at the same time. Charlotte types: ???

His computer bores me to tears.

"No pictures of murdered women on Pemberton's computer, and my brother calls that bad news," Luke says.

You finally got in? Charlotte types.

With help.

Luke makes a low sound in his throat; the same sound he's started to make every time Bailey references the other hackers he may or may not be working with and they'll never know because he doesn't discuss procedure and they should stop asking already or they'll risk sounding like tools of the establishment.

But it's what's not there . . .

Luke types, What would that (not) be?

No porn.

"Well, that's suspicious," Luke says.
"Seriously?"
"A man with no porn on his computer? That's full-on weird."
"Uh-huh. Maybe you have a porn problem and you're projecting?"
"Single man, living on his own. I'm just speaking truths; that's all. The only men who don't have some form of porn on their computers are superreligious or they share a computer with their wives."
"So wives can't have porn? Wait. Does Tumblr count as porn?"
"If you have to ask . . . Wait a second, though."
Did you check his web history? Luke types.

Do you think I started doing this yesterday? I'm wanted by the FBI, genius.

"I guess that's a yes," Charlotte says. "So why are we talking about Pemberton and porn?"

Luke points to the phone to indicate he wasn't the one who raised the issue. *Good point.* She asks Bailey the same question.

Makes me want into that country house more, but there's no way in . . . yet.

What about his office? Charley types.

Harder. More secure. Probably because of patient info. Not impossible, but harder.

"So he's not volunteering to hack his office," Luke says.

"I'm still not sure on the etiquette here. Should I ask him? Offer to send him a fruit basket?"

"He hacks satellites, but suddenly a doctor's office is hard."

"Maybe he's getting tired. And cranky."

"Tell him what a good little hacker he is and how he's changed your opinion of hackers forever and ever and you promise to be less hackerphobic in the future."

Charlotte laughs.

There's a ping from one of the tablets.

"Doc's on the move," Luke says.

She studies the map.

"He's not headed home."

"Maybe the gym?" he asks.

Bailey had sent the name and address of the doc's favorite fitness club before they left Altamira. They'd cruised past the place that morning after it became clear Pemberton was going to be in surgery for a while. It's one of many businesses inside an upscale corner minimall with big walls of glass and escalators traveling all four floors.

"Looks like it," Luke said.

"Let's go."

A few minutes later, the tracker shows Pemberton's motorcycle has stopped in what appears to be the dead center of Barry Fitness, probably because it's in the parking lot below. As he closes in on the place, Luke eases his foot off the gas and gives her a long glance that tells her he's awaiting instructions. It's almost dusk, and she's got a baseball cap tucked low over her head. Together with a black hoodie Luke brought, it's a passable disguise.

"I'm gonna hop out. Circle until I text."

"Charley." He brakes, grips her elbow gently. "If you're gonna use yourself as bait, he can't see you until it's time. It's not time, is it?"

"No. I need a good look at him."

Luke wants to ask more questions; she can tell. But he restrains himself. Maybe something about her tone conveyed a meaning she wasn't aware of even as she spoke. Early that morning, they'd reached Pemberton's high-rise just in time to see him roar out of the parking lot on his bike. But he was helmeted. Faceless. And she'd found herself disappointed that she didn't get a chance to look into his eyes, to see if she could glimpse something that reminded her of the Bannings. Something predatory, feral.

Luke's right. Looking into his eyes now is too much of a risk. But she needs to watch him, if only for a few minutes. Needs to observe him when he doesn't know he's being observed.

"Be careful," he says.

She nods and jumps from the Jeep.

Barry Fitness is on the mall's second floor, with giant walls of glass overlooking the street and the escalator atrium. It's a small gym, but the equipment inside looks pricey and new. A row of flat-screen televisions hangs from the ceiling, angled down slightly so they can easily be watched from all three rows of cardio equipment.

First she tries the floor above the gym to see if that'll give her a good vantage point through the escalator well. All she can see is the registration desk, the bored-looking attendant on her smartphone, some weight machines behind a glass partition.

The same spot one floor down gives her a better vantage point, with a greater risk of being seen. From here the gym looks like a glass bubble attached to the mall's facade. No doubt the design of the place is intended to tap into the exhibitionist tendencies of its clientele, of which there aren't very many at present. A few women of varying ages and sizes work themselves tirelessly on the treadmills and striders. Even fewer people are on the weight floor, which extends from the first row of cardio machines all the way to the glass wall overlooking the street.

She's about to scan the surrounding businesses. Maybe Pemberton came here for something besides a workout.

Just then one of the men inside the gym stands up from the shoulder-press machine and rises to an impressive height of over six feet. Bike shorts hug his armor-plated thighs, leaving his carved, veiny calves exposed. A black spandex shirt accentuates his V-shaped torso, particularly the muscular swell of his upper back. Unlike some of the other men pumping iron around him, his body doesn't have the bulbous curves of the chemically enhanced. Rather, it looks naturally sculpted by hours of grueling work.

His black baseball cap casts some shadow on his face, but she can tell it's him. It's the nose that clues her in—the impossibly perfect nose that doesn't seem to match the rest of his face. Now, with the retouching on his headshot removed, she can clearly see his long mouth that doesn't seem to close all the way over his tongue, the tiny eyes that make him appear like he's squinting nervously even as he settles into a new machine and begins confidently hammering out a series of chest presses that sends a stack of metal plates as tall as her knee shooting up and down the cable in quick, smooth repetitions.

Against her will, she feels an almost blinding surge of pity for the man. The quiet gravity with which he expertly goes about his workout seems fueled by neither a love of fitness nor a desire to be healthy; he moves with an angry, bitter determination to be free of his own face. A face, despite his skill and his nose job, he can't alter to his satisfaction.

Why should she view him any differently than the girls she went to high school with who were driven to eating disorders by their own insecurity about their bodies?

Because he might have killed two women, that's why.

She realizes she's been staring too long. Glances down at her phone. There's a text from Luke.

Eyes on him, she writes back.

Good, comes the response.

She gives Pemberton her full attention again. Tries to see past the muscles, past the facial features. Tries to see what type of man his casual mannerisms suggest. She's not a gym person, but his workout seems challenging, and he's not getting tired. He's barely sweating.

Now and then he pauses to sip water from the bottle he carries in a holster built into his waistband; a waistband that also holds his cell phone and what looks like his wallet. There's even a pouch big enough for his keys.

Maybe he avoids the locker room. Just like he's avoiding the crowd at a bigger, trendier, name-brand gym by coming here.

She's changed positions twice, even pantomimed a phone call, just in case he notices her, by the time she realizes he's emptied his bottle.

He heads to the nearest water fountain, starts to refill. That's when something catches his attention, something on one of the TVs. As if in a mild trance, he walks to an empty bicycle in the second row, leans against it as though he's about to get on, but instead stares up at the row of screens overhead. From her new position, she can barely see his face, but she can see the TVs and their predictable buffet of enter-tainment options. A reality-TV catfight in a crowded nightclub, a football game, a syndicated cop show she remembers Luanne watch-ing when it was new.

It's the local newscast that's caught his attention.

Parked police cars. Shots of bicyclists and hikers entering and exiting the woodsy entrance to some sort of wilderness trail. Shots of local signage: Whiting Ranch Park. And then, as if these details weren't dread inducing enough, a black-and-white image, taken in a crowded restaurant, of a plain young woman with brown hair and an uneasy smile. The group of friends she's leaning into, as well as the drink she's probably holding in one hand, have been cropped out. Then she's replaced by images of Kelley Sumter and Sarah Pratt. Faces Charlotte last saw on a smaller, grimier TV inside that horrible bar where she almost killed two rapists.

The chyron on-screen confirms her suspicion about the news report.

Is MISSING OC WOMAN THIRD "MASK MAKER" VICTIM?

She steadies herself with a deep breath, reminds herself she's there to watch Pemberton, not the news. But when she focuses on him, she sees that he's staring up at the screen like a dog whose owner has a treat in hand.

She changes positions again. Tries for an angle on his face with-out exposing herself. She finds a reasonably decent one. It gives her a better view of the bike seat, and the hand he's stroking it with. There's no better word for what he's doing. *Stroking.* Stroking the seat while he gently presses his crotch to the back of it.

Not just pressing, she realizes. *Rubbing.*

Pemberton seems to realize it at almost the same moment she does; he's become fully erect in his skintight bike shorts in the middle of a gym while watching a news report about a woman who might have been murdered.

He swallows, glances behind him, and manages to keep his cool as he makes a show of stretching his arms, which gives him an excuse to drive himself against the back of the seat. He's not trying to cause himself more pleasure; he's trying for the opposite. Maybe that's why he's biting down hard on his lower lip. She can't tell if any of it works. But at least he's embarrassed by his display.

At the very least.

Quickly, he turns his back to her, heads in the opposite direction. She figures the hallway he's turning toward now leads to the locker room. Next to him, there's a shelf lined with fresh hand towels just like the kind the women on the cardio machines are using to mop their brows. He whips one off without slowing his pace and holds it against his stomach so that it covers his crotch as he walks.

As she heads for the nearest escalator, nausea and dizziness are doing a joint number on her, but she manages to stay upright and text Luke.

Pick me up same spot, she writes.

Then once she hits the sidewalk and takes a deep breath, she adds, It's him.

37

I didn't know.

They're following Pemberton back to his condo, which at this hour of the day, makes her feel like they're about to be swallowed by the sunset's blaze.

When did this break? Charley types.

An hour ago, Bailey responds. No word of this at LAPD this weekend. Elle Schaeffer's only been here a few months. Moved here from Wisconsin. No family in SoCal, and her parents passed away a few years ago. No one reported her missing until Monday when she didn't show up for work.

Where are you getting this info? she types.

Um. The *LA Times* website.

The blood left Luke's cheeks as Charley had described what she saw in the gym.

He's been silent ever since, his focus on the road, his jaw working as if there's something stuck in the back of his teeth. Maybe he was just indulging her, holding out hope they were following the wrong guy, and now the reality of this is sinking in.

Pemberton uses his remote to get through the entry gate to his building.

Luke keeps driving, bypasses the spot they parked in that morning, then onto side streets. Meanwhile, the blip indicating the doctor's motorcycle goes still as he parks.

"If he has someone alive, this changes everything," Charley finally says.

"It does." For once he's not disagreeing with her.

Lag time between abductions and masks. Three weeks, right?

Longer, Bailey answers. A month.

"Jesus," she whispers.

"A month. A month goes by between the abduction and the mask. Luke, if he's got a captive, we can't just keep watching him like this."

"I agree, but we don't have evidence that he does."

"I told you what I saw at the gym."

"You did, and it's revolting, but it's not proof he abducted Elle Schaeffer."

"He was literally aroused by the story of her disappearance. As in the actual definition of *literally*."

"Which is proof that he's a sexual sadist, and maybe even the Mask Maker. But it doesn't connect him to Elle Schaeffer. The news could just be speculating about her being a victim. People go missing all the time. You really think he's got a woman up there in that condo?"

"No, I think if he's got her anywhere it's at the Temecula house. I'm calling Marty."

"OK. Once you do, I've got a question I want you to text Bailey."

When Marty answers, he tells her he just got to the RV down at the casino, that he left the surveillance post about twenty minutes before. There's been no sign of life from inside the house all day. The

361

guy who feeds the dogs came back at the same time, obeyed the same routine. In short, nothing seems any different from the day before.

"You don't sound good," he says.

"Call me right away if it seems like anyone's inside. Or anyone else shows up."

"Sure thing, Charley."

As soon as she hangs up, Luke says, "Ask Bailey how long this plastic-nation—"

"Plastination."

"Right. Ask him how long the process takes."

She does. Bailey's response comes a minute later.

An entire body takes fifteen hours of work. But I don't know what percent of that is just posing limbs. If you're just dealing with a face separate from a body, a lot less time, obviously.

"He doesn't know."

"But a while, right?" Luke asks. He's found a parking spot two blocks away. They can't see the high-rise, but they can see the entry gate, and both trackers are stationary and right next to each other now. "Charley?"

"Yes, a while," she says. "Just tell me what your theory is."

"I think the lag time between the abductions and the masks is about the process he needs to actually make them. My guess? He kills his victims right away. Because if he did abduct Elle Schaeffer on Saturday, and we don't have proof that he did, look at how he's acting now. He's been at work all day. He did . . . what? A two-hour workout at the gym?" She nods. "And there's no sign of life at his country house. This isn't the behavior of a man who's got a captive somewhere. Also, the mask-making process is complex. I can't see him making one mask while tending to a different captive in another room while also holding down what looks like a pretty kick-ass career as a plastic surgeon."

They're good points, all of them.

"And if you're wrong?" she asks.

"Then we treat Graydon to a show of you fighting off some really mean Dobermans. Think you're up to it? I mean, it might be an off-label use, but last time I checked, they didn't exactly have FDA approval for this thing."

"I'm glad I have you around for comic relief."

"Hopefully, I'm worth more than that."

"You are . . . I think."

"You think?"

She reaches into her pocket, pulls out the case for the contact lenses, which looks somewhat like a normal case for normal contact lenses, except for the fact that it's made out of stainless steel.

"Are we ready for these?" she asks.

"I don't know. Are we? I mean, seems soon."

"Maybe I just want them to know who we're after. And why."

"Runs the risk of them shutting us down if they think it's too dangerous."

"Maybe. Or maybe Graydon will step in and take down the dogs for us if they can tell he's got someone alive in that house."

"Good point, but . . ."

"But what?"

"Might I suggest a backup plan?"

"I'm listening."

"Have Bailey ready to dump all the documents he found from the Bryant Center hack. That way if Graydon does shut us down, Pemberton and his rich friend won't be able to hide behind that warrant anymore. Or lack thereof."

"That's not a bad idea."

She's getting ready to text Bailey when one of the trackers starts moving.

"Well, that was a quick shower," she says.

"It's the Cadillac."

A few seconds later, she sees it leave the entry gate and turn inland.

Luke eases his foot off the brake and follows.

By the time they've followed Pemberton onto the toll road, she's got the lenses in, and she's used the passcode key to open the feed. The hall of mirrors effect when she looks directly at the receiving tablet turns her stomach.

"Which way's he headed?" she asks.

"South—5 freeway."

"Temecula?"

"Possible."

And though she doesn't say it, it's also possible what they're seeing now actually is the behavior of someone with a living captive who needs tending to.

By the time they're skirting Camp Pendleton, she and Luke agree there's a 75 percent chance they're headed for the Temecula house, which is cause enough to call Marty.

When she asks him to head back to the surveillance point, Marty doesn't complain, but the request still gives her a twinge of guilt. It's his first break of the day, and she figures he was up there for hours already. But even though Marty vouches for all of them, she doesn't know any of the guys currently on watch; she needs someone she can trust with eyes on the property.

Worse, after studying the map earlier that day, Luke's assured her there's no way in hell they can follow Pemberton up the twisty mountain road to his place without being detected. The road leads to only one place—Pemberton's. They'll need to fall back at the entrance to the narrow valley that contains his house, stay in phone contact with Marty, and hope the signal from the tracker doesn't drop out.

If they're given cause to approach the house on foot, the best plan will be to meet up with Marty at the surveillance point and strike out from there. It's a downhill walk most of the way, and the brush is thin. The downside of this plan? If Pemberton leaves by car quickly, catching up with him from the surveillance point won't be easy. Again, it will all depend on the strength of the tracker. Thank God they bought the priciest model.

They're silent now. Suppressing nervous tics. Doing mental battle with worst-case scenarios. And, she's sure, wondering what comes next if it seems Pemberton's got a live captive.

To their right, the Pacific, glittering in the moonlight. To their left, the long, dark expanse of the Marine Corps base and its rear fortification of dark mountains. When they reach Oceanside, a small town right at the base's southern border, Pemberton's Cadillac takes a right onto Highway 76, and Luke says, "Seventy-five percent just went up to ninety."

Low, rolling hills plated in night darkness. The occasional terrace of lights from a subdivision. Then, suddenly, Interstate 15, a blazing ribbon of red and white twisting through the night's darkness, past the hill-nestled town of Fallbrook. By day it must be beautiful countryside. At night it's like they're driving in between frozen ocean waves.

They cross I-15, head into even darker and more rugged countryside.

"Valley entrance or surveillance point?" Luke asks.

"Valley entrance, until we're sure he's staying."

The taillights of Pemberton's Cadillac vanish onto the side road up ahead. Luke keeps driving, toward the Pala Indian Reservation and the blaze of lights from the casino resort up ahead. When he pulls over onto the gravel shoulder, she calls Marty, tells him how far up Pala Temecula Road Pemberton's tracker is.

"Got him in sight," Marty says. "He's coming up the road. Opening the gate, dogs are going nuts."

The fact that she can't hear their barking through the phone tells her how far the surveillance post is from the house. Not good if they're actually going to have to approach the place.

"Pulling into the garage," Marty says.

"How big?"

"The garage? You could fit about four cars, I guess."

"And it's behind the gate?"

"Yep. Everything is except the old vineyard fields, and it doesn't look like he's using those."

"All right. What's he doing now?"

"No sign of him."

"Is there enough light to see by? Maybe he walked to the main house and you—"

"Nope, nope. He's backing out. Or someone else is. No, it's him. But he's in a brown Toyota Camry now."

"Shit," she whispers.

"What?" Luke asks.

"He switched cars."

Luke curses under his breath, takes the Jeep out of park.

Charlotte asks, "Which way's he headed?"

"North on Pala Temecula Road," Marty says.

"Fuck," she whispers. "Go. He's headed in the other direction."

Marty says, "License plate's six, alpha, Juliet, bravo, three, nine, six."

Luke spins out into a U-turn, races for the entrance to Pala Temecula Road. There's no need to point out what they're suddenly up against. New car. No tracker. Unknown direction.

"Careful," Marty says.

She thanks him and hangs up. Suddenly they're speeding through the dark valley, Luke taking hairpin turns faster than any driver should.

"I need to do something scary, but it'll help," he says.

Before she can answer, he kills the headlights. She grips the oh-shit handle, sinks her foot into a phantom brake pedal at her feet. They're gaining slowly on a set of taillights now. As they get closer, she sees the plate number Marty just read to her. Luke keeps the headlights off. Then the city of Temecula appears up ahead; another circuit board of light amid the black, lumpy suggestions of hills.

"A Camry. Does that really seem like the doctor's style?" she asks.

"Nope, but it is one of the most popular cars on the road."

"Perfect for blending in."

"Yep."

They both sigh when he gets on the 15 North. No more twisting through mountain roads in the dark. For now at least. And he's hanging out in the middle lane, obeying the speed limit, which allows them to fall back. They're just past rush hour now, that magical California hour when the traffic starts to thin and the freeways make drivers feel unstoppable instead of trapped.

Murrieta, Wildomar, Lake Elsinore. He's leaving them all in his wake.

"He just passed the Ortega Highway, so I doubt he's headed home," Luke says.

"Or maybe he's taking the long way."

"In that car? I doubt it."

More silence. Pemberton doesn't deviate. Luke manages to maintain a perfect, steady speed in response.

"Charley," he finally says.

"Yeah?"

"You should probably take your medicine now."

"You think?"

"I think he's headed to points unknown in a car designed to blend in. A car he keeps hidden from the world. It's your call. But that's my honest assessment."

And there's no arguing with it, she feels.

By the time they reach Corona, she's taken her pill, just like he suggested.

Bailey texts, asking for an update.

Question, she types back. If this all goes to shit, can you be ready to dump the Bryant Center hack docs?

Define "goes to shit," he answers.

It'll be when I text you and say, "It just went to shit."
Feels like there's a ghost in the room with us. Has been since we started. You want to tell me their name?

Safer if I don't, she answers.

Safer for who? Thought you told me not to be afraid of people you're afraid of. My patience for irony is wearing thin.

"That doesn't sound like it's going well," Luke says.

"Don't worry about it. I got it."

Fine, she types. It's your call. You did the hack. So I guess by your logic, you own the proceeds. But if someone stops us from doing what we're doing out here, you can decide whether you want a serial killer to get away with more murders.

Luke starts shifting lanes. Seconds tick by without a response from Bailey.

Maybe I'm worried about you guys, he writes.

That's sweet. But right now there's only one thing to worry about.

?, he responds.

Pemberton getting away.

She looks up, sees the Camry leading them west onto 91, a different toll road. Orange County spreads out before them in a seemingly never-ending blanket of lights, too vast to be called the suburbs, too flat and diffuse to be considered urban sprawl.

Another turn north, this time onto Interstate 605, then, in what feels like an instant, a turn west again onto I-105. Never before has Charley had such a hatred of Southern California's seemingly non-sensical network of freeways.

"I think I know where he's going," Luke says.

"Where?"

"Won't say yet. Don't want to jinx it."

Whatever that means, Charlotte thinks. But he's doing such a good job of tailing Pemberton, she doesn't want to say anything to distract him.

They keep heading west; then Pemberton's right-turn blinker starts flashing.

"Shit," Luke whispers.

And that's when Charley sees the sign for the exit Pemberton's about to take: Los Angeles International Airport.

"Shit on a stick," she adds.

38

They follow Pemberton across Century Boulevard and into one of the vast and uncovered long-term parking lots right beneath the airport's final approach path.

He bypasses several open spots close to the entrance. Heads for one in the middle of the shadowy sea of parked cars.

"Look at it this way," Luke says. "At least I'll be able to put a tracker on the Camry now."

"What good will it do if he's leaving town?"

Instead of answering, Luke drives past Pemberton's freshly parked car. Slows as he comes to an empty spot two rows away.

"Besides, I thought the extras were replacements for his bike and his Caddy. They only have a sixty-hour charge, right?"

"Yeah, well, best-laid plans and all that."

He's parked them between an SUV and a van.

"Can you see him?" she asks. Her view is blocked.

"Yep. Oh, look. How handy? He already had a carry-on packed in the trunk."

"Well, that's some forward thinking. If he's going to the terminal, we need to follow him."

"No, *I* need to follow him," Luke says. "You need to put the tracker on the Camry."

"Which I don't know how to do."

"If he's getting on a shuttle, you're not getting on with him. Too confined. He'll see you for sure."

"What if he's about to abduct someone?"

"Then he's an idiot. LAX has their own intelligence service, and cameras everywhere. If he's actually going to the airport, there's no way. He's either leaving town or . . ."

"Or what?"

"I don't know. He's walking to the shuttle stop. I'm going after him. At least I can find out what airline he's taking."

"You don't have a bag."

He reaches into the back seat, pulls out the backpack he's been using to carry all the surveillance devices they've acquired over the past few days. He digs in it with one hand, pulls out a spare tracker, and hands it to her. But she still has no idea how to install and activate it, much less connect it to the tablet.

"I'm not fucking this up," she says.

"Fine. Just wait till I'm back. But I need to go now, or I'm going to lose him."

She nods.

He hops from the Jeep, slides the empty backpack up onto his shoulders as he jogs toward the shuttle stop. *The bag looks too empty,* she thinks. But there's no fixing that now.

She steps from the Jeep and inches down its side until she can see Pemberton standing several deliberate paces away from the small group of suitcase-toting travelers waiting for their ride to the terminal.

A thought occurs to her. She pulls out her burner phone.

Still in Pemberton's computer? She asks Bailey.

Yep.

Any evidence of travel arrangements?

Checking.

Luke's made it to the shuttle stop. Like Pemberton, he's standing several paces away from the other travelers, but on the opposite side of the group.

From a distance, he's doing a decent job of looking like a nervous traveler; checking the time on his phone, pulling out some folded-up papers he found inside the bag, checking them as if they're boarding passes.

She waits. Pemberton waits. Luke waits. The other travelers wait.

Then there's a sharp hiss of bus brakes that makes the entire group straighten in anticipation. A few seconds later, a shuttle comes bouncing into the lot.

Almost too late, Luke seems to realize Pemberton is determined to board last. For a few seconds, she's afraid his hesitation might give away his attention. But Luke recovers and steps up onto the shuttle, allowing a young couple and their two small children to fall in between him and their target, who's now bringing up the rear.

Another hiss of brakes and the shuttle lurches forward. Once the low bellow of its engine fades, she's left in unnerving silence. Then a wide-body jet blasts by overhead, so close she can read the codes painted on its belly, engines loud enough to make her teeth rattle.

She approaches the Camry.

It's parked well outside the halo of the nearest sodium vapor light. Maybe that's why he bypassed the first two open spots after entering. She looks around. In general the parking lot is badly lit. Badly lit and huge. And according to the posted rates, not all that expensive, either. And it's hardly secure. The exhaust from the jets can't be good for your paint job.

She peers through the Camry's window. Gives her eyes a minute or two to adjust to the shadows.

There's nothing inside. Nothing. Not a scrap of paper. Not an empty packet of gum. Nothing.

Even though it feels dangerous, she places her hand against the trunk.

She even knocks.

But it's crazy, what she's thinking. According to Luke, Pemberton just opened the trunk and pulled out a carry-on, and besides, he's never dumped an entire body before.

The only part of one of his victims he allows the world to find is her face.

The terminal is packed.

Pemberton bypasses the long lines of customers trying to figure out self-serve ticket kiosks that seem to confound everyone equally regardless of their educational background.

He's strolling, Luke thinks, and for some reason, it's harder to maintain a tailing pace on foot than it was on the freeway.

He pulls a plain black carry-on that looks like almost every other carry-on in the airport. Just like the Camry looks like almost every other car on the road. His outfit, however, is startlingly bright. White jeans, one of those rumpled tan fisherman's hats that reminds Luke of his late grandfather, a cream-colored T-shirt, and a tan windbreaker. It doesn't seem to fit with the rest of his incognito routine. Then Luke imagines what the ensemble looks like against the polished white floors on a black-and-white screen, and the outfit choice makes sense.

So far Pemberton's walked past one major airline, two regional ones, and the entrances to two different security checkpoints. He's made no effort to weave around even the most sluggish of passengers who cross his path. In fact, he seems to stick with the nearest crowd wherever possible, as if he's being gently sucked into the wake of every family or tour group or excited gaggle of college students.

Even if he is taking his sweet time, Luke's still confident there's not a chance he'll strike here or anywhere else inside the airport. The minute he stepped off that shuttle, he gave up all hope of an abduction.

So what is he doing?

They arrive at the entrance to another security checkpoint.

Pemberton slows. So does everyone else around him. They're pausing to debate whether or not this is the checkpoint for their gate. Digging in their bags and purses for their photo IDs. Using the little crowd as cover, Pemberton slips into the nearest restroom. Luke pauses, looking for some way to look busy without having to commit to any of the actual rituals of travel.

He walks past the bathroom, then out the nearest exit. There's a wall of glass that allows him to see the bathroom entrance when he doubles back. Once inside again, he walks up to the spot where travelers are showing their IDs to the TSA agent, looks up at the nearest bank of arrival and departure screens. Then he looks back and forth between the screens and his burner phone as if he's comparing what he sees on each.

After ten minutes of this, and no sign of Pemberton, he needs a new charade. There's no Starbucks, no magazine stands, no stores of any kind this side of security, so it won't be easy. And there's still a good chance the guy's about to fall into the security line and board a long flight. Maybe he checked in online. But why get off the shuttle at a stop so far from his gate? Why walk two and a half terminals first?

He almost misses the man who emerges from the bathroom. And that's the idea, apparently. It's Pemberton, but the fisherman's hat and cream-colored outfit is gone. Now he's in black running pants, a black baseball cap, and a black windbreaker with white stripes on the arms. He's also added a pair of thick-framed glasses, and he's moving at a different speed. Not rushed but clipped. He changed not only outfits but also demeanors; Strolling Leisure Traveler has been replaced by

Just Landed and Have an Appointment First Thing in the Morning Traveler.

Luke follows him down the escalator to the arrivals level.

If he changes cars again, I'm gonna grind my teeth to dust, he thinks.

Pemberton heads to the nearest taxi line. Luke allows some space to develop between them, then joins the line himself. Is Pemberton actually going to get in a cab? At this point Luke wouldn't be surprised if the guy whipped out a saxophone and began playing tunes for change.

The burner phone buzzes in his pocket.

It's Charley. Update?

Luke types, Walked two terminals. Never checked in. Changed outfits in a restroom. Now he's in the taxi line.

Charley answers, He's going home.

How do you know?

There's only four people between Pemberton and the head of the line now. What should he do once Pemberton gets inside a cab and leaves the curb? In this day and age, if you tell a cabdriver to follow another cab, he probably calls the cops on you.

No e-mails from airlines or travel agencies on his computer. And he's scheduled for surgery tomorrow at 11:00 a.m. He's going home. Trust me. Come back.

Bailey, he thinks. Someday soon he'll get used to the fact his brother can see into almost every corner of the world.

You sure? he types. I don't want all this to be for nothing.

It wasn't, she answers. We found his next abduction site.

"So all of this was just to plant the getaway car?" Luke asks.

After taking the shuttle back to the parking lot and planting the tracker on the Camry, he and Charley are sitting in his parked Jeep. He wants to be more relaxed than he is, but the fact that Pemberton's slipped off into the night has left him with a weight in the pit of his stomach. He's not as convinced as Charley is that the guy went back to Newport Beach.

He's angled the rearview mirror so he can see part of the Camry's roof.

"Just?" she asks. "It's probably the most important part of his plan. Look at it this way, a parking lot like this, same-day entry and exit's going to be suspicious, and it'll be the first thing they look for on the cameras once they figure out the abduction happened here. This way, the car stays here for several days like the rest of them, and when he rolls through the exit, presumably with his victim in the trunk, it looks like he's coming home after a trip."

"With *you* in the trunk, you mean. Presumably awake, since twenty milligrams of Xanax has no effect on you."

"Yep."

"Why not just fight him off here in the parking lot? Why let him take you all the way back to Temecula?"

"Remember the plan?"

"Overpower him; restrain him. Leave him right next to the evidence of his crimes."

"Yep. I can't do that here. Best I can do is scare the shit out of him."

"Or kill him."

"Which I'm not interested in doing," she says sharply.

"I didn't say you were."

"I didn't say you did. This is about stopping him. This is about making sure it's me he pulls out of this lot and not someone else, not someone who doesn't have my . . . abilities."

He remembers a little speech she made the other night about how she wanted to stare into Pemberton's eyes and enjoy the fear there when the man realizes she's the *end* of him, but no sense bringing that up now.

But is there any way to point out to her that, yes, there is an easier way to do this? She could overpower him here in the lot. They could call the cops. Once the cops realized they had an attempted abduction on their hands, they'd haul him in, have cause to search his houses.

You didn't agree to stop Pemberton, he tells himself. *You agreed to help her do whatever she wanted, so here you are, hotshot. Enjoy the ride.*

"I don't know," he finally says, surprised to hear he's kept his thoughts from shaking his tone. "You really think this parking lot is where he's going to strike next?"

"Well, what else was he doing tonight?"

"Setting up his escape plan if he's about to get caught. I don't know. It just seems crowded here."

"Look around. It's one of the biggest and the cheapest lots. Almost every other light's burned out, and I haven't seen a single security patrol since you left. Just a bunch of exhausted people, most of them smelling like cheap airline booze, stumbling off that shuttle bus every time it pulls up and walking to their cars in the dark. This is why he drove clear across SoCal tonight, Luke. It's why he switched cars, walked half of LAX, changed outfits. Because *this* is his next abduction site."

"Maybe. Why go to the terminal at all?"

"Shuttle stop's got a camera on it. Look." He follows the direction of her finger; she's right. "If he pulls in and never boards the shuttle, that looks suspicious. If he hails a taxi close to the airport but not at the airport, that's also suspicious, and something a cabdriver might remember later. If he goes straight to the taxi line without changing clothes, he'll stand out when they review the footage. I'm telling you,

Luke, tonight we saw firsthand why this guy doesn't end up on cameras unless he wants to. Everything he's done is about blending into crowds. Going with the flow. Not popping out later when some cop has to watch thirty-some-odd hours of surveillance footage. And he has to do all this because of his face. It's distinctive and weird. The nose doesn't match the rest of it. It's the kind of thing a lone cabdriver late at night might remember later, especially if the pickup place is odd. But in a crowd, in a cap and glasses, he just blends in."

"So he ends up on camera. They just don't notice him when they review the footage."

"Exactly."

Neither of them says anything for a while.

"He's smart. He's resourceful. He has money and means, which gives him time to plan. And he's figured out a way to get his message across to the public without escalating his crimes. In other words, he is the worst-case scenario when it comes to a serial killer."

"And it looks like we're about to get him," he says.

Maybe it isn't the first time he's seen her smile since they were reunited, but it certainly feels that way.

Their burner phones both buzz at the time.

It's Bailey.

Finally found something in his computer that might help.

39

He's on the move.

When Luke's text message arrives, she starts in the direction of the nearest escalator. Friday night at LAX, just after 9:30 p.m. Traffic oozes through the airport's U-shaped departures level like a mudflow. The worst of it's outside Tom Bradley International. There, hordes of passengers are arriving to check in early for their overnight flights to Asia, some pushing carts loaded with enough luggage to provide a family of four with a fresh change of clothes for a month. For the past few minutes she's been weaving through the crowd outside, taking cues from Pemberton's stroll through nearby terminals several nights before. Trying not to stand out on security cameras in case she has to make another visit tomorrow night.

Now she moves with more determination.

Even though she hasn't been anywhere near a plane since they got to the airport hours before, she's dressed like Luke's idea of a weary college student: a loose-fitting canvas jacket from a thrift store, a baggy green blouse from T.J. Maxx. The blue jeans she wears are from her own wardrobe, but the Velcro tennis shoes are brand-new, bought for the occasion, easy to take on and off at a security checkpoint she's never going to pass through. The backpack was new once, but it's also from a thrift store, handpicked because its straps are tattered and it smells of cigarette smoke. The carry-on she pulls is cheap and plain, bought used from one of those stores near the airport that sells off unclaimed luggage, and she's divided a passel of her own clothes and toiletries between it and the tobacco-infused backpack.

Once she reaches the arrivals level, she starts for the nearest shuttle stop. She's memorized the location of each one.

An hour and a half before, at the Westin LAX, Pemberton finished up a talk on how platelet-rich infusions can provide contours during facial surgery. Even though his next conference event isn't until Sunday at 3:00 p.m.—he's listed as a "special guest" at the closing night cocktail party—he reserved a room for both nights with a guaranteed late checkout Sunday evening.

Bailey discovered all this in the doctor's in-box. Initially he'd searched for e-mails from airlines and travel agencies. When he came up short, he moved on to hotel chains; that's when he found the hotel reservation and registration info for the SoCal Regional Medical Suppliers Conference. As Luke put it, 8:00 p.m. Friday to 2:00 p.m. Sunday is the red zone; the time when the conditions for the doctor to slip off and make his abduction are ideal. Winnow those down to nighttime hours, when arrivals and departures are steady, and they've got a nice, tight window to work in.

And now, according to one of the guys Marty's stationed around the Westin, the doctor's on the move.

Which exit did he take? Charley types back.

Point A. It was Luke's code name for the main entrance.

Earlier that day, she and Luke met Marty and two guys he introduced as his *best dudes* at a gas station fifteen minutes from the hotel: Trev Rucker, a wiry former marine sniper who seemed to have no use for blinking, and whose new and starchy-looking long-sleeved shirt hid ornate tattoos, and Dave Brasher, a towering, bald-headed wall of muscle who'd apparently learned a mix of patience and perceptiveness doing things Marty didn't want to mention aside from the fact that they'd earned him a stint in Lompoc. Both men had what Marty called *long-term sobriety*, and both seemed willing to do anything Marty told them to. Charley cared more about the latter.

The departure of Brasher and Rucker from Temecula has left a crew of three at the surveillance point above the vineyard; one of whom rotates down to the RV at Pala Casino for a five-hour nap before returning to relieve the next in line.

Here at the airport, Brasher's on Point A, the Westin entrance; Rucker's on Point B, the hotel's service entrance connecting to a sidewalk that travels most of the way to the long-term parking lot; and Marty's at Point C, halfway between the hotel and long-term lot.

Luke's at Ground Zero, casing the lot on foot, keeping eyes on the brown Camry. As soon as the shuttle she's about to board gets within striking distance, she'll text him, and he'll head back to his Jeep, which is parked inside the lot, and monitor the feed from her contact lenses.

But for now the shuttle is taking its sweet time to show up.

Marty says definitely headed for the lot, comes Luke's text. All three guys tailing.

Tell them not to get too close.
They know.
Tell them anyway.
K.

She waits, bouncing on her heels, running through everything she doesn't know.

What's the Camry's fate once the abduction's done? Bailey's figured out the plates are registered to a woman who died of a stroke at the age of eighty-one last year in Santa Clarita, a woman with no evident connection to Pemberton aside from the license plate. Will Pemberton ditch the car, torch it? Has he used a different car each time? If so, how's he planning to get back to the hotel for the cocktail reception if he's got no wheels and his car's still at the Westin? What a relief it was to have him back in his Cadillac for the drive up from Newport Beach that afternoon. Once again they could follow from a safe distance and use the tracker as a guide. Luke had placed a fresh one under the bumper just before dawn.

In the week since the Camry stash, while Charley and Luke were changing motels to avoid suspicion and Marty was rotating out the guys on his watch crew with actual jobs they had to show up for back in Altamira, Bailey's tried to fill in the holes in what they know of the doctor's plan by searching the man's web history. But he hasn't turned up anything useful. Charley was hoping he'd find searches for shuttle routes or bus services between potential dump sites for the Camry and the Westin, but as Bailey put it, the guy's as good at cleaning out his cache as he is at switching cars and abducting women.

That doesn't mean he hasn't done the research, though.

But why should she care? If everything goes to plan, Pemberton won't make it back to the Westin.

Luke texts, Stupid question but you took it, right?

Right when his talk ended. Yeah.
K. How many left?
Six. But I'm sure they'll give me more if I keep working.
They're reading these right now. Aren't they?
Yep. Hi . . . whoever the hell you are.

A few seconds later: Eyes on him. He's headed for the Camry. The shuttle's stuck in traffic two baggage claim entrances away.

Doc's at the Camry. Pulled some stuff from trunk, got in car. Think it was a jacket. Something else. Just heard from Marty and crew. All lot foot exits covered.

Great, but that asshole's not leaving that lot on foot, she thinks.

The bus pulls up. The door opens with a hiss. She smiles at the driver as she boards, but he ignores her; already looking for an opening in traffic he can pull in to.

The shuttle's mostly empty.

They start forward, two more stops before they're free of the terminal and bound for the long-term lot, and the traffic's getting thinner the farther they get from the international terminal.

Bus showed up, Luke says.

Not mine. Just got on. Still in terminal.
I know.

Several seats away, a woman frees her pug from its carrier. The dog scans the bus, eyes glassy from whatever drug kept it docile at thirty thousand feet. The question from the man across the aisle about when the dog ate last is too familiar to be chitchat from a stranger; he's her husband or boyfriend. A few rows up, a mother argues cheerfully with her two young sons about whether or not Xbox is on the agenda when they get home. Apparently the boys didn't get a lot of rest on the flight from Chicago.

She's the only single woman on the bus.

But another bus has just pulled into the lot. And she's not on it.

He's on the move, Luke writes. Added a jacket and a baseball cap.

Where he's going?
Lurking. Checking out ppl coming off shuttle.
Can you see the passengers?
Some.
Women alone?
One.

Then a few seconds later:

He's going for her.

She feels dread tinged with a disappointment that feels noxiously selfish.

They knew this might happen. They've discussed what to do. No way can they stand back and let him abduct another woman. Luke will have to intervene; he's got his service revolver just in case. He'll wait till the woman's in the trunk, draw the gun. Then they'll have Pemberton on something real; something other than a creepy snatch and grab or attempted assault. It's not the way they want him, and it's probably not the show Graydon wants to see. But they'll stop another murder, and another mask, and maybe that will make this all worth it.

Until it's time to look for another bad man.

He walked right past her.

Details? she types.

Didn't come up behind her. Walked toward her. Watching her. She said hi. Very cheerful. He said hi back. That was it. Now he's headed back to the Camry.
Size?
Tiny. And her car's in the middle of the lot. Close to his.
Sara Pratt, 5' 6". Kelley Sumter, 5' 2". Why not take her?

Her shuttle lurches toward the second and final terminal stop. Nobody else gets on.
In terms of arrivals, this is in the in-between zone.

Right now most of the airport's traffic is international check-ins. In another hour, baggage claim in all the terminals will get swamped with people arriving from points east, folks who took advantage of the time change to enjoy another full day at their destinations before catching the last flight west.

If he's as smart as she thinks he is, if he's researched the arrivals schedule like she has, he'll know this is his golden hour. Another hour and too many passengers will start pouring off the shuttles at once for him to make a quick, clean grab. An hour after that and arrivals traffic goes down to a trickle. Hunting will be poor, and any wrong move could draw the attention of the bored graveyard shift. And this guy doesn't call attention to himself—not until it's time to leave one of his creations in public. So far he's been about balance, precision, a true surgeon in all his affairs.

Why reject her? Luke writes. Is he just scoping?

Thinking . . . she writes.

She's imagining the steps Luke described.

Woman emerges from bus.

He starts for her.

Approaches her from the front, not the back.

And then she says hi, and he says hi, and he keeps walking.

Another one, Luke types.

Her shuttle's left the terminal. They're cresting Aviation Boulevard, angling for the canyon of airport hotels—bus bouncing, passengers chatting excitedly now that they're picking up speed.

Another shuttle? she asks.

No. Another woman. She just parked. Alone. Heading for the shuttle stop. He's seen her.

A few seats away, the pug yips, obviously regaining strength after its drug-induced nap.

Same deal, he writes. Coming up on her from the front.

The shuttle turns a corner; she figures they've got about another ten minutes until she reaches the lot.

Luke. What's happening?

They're talking.

What???

She's asking him where the shuttle goes, and he's answering.

Watch them. And draw your weapon.

Can't text with a gun in my hand :)

This isn't fucking funny, she wants to say, but she also needs to trust him. If he's joking, it's because he doesn't see or sense danger.

She's headed off now. He's not following. WTF? Two easy targets. Doesn't go for either. I don't get it.

Charlotte takes a deep breath. Tries to clear her head. Runs through his script again in his head.

Approaches from the front, not the back.

First one smiles, says hi. He says hi back; lets her go.

Another one approaches him, asking questions.

Letting him know she doesn't know where she's going. Letting him know she's vulnerable. A target of opportunity if there ever was one.

And he doesn't take her.

Why?

Is he hunting for a physical attribute?

She and Luke have spent days now studying everything they could find about the victims, including Elle Schaeffer, even though her connection isn't definitive yet.

Sarah Pratt, Kelley Sumter, Elle Schaeffer. All three midtwenties and white.

At five six, Sarah Pratt was the tallest of the bunch, with Kelley and Elle coming in right behind her, at five two and five four, respectively. The physical similarities end there. Hair color, eye color, facial features—they're all wildly different. Kelley Sumter was a stick figure with a great mane of bottle-blonde hair and a love of cheap, flashy jewelry; Sarah Pratt, a svelte fitness nut and redhead who kept her hair military-grade short and wore halter tops that proudly flashed a tattoo on her shoulder inspired by a series of vampire romance novels she loved. As for Elle, she was a full-figured tomboy who eschewed dresses and had trouble smiling in pictures; the jog that might have ended her life was, according to her work friends, one of her first.

It's not about them, she realizes. *It's about* him. *He approaches them from the front so they can see* him.

The bus makes a dramatic left turn.

It's time to text Luke.

Coming into the lot, she writes.

OK. He's getting out of the Camry.

The bus is slowing down.

I need to put the phone away, she writes.

OK.

She's already deleted all the text messages from earlier that week. Now it's time to delete the ones from Luke. But her finger hesitates, and another one pops through just as the breaks hiss, and the shuttle slows to a gradual halt.

Charley?

Yeah.

Whatever happens, knock him dead ;)

Hey Luke, she types back.

Yeah.
Thanks for doing right by me.

A few seconds tick by, and then, XO.

The shuttle stops. The other passengers get to their feet. She hangs back, letting them wrestle their suitcases out from the racks on either side of the middle exit door. She deletes all of Luke's messages from that night. First the mother and her two sons head out into the dark, then the couple with their now-energetic pug. She feels a twinge of guilt, as if she's allowing these unsuspecting travelers to swim out into waters where a shark lies in wait. But this shark doesn't have a taste for people like them.

Will he have a taste for me?

Amazing, that this is what's occupying her mind in this moment, that her life has brought her to this point—desperate to snare the attention of a human monster. But if he passes her by like he did the other two, they'll have to start over. Once he's laid eyes on her, assessed her, and for some reason judged her wanting, her hopes of baiting him will be forever dashed.

Luke's left the Jeep empty, and she's got a key to it if she has to walk that far. But for now she walks slowly, with a bowed head. Eye contact seems enough to drive the guy away. Eye contact and engagement. But still, he approaches the women from the front.

He's got a trigger, just like Zypraxon does, she thinks. *He's not rejecting these women because of what they are, but because of something they do. Or something they* don't *do.*

She hears footsteps approaching her through the dark.

She grabs the straps of her backpack, keeps staring at the ground, lifts her view just enough that she can see a man's legs approaching. And the sight of his legs reminds her of the way he moved through the gym the other day. Of his perfectly muscled body—his perfectly muscled body contrasting with his imbalanced, slightly altered mess of a face.

With a surge of excitement that borders on giddiness, it comes to her.

He rejected them because they were nice.

They're paces from each other now.

He rejected them because they didn't reject him.

She looks at his face, looks right into his eyes. He's watching her with an intensity that belies his quick, confident steps.

And that's when she winces and quickly looks away as if repulsed by what she sees.

They pass each other, and then she hears his footsteps stop.

I got him, she thinks. *I fucking got him.*

Too late she realizes what she forgot to do.

She forgot to be afraid.

The impact is swift, instant, and skull rattling. Suddenly her torso, neck, and head seem to weigh nothing at all. The next thing she knows, she's kissing asphalt with no memory of the face-plant itself.

Her mind grabs for terror. Nothing is there. She's hollow, vacant. Never in her life has she been truly stunned in the most literal and physical definition of the word. Terror seems like a rational thought process her body can't accommodate, and the more she tries to summon it, the more she pushes it away. As if she were trying to meditate on the calm in the middle of a thunderstorm.

It's like she's breathing through a straw. Her knees scrape the asphalt. He's dragging her in between two parked cars. A sudden rush of fumes makes her eyes water. He stuffs something in her mouth; something soaked in a noxious chemical. She feels it the way you feel your bedsheets when you're first coming to in the morning.

And then the prick of a needle.

My neck, fuck. My neck. He just . . .

And when the darkness closes in around her, she realizes he beat it. He beat the Zypraxon, and whatever he's injected her with is flooding her system. He beat it because she was too busy playing detective and psychologist. She forgot her most important role: victim.

Luke knew this part would be hard.

They discussed it multiple times. What it would mean to watch her go limp and not react. What it would take to just sit there and watch her give herself to the guy so he'd feel safe stuffing her into his trunk.

But the hardest part is watching Pemberton's speed and efficiency. It would be easier if he growled or snarled like a monster, but for him this is just routine, jamming a woman in his trunk like luggage. Even the way he brought the blackjack down across the back of her head was clean, precise. Now he's placing her carry-on in the back seat as if it's his.

The Camry's headlights wink on.

To Marty, Brasher, Rucker, and the two guys on watch in Temecula, Luke texts: We're a go. En route.

Luke waits for the Camry to head for the exit, then brings up the brightness on both tablets affixed to the dash. A few seconds later, there's a knock at the window. It's Marty and his boys. Luke unlocks the doors. The boys slide in back, Marty in the front.

"Motherfuck, man," Marty growls. "Mother*fuck*. I mean, this better—"

"Easy," Luke says. "I know, I know. I watched it, too."

The Camry's tracker is live on one tablet; he's logged in on the second, as evidenced by the square of lighter darkness in the center of the screen. The contact lenses are live, he's sure of it. The trunk is just dark.

"Her head man. He hit her in her fucking *head*, man."

"Marty," Luke says firmly. "Take a breath, OK? I get it. But take a breath. This is what was supposed to happen."

Marty's lips sputter, and he grips the handle next to his arm and nods.

"We're good," Luke says, starting the engine. "Everything's good. We're rolling, and we'll have him soon."

Luke pulls out of the parking spot. As the exit booth comes into view, he sees the Camry's taillights swing out onto the service road.

"Something's wrong."

It's Ed Baker who says it first, but they're all feeling it. The entire crew sitting in front of the bank of computer screens. The warehouse is air-conditioned, thank God, otherwise their combined sweat would be stinking up the place. And if there's anything Cole hates more than waiting, it's body odor.

They were able to watch most of Charley's walk through the terminals on hacked airport surveillance cams as well as through her TruGlass. But only once she made it to the parking lot did Cole stop pacing. It's not just the suspense of watching. He's never worked this closely with these team members before, and that makes Ed nervous. And Ed getting nervous makes him nervous. No compartmentalization means no plausible deniability if things go wrong, if certain hacks are discovered.

An airport, he kept thinking. *Why did all of this have to focus on an airport?* No way can he launch microdrones yards away from two major active runways.

Now they're staring at the hazy black square offered up by Charlotte's TruGlass.

"We sure it's live?" Ed asks.

One of the computer techs says, "It shows as live, and I don't see any interruption in the signal since she left the terminal."

"The center of the screen's lighter than everything around it," Cole says. "She's live—she's just keeping her eyes closed for some reason."

"Why?" Ed asks. "Why is she keeping her eyes closed? She's in the fucking trunk. He can't see her."

"Maybe she's opening them and there's no light source?" another tech asks.

"Something's wrong," Ed growls.

Cole's phone rings. He expects it to be another call from Dylan, another call he plans to ignore. But it's not. It's a call he should have prepared for, but he's had a lot to prepare for over the last few days, so this particular possibility didn't get a dress rehearsal.

Julia Crispin says, "Tell me you have teams in place." No doubt she's been sitting in front of her laptop in her mirrored basement office in Rancho Santa Fe, sipping her drink of choice while tending to paperwork and occasionally glancing over at Charlotte's feed like it's a nostalgic TV rerun.

From the tone of her voice, it sounds like she's just realized this won't be an episode of *The Golden Girls*.

"So you've been checking in on us?" Cole asks.

"It's my technology. I'll do whatever I want with it. Tell me you've prepared for this, Cole."

"A lot has gone into this night, Julia, and it's better if I don't tell you about any of it. That way if something doesn't go exactly as planned, then—"

"Cole."

Her voice is frosty enough to silence him.

"If something happens to that woman, there will be consequences."

"Well, I'm sorry, but something is happening to that woman, and it's the result of a series of choices she's made."

"Choices forced on her by Dylan Cody, and now you. If you don't have teams in place, get them in place now, Cole. Because if that woman doesn't make it out of this, I will fucking ruin you and your family's company and every last member of your family. Do you understand me?"

But it must be a rhetorical question because she hangs up before Cole can answer, and before he can point out the potential self-inflicted wounds inherent in such an endeavor.

When he turns back to the monitor bank, Ed's studying him.

Cole waves his concern away.

"Do we have real-time traffic?" he asks.

The web tech says, "Yeah. They're forty-five minutes out."

"Good. My bird's gassed up, right?"

Ed nods.

"Good," Cole says, as if everything's going to plan.

"Get closer," Marty says for what must be the tenth time.

"Marty, we talked about this." Luke's trying to focus, even relax himself a bit. They're traveling the reverse of the route Pemberton took on the night of the Camry stash, and that's good. That means he's behaving as expected, taking them to the Temecula house. This is the time to focus, get their breath. But Marty's decided it's time for a freak-out.

In the back seat, the boys are quiet, but in the rearview mirror, Luke catches glimpses of their eyes moving back and forth between him and Marty like dogs following a tennis ball.

"We can't see her, for fuck's sake," Marty barks.

"We can see her right there," Luke says, pointing to the GPS tablet. "Marty, I've been tailing him for days, if he recognizes the Jeep and panics when he's got her in the trunk, we're in uncharted territory. That's what the tracker's for."

"Why's it dark, though?" Marty points to the contact lens feed. "Why's it so damn dark? Shouldn't she be blinking? Doing something we can see?"

"If he's moving bodies in that trunk, he's going to take out the light sources, if there are any."

"But not even any cracks, maybe light around the edge of the roof? Come on, Luke."

For the first time, he thinks Marty's got a point. But he also thinks Marty's reactive and maybe not as cut out for this kind of operation as he thought he'd be. Charley's objective could not be any clearer: make the guy believe she's a prostrate victim until she can overpower him when he's surrounded by evidence of his crimes. Any sudden moves before then could blow the whole thing, pitching their operation into a half-assed arrest of Pemberton, a bullshit cover story, and potential evidence lost to rich lawyers and more denied warrants.

But there's something else's that nagging at him.

The drive time. If they continue at their current rate, Charley will only have a little less than an hour left on her Zypraxon after they reach the vineyard.

"Your guys at the surveillance point," Luke says. "What'll it take to get them close to the house?"

"Not much. We staked out possible positions yesterday. Wasn't much else to do up there."

"They're armed?" Luke asks.

"Oh yeah."

"Tell them to get in place. Just in case."

Marty sighs, starts typing into his burner. Relieved and calmed some, it seems, just to have something to do.

And he's relieved that Marty's not still pressuring him to ride the Camry's ass.

He sees the sign for CA-79. A short stint on that will bring them to the entrance to Pala Temecula Road. Ahead of them, the tracker takes that very route.

More good signs.

On the GPS map, the mountain road looks like a slender thread laid across an ocean of black, the Camry a flashing blip slowly traveling its length.

"It does look dark." Luke hasn't heard Brasher say more than a few words since they met earlier that day; he has to check the rearview mirror to make sure it's him. "The other screen, I mean. Is that thing working over *cell* service?"

"Nope," Luke says.

"You got Wi-Fi in this car?"

"Nope."

"How's the signal getting to that thing then?"

"We don't know," Marty answers. "We just enter a code."

A few seconds go by before Brasher says, "Well, shit."

"Going dark," Luke says, before killing the headlights.

There's a collective sphincter clench throughout the Jeep, and then they're twisting up the road without headlights. Up ahead he sees a brief, teasing glimpse of the Camry's taillights. But they're far enough away to seem like the wing lights of a plane at cruising altitude. Later he can brag about how well he memorized the map of this particular stretch of road, but only if this next part goes well.

"How are your guys?" Luke asks.

"Fifteen minutes out."

More silence, more strained breaths and the plastic creaking sounds of Rucker and Brasher grasping their oh-shit handles in the back seat as the Jeep weaves through the dark.

"His access road's coming up on the right," Marty says.

Luke slows, drives right up onto the rock-strewn shoulder. A good distance uphill he catches a glimpse of the Camry's headlights flashing across an automatic gate sliding to one side. Then the car disappears inside. A few seconds later, what he assumes are motion-activated lights die, and his small glimpse of the gate disappears.

Now it's just darkness.

A minute later he hears barks echoing through the canyon; their ghostly distance does nothing to muffle their ferocity.

Then the dogs go quiet, perhaps recognizing their owner. More darkness. More breathing.

And darkness on the tablet that should be showing them everything Charley sees.

With each passing second, Luke's stomach gets a little bit colder.

"Something's wrong," Marty whispers.

"The lenses are working," he says. "The signal's live. It's just . . ."

"It's not the lenses. It's the drug. We're not seeing anything 'cause *she* isn't seeing anything."

"Give it a minute."

"The garage is ten paces from the house, Luke. They're inside by now."

"Text your boys. See what they see."

Marty complies.

A minute goes by with no response.

And another.

And another.

"Nothing," Marty says. "They've gone quiet."

"Bad cell service?"

"We were fine at the surveillance point. We figure the casino down valley's got extra towers. Luke—"

"All right. Everybody. Guns out. Let's go."

Rucker says, "What about the dogs?"

"If they don't sit when you say, shoot 'em."

"I don't hurt dogs," Rucker says.

"Seriously?" Luke whispers.

"Dogs didn't abduct Charley. Men did."

"Then fire over their heads. Just not at one of us."

There's no argument. Luke grabs the tablet from its holster. If it hasn't come to life by the time they reach the gate, he'll junk it and focus on his weapon, but God willing . . .

Somehow they're all following Brasher, who pumps his giant arms as he runs uphill. Later Luke'll think the fact that Brasher somehow outpaced all of them is hilarious given the guy's not exactly streamlined for speed. But he's not sad to have a human tank in the lead; that's for sure.

And then suddenly the tablet flashes in his hand. A bright pulse of light that blinds him. He almost trips, finds his footing.

The other men notice and turn.

The tablet flashes more. Not flashes.

Blinks.

"She's awake!"

Two thousand feet above the Cleveland National Forest, Ed Baker stops reciting the report he was just given by Ground Team A and falls abruptly silent.

A flash of light just pulsed through the helicopter's passenger compartment, followed by another, then another, each one giving his face a ghoulish cast.

For a few seconds, he and Cole blink their surprise at each other; then Cole pats the empty leather next to him, and Ed awkwardly settles his bulk onto the forward-facing bench seat so he can see what now fills the screen of the MacBook resting on Cole's lap.

Charlotte Rowe is finally opening her eyes.

First she becomes aware of a deep, throbbing ache in her temples. As it lessens, she feels a second sensation stretching across her forehead. This feeling isn't in her bones. It's on her skin. It's scratchy and rough.

A strap, she realizes.

These thoughts struggle against a narcotic haze. But it doesn't feel like she's rousing from a long nap. Rather, it's like a chunk of time has been stolen from her. The exact same feeling she experienced when she came to after wisdom tooth surgery.

Surgery.

The word surges through her. The muscles in her neck tense, but they're the only ones. That's when she feels straps on her wrists and ankles. Leather, thick, securing her to the operating table. She's blinking up into a bright glare; against it, she sees the outline of a bulging, transparent IV bag on a stanchion. There's writing all over it—warning labels, she realizes—and one word bigger than the rest: ACETONE.

While physical sensations are returning in stages, her emotions aren't coming back as quickly, and she needs them to. Desperately. Instead her mind floats between a vague sense of alarm and a dull awareness of her situation.

Something burns in her upturned right arm. Two IVs—one small, one large. Neither one is connected to the bag of acetone; the smaller one's connected to a short cord, with a port for injections. Maybe he used that port to bring her back to consciousness.

Something tugs at legs that still feel mostly numb. As if from a distance, she hears rustling sounds. Looks down at her body as much as she can without moving her head. It's not rustling; it's shredding.

Pemberton stands over her. He's lost the jacket and hat, and he's slowly cutting up the right leg of her blue jeans with surgical scissors. The left one's already been cut, the flaps primly laid aside so that her entire thigh is exposed.

"Hello, Charlotte." She's blinking up at him as he traces a finger down the side of her cheek.

He's gone through her things; that must be how he knows her name.

She goes to speak. She can't. There's a ball gag tucked in her mouth. Now that she's aware of it, she can feel the saliva gathering around it, coating the back of her throat. She coughs, but it's a weak effort that forces her nostrils to suck half breaths.

With each new returning sensation, she prays for the return of terror, for the arrival of bone music. But it's like grasping for hunger when your body knows it's full. Somewhere within her the Zypraxon's locked in a cage or stuck against a filter it's too large to slip through. Undissolved. Untapped. Untriggered.

"I assume you know who I am, or you're figuring it out now." He seems as steady and focused as if he's prepping her for a common, beneficial procedure. With the first three fingers of his right hand, he presses down softly on her cheek, as if assessing the fat content, the durability of the skin. "And that means you've probably figured out what you're going to become." He smiles primly. "And you're not panicking, which is either a side effect of the drugs or you think being strong will change the outcome of this." He looks into her eyes. "It won't.

"You see, this face of yours, Charlotte. You realize what it is, don't you? It's just a collection of accidents, really. Genetic accidents that created the shape of your nose, your lips, your chin." He grazes each feature as he references it. "So much of your life has been determined by this face. *Granted* to you by this face, by how people respond to it. But it doesn't have inherent meaning, you see? It's cartilage, really.

Cartilage and privilege. What I do—now *that* gives it meaning. It gives *you* meaning, Charlotte Rowe."

He gives them all this speech, she realizes. *This is what they all saw and heard before they died. He terrifies them like this on purpose. Because he is just like every other human monster, twisting truths and perverting philosophies to justify his desire to inflict pain.*

He traces a path down her upturned forearm, lingering at the IV injection site for a few seconds.

"But I work with the whole body, you see. Your face, I give to the world. Your body stays with me so I can remember the amount of effort I put into it. Into you, you ungrateful little bitch. Tell me." He bends forward, looks into her eyes. "Did you have any sense of the man I really was when you turned up your nose at me in that parking lot? Any sense of the magnitude of what I contain, of what I can do?"

He keeps the bodies, she thinks. *Then the bodies are here. The bodies are the evidence.*

She feels acutely nauseated now. The aftereffect of the blow he delivered to her head in the parking lot throbs persistently in her skull, rings in her ears. And that's good. That means her body's coming back. Rousing. Her thoughts are coming quicker, clearer.

"No?" he asks. "Well, let me tell you what I'm capable of, Charlotte. I'm going to fill your system with acetone. It's going to drive out your blood, replacing most of your body fluids, and it's going to do it while you're alive and awake and remembering this moment. The moment when you realized who I am. This moment, when you finally knew truth."

She blinks, sees the IV dangling from the acetone bag, waiting to be connected to her arm. Her heart races at the sight. Something's missing. The acetone goes in through the big IV, but her blood, her body fluids, how will he push those out?

She feels the cool air—subterranean air, she realizes—kissing her exposed thighs, and that's when terror sends rivers of ice through her body from head to toe. She remembers a term from one of Luanne's hospital stays, when they'd needed to draw blood and the veins in her arm weren't strong enough. *A femoral stick.*

Pinpricks. Not from him. And then shaking in her bones. He sees it, mistakes it for pure fear, and smiles. He can't hear the bone music, but she can.

"They say beauty hurts. But trust me, Charlotte. Achieving meaning hurts so much more."

He turns to the supply table next to him. He gloves his hands, then picks up a loop of clear tubing that's long, thick, and attached to some kind of plunger. There's another waiting on the supply table. Two of them. One for each leg.

"And when I'm done," he says, "you will be very, very beautiful."

A distant, grating sound stills him.

Dogs. Barking dogs.

That's when she quickly and silently pops her left hand free, as if the strap were suddenly made of paper. That's when the strap across her forehead pops off as she goes to sit up, and that's when Frederick Pemberton spins to face her.

He's so stunned to find her sitting upright, so stunned to find them eye to eye, he doesn't notice when she reaches out and grabs his hand. She spits the ball gag she's bitten in half onto her lap, and he looks desperately from it to his own wrist, now clamped in her impossibly strong grip.

"You are a bad, bad man," she whispers.

The bones inside his hand crunch like popcorn. A miserable yowl seems to emanate from deep within his belly. It turns into a high barking when she snaps his wrist.

She swings her legs off the table. His knees hit the floor. He's shuddering, drool flying from his yawning, moaning mouth. Standing over him now, she finds her footing and squeezes down harder on his shattered wrist, drawing the limp and lifeless arm out from his body so she can keep him upright on his knees. Part of her is waiting for the same revulsion she felt when she broke Jason Briffel's shoulder, but it's not coming. All she feels is the bone music and, thanks to the terror in Pemberton's eyes, the sense that she has become not darkness but a great fire, bringing a sudden, blazing end to it.

"Did you give them all that little speech, Dr. Frederick Pemberton? Did you say it to them all so that you could see their fear?"

Tears of agony spit from the corners of his squinting eyes. His breaths are wails. And the wet spot darkening his pants isn't blood, she's sure.

She leans in close, until they're nose to nose. He shudders. "Do you see any fear in *my* eyes, Doctor?"

His answer is a trembling groan.

Another bone, possibly his shoulder, snaps as she yanks him upright by his already injured arm. His head rolls on his neck; his feet graze the floor like a dangling puppet's.

"This is my meaning, Doctor," she says. "This is the truth of who I am. I'm not here to show you fear. I'm here to see yours."

She releases his arm and gives his opposite shoulder a light shove that sends him stumbling backward into a coffinlike vessel sitting a few feet from the operating table. Now that she's free, she's seeing it for the first time. It's a vacuum pump chamber—just like the one she saw online, the one he probably stole from the Bryant Center. The entire thing tilts away from her. From his wheezing breaths and glassy eyes, it's clear the impact has stunned Pemberton as badly as his blow to the head stunned her in the parking lot. The chamber's tilting. When it goes over to one side, he goes with it like a pile of bones.

She starts toward him.

The dogs are barking their asses off, but none of the men could give a shit. *Later I'll laugh about this,* Luke thinks. They'll all laugh about how they stood in the dark outside a serial killer's gate, ignoring vicious dogs while they watched Charley beat the living shit out of Pemberton on a tablet Luke held in his sweaty, trembling hands.

It wasn't like they weren't ready to break in. They were. The problem was, the damn gate didn't have a pedestrian entrance. Just a sliding one for cars. So there was no lock to shoot off. They were trying to figure out how to distract the dogs while one or more of them jumped the fence, Luke trying to hide the tablet from the guys so they didn't panic with each moment Charley didn't fight her way free of the table.

In other words, they were about to kill the dogs.

Then Charley broke the serial killer's wrist, and Luke started shouting at everyone to stop, and everything changed.

And now they're just standing there, watching. Watching what shouldn't be possible.

And Rucker's saying the Lord's Prayer under his breath.

Or maybe it's a Hail Mary; Luke isn't sure. He's never been religious.

Maybe he will be after all this.

Suddenly the dogs' attention shifts. They start running toward the fence off to their left, the one that faces the downhill slope. It takes all Luke's effort to look away from the tablet, and he has to blink in the darkness. It looks for a moment as if the brush on the far side of the fence has come to life. He thinks maybe it's the guys from the surveillance post, the ones who stopped responding after they were fifteen minutes out.

But these are not the guys from the surveillance post.

These guys are outfitted for war.

The first dog goes down with a high-pitched whine. Felled by something swift and silent. Not a bullet, some kind of dart. Apparently Brasher's not the only one averse to hurting dogs. Then the second and the third. As soon as the barking fades, Luke hears a growling, chest-rattling sound. Realizes it's coming from above.

There's a blast of air and a blaze of light, and suddenly the four of them are grabbing on to each other and stumbling backward as a giant helicopter barrels down on them, runners extending in the moments before it touches earth. The downdraft deafens him. Marty's gray mane has come loose from its ponytail. It dances up into Luke's face, forcing him to bat it away.

The chopper lands in such a way as to pin them in between the gate and wherever the thing's spinning blades end. He'd love to know where the fuck that is exactly. They all would, so they keep stumbling backward toward the gate. Just then there's a fireworklike blast off to his right. The falling spikes of the steel gate force them all to jump back in the direction of the chopper, which causes Marty to scream, "Jesus Fucking Christ. Make up your goddamn minds, assholes!"

The soldiers from the brush are streaming across the house's yard now, automatic weapons raised. Helmets, visors, maybe even night vision goggles, Luke can't be sure. He counts five or six of them at least. And not a single one has the insignia of a law enforcement agency.

Then the door to the helicopter opens, and the man who steps out looks vaguely familiar. He's dressed in a long black trench coat like something out of *The Matrix*—a powder-blue button-up, collar flapping in the wind—and big, chunky black boots that are probably some designer's expensive imitation of Doc Martens.

Cole Graydon, CEO of Graydon Pharmaceuticals. He read about him in the file Kayla brought.

Cole approaches him. For a delirious second, he thinks the guy's actually about to shake his hand. Three SUVs pull up behind the chopper. At least seven men emerge. All military-grade scary. Not combat ready like the guys who just took down the dogs and poured across the yard. But they're packing. And maybe that means if Luke doesn't shake the guy's hand, he'll end up with one right between the eyes.

"Your passkey," Cole Graydon says.

Luke's genuinely stumped.

Cole points to his own eyes and gives Luke a broad smile.

Luke digs into his pants pocket, hands Cole the digital key.

Cole takes it, extends his other hand.

The tablet. He wants the tablet.

He wants their connection to Charley.

As if reading his mind, Cole says, "Don't assume the worst of us. It will serve no one."

"Too late," Luke says.

Cole laughs. "How's this? Stay out of our way, and no one will die."

Behind Cole, three of his guys part their windbreakers, revealing Glocks in hip holsters.

Luke hands over the tablet.

"Thank you," Cole says with a smile; then he turns and starts walking over the fallen gate toward the house.

"I wouldn't mess with her if I were you," Luke calls after him. "She's in kind of a mood."

"Oh, I won't." Cole turns. "Far from it. Quite the opposite in fact."

Then with another smile as gracious as the one he probably gives at board meetings, he starts for the house, his own private army on his tail.

"Where is Elle Schaeffer?" she asks him for the fourth time.

She's not sure if his spine is broken. She's not sure if she cares.

He's sprawled on the toppled vacuum chamber, still blubbering like a baby. The pleasure's going out of it for her. The delight she's been taking in his misery is fading. She toys, briefly, with the idea of trying to provoke him in some way. To draw out some evidence of his evil so she can pounce on it. Pounce on him. But he's broken. If not physically, then mentally. She's never seen someone truly snap, never borne witness as another human loses his mind in the course of one swift and devastating episode. How many victims of the Bannings did just that during their confinement and rape, yards from where she ate, slept, and daydreamed?

Does this square that terrible debt in some way?

She's been prodding his face. Grazing it. Treating it just the way he treated hers. Now she grips both sides of his chin in her open palms. Gently. But even that makes him shudder and sob.

"*Where* is Elle Schaeffer?"

His bloodshot, tear-filled eyes cut to the left.

For the first time, she really surveys her surroundings, surveys this basement of horrors where at least two women lost their lives in a brutal, agonizing way. One wall is dominated by a utility sink and lockable metal supply closets that look like they could survive a bomb blast. To the left, the direction he just looked, are double doors to what looks like a giant walk-in freezer.

She heads to it, observes the lock, grabs both handles, one in each hand, and pries the doors open with minimal effort. The lock mechanism tears in half and falls to the floor at her feet. A blast of refrigeration hits her. The space is large enough to park a car in. And they're all in there. All three of them. Elle's body is still strapped to an operating table just like the one Charley escaped from, but her face is missing.

Toward the back, what remains of Sarah Pratt and Kelley Sumter sit side by side on a bench. Their missing faces reveal frozen eyeballs staring out from exposed muscles and tendons. But the rest of their flesh is intact. They sit upright, held that way by lengths of wire that secure them to the ceiling overhead. They are something between mannequins and puppets. Still being molded and formed into their final poses, destined perhaps for a rendering similar to the exhibit at the Bryant Center, only for the depraved delight of one man.

Charlotte is amazed to discover that even in this heightened state she is still capable of tears. That even as she lays her hand gently on Elle Schaeffer's collarbone, as she wishes the woman some peaceful rest, that Zypraxon in full bloom in her veins does not rid her of grief or pain, for these women, for those who met their end in the Bannings' root cellar.

For her mother, who loved "Angel of the Morning." Who might have patched things up with her father again, if only for her sake.

She hears him behind her. Coughing, wheezing, struggling to his feet. She knows even as she turns that he's going to try some pathetic, last-minute defense.

She also knows that she's going to kill him.

He's yanked the acetone bag from the stanchion; he holds the long rod of steel in his unbroken arm as he runs for her like a gutter drunk trying to scare off the cops. She reaches out and seizes his throat with the gentlest of grips. It's enough to choke off his air and drive him backward as she walks out of the refrigerator.

She carries him by his throat to the operating table, slams him to the metal. Carefully straps his unbroken wrist, then realizes she tore through the other strap when she broke free. She secures his ankles instead. He barely manages to catch his breath by the time he realizes he's restrained.

"Tell me, Doctor," she says. "What happens if it's all got nowhere to go?"

Goggle-eyed, he stares at her, shaking his head, wheezing, no idea what she's talking about, until he sees her reach down and slide the large IV port from her arm with the press of one finger against the plastic. She studies the bloody needle briefly; then, with her other hand, she grips his left forearm just above his shattered wrist. There's enough power in even this light grip to bring his vein pulsing to the surface of his skin.

She sticks him with the IV, reaches for the cord dangling from the acetone bag. "What happens if the acetone goes in and all your blood and body fluids have nowhere to go? Does it just fill you up, Doctor? Does it fill you with *meaning*?"

She's never seen someone pass out from fear before, but that's exactly what he does. Nods off like exhaustion's overtaken him, when really it's shock. She's considering ways to wake him up when another man's voice calls out to her from across the room.

She looks up, instantly recognizes him from the magazine profile of him she read only days before.

Cole Graydon.

He stands at the foot of the staircase. Two bulky men in black windbreakers with military-grade buzz cuts have preceded him into the basement, guns raised. Are they aiming at her or Pemberton or both of them? It's impossible to tell. Because both men have seen what Cole hasn't. They've seen Kelley Sumter, Sarah Pratt, and Elle Schaeffer.

"Don't do that, Charley," Cole says. "Whatever you're about to do with that IV, just . . . take a step back from the table so we can talk."

"Come closer, Mr. Graydon."

"Let's avoid threats if we can. And please. Call me Cole."

"Come closer so you can see what your men are seeing."

He complies, leaving the bottom step. When he sees what's inside the walk-in refrigerator, he goes as still as if a snake were coiled at his feet. The confidence that sparked in his eyes when she first saw him fades. His nostrils flare. She doesn't delight in his silent, muffled terror, but she thinks maybe it's just. If he is one of the architects of all this, if, like Dylan, he's tried to use her past to manipulate her, he should at least have to stand nose to nose with what that past is really made of.

He turns to face her, trying his best to compose himself. It isn't working.

"Come with me, Charley. We have much to discuss."

"And this . . . thing?" she asks. "What should I do with him?"

"We'll take care of him."

"I don't want him taken care of. I want him dead."

"No. No, that's not true, Charley. You want him to have never killed at all. And that's not an option. But you've done the next best thing. You stopped him."

"Now you're trying to read my mind. Bend me to what you want. Just like Dylan Cody."

A flash of something in his eyes when she says Dylan's name. He's still so shaken by the scene inside the refrigerator; he can't hide it from her. But this is different from horror, this feeling that flares bright in his piercing-blue eyes. Hurt, betrayal.

"I am not just like Dylan Cody." There's a tremor in his voice. "And I didn't want any of this."

She believes him.

Maybe she shouldn't, but she does.

"Come with me. We'll talk. Things will become clearer—I promise."

She looks down at Pemberton. So twisted and deformed by terror, agony, and pain as to be almost unrecognizable from the man who strapped her to this very table only moments ago.

She backs away from the table, rounds its foot, and starts toward Cole and the staircase. Instantly one of Cole's men aims his gun at Pemberton. The other takes aim at her, even as he sidesteps closer to his partner and the operating table, allowing her to join Cole.

Cole gestures for her to go first.

"I could tear you apart," she says. "You know that, right?"

"I do. And I trust you not to. Just as I hope you'll trust me not to do anything to harm you or your men."

My men. So he's reminding me he's got Marty and Luke, she thinks. *So much for avoiding threats.*

She steps forward. Takes the stairs carefully, one at a time. They're rickety. Too much pressure might punch a hole through them.

For a moment, she thinks she's stepping into a quiet house. Pottery Barn furniture; bland hotel-room-ready art on the walls. It's all a front for the work Pemberton did in the basement; most of the rooms seem as neglected as the vineyard fields beyond the fence. Then she sees the glass doors to the backyard have all burst inward. There's a regiment of rifles pointed at her from all sides, through every opening, through every possible escape. Helmets, visors, goggles. Black tactical gear, sticking out amid the house's beige walls and clay pottery like some infestation from an alien world. It all reminds her of the SWAT team that burst from the woods and tore her from Abigail's arms.

She isn't frightened, but she feels numb. Dislocated. As if she's crossed a barrier into a world trying as hard as it can to deny the existence of the one she just emerged from. *There will be order here,* the guns of the helmeted men in black seem to say. *There will be order and structure and rules. Maybe not laws, exactly. But rules, at least.*

Fat chance, assholes, she thinks.

Cole walks out from behind her and into the foyer. The house's front door stands open to the driveway. Beyond, more rifles, more men in combat gear, and farther out, impossibly, the giant hulk of a helicopter that's somehow landed just outside the house's front fence.

With each rifle she walks past, with each soldier down in a crouch, ready to fire, the momentousness of what she's capable of is somehow more apparent to her than it was as she broke Pemberton's bones. Down there in the basement, the twisted laws of his madness ruled.

Up here she is a terrifying aberration amid firepower that could have overpowered her only an hour before.

She follows Cole outside.

When they reach a fallen section of fence, she sees Luke, Marty, Rucker, and Brasher standing in a huddle off to one side of the driveway, watched over by windbreaker-clad guys like the ones she assumes are taking Pemberton into custody down in the basement right now.

She stops.

Cole stops.

"I'll bring them to you once we're done," he says. "They'll be safe. I promise you."

Luke makes eye contact with her, nods. His expression is stone cold, jaw tense, but the nod's slight enough to say it's intended just for her. She figures he's telling her to do whatever these people have said. Telling her he doesn't feel like the group's in any immediate danger if she leaves. She doesn't know whether or not to trust his judgment. For the first time, she sees the rest of Marty's crew, the guys who should have been up at the surveillance point. They're huddled with the group, too. How they got rounded up, she has no idea. But seeing them all together frightens her. Yes, she has strength. Impossible, almost otherworldly strength, but to fight off an army of this size would require coordination and skills well beyond that.

"Charley?" Cole calls.

"What do you want from me?" she asks. "Why can't they come with us?"

"Because there isn't room." He smiles and gestures to the helicopter, as if he's inviting her to dine with him at an exclusive restaurant. He starts toward her. She feels every man in her vicinity stiffen and raise his weapon by an inch or two. "Charley, do you really think I'm going to try something stupid at two thousand feet with you in your current condition?"

"You get thirty minutes. If you don't put me down after thirty minutes, with *them*, we'll all get to see how I fare in a crash landing."

"Deal." His smile is bright, confident, as if he's never seen the horrors in Pemberton's basement, as if he's the type of man who'll be able to stash them away for the rest of his life. Maybe he is.

There are two other men standing next to the chopper's open door. The tall bald one radiates a quiet confidence that some of the other men lack, even as they point guns at her. The other is short, bespectacled, and his rigidity and vacant-eyed stare as she approaches could either be terror or a laserlike focus that borders on sociopathy. Or he's terrified of whatever's inside the thick briefcase he holds in both arms.

Cole steps inside the passenger compartment, which she sees is much more spacious than she thought.

The other two wait for her to go first. The bald one gives her a polite nod as she steps past him, as if she were any other guest. As if this were just another corporate flight on a busy CEO's calendar.

Careful not to touch anything, she takes a seat on the leather-upholstered bench seat across from Cole. The engine starts up. The blades spin, slicing the glare cast by the house's security lights. The other two men pile into the helicopter after her, taking seats on opposite sides of Cole.

The bald one slides the cargo door shut. Soft golden light fills the cabin from running lights along the roof and the floor. It's insane, this juxtaposition. The distance she seems to have traveled between one world and another in no more than a few paces.

Then, suddenly, they're rising into the air. Her heart lurches as Luke, Marty, and the rest of them disappear under tree cover. As they ascend over the valley, she wonders if the unreality of this, rising into the air this suddenly, watching the house of horrors below shrink down to the size of a child's dollhouse, will somehow separate her from the nightmares in that basement.

No, she realizes, *but the memory of Pemberton's sobs will make the nightmares bearable.*

For the first time since liftoff, she looks into Cole's eyes.

He introduces the bald man sitting next to him as Ed Baker, his director of security. Ed wisely doesn't attempt to shake her hand. When it's clear he's not going to introduce the shorter guy in spectacles to his left, Charley says, "And who are you?"

The man just stares at her.

"This is Mark Hetherington. He's also with my security team, but he has a background as a registered nurse, and when it's appropriate and you consent, he'll take a sample of your blood."

Now Cole's staring at her, too.

"Will you allow me to do that, Charley? Will you allow me to take a sample of your blood?"

"I'm thinking about it."

Cole smiles, taps the briefcase Mark now holds on his lap. Mark pops it open. She glimpses thick foam padding with indentations holding several different vials. They look empty, but she can't be sure. Mark opens up a second compartment within, removes a thick file folder, and hands it to Cole. In turn, he hands it to her.

"Let start with this," he says cheerfully. "I think you'll be very interested in what's inside."

40

"I'm not really good at flipping pages right now," she says.

Her voice sounds like someone else's—something between a growl and a whisper. They seem to be heading east, toward the Arizona border, over mountainous terrain that will soon yield to the Anza-Borrego Desert.

The cabin is surprisingly quiet given the size of the rotors overhead: a floating, padded cell.

Cole reaches across the space between them, presses a button just over her shoulder. A pin-spot light clicks to life, shining a bright halo down on her lap, revealing the bloodstains on her jeans, the loose flaps where Pemberton sliced the legs. Cole's nose comes within inches of hers as he withdraws. Kissing distance, almost. She's not sure if he genuinely wants her to read the file, or if he wants to show her he's not afraid, that he trusts her not to tear his arm off.

With all the effort she can manage, she opens the file without ripping it in half. Finds herself staring down at a page printed with large side-by-side photographs, one of a toddler-aged boy who strikes her as immediately familiar. The other's Dylan. The resemblance between the two is undeniable; they share not only Dylan's sculpted chin but also his relaxed, attentive gaze.

"I can summarize the contents if you like," Cole says, "but the file's yours to keep."

She tries to nod but can't manage it. It's sinking in suddenly, what the page before her means, and maybe if her veins weren't enflamed with impossible strength, she'd feel like an idiot for not having seen it sooner.

Of course Dylan didn't pick the Saguaro Wellness Center at random. Didn't even pick Scarlet, Arizona, at random, and now, it's clear, most certainly didn't pick *her* at random. Why didn't she see it the other night when she was journaling about all the victims? The boy who was whisked off to a foreign country. Given a new life so different from hers. Or so she thought.

"Lilah Turlington," she says. "He's her son."

"Yes. The Bannings killed his mother and her boyfriend just like they killed your mother. After their disappearance, he was taken out of the country, given a new identity."

"The uncle. The one who works in gas pipelines."

"Exactly. Dylan was protected from things you weren't. But given my experience of him, I don't imagine it was a very pleasant upbringing."

She gently slides the picture page to one side; sees what looks like the records of Dylan's military service Kayla couldn't find. References to kills and assassinations with the word CLASSIFIED stamped across the top, which seems pathetic. The word should be red, but instead it's black and white, which means these documents are photocopies made by someone who wasn't supposed to have them. Too dense to read through now. But it's something. Far more than she expected out of the guy sitting across from her.

"And what's your experience of him?" she asks.

"Dylan was one of my father's last hires before he passed away. When I became CEO, Dylan came to me with video evidence of animal testing he'd done on a new drug. He'd been trying to advance antianxiety medications beyond what he called the realm of alcohol in a pill. He was searching for a compound that suppressed certain panic responses in the brain that can lead to paralysis and other fear responses he deemed . . . *ineffective.*

"Given what I've just shown you, it's not a mystery where this obsession came from. I know you were very young, and I know you weren't involved in any of their murders, so I'm not sure how much time you spent researching the details of their crimes, the statements Abigail has made in prison." She nods weakly. "Then you're probably aware Abigail Banning told authorities and several journalists that Lilah Turlington froze up when they attacked her boyfriend. That they almost bungled it, and there was a moment when she could have got away, maybe even saved Eddie Stevens. But she was paralyzed by the shock of it all. Two perfectly nice people she thought were fellow backpackers sharing a campfire suddenly turning on her boyfriend with a rock. She froze."

"Abigail lied about a lot of things."

"Even so, the story seems to have had a particular effect on the man we know as Dylan Cody, born Noah Turlington in Asheville, North Carolina."

"I knew him as Dylan Thorpe."

"Indeed. It's been hard to keep track of everyone's name of late."

"I only have one, and it's Charlotte Rowe."

Cole smiles nervously, nods. "Of course."

"These animal tests. What did they show?"

"In two hundred of them, Dylan matched prey and predator in a contained environment after dosing the prey subject with Zypraxon. In only five of them did the predator survive."

"What did you do? After he showed you these tests?"

"I made arrangements to begin human testing. On *willing* volunteers."

"I'm going to assume this trial was off the books."

"It was."

"How did it go?"

"Not well."

"How not well? Is that explained in this file?"

"It went so badly I shut down Project Bluebird six months later. Pulled all Dylan's funding and denied him access to his labs."

Bluebird. The word lances through her. The bird in the cage. The bird waiting to be set free. The bird she almost killed as a child. Anyone who knows her story would know the symbolism, and Dylan picked it as the name for the most important work of his career.

"So, very badly. What happened to the subjects? These willing volunteers?"

"Charley—"

"I thought we were trusting each other," she says.

While none of the men across from her reaches for a weapon, they stiffen at her volume; this subtle reminder of what she's capable of, and how they're trapped in a confined, airborne space with those skills.

"They tore themselves apart," Cole answers. "Quite literally. We called it going lycan."

He lets her absorb this. Lets it sink in—how much danger Dylan put her in by giving her the drug without her consent. The possibility of being raped by Jason Briffel was the least of it.

"We conducted extensive psychological profiles on each man to determine what his fears and phobias were. We tried to avoid asking the question directly, because we didn't want them to anticipate the tests that lay ahead. Once the profile was complete, we took them to a secure location and set them loose in a kind of obstacle course, where they were presented with different physical variations of their greatest fears. For some it was confined spaces; for others it was the possibility of drowning. A snake in an unexpected place. We called it the Fear Matrix."

"But it worked," she said. "They each got triggered."

"Yes. But unlike in the animal testing he'd done, they didn't direct their aggression outward. They directed their aggression at what they saw as the real source of their fear. Themselves. Their minds and the bodies those minds controlled. We did everything we could to stop them. But imagine the strength you just showed Frederick Pemberton channeled entirely into self-destructive impulses, along with aggression toward anyone or anything who tried to block those impulses once they were triggered. And imperviousness to any drugs we could dart them with. Imagine that, and you will have some sense of the nightmare Dylan Cody unleashed in our labs."

Our *labs,* she thinks. *A secure location. Where? An island?* She doubts that's in the file, and she doubts he'd tell her the truth if she asked.

"You tested all these men at once?" she asks.

"No. The second, third, and fourth all went in believing there was something inherent in their character that would allow them to improve on the results of the man who went before. After Dylan convinced them of this, of course."

"And then you shut it down?"

"And then Dylan came to me and told me he thought the problem was that we were only testing it on men. And that we should start testing it on women. And *then* I shut it down."

"So he left the company?"

"Yes."

"You didn't have him followed?" she asked.

"For a time. He bounced from city to city. Worked odd jobs so far beneath his pay grade I thought he might disappear forever. He was drinking heavily. It was clear there was no connection to family. No friends. His uncle passed away several years ago. There's an inheritance of some kind stashed away. But he doesn't spend it very often. If there's a lot to spend, that is."

"Not a lot to a man with his own helicopter, probably," she says.

"Touché." Cole smiles, but his smiles are becoming more strained with each passing minute of this flight. "I thought his failure, what happened to those men, had broken him."

"And you were wrong," she says.

Cole sits forward, resting his elbows on his knees and staring directly into her eyes. "If I'd had one inkling of what he was going to do to you, Charlotte, I would have stopped him. You must know this. You must *believe* this."

"How?"

"I would have had no shortage of ideas on that front. I guarantee you. I don't run a convenience store. I'm the CEO of one of the most powerful companies in the world."

There's no arguing with the icy conviction in his tone.

"So that's why Zypraxon works on me?" she asks. "Because I'm a woman?"

"No."

She must be visibly startled by his answer. He gives her a few seconds to recover.

"Dylan says he altered the formula a bit and tested it in another woman before you. The results were apparently as catastrophic as he should have expected."

"Did she . . ."

"He says she agreed to it, knowing the risks. But I no longer put much stock in anything Dylan *says*. Do you?"

"You tell me. Your history with him is . . . longer than mine."

Is he wincing or smiling or both? She can't tell.

"What do you want from me, Cole Graydon? Just my blood?"

"You're angry with me. Even after all I've told you. Can you tell me why?"

"You allowed him to do this."

"That's not true. I told you, I had no idea he was even in Arizona, much less that he'd made contact with you under false pretenses. When he came to me after the mess he made with those bikers, he was desperate. He was pretending like he'd planned it all, but it was clear he hadn't. He'd lost you, and he was on the run, and he knew that both of you would be in serious trouble if I didn't step in right away."

"You put me under constant surveillance. You allowed him to watch my every move."

"No, *I* watched your every move, because you were a miracle, Charlotte, and even you knew it. Because the drug was working for the first time, and on top of that, you seemed determined to actually use it. As for your surveillance, I fed him only what I wanted him to see, which was almost nothing. I also kept law enforcement from following a trail from that biker massacre to your uncle Marty's front door in Altamira. Right now Dylan's holed up in a shack outside of Tucson under constant surveillance, and he'll be there for the rest of his natural life if I so choose. Or someplace worse."

"He said I had to perform. He said I had to put on a show for all of you. He said you were so rich and powerful there was no outrunning you."

"He was wrong, and I'm here to tell you how."

"I don't understand."

"I'm here to tell you how to make us all go away, if that's what you want. If that's truly what you want. I'm here to do the thing Dylan didn't do in Arizona."

"What's that?"

"Give you a choice."

"I'm listening."

"What you did tonight, it was remarkable. It required a level of bravery unlike any I've ever seen. And if you would like to keep doing it, I can make that happen. I can make it happen in a much safer and more controlled way. I can provide the support and the tools you need to remove all the kinks, shall we say, in tonight's operation, so that you can take some of the worst human monsters out of circulation for all time."

"And what do you get out of it?"

"You would, in essence, of your own free will, become our test subject. But in that capacity, we would treat you with the utmost care and respect, provided you followed certain guidelines."

"Such as?"

"Extensive medical testing after each use of the drug. Allowing yourself to be monitored as well. When you're not pursuing a subject like Pemberton, your life would be your own. Altamira. Marty. Luke. The new resort that's set to open soon. I imagine there will be employment opportunities there. For all three of you. If you're interested."

Because you own the place now, she thinks.

"And what about Dylan? Will I be working with him?"

"Not directly, no."

"But what's the point? What will the testing be *for*?"

"The goals remain the same."

"You're gonna find a way to sell this drug? To make it work in everyone? That's insane."

"Of course not. The goal will be a stable, restrained, marketable version of Zypraxon that will do nothing more than inhibit those elements of the panic response that are counterproductive to survival mechanisms in populations at risk of being exposed to severe violence." He seems comforted by this string of buzzwords and marketing speak; he smiles wistfully, like a man who's just recounted a fond memory of his hometown. "The goal will be a drug that could have saved your mother's life."

"You're gonna start marketing a drug that allows women to rip men in half?"

"Stable. *Restrained.* It won't happen overnight. It will be years before we get there. But with you, we're closer than we've ever been. And I imagine the breakthroughs along the way will be considerable. To say nothing of the women whose lives will be saved by your work before then. How many more *masks* do you think Pemberton would have made if you hadn't stopped him tonight?"

"I don't actually know what you've done with him, so he could still end up making more."

"One thing at a time, Charley."

"OK. And the other choice?" she asks.

"Walk away. And we all pretend the last week or so never happened. I might keep some tabs on you, but only to make sure you aren't sharing too extensively about our time together. But your life will be your own, albeit . . . a little less exciting than if you had chosen to work with us."

"You'd let me just walk away after everything you told me?"

"After everything you've *done*, for sure, Charley." She can't tell if he's referring to her so-called bravery or the multiple hacks Bailey's committed on her behalf.

"OK. And Dylan?"

"He would have to die."

At first she thinks his gentle, conciliatory smile is a sign he's kidding, but as it fades and his eye contact doesn't waver, she realizes he's absolutely serious. For the next few seconds there's only the muffled chop of the rotary blades overhead as the helicopter swings back to the west.

"You're serious?" she asks.

"Yes."

"So if I refuse to work with you, you'll let me go back to my life, but you're gonna . . . what? Hunt Dylan down and shoot him?"

"It'll be more elegant than that, but that's the basic idea, yes."

Everything else the man has said to her tonight has felt clinical, rehearsed down to the last word, but there's something in his expression now that seems raw and electric. She wonders if she had a similar look in her eyes when she snapped Pemberton's wrist. He's out for some kind of revenge, and he's using her to do it.

"Why?" she asks.

"*Why?* He gave you a drug without your knowledge that might have caused you to tear yourself apart."

"You don't care about me. You don't even know me."

"For two years, he developed that drug with my complete support. That makes me responsible for you."

"Right, but if you were so outraged by what he'd done, why not kill him the minute he told you?"

"I wanted to see if he was telling the truth."

"You didn't need him alive to see that. You could have just followed me like you did."

He nods. He's surveying her. Maybe if she wasn't capable of bashing his head in, he'd have her killed for speaking this kind of truth to him. Maybe he's just that kind of guy. Maybe that's how he got his own helicopter.

"Forgive me, Charley, for the speech I'm about to make. And let me qualify it by saying I really do believe that all people are created equal, even if a fair amount of them go to shit not long after they're created. But you need to know this.

"I'm not like you. I'm not like anyone you know, and I'm not like anyone you will ever meet. I sit at the head of a company that will make more money in the next five minutes than most people would be able to earn in ten lifetimes. The products that I deliver to the world save thousands of lives every minute, all over the planet. And the development and manufacture of those products, products that people now demand at the drop of a hat for almost nothing, comes at a cost those same people cannot bring themselves to examine. It's my job to deliver those products while concealing that cost at all times. That's my duty. That's what I go to bed with every night.

"Now, I realize we live in the age of the social justice warrior who thinks he can ferret out all the corruption in the world just by doing some Google searches, but the fact of the matter is this. While everyone points the finger at Wall Street and Goldman Sachs and the like, it's companies like mine that actually shape the world, and we have this responsibility because people gave it to us. Because they expect to be relieved of every ache and pain and bad mood, as if being alive itself is a pathological condition, and someone, somewhere is responsible for fixing it. And we meet that need. We meet that need in the hopes that we can someday wrest enough financial gain from this neurotic hunger that we end up developing a cure for cancer. Or a drug that stops strokes once and for all. Or a drug that allows people at risk of violence or abuse to defend themselves in a competent, focused, and effective manner. Something that's truly important, not just easily marketable.

"That's my job, in a nutshell. That's my responsibility, and it was my father's before he left it to me. And if you decide to wash your hands of all of this, then Project Bluebird is dead forever. I've got no more to give to it. And that's fine. But that also means Dylan Cody or Dylan Thorpe or Noah Turlington or whatever he chooses to call himself tomorrow has no more to give me or my company except dangerous and unacceptable risks. And I can't have that. I can't have that at all."

The pictures still stare up at her from the spread of pages on her lap: the boy with the murdered mother and the mad scientist he became.

"Why tell me?" she asks. "Why make me responsible for his life? Why not just deal with Dylan the way you want to?"

"If you do decide to work with us, I don't want to jeopardize our new relationship. For all I know, you might have developed a real attachment to him."

"You certainly seem to have one."

"I'll show you some footage of what happened to the test subjects in our labs. That way you'll appreciate the magnitude of the danger he placed you in."

"Or you could admit that you just want him dead, but you can't bring yourself to do it unless you use me as an excuse."

"I'd dismiss that as glib if you didn't speak from experience. After all, you're the one who used me and my surveillance and Zypraxon as an excuse to hunt down a serial killer who reminded you of the people who killed your mother."

"I didn't do it for revenge."

"Coulda fooled me, Burning Girl."

"I'm not interested in being part of your revenge, either."

"That's not what it is, but I can certainly understand why you'd see it that way."

"What is it then?"

"Management." He sucks in a deep breath. "That said, this isn't a decision you need to make tonight, or the next night, or the night after that. Take your time. You've been through a great deal these past few days. But, Charlotte, right now I need your blood."

Maybe this was his strategy, to sideline her so she'd offer up her arm without a struggle even though she's currently capable of snapping his neck with one hand. It works. She gives them her left arm; the wounds from where she tore out Pemberton's IVs are still fading on her right.

Mark, the spectacled former nurse, springs into action, opening the briefcase, revealing the vials in their foam slots. Only when he brings the syringe close to her flesh does she notice that his hands shake slightly and his nostrils flare with each breath, as if he were preparing to inject a growling tiger.

Once her blood starts to fill the vial, Cole knocks on the partition behind his head. The chopper banks again, and they start flying back toward the rivers and lakes of twinkling lights beyond the dark mountains.

By the time they start to descend, Mark Hetherington has filled five vials.

When he removes the last one, she glances out the window. They're close to the Pala Casino Resort; it rises like a gatehouse to the network of mountain valleys they just took off from. Their landing spot is the empty parking lot of an unfinished shopping mall.

Approaching on the nearest service road now are two large black SUVs she recognizes from outside the vineyard's gate, and Luke's Jeep in between them. As the three cars pull in to the lot, she's surprised to see Luke and Marty emerge from the back seat of the first SUV and not the Jeep. Apparently Luke's vehicle has been commandeered by more of Cole's windbreaker-clad Glock aficionados, like the guys now fanning out across the perimeter of their impromptu helipad.

The man driving Luke's Jeep hops out, then disappears into the back seat of the SUV in front. Whatever's about to happen, it's going to be a quick transfer, and as the chopper's runners come to rest on the asphalt, she realizes most of the men and the firepower are still up at Pemberton's place.

But her people are all here: Luke, Marty, Brasher, Rucker, and the three guys who were supposed to be at the surveillance post. They don't look traumatized, just shaken and confused—like students evacuated from a school after a phony bomb threat.

The Windbreakers, as she now thinks of them, are falling back and piling into the SUVs.

Ed Baker slides open the door to the passenger compartment, allowing in a blast of air as the blades roar by overhead. This time, she realizes, the helicopter won't be shutting down.

"I'll be in touch, Charlotte," Cole says. "Not with quite this much fanfare, of course. But soon. I would offer you my hand but . . ."

She reaches out and grips the edge of the door, careful not to bend the metal. In her other hand, she holds the file.

"Oh, and Charley?"

She looks at him.

"In another few hours, Frederick Pemberton is going to tell a very strange story to the authorities. We'll do everything we can to make sure they don't believe it. But I wouldn't stick around if I were you."

She wants to ask him more questions, but she doubts he'll give her the whole truth.

"You and Dylan make a great couple," she says. "It's a shame you want him dead."

No sooner has she stepped from the helicopter than Baker slides the door shut behind her, and suddenly it's lifting into the air over her head, the downdraft plastering her hair to one side of her face. But of course her grip, magnified by Zypraxon, is more than enough to keep the contents of the file from blowing out of her hand. In time with the helicopter's departure, the two SUVs speed back onto the service road, leaving Luke's Jeep all by itself several yards away, its doors standing open.

Luke is walking toward her. Too fast.

"Wait," she says.

"No," he says.

Suddenly his arms are around her.

"If you can't hug me without crushing my spine, then just don't hug back," he whispers.

She leaves her arms at her sides. She leans into him. She can do that, right? Just a little lean. A little movement that allows her to shift some of the weight off her heels and onto the balls of her feet, to breathe deeply for the first time in hours.

For the first time in days.

For the first time in weeks.

She blinks against his chest, sees the rest of the group headed toward her.

"I'm gonna wait if that's all right, darlin'," Marty says, "maybe another hour and a half or so. I'm not quite as brave as him."

She smiles, nods against Luke's chest. She's allowed her eyes to drift shut again when she hears one of the other guys say, "We need to get her some new jeans."

IV

It's been two weeks, and this is what the world thinks happened that night.

They think the Mask Maker, aka Frederick Pemberton, was rearranging equipment in his surgical lab of horrors when he accidentally pushed one of the operating tables into the vacuum pump chamber he used to create his masks, knocking the giant chamber onto its side. They think he almost pinned himself underneath it, breaking several bones in the process. They think he was so afraid a trip to the hospital would expose the source of his injuries, he chose instead to inject himself with a powerful pain medication until he could figure out what to do. And because he was in so much pain, he made the mistake of dosing himself with one of the tranquilizers he used to subdue his victims, knocking himself unconscious in the process.

After he passed out, his dogs escaped through a driveway gate he'd failed to close all the way behind himself earlier that evening. Given their reputation as fearsome beasts, it took only one or two sightings of the dogs running along Pala Temecula Road before neighbors placed concerned calls to local law enforcement. A little while later, a routine door knock ended up unmasking one of the most sadistic serial killers in American history.

Since then cable news has been filled with criminal justice and forensics experts who can't get enough of this story. Of its crazy irony. The killer being brought down by the implements of his crimes. None of them have paused to wonder if it's all too neat. If perhaps the whole thing was staged.

Maybe they do, just during commercial breaks.

If Cole Graydon's men left behind any evidence that a combat-ready team of soldiers had practically blown the place apart in the minutes before I was triggered, local law enforcement hasn't found any of it.

As for Pemberton, the contents of his confession have not yet been made public, aside from the fact that it's most definitely a confession. What other choice did he have? the experts ask. Was he really going to insist that the entire contents of his lab, right down to the three faceless corpses in his refrigerator, were somehow carted in and staged there while he slept on the floor? How would he explain the fact that all of it was slathered with his fingerprints? Maybe he's told them some crazy story about one of his victims overpowering him, but if he has, the police sure aren't acting on it. I'm sure I have Cole Graydon and his men to thank for that.

Defeat.

That's how, in the eyes of the world, the story of the Mask Maker has ended. Total, pathetic defeat.

And I'm not going to lie.

This satisfies me.

It does more than that, to be honest.

It makes me very happy.

So happy that I'm not afraid to admit to myself—and to Luke and to Marty—that my memory of the fear in his eyes, the pain in his expression as I snapped his wrist, does not fill me with guilt. Every now and then I feel like it might. But then I close my eyes and try to imagine the faces of the women whose lives I probably saved, going about their daily business. Laughing. Loving. Crying over silly movies. Future victims of the Mask Maker who might have looked away too quickly from Frederick Pemberton's unusual features.

I removed from the world the hours of agony and torment and terror Pemberton's next victims would have suffered at his hands. Save the world? Maybe not. Make it a better place? I think so.

It took me about three days to realize this.

You could say I was in shock. But it wasn't the kind of shock I've heard described by car accident victims. I wasn't speechless or paralyzed. It was like I was skating across the surface of what had happened. Like if I just didn't talk about everything I'd done, it would eventually seem perfectly normal. So I went about my days at Marty's house, then at Luke's, because his place was bigger, showering, eating, and watching cable news coverage of Pemberton's arrest.

It was strange, logging in to my e-mail, but it didn't bring me back to reality the way I expected. The messages waiting there just seemed like terse dispatches from a life that wasn't mine anymore, most of them inquiries from the travel agency I worked for. The first message was politely curious, the second, concerned. The third, arriving after I'd missed my second shift in a row, was all disciplinary talk of probation. In the fourth, I was fired.

And then there were the voice mails on my cell phone. Several from the Scarlet Police Department, from one of the cops I'd met when I went to register my alarm. Poor guy, he'd sounded so halting and nervous. Probably overwhelmed by federal agents. I thought I could hear some of them talking in the background.

He just wanted to know if I was out there, is all. They'd tried knocking, ringing my buzzer. There'd been a big mess out in the desert nearby, if I hadn't heard. Could I get back to them as soon as I could?

Five calls over the course of two days. Then they'd stopped altogether as the attention of the federal agencies involved was directed to other sources by an invisible, powerful hand.

Thanks, Cole.

Did he call politician friends and get them to look away? Did he blackmail federal agents into extending their investigation south toward Scarlet and not north toward my house? I'm in no mood to ask the guy.

If I ask him anything, I'll be required to answer his question first, and I'm not ready for that. Not yet.

Around sunset one night, Luke drove me out to the beach and Bayard Rock. He told me it was where he used to bring Bailey when their mom was sick.

Bailey's got no interest in coming home, apparently. This has hurt Luke's feelings all over again. Apparently the fact that we've made powerful new friends who could probably get Bailey back in the country, maybe even keep the FBI off his back, means nothing to him. Wherever he is, whoever he's working with, he's happy there. And it's hard for Luke to argue with him. Because wherever Bailey is, whoever he's working with, allowed us to take a vicious monster out of circulation. So can we really complain?

There are already construction vehicles out at the old resort. Clearing out debris. Getting ready to pick up where they left off. There are advertisements for job fairs in town. Mostly construction stuff, but they're also interviewing for positions at the hotel once it opens. Kitchen staff, housekeeping. Stuff like that. It makes me dizzy to think all that might go away if I turn down Cole's offer.

For a while Luke and I sat watching the sunset. I've taken his physical affection for granted these past few days. At first it just seemed like a natural outgrowth of what we'd been through. Now it's constant. And welcome. And so when I rested my head against his shoulder as we sat together on the sand, it didn't seem like a big deal. And when he took my hand in his and held it against his chest, it didn't seem like a big deal, either.

When our lips finally met, it felt necessary. Essential. Not the forceful, desperate thing I'd seen in movies, and nothing like the hesitant, exploratory hour I'd spent with that guy I met on my road trip. It felt like an extension of what we'd been through. To kiss him. To get as close to his woodsy smell as I possibly could. To learn that his lower lip is sensitive, and if I lift my hands to the sides of his neck and just graze my fingers gently across the muscle there, he gets shivers all over his body. He doesn't just laugh. He giggles, and then he gets embarrassed that he's giggling, tries to turn it into a manly laugh, and ends up coughing. Which I really like. A lot.

I never anticipated that just kissing someone could be an event. With different stages and acts. The slow approach. The commitment. The taste. The smell. The withdrawal and then going back in for a second taste, a deeper one. It's happened three times, and we haven't had some big talk about it. We haven't named it. And we haven't tried to get each other's clothes off. For now it's just something we need, even though it's brief. Even though it's nameless.

For now.

We're together right now as I write this, on a plane headed for Atlanta.

The e-mails from Cole have been pretty steady the past two weeks. They all say the same thing: "Ready to hear your decision when you've made it. —C."

But there's only been one e-mail from Dylan and it arrived yesterday: "Let's meet. So much to discuss, it seems. —D."

Followed by a screen cap of a Google map of an area I knew all too well.

Marty offered to go with me, but I could tell he was at risk of losing several jobs given how much time he'd spent away. Luke had put in regular shifts ever since we got back, and he'd told Mona a good enough cover story to explain his absence.

Twenty-four hours. That's how long we've scheduled this trip for. Twenty-four hours that could decide my fate.

And Dylan's.

It seems insane to be writing in this notebook again.

What if I dropped it or lost it? Whoever picked it up would probably think it was someone's idea of a novel, that's what.

Maybe it's as simple as I can't really think of anything else to do with my hands right now. It's a long flight, SFO to Atlanta. About four hours. And Luke's only pretending to watch the movie on his phone; I can tell.

Still, it's comforting to have him next to me. It's comforting to know he watched me do what I did in Pemberton's basement and he doesn't recoil from me. He isn't afraid of me. He doesn't believe some incurable darkness has been unleashed in me. He looks at me with a protective-ness and steadiness I've never seen in the eyes of another man. It's not like the way Marty looks at me, with a lot of smiles and winks to hide how worried he is. Luke is there. Present. Constant. Ready.

Which is good.

Because I need him.

I need this journal, too. I need these words. They're mine. They exist between all the other versions of my life that have been forced on me over the years. They exist outside the terrible choice Cole Graydon has given me.

Maybe this really will be the last chapter of the story that began with my mother's murder. Maybe I really will walk away, no matter what that entails.

If I do, does this mean I should keep this book, or burn it?

Cole sent me another e-mail this morning. I got it as we were boarding: "Hope you have a productive meeting. I look forward to see-ing your decision. —C."

I showed it to Luke. "Seeing," he said back to me. So I wasn't the only one who noticed the unusual wording.

"So they're gonna be watching us," he said.

I nodded. Watching us today.

And maybe always.

If that's the price of being able to bring Pemberton's madness to an end, of saving the lives of his future victims, is it worth it?

If I had an answer, I wouldn't be asking you, journal.

41

Her arrival at the farm is relatively painless at first because she doesn't recognize anything. It's all so overgrown. On the drive in from Atlanta, the seas of rolling green mountains reminded her more of the grave-site tour she took right before she moved to Arizona than it did her fragmented recollections of early childhood.

By the time she and Luke reach the old chain where the entrance to the access road used to be, they've been trespassing for about twenty minutes. But she figures if the owners of the farm that bought up all the Bannings' property years ago come bursting out of the trees with shotguns raised, Cole will somehow intervene.

What tipped him off? she wonders. Was it that they booked their airline tickets in their own names? Or has he been tracking Dylan's e-mails? She figures it's the latter.

It's cold at this altitude, colder than it was in Atlanta. Their breath fogs the air. Luke pushes brush back with gloved hands. Someone, probably morbid hikers, and if the rumors are true, the owners of the property who lead them on guided hikes here, have beaten a trail through the brush to the front steps, where she used to sit with Abigail and watch for birds. She and Luke follow it now.

They're several yards from the house when someone steps out onto the porch.

Dylan's dressed like a preppy backpacker; a new-looking waffle-print coat, lightly scuffed jeans, and shiny black boots. This is how Dylan Thorpe, the privileged but kindhearted therapist she knew in

Arizona would dress if he took off on a hike in a colder climate. She reminds herself not be fooled by the outfit. By the look.

He's not Dylan Thorpe, she thinks as they stare at each other. *He's not even Dylan Cody. He's Noah Turlington. Think of him that way, and it will be easier not to hate him. Or at the least your hatred won't show.*

He gestures for them to follow him inside.

When she first spotted the remains of the farmhouse, she assumed it had been through several fires. Now that she's inside, she can see it's time and weather that have eaten away at its roof and walls, leaving holes so large they look like evidence of cannon blasts. The fireplace has been conquered by a blend of vines and weeds, watered, it looks like, by a steady diet of rain. The center of the brick mantel gave way a long time ago. Below, the bricks sit where they landed, black as coal where they aren't covered by leaves.

One entire corner of the house, including the large window from which she used to watch snow fall and birds congregate at the feeder outside, has collapsed, flooding the interior with sunlight that exposes the morbid graffiti along the walls. It's the same bargain-basement poseur satanist crap she's seen in pictures of the place online. Skulls, upside-down stars, crude outlines of heads she only realizes are supposed to be the devil when she finally sees the crooked horns on top. At floor level tiny altars left by the visitors line the walls. Defaced stuffed animals, some of them tied to black pillar candles. Like so many of the tributes to the Bannings that persist on the Internet, the offerings here are a crazy mishmash of grief for the victims and a perverse celebration of their killers. As if her mother and Noah's mother weren't claimed by maniacs, but by a dark god who demands constant reverence. She can imagine Jason Briffel crouching down in these shadows, maybe with some of his letters from Abigail tucked in his pocket, lighting one of the intact candles. This would be his church.

For her, this house, the fields outside, the entire property, is a gory delivery room where her true self was yanked from the womb by a well-armed SWAT team acting as OB-GYNs.

But what is it for Dylan?

For Noah, she corrects herself.

There are maps online that claim to show the locations where each body was buried before her rescue, so maybe he spent some time standing over his mother's first, forced grave. If the victims were taken from an isolated location like her mother, their car was buried here, too. Even today, the most popular crime scene photos are aerial shots of the so-called automobile graveyard, where the rusted skeletons of the freshly unearthed cars looked like fossils emerging from the sands of history.

Has he never been here before?

Was he saving it for their reunion?

As they stand together inside this crumbling ruin, she feels exactly the type of kinship with him she had hoped to avoid. *It's the expression on his face as he studies these walls,* she thinks. Unguarded, wide-eyed. Free of anything that looks like calculation.

Behind her, Luke stands just inside the front door, watching Dylan's every move.

"I have something for you," Dylan finally says.

When he extends one hand toward her, Luke takes a step, boards creaking underfoot. A link of shiny gold dangles from Dylan's outstretched fist. She recognizes it instantly, extends her hand, gesturing with the other for Luke to stay back.

Jason Briffel's necklace, the one he wore to her house, drops into her palm. Most of it is blackened from intense fire, the ends melted from the heat. The sight of the tiny medallion of flames, now soot covered, makes Jason's break-in seem like minutes and not weeks ago.

"I would never have let him hurt you."

She looks at him in disbelief. Not because she thinks he's lying. Because she didn't expect his candor.

"So you were outside the whole time?" she asks. "You followed me home?"

He nods.

Without thinking, she tosses the necklace toward the nearest grim altar. When his gift lands atop a rotting pile of burned offerings, Dylan flinches.

"You have every right to be angry with me." But he doesn't sound like he believes it, only that he thinks he should. "How much did Cole tell you about me?"

That your life hangs in my hands, she thinks. *That if I refuse to keep being a guinea pig, he'll probably shoot you dead. Right here, for all I know.*

"Did he tell you that when I came to him with the first animal tests of Zypraxon, he'd squandered millions of research dollars hunting for common links between orphan diseases? That he was losing the confidence of his board and he'd only been CEO for a year. Do you know what that phrase means? *Orphan disease*?" She shakes her head. "It's a disease so rare there's no real financial incentive for a company like Graydon to find a cure for it, or even a treatment. But Cole, for some crazy reason, got it in his head that with the right amount of money and determination, and as it turned out, *ignorance*, he'd find some commonality between random, isolated, rare diseases and somehow develop treatments for them. His Umbrella Theory. That's what he called it. It was complete nonsense, and he almost ruined his father's company over it."

"And then you came to him with a cure for something else," she says.

"A cure?" he says. "Maybe. More like a weapon."

"A weapon that could have saved your mother."

"And yours."

"And you killed four men to make it work."

"Four willing volunteers gave their lives so we could *try* to make it work. We weren't out to create a Superman pill. We wanted to formulate something that could seize on the biochemical process of panic itself and transform it into efficiency, competency, responsiveness."

"Survival," she whispers before she can stop herself.

He looks into her eyes, smiles slightly. Pleased, no doubt, that she's just parroted the word he used to justify his actions the night Jason almost raped her.

"Exactly," he says. "The strength was an unexpected by-product. And one with undeniable defense industry implications that I will admit I did use to secure funding for our further development."

"But it didn't work. So you decided to put my life at risk."

"I knew it would work in you. I had a theory. I was right."

"What was your theory?"

"Our tests used combat veterans. People who'd been through extreme physical trauma. Trauma so severe it had reshaped their neural pathways. With you, that wasn't a concern."

"You're saying my life's been free of trauma?"

"Your life is full of grief, betrayal, and loss. But the only time you were ever held down against your will was when the SWAT team saved you from this place. You've never been shot or even shot at, much less beaten, violated. The threat of those things has been ever present in your life, as it is in so many lives. But it never manifested."

"Until you sent Jason to my house."

"Yes. And we all saw how that went."

"I don't believe you, Noah."

He closes his eyes at this use of his old name. What's he trying to summon? Patience or violence?

"Which part?" he finally asks quietly.

"I don't believe you were so confident your pill wouldn't kill me. I think you thought I was expendable."

"How, Charlotte?"

They're thoughts that have only come to her in the past few days, so she's afraid she might have trouble articulating them now, but when she starts to speak, the words come easily. Is she saddened or relieved to be saying these things? "I think you tracked me down because you knew who I was. And you hated me. You thought I'd made money off the Bannings, off your mother's murder. You'd already lost a female subject. Maybe it was someone you cared about. Now you needed one you wouldn't care about at all."

"Interesting," he says. "So naturally I spent three months getting to know you so that I wouldn't be attached when you went lycan on me and I had to destroy you?"

"Those three months gave you everything you needed to set up your test."

"Two weeks gave me everything I needed to set up my test. You were desperate for someone to talk to, and after our first session you rarely held back."

"Better for you then."

"But that's not why I was there. Not in the beginning."

She's startled by his conviction, but he doesn't rush to say more.

"Why were you there?" she asks.

"I wanted to know who you really were. You're right. I hated you. Ever since I found out who my mother really was, what had happened to her, I hated you. I'd read your father's crass, manipulative, disingenuous book. I'd watched every single one of those disgusting films, knowing you got a share of the profits. And I'd never believed a word you'd said in front of a camera. I thought it was all for show, all for money. Even storming offstage on your father like that. Just a teenager getting bored with her old act. And I thought deep down, you probably hated your father because you loved them more. Abigail and Daniel. Your real parents. In short,

I believed everything about you that you didn't want the world to believe."

She's never seen him this angry. It takes a form as penetrating and focused as every other intense swell of emotion he's displayed.

"And then?" she asks.

"And then, one day, I saw you standing over my mother's grave."

For a second she's got no idea what he's talking about. Then she remembers. *The road trip.* The road trip she wrote about in her journal only days before.

"After Cole shut down the project, it was like my one connection to my mother died. I wandered around for a bit, but I ended up in Asheville, where she lived. I was trying to put together pieces of her life. And then one day, I walked out to her grave, and there you were. Burning Girl. And you were crying.

"I'd seen the news. I'd read about the lawsuit. I knew you'd won. But you weren't off vacationing on some island. Instead you'd traveled across the country to bring my mother her favorite flower. And that's when I realized, we don't get to pick the other survivors of the shipwreck, and on our darkest days, they're all we have. So I decided to find out who you really were."

"You followed me all the way to Arizona?"

"I followed you back to Asheville. Heard you use your new name. I used that to do the rest."

"The rest . . . pretending to be a therapist. Lying to me."

"It was not my best plan. In the beginning, it wasn't really a plan at all. It was . . ."

"What?" she asks. "What was it?"

"Hope."

"For what, Noah?"

He whirls, a visible pulse in one corner of his jaw. "I call you by the name you've chosen. Can you do me the same favor?"

"You didn't do me any *favors*, Dylan."

His shame, if that's truly what it is, shows itself in the quick breath he sucks in through his nostrils, the speed with which he looks out into the woods beyond.

Should she tell him they're being watched? Shouldn't he already know? After all, he's worked with Cole Graydon far longer than she has.

"So who was I?" she asks. "When you finally got to know the *real* me, who did I turn out to be?"

"You were everything I said you were during our sessions. Brave but deluded. Convinced you were weak simply because you were grief stricken and exhausted. But on a fundamental level, what you'd been through had turned you into something I'd never anticipated. Someone resourceful, determined, honest. But in need of a push."

"A *push*?"

"Do you regret it, Charley? Not our sessions. Not what I had to do with Jason. The Mask Maker. Do you regret it? Do you regret bringing him down?"

"Is that what you expected me to do?"

"Never in a million years," he says with a warm, contented smile.

"Then maybe you didn't get to know the real me after all."

"Maybe," he whispers, his smile fading but his stare growing more intense, as if he's convinced he might learn more about her in this single moment than he did during those three months.

"You said in the beginning, I was hope. Not for . . . your drug, but for something else. What, Dylan? Hope for what?"

He's studying the view beyond the collapsed walls now. He's searching the woods; she's sure of it. Searching for the glint of sunlight off binoculars or a rifle's scope. But he doesn't seem frightened.

"Dylan?"

"I thought you might have seen her. When they brought her here."

"Your mother?" she asks.

He nods.

"I didn't," she whispers. "I never saw any of them. I'm sorry. I would tell you the truth if I had."

"I know," he whispers back. "I know."

Either he hasn't seen what he expected to out in the woods, or he's given up looking for it. He turns to her now.

"Forgive me, Charley. It wasn't my plan to involve Cole and Graydon right away. I didn't want to snare you in their net so soon. I thought we'd have time. I thought we'd have time to work together. To come to an understanding.

"I knew you'd see the worth of what I was trying to do. The implications. For our mothers. For women everywhere who live in fear. For *people* everywhere who live in fear, overpowered and silenced and erased by those who lack morals or possess brute strength . . ." He studies the altars all around them, and she wonders if these general, academic words are the closest he can come to describing his mother's murderers in any kind of detail. "Or are pure evil."

There's a tremor in his voice when he speaks these last two words. He's turned in to the shadows so he can face her. If there are tears in his eyes, she can't see them.

"I take it Cole's made it clear he has a continued desire to work with you," he says.

"He has."

"Has he said what will happen if you turn him down?"

She can't bring herself to lie, but she can't bring herself to answer, either.

He looks up, stricken by her silence.

"What has he said to you?" she finally asks.

"That your decision will determine everything." She nods, avoiding his stare for the first time since entering the house.

"Has he offered you a graceful exit plan by chance?" he asks.

I look forward to seeing your decision. Black and white. Staring back at her from her phone's screen. She imagines a bullet striking

Dylan between the eyes right there if she . . . does what? Runs from the cabin in tears? Slaps him? Or is the place bugged and Cole's listening to their every word right now?

"Not graceful," she says. "No."

He steps forward. Behind her, Luke stiffens and matches Dylan's step with two of his own. But Dylan doesn't go any farther, and she realizes he's searching her expression as intensely as he did the woods outside.

"So if I had given you a choice, if I'd told you the risks, would you have said yes?"

It's an impossible question, but she's closer to an honest answer now than she was just twenty-four hours before. It's what she wrote in her journal.

She closes her eyes, imagines those twinkling vistas that stretched out before her and Luke as they chased Pemberton across Southern California. She tells herself that somewhere out there in those glittering lights are young women, about her age. They're settling in for the night or getting ready to head out on a first date or maybe even driving to pick up their kids from the movies. Because of Charley, they will make it to their destinations. They will hear the delighted laughter of their children as they slide into the back seat of the car. Or they will lock eyes with their date across the table and have the privilege of asking themselves if this person is the one. They will have a night full of dreams before the sun rises, and they will wake in their own beds. In their own rooms. Not in Pemberton's basement. Not in the Bannings' root cellar. Someday they will die, of course, but until then they will be spared the degradation of dying at the hands of someone who derives sexual satisfaction from their agony.

She answers before these images can leave her mind and be replaced by her current, decaying surroundings.

"Yes," she says. "I would have said yes."

It's like she's slugged him in the center of his chest.

He blinks, stares at her. He works his jaw suddenly to hide the fact that it just started to quiver. Does he think she's lying? She isn't. It's the truth, as much as she's capable of telling the truth about a possibility that no longer exists, an opportunity that was stolen from her by a man who's only just now realizing that his belief in what's best for others can bring him close to committing the kind of violent acts that destroyed his life. Or *one* of his lives. A life that will never be, with a mother he never got to know.

So what if he doubts her answer? That's his burden to bear. He's the one who stole the choice from her. He's the one who made sure they'll never truly know if she would have accepted the risks, the challenge. The opportunity.

For the first time since she's met him, he looks miserable.

Maybe he regrets it all. The loss of life—the slaughtered bikers, the chaos that followed. Maybe he really does regret stealing the choice from her, putting her through hell in the name of his warped view of scientific research.

Maybe he cares about her as much as he's capable.

It doesn't matter.

What matters is that she has the answer she came here for.

She can't let him die.

"So," he finally says, voice shaky. "What will you tell our mutual friend about our meeting?"

"Nothing he probably doesn't already know," she answers.

With a smile, he looks to the woods, nods. "Makes sense. You're one of his most valuable investments now. I'm sure he'll do anything to protect you."

"Maybe," she says. "He took some of my blood after I was triggered. He'll be able to work with that for a while even if I choose not to do any more tests."

"And what about me?" he asks.

"What about you, Dylan?" she asks.

447

"If you decide to go no further with him, what did he say about me?"

"Don't ask questions you don't want the answer to."

"I never do," he says.

"You played the therapist for me. What did you play for him?"

"I didn't *play* anything. I just offered him a release of his tension; that's all. So that he could focus."

"A well-timed one, given what you were asking of him."

"Cole Graydon doesn't fall in love with people. If he's threatened me it's because of the risk I pose to his company. And to his secrets."

"Or that. But you're both more alike than you realize."

"How's that, Charley?"

"You're both more human than you'd like to be."

He nods, tries for bitter laughter, but it gets caught in his throat. "I see," he says. "So he did give you an out, just not a graceful one. He said you could walk away, but that it would be the end of me."

Her expression confirms his suspicions. He laughs, looks to the woods outside again.

"It's genius, when you think about it." He approaches what remains of the nearby wall, which only comes up to his knees. He steps into the shafts of bright sunlight pouring through where one corner of the roof used to be. "This way, you can agree to go along with him out of a crushing sense of obligation. You *almost* killed Jason. You *almost* killed Pemberton. And you may very well lose control and kill someone during a future test. And so even if things do get bloody in the months ahead or the years ahead or however long it takes us to isolate whatever it is about you that makes this drug work, you'll always be able to console yourself with the fact that you spared my life. It will keep you going. For him. And you think *I'm* the master manipulator."

"I think you two were made for each other."

"Well, he's wrong," Dylan says, turning on her now. "You're not going to do it to spare my life." When he digs into his pocket, Luke steps forward. "Easy, Cowboy. It's just this." Dylan rattles a small pill-box in one hand and stops. He's several feet away from her, back turned to all the shadowy hiding places in the landscape outside. He extends the box to her. It's shaking. It's shaking because his hand is shaking. "You're going to do it for everybody who was buried on this farm. You're going to do it for my mother, and you're going to do it for yours."

When she reaches for the pillbox, she feels a firm pressure in her shoulder, so sudden and strong she wonders if Luke just grabbed her. But when she looks over her shoulder, he's still several paces away. Studying her. Ready to react, to what he's not sure, but he's ready. Ready and watching.

Now she can see the tears in Dylan's eyes. But he doesn't blink them away, and he doesn't stop staring into hers.

"*Don't* do it for me," he whispers. "I don't need you to spare my life, Charlotte Rowe. Make the choice for yourself and for the other women you can keep alive. Do that for me, if you can find it in your heart to do anything for me at all."

Pam, she thinks. *Jessica, Sara.* Maybe they have ordinary names. Maybe they have ordinary lives. Or maybe they're currently living lives that seem ordinary on the surface but will ultimately unveil some extraordinary purpose. Maybe they will invent something or one day become a senator or a president. What matters is that they are alive. A mass of dreams and potential, vulnerable to fate but pro-tected from Frederick Pemberton. But she's not just thinking of them, of the women whose lives she's saved. She's thinking of ordinary-looking human monsters. Men like Pemberton, women like Abigail. She's thinking of other basements and closets keeping untold horrors just out of view until they are revealed by a gate left open or a cop responding to a noise disturbance or the accidental sighting of a girl who went missing years before.

She extends her hand toward Dylan's, allows him to drop the pillbox into her open palm. They're in full view of whoever might be watching from the woods, but she hasn't closed her fingers around the box yet. She's studying it, as if unsure whether or not to pocket it and the responsibility it contains. But all she sees are the faces of these bland-looking killers, with placid half smiles and faraway expressions. They're inventions of her mind, of course, but they're born from the mug shots of dozens of depraved human monsters, of which the Bannings were only two. People who spent most of their midnight hours on the sadistic manufacture of fear and agony so that one day the mere mention of their names would send a shiver through anyone who hears them.

It's these monsters she's thinking of as she closes her fingers around the pillbox and slides it into her pocket. It's these monsters to whom she silently says, *I know you're out there. And I'm coming for you.*

ACKNOWLEDGMENTS

Like most of my novels, this title had several editors, and I owe a big debt of gratitude to each of them, beginning with Jacquelyn Ben-Zekry, who helped bring Charlotte into existence, and continuing on through Caitlin Alexander and Thomas & Mercer's Liz Pearsons. A big shout-out to the rest of the Thomas & Mercer / Amazon Publishing team, specifically Grace Doyle, who showed great faith in this book from the beginning.

A big thank-you to my good friend Dr. Peter Scheer, who provided priceless research guidance in the areas of plastination and facial surgery. He's a brilliant doctor and a wonderful man who bears no resemblance whatsoever to any of the multiple mad doctors in this book. The same can be said for Geoff Symon, who provided invaluable insight into law enforcement technique, particularly at the federal level, and who bears absolutely no resemblance to certain shady government agents referenced within these pages.

Thanks as well to Paul Shreve, who provided insight into computer hacking and keeping online communications as private as possible, and additional gratitude to his insanely talented wife, novelist Meg Gardiner, for being willing to loan out his brains to another writer. *Bone Music* is a novel that walks the line between thriller and science fiction, and any creative license within should be seen as just that, and not the result of misinformation offered by the very smart and skilled individuals mentioned above.

Invaluable early reads of the manuscript were provided by Jillian Stein, Eric Shaw Quinn, and Becket Ghiotto. And, as always, thanks to my own team that makes it possible to write early and often; my agents, Lynn Nesbit at Janklow & Nesbit and Elizabeth Newman at CAA; my attorney, Christine Cuddy; my mother, Anne Rice; and again, because he likes it when I mention him a lot, my best friend and partner over at www.TheDinnerPartyShow.com, Eric Shaw Quinn.

Scarlet's a made-up town, so don't go looking for it on a map. So's Altamira, along with many of the locations I describe as being nearby, including State Mountain Road 293, Bayard Rock, and the Copper Pot, which stinks because I hear they have good pie.

ABOUT THE AUTHOR

Photo © 2016 Cathryn Farnsworth

Christopher Rice is the recipient of the Lambda Literary Award and is the *New York Times* bestselling author of *A Density of Souls* and the Bram Stoker Award finalists *The Heavens Rise* and *The Vines*. He is the head writer and an executive producer of *The Vampire Chronicles*, a television show based on the bestselling novels by his mother, Anne Rice. Together they penned *Ramses the Damned: The Passion of Cleopatra*. With his best friend, *New York Times* bestselling novelist Eric Shaw Quinn, Christopher hosts the YouTube channel *The Dinner Party Show with Christopher Rice and Eric Shaw Quinn* (#TDPS). He lives in West Hollywood, California. Visit him at www.christopherricebooks.com.